THE
KEY TO
SUSANNA

THE KEY TO SUSANNA

Hilary Norman

A DUTTON BOOK

DUTTON
Published by the Penguin Group
Penguin Books USA Inc., 375 Hudson Street,
New York, New York 10014, U.S.A.
Penguin Books Ltd, 27 Wrights Lane,
London W8 5TZ, England
Penguin Books Australia Ltd, Ringwood,
Victoria, Australia
Penguin Books Canada Ltd, 10 Alcorn Avenue,
Toronto, Ontario, Canada M4V 3B2
Penguin Books (N.Z.) Ltd, 182–190 Wairau Road,
Auckland 10, New Zealand

Penguin Books Ltd, Registered Offices:
Harmondsworth, Middlesex, England

First published by Dutton, an imprint of Dutton Signet,
a division of Penguin Books USA Inc.

First Printing, May, 1996
10 9 8 7 6 5 4 3 2 1

 REGISTERED TRADEMARK—MARCA REGISTRADA

Library of Congress Cataloging-in-Publication Data

Norman, Hilary.
    The key to Susanna / Hilary Norman.
        p.   cm.
    ISBN 0-525-94042-1
    1. Married women—Psychology—Fiction.   2. Models (Persons)—
Psychology—Fiction.   I. Title.
    PR6064.O743K49   1996
    823'.914—dc20   95–39424
                                                                    CIP

Printed in the United States of America
Set in Janson Text
Designed by Leonard Telesca

For Jonathan

Acknowledgments

I never cease to be thankful for the generous and valuable assistance given to me while I'm researching and writing a novel. My experiences during the preparation of this book have been no exception. Special gratitude to the following (in alphabetical order):

Dorothy and David W. Balfour, for their great kindness, patience and expertise; Howard M. Barmad, for coming through yet *again*; Carolyn Caughey, my wonderful editor at Hodder; Howard Deutsch; Sara Fisher, whose opinions I so greatly value; John Hawkins, the best New York agent and friend one could have; Audrey LaFehr, my equally wonderful editor at Dutton; Herta Norman, always the first to read and give excellent advice; Helen and Neal Rose; Dr. Jonathan Tarlow; Michael Thomas of A. M. Heath, also the very best agent and good friend; Norman Waterman at *Vogue*; and the staff at the Dan'l Webster Inn, Sandwich, Massachusetts.

PART ONE

PART ONE

CHAPTER 1

~

Pete Strauss wrote in his journal most nights. On March 22, 1991, he wrote slowly, pensively, about Susanna. He had long since become aware that many of the entries he had made over the past four years concerned her.

> The key to Susanna, to really understanding Susanna, appears to lie somewhere in the dunes of Cape Cod, tucked someplace between those endlessly shifting hills and valleys of sand and grass that I visited once, as a boy, with my father. I remember thinking then that some of it looked like the Sahara, some of it the way I had pictured a moonscape; but then Dad and I clambered up and over one of those dunes, and suddenly there was the beach, just a regular beach after all, and there were kids building castles, and dogs chasing sticks and balls, and families eating their picnic lunches, and I forgot about the moon and we might have been on any happy summer beach, any place, any time.

He wrote in an easy, sloping hand, looping gently, an average kind of handwriting common to well-educated young American men. He sat in his study at an old oak desk, ink-stained and carved in two places, to the left of his blotter, by some anonymous child leaving its poorly executed smiling face marks. Outside, on Eighth Street, young voices laughed, and a woman sang, not too badly at all, a strange and jazzy rendition of "Che gelida manina" from *La Bohème*. The window was open, and the March breeze was a little cool for comfort, but Strauss, being a two-pack-a-day man, liked to give his lungs a fighting chance when he could, and even in January he turned the heat on high and kept the windows open at night.

Susanna and I have been talking now, off and on, for almost four years, and I know so much more about her and her turbulent, extraordinary life than when we started, and yet sometimes I am aware that I still know next to nothing. When she began to speak about the Cape, I don't believe it was just my imagination that she actually seemed to change a little, to open up—just a tiny crack more—that long-sealed space deep inside her that I sense, these days, she is ready to open now, to expose, if she can bring herself to. For though she has told me so many things, terrible things, I know there is still more to come.

Sometimes she speaks about the place itself, not just about its relation to herself. Her voice is hushed and low as she talks about those wild, untamed, rolling lands at the constant mercy of the ocean and the elements. Some of the time she keeps her eyes closed as she talks; other times they're open but unseeing, and I imagine I almost see the sea and the sky deep in their lovely blueness. But then the truth is that I'm always seeing things in Susanna that I never have in other patients or other friends, no matter how intently I'm focusing. Things that maybe, even after all this time, I still have no business seeing.

It was past midnight when he closed his journal and locked it inside the top drawer of his desk. He turned out the light, stood up, closed his study door, and went into the living room. His apartment had three main rooms: the study, which he used as his office when he saw patients at home; the largest room, in which he lived, ate, and slept; and the third, in which he painted. Had his life been a little more normally structured, it would have been a spacious and more than comfortable home, but the oddness of using what was intended to be a bedroom or dining room for a pastime for which he had no talent was an indulgence that he felt kept him well balanced, if not wholly sane. Strauss painted very badly, but he loved doing it so much that even when he regarded a finished canvas and understood its poorness, he had such an affection for the work, such a profound gratitude for the pleasure it had given him that he felt it only right to do what should be done with paintings, to hang it on his wall. He used his works as a kind of relaxation barometer with his patients; depending on how long it took them to pass some kind of bemused comment on the paintings in his office, he knew how relaxed they were with him, and how honest.

Tossing his shorts into the laundry basket, Strauss tried his nightly exercise of pushing Susanna out of his head, knowing it was a lost cause. Many nights, over many months, he had gone through the same tug-of-war, the same split-personality third degree, asking and answering his own questions about the morality of allowing himself to continue seeing her in this semiprofessional, semifriendship no-man's-land. It happened from time to time, he knew, normally professionally detached psychologists suddenly, lethally incapable of leaving a patient in the office, but this degree of personal emotional involvement had never happened to Pete Strauss before Susanna.

He'd known nothing about the dunes back in 1987, on that day in the hospital when he had first sought her out. His intention then had been to help, but his prime concern had been for Hawke, not for Susanna, her own emotional state of interest to him only because of the way it might affect her husband. Pete had approached her cautiously, a little tentatively, and with—he was still ashamed to admit it now—a bunch of preconceived and idiotic prejudices about the empty-headedness of women like her, women who achieved fame and wealth because of their beauty. That beauty, in fact, had almost slain him on the spot, but recovering himself swiftly, Pete had seen, in just a few more seconds, how greatly she loved Hawke. Since that day he had come to learn, with excruciating slowness, how much she had suffered, then, and after Hawke. And before.

Hawke had been gone for three years now, and Pete and Susanna shared a friendship outside their professional relationship. Pete knew that Susanna trusted him, yet even after all this time, after all the sessions in his office, all the meetings over dinners and lunches and endless cups of coffee, he was aware that he still knew only what Susanna wanted him to know, what she was ready to tell him. That was the way it mostly went with patients, a laborious, mesmerizingly vague shading in of the life's landscape, occasionally, fleetingly, spattered with a precious splash of deeper, brilliant color. But then again, Pete figured, that was the way it went with most people he knew in real life too, and it didn't really matter if you were a psychotherapist or a bus driver or a politician or a plumber. Everyone hid inside himself or herself, the extroverts often even more than the introverts; everyone shared their innermost secrets as and how they chose, doling them out in big, generous, sometimes gruesome bowlfuls or in tiny, tantalizing morsels.

In Susanna's case, Pete knew that there was still a missing piece to the jigsaw, without which the whole could never make sense. She wanted to be unlocked, unraveled, released. But she said that she had been hiding the truth from herself for a long, long time, that she had chosen, she thought, to forget, to bury it. She said she had always known that, but until recently there had been no real purpose in forcing herself to face it, so she had simply excused herself, in the same way that an unathletic child uses a head cold or a nosebleed to get out of a PE class.

Of course Susanna's excuse had been, at least in her mind, more substantial than a nosebleed. It had been survival.

CHAPTER 2

~

Susanna was sitting in the waiting room, taking time out from being with Hawke, when she saw Pete Strauss for the first time. She noticed him before he spoke to her. He was around thirty years old, wearing blue denims and a Yankees T-shirt. His hair was fair, straight, and well cut. His eyes were green; his mouth was a little thin, his nose small, and his chin pointed and clean-shaven. He was a slim man of about five-nine, five-ten, and he looked okay. Nice. And though he looked a little tired, he also looked healthy. She resented him for that.

There were two other people in the room, a man and woman, both sunk in private misery, not speaking. Susanna was over by the window, half hidden by a tall and ailing rubber plant. An orderly at the nurses' station had told Pete that Mrs. Hawke had gone into the waiting room, but it was a full ten seconds before he saw her. Face of dreams. Body to match. She wore cream-colored chinos, a big blue cotton pullover, and loafers. It was June, and warm outside, but Susanna Van Dusen Hawke looked cold. Pete knew he was guilty of a certain bigotry when it came to beauty that had begun with his stunning wife Leigh's betrayal of him. He made assumptions he had no right to make; he thought that women capable of selling their looks the way this one did, these strong, bold, fuck-you women, had to be hollow somewhere deep inside, where it counted most.

He walked toward her.

"Mrs. Hawke," he said.

"Yes?"

She was leaning up against the wall, and her arms were wrapped around herself, and she didn't move when he spoke to her, and for a split second he thought it was rudeness or arrogance, and then he realized that she had frozen at the sound of his voice, at his approach, and that she was afraid. He had seen the look many times in hospitals, when doctors approached relatives. It was a defense mechanism of a look; it said, "Don't say another word, and maybe it won't be so; just turn around, and walk away and don't *say* it." She thought he was a doctor.

"I'm Pete Strauss," he said. He saw no recognition at his name. "I've been spending time with your husband. I'm a counselor."

Some of the fear went away. Pete had seen a zillion photographs of her, but she looked different two feet away, in the flesh. Her hair, always so sleek and gleaming on magazine covers, was several shades of gold, an inch or so shorter than shoulder length and mussed up, perhaps from running her fingers through it, the way people did when they were stressed out or just bone tired. Pete had expected the toughness of a performer, but this woman looked frail and vulnerable. He was no expert, but so far as he could tell, she wore no makeup except a touch of pale lipstick, and there were shadows under her eyes. He had anticipated superficial beauty, but she was utterly real, entirely human, and her pain, when he looked into the famous deep lilac blue eyes, nearly knocked him sideways.

"What can I do for you, Dr. Strauss?"

He recovered himself quickly. "Can we talk?"

"Of course."

Her voice was quiet, so low that he had to strain to hear her. "There's an office they let me use," he said, glancing at the tragic-looking couple on the settee. They didn't appear interested in the famous Susanna Van Dusen, but he preferred to be sure. "It'll be more private."

She hesitated. "I told Hawke I'd just be a few minutes."

"We can drop by and see him first if you like."

"No." She shook her head. "He'll sleep for a while. He tries to fight it when I'm there, toughs it out."

"He's a brave man."

"I know."

They left the waiting room, walked in their silent shoes through the long linoleum-covered hospital corridor. When they passed Hawke's room, Susanna glanced at the closed door but did not stop. She had longer legs than Strauss and slowed her gait to accommodate him. He was not a clumsy man, but beside this woman's grace, Pete felt like an elephant. Her walk had nothing of the studied, runway stride that she undoubtedly had down to perfection; this was easy, slightly swaying, purposeful but natural, calming. When they came to the stairwell and Pete automatically held the door open for her, Susanna smiled at him, and there it was, her entire face gently lifting in the warm upward curve that had illuminated magazine covers across the world.

"Just one floor down, okay?" he said.

"Sure."

The office had no window. It was dingy, stuffy, and over-crowded with file cabinets and broken chairs, a dumping ground for the discarded. Pete dusted off a chair and held it out for her.

"Thank you," she said, and sat down.

"How about some coffee?"

"Not for me, thank you, but don't let me stop you."

"I'm okay," he said. "I drink too much of the stuff anyway." He sat on the other side of the old fake teak desk. "Do you mind if I smoke?"

"Not at all."

He pulled out a pack of Marlboro. "Do you?"

She shook her head.

He lit a cigarette with a match, picked an old dirty ashtray out of an empty plastic filing tray, and inhaled deeply.

"A lot of doctors smoke," Susanna said. "It puzzles me, know-ing what they must see all the time."

"I'm not a medical doctor," Pete said.

"What are you, exactly?"

"A psychologist. I practice psychotherapy." Pete paused. "And I do this on the side."

"AIDS counseling."

"Yes."

"Why?"

"Because it's needed."

Susanna nodded slowly. Her face was filled with sorrow. "They tell me there are worse ways to die," she said softly, "and I guess that's true, but right now it's hard to believe."

"Hawke's getting stronger."

"Stronger." She made a small, scornful sound, just a soft exhalation through her fine, straight nose, but very eloquent. She was remembering Hawke at full strength. Not so very long ago. Just two years. Away from him, it was easy to remember him that way, but with him, seeing him struggle for breath, observing his weakness, she found it almost impossible to believe it had ever been different.

She looked up and saw Pete Strauss watching her. "I'm sorry," she said.

"What for?"

"I was thinking about Hawke."

"How could you not be?"

A sudden wave of irritation swept Susanna. "Dr. Strauss, what do you want? I assumed you wanted to talk about my husband, so can we please talk?" Then she flushed, embarrassed. She hated rudeness, but lately she found it seemed to burst out of her without warning. "I'm sorry," she said again. "It's just that time seems very precious these days."

"I know," Pete said. "I don't want to waste your time, Mrs. Hawke."

"Call me Susanna."

"Okay."

He hated these first encounters, these intrusions into privacy. "I'm afraid I always find beginnings hard," he said.

"Beginnings of what?" she asked, trying but failing to sound patient.

"Sometimes of nothing," Pete answered. "It's up to you." He took a drag of his cigarette, then balanced it on the edge of the ashtray. "I've been spending time with Hawke since he's been here. He didn't want me there at first, but he seems to have gotten used to my visits now. He talks to me more than he did."

"About what?"

"About the way he feels. About his fears. About AIDS."

"He never talks to me about any of that," Susanna said.

"I know."

Her eyes flickered. "Does he talk to you about me, Dr. Strauss?"

"Pete, please."

"Does he talk about us?" She was accusing.

"Hardly at all." Pete felt guilty. It was his job, but an intrusion nevertheless. "Susanna, Hawke does want to share these things with you."

"Then why doesn't he?"

"He's afraid."

"Of what?"

"Increasing your pain, mostly. And his shame."

"He has nothing to be ashamed of." Susanna was aware that her own pain was reflected in her eyes. Hawke had always told her how they betrayed her. He said that some blue eyes could stay cool, no matter what, but that her dark-rimmed deep blue irises spilled her emotions for all to see.

"He feels he has." The small, cluttered office seemed to fill to stifling point with awkwardness. "I'd like to help, if I can."

"In what way do you think you could help?"

"To try to ease the lines of communication between you, if that's what you want." Pete looked right into her eyes, kept his gaze steady and even. "Or you can tell me to butt out."

"And would you?"

"Of course. Though I'd still be there for Hawke, if he wanted me."

For a moment Susanna was silent.

"It's true about our not communicating enough," she said, "about the illness, at least." She paused. "I'm sorry, but confiding in strangers doesn't come naturally to me."

"That's understandable."

"In my world—in our world—you have to be careful about sharing private things. There aren't that many people you can trust."

"I think that goes for most worlds," Pete said.

She looked away from him, inclined her face to the sordid wall of rusting cabinets. "Do you want to counsel me? To make it easier for Hawke. Is that what you're suggesting, Dr. Strauss?"

"Pete."

She turned her face back to him. "Is that what you want to do?"

"I'd like to make it easier for you both."

"Can you make him not die?"

"No."

"Can you make it painless?"

"No."

"Can you turn it into a more acceptable disease?"

"That's a part of what I'm trying—what many people are trying to do."

Susanna nodded again, the same slow, thoughtful nod.

"And you think that Hawke trusts you."

"I believe so."

"Do you mind if I talk to him about you?"

"Of course not."

"Okay." Susanna stood up. "Do you have a card?"

Pete took a last drag on his cigarette and stubbed it out. Then he picked up the matchbook he'd just used and wrote his telephone number on the inside. "If I'm not there, the answering service will reach me. Any time, day or night." He rose and gave her the matchbook.

Susanna glanced down at it and smiled again, a wistful little ghost of a smile this time.

"You know Amerigo's?" Pete asked.

"It's one of our favorites," Susanna said. "You look surprised."

"I guess I didn't picture you dining in the Bronx."

She chose to ignore the unintentional insult. "They serve the best osso buco I know."

Pete's taste buds churned. "Have you tried the shrimp with mussels?"

"Hawke has it every time." She remembered him lying in his room, one floor up, trussed up with IVs and gulping oxygen. "Or he did."

"He will again," Pete said gently. "He's winning this round."

"Yes," Susanna said.

Hawke was sleeping when she returned to his room. She shut the door softly and sat down in the armchair to the left of his bed. He always looked better asleep these days, much less sick than in his waking hours. Susanna came back to the hospital sometimes late at night and crept into his room, after his sleeping pill had taken effect, just to watch him. She always marveled at the way so much of the fear and bad stuff disappeared from his face as soon as he drifted off. It was still such a remarkable face, pugnacious yet gentle, intelligent yet youthful, at least in sleep. Even with those all-seeing, clever gray eyes closed, Hawke's character seemed stamped on every feature: clean, firm mouth, long-ago broken, unset nose, scarred left cheek, vigorous, stubbled chin, wavy brown hair, threaded with gray—more and more gray, Susanna noticed. Hawke, the man with just one name. Her passionate, tender Englishman.

She sat in the armchair and thought about losing him. The pain rolled through her mind in great, agonizing breakers, and she listened to the traffic noise far below on the New York streets and longed for the old familiar sounds of the ocean to crash over her pain, to wash it away, slap it into submission, rub it out. She still often missed the waves during long, sleepless nights at home. The surf, the roar from the deep. Her lullaby. Its very constancy, even with all its inconsistency, its unpredictability, its omnipresent menace, had come to soothe her to rest in the dark hours, during the time she knew now she had not, after all, forgotten. Would never forget, no matter how she wanted to.

Susanna knew that the counselor was right about her inability to communicate with Hawke about his illness or his inevitable death, and she knew, too, how grossly unfair it was to Hawke not to let him talk about it when he needed to. But then Susanna had spent most of her life not sharing her own depths, unwilling and unable to share them, not with Hawke, or with Abigail, or with Bryan or Connie or Tabitha. She knew how to share good things, had a talent for loving, for distributing the warmth and generosity and laughter that came into her world, but darkness remained locked inside her. Susanna thought that she was by now a habitual noncommunicator. She wondered, not really convinced, if Pete Strauss might find a way to help her change that. If she would let him. If she wanted him to. She thought that she was willing to try, for Hawke's sake. But she was not sure.

CHAPTER 3

～

"We met at a preview of Connie's one-woman exhibit—Connie Van Dusen's my foster mother."

"You took your foster parents' name."

"Not legally, but it's the name my sister and I go by." Susanna paused. "Connie's a photographer too. The exhibition was at the Groentken Gallery on Madison."

"I know it."

"Seven years ago. May twenty-sixth, 1980."

"You were what—eighteen?"

"Almost. My birthday's June third. Hawke's ten years older."

Susanna and Pete were walking in Central Park, near the zoo. He'd asked her if being recognized was a problem for her, but though it was easier in winter, with hats and scarves and big coats, Susanna had become adept at disguising herself in all seasons. She liked Pete's idea of talking in the park better than in his office or at home; it was less like. being counseled, less formal, and the notion of being able simply to walk away at any moment made her feel easier. They had met outside the Pierre, and it had taken Pete several seconds to recognize her in her short brunette wig and dark Ray-Bans, but then Susanna had laughed at the success of her disguise, and that wonderful curving smile had again taken his breath away.

"We were all there; we'd all driven down from Cohasset—that's on the Boston South Shore. The Van Dusens—that's Bryan and Connie and Tabitha, their own daughter—Abigail, my little sister, and Lucy."

"Lucy?"

"Lucy Battaglia's Connie's assistant—well, more of a friend. She helps Connie when Bryan's not around—Bryan writes local interest books, so he's around quite a lot—but Lucy helps Connie with just about everything from housework to darkroom work to looking after Abigail. Connie was paralyzed in an accident thirteen years ago. She was taking photographs of gulls from the top of a stone wall between their house and the ocean, and she lost her footing and fell backward onto the road. She broke her spine."

"Poor woman."

Susanna nodded. "She's an amazing person, though. She has the use of her arms and hands, thank God, and she's very strong. She hates that the accident happened through her own carelessness; she says that she'd have preferred something more glamorous, like being shot by terrorists."

"But it hasn't stopped her from working?" Pete asked.

"Far from it. In fact more than half the photographs shown in that exhibit in '80 were taken after she was paralyzed, and she really laid herself on the line before the opening by giving an interview to the *Boston Globe* and insisting that her work should be judged on its own merit. Connie can't stand the idea that people may make allowances for her disability."

"Did the critics like the show?"

Susanna nodded. "Mostly. I remember Connie was very happy."

They circled a small crowd watching a pair of jugglers. Close by, an old man in a shirt and tie played a trumpet, battered but gleaming, for no one in particular. He might once have been a good musician, but his breath control had gone to hell, and Pete, looking for a hat or something into which he could have tossed a dollar, saw nothing and kept walking.

"What was Hawke doing there?" he asked.

"He'd known Connie for a few years, I think."

"So it was a parental introduction, you and he."

"Not exactly." Susanna smiled.

"Tell me." Pete paused. "If you want to."

"What I'd like is something to drink."

They stopped, and Pete looked around.

"You want to go to the zoo cafeteria?" He sounded dubious. "Or the Plaza's not too far."

Susanna shook her head. "Why don't we just get something off a stand?" Her eyes brightened. "What I'd really like is a hot dog."

"You're sure?"

"If you don't mind."

Pete grinned. "The day I refuse a hot dog, you'll know the body snatchers have got me."

They got two Cokes and two dogs with everything and sat on the grass under a tree. Susanna bit into her roll and sighed with pleasure.

"The best," she said. "And strictly against the rules."

"I can't believe you have to worry about your weight," Pete said with undisguised admiration.

"In my world? Always." Susanna gave a shrug. "Though the way I look at the moment, my waistline's the least of my problems."

"You look wonderful to me," Pete said.

"Thank you."

"Anyway, you have to keep your strength up right now."

"For Hawke's sake," Susanna said.

"And for your own."

Hawke was at the Groentken Gallery on the evening of May 26, 1980, partly because he liked Connie Van Dusen and respected what he had previously seen of her work, and partly because the invitation had coincided with a meeting seven blocks down Madison. His expectation was to spend about fifteen to twenty minutes checking out the exhibit before going home to his own darkroom. For the first ten minutes things went as planned; he was impressed by the way Van Dusen had refused to allow her horizons to be curtailed more than necessary by her accident. A series of underwater studies, for example, gripped him both for their technical expertise and for their crepuscular, dreamlike quality. Hawke thought Connie had probably achieved what she had intended to, had made him want to get right into that water with her, get behind that lens to glimpse what lay beyond the next swirl, the next dark, impenetrable shadow, and glancing back at the photographer sipping champagne in the damnable confines of her wheelchair, Hawke guessed how much courage and physical strength it must have taken to get those shots.

In the eleventh minute, a whole lot more than just his plans for the rest of the evening were blown away. There were three photographs hanging on the west wall of the gallery, all of the same young golden-haired girl. Two were black-and-white, one of the girl walking on a beach, the other of her sitting in a cane chair, wearing frayed shorts and laughing into the lens. The third portrait was in color, with the girl giving a piece of Red Delicious to a small child. The girl's laughter was infectious, and her movements were stunningly graceful, even in the immutable silence and stillness of the photographs, but it was her eyes that compelled Hawke most. Blue eyes with a hint of lilac, tender, soft, warm eyes, sharpened to intelligence by the irises' vivid dark outline and penetrating black pupils.

"Lovely, isn't she?"

Hawke turned. Bryan Van Dusen, Connie's husband, stood beside him with a young girl who had to be his daughter—same reddish brown hair, same hazel eyes, same handsomely curved nose.

"I don't think you've met Tabitha, my daughter, have you, Hawke?"

"I haven't had that pleasure." Hawke gave the girl his hand. "Glad to know you."

"Hello, Mr. Hawke." The girl's eyes were shy, but she shook his hand strongly. She was, Hawke estimated, about fourteen, with the vigorous, healthy bloom of a tough young sportswoman. He imagined her leaping on a tennis court or knifing through an Olympic-size pool. He wondered whether Connie had taken her daughter along on her subocean shoots.

"It's a good show," Hawke said to Bryan. "Connie must be happy."

"She's still holding her breath, I think." Bryan, a big, warm man, didn't trouble to disguise his pride.

"Who's the girl on the beach?" Hawke was looking back at the first photograph.

"That's Susanna."

"Friend of Connie's?"

"Our foster daughter." Bryan grinned. "And the little one's her sister, Abigail."

"Two more beauties," Hawke said, smiting Tabitha with a sidelong smile that turned her into his slave for life. "Are they here today?"

"Somewhere," Bryan answered.

"Abigail's eaten about sixty canapés," Tabitha said.

"Let's hope Lucy doesn't let her jump about too much," Bryan said.

"Do you know where Susanna is?" Hawke asked Tabitha.

"Gazing at the ocean, I think."

Connie's photographs looked more imposing to Susanna up on the sleek Madison Avenue walls than they had at home. There were the glorious full-color shots of the woods near their house, and a half dozen flower photographs, of which Susanna's personal favorite was a single dew-filled daffodil. And then there was the underwater series. Susanna stood and stared into the depths, mesmerized, losing herself.

She felt his eyes on her, before she turned around and saw him. He was tall and lean and a little rumpled, with a nose that looked as if it might have been broken, a fine scar on his left cheek, and piercing gray eyes. He wore faded denims, a well-cut but clearly aged charcoal linen jacket over a white T-shirt, and Susanna felt that he might have been watching her for some time.

"You looked as if you were drowning," he said.

She looked back at the photographs. "It was a very comfortable, gentle kind of drowning," she answered.

"I know what you mean. They're very fine."

"You're English," Susanna said.

"You're Susanna."

"Yes." She was surprised.

"Bryan told me," Hawke explained. "He saw me looking at Connie's photographs of you and your sister."

"Abigail." She smiled. "Isn't she gorgeous?"

He was silent for a moment. "You have an extraordinary face," he said, at last. "I'd like very much to take some pictures of you."

Susanna stared at him. "Who are you?"

"I'm Hawke," he said.

"*The* Hawke?"

"Guilty."

"Isn't he a dream?" Tabitha whispered in Susanna's ear as they watched Hawke speaking to Connie about a half hour later. The gallery was swarming with people, the air filled with a deliciously piquant brew of champagne, tobacco smoke, and blended perfumes, and the buzzing harmony of mingling voices and the swishing of clothes and the soft tread of feet on the carpet, moving and pausing, while eyes roamed over pictures, then moving on again.

"He looks nice," Susanna said.

"Nice?" Tabitha gave a small snort of teenage disdain. "He's the sexiest man I ever saw. What was he saying to you before?"

"That he wanted to take my picture."

"You're *kidding*!"

Susanna shook her head. "I'm sure he didn't mean it, but that's what he said."

"What did you say?" Tabitha's eyes were huge.

"I didn't say anything."

"Why not?"

"Because I didn't think he meant it."

"But he's famous."

"I know he is."

"I mean, he's *really* famous."

"I know."

Tabitha saw Hawke and Connie look their way and gripped Susanna's right arm tightly. "They're talking about you."

"No, they're not."

"I bet you your cowboy boots they are."

Tabitha knew that Susanna's boots would not fit her, but that knowledge did not stop her from coveting them, as she coveted most of Susanna's wardrobe. Not that the clothes themselves were all that hot; it was just the way they looked on Susanna. Her own strong, sporty physique was a constant source of dismay to Tabitha, who wanted, more than anything, to look like her older foster sister. Susanna was tall and slender as a birch, with the longest, most divine legs on the whole Boston South Shore, while Tabitha sometimes felt like a quarterback. Susanna had those glorious eyes and mouth, while Tabitha was saddled with boring hazel eyes and braces. Susanna looked gorgeous first thing in the morning, even better when she stepped dripping from the shower, and her hair gleamed like angel's wings after just a few minutes' rough drying. When Tabitha woke up, she had creases on her face, she looked like a drowned rat after a shower, and it took the best part of an hour's hard labor to pulverize her curly hair into submission, and even then, though Susanna told her it was the color of fall leaves, Tabitha knew that her blusher brush had more style than her hair did. Yet not for one single minute had Tabitha Van Dusen ever resented Susanna since she and Abigail had come to share their home and, ultimately, their name. Little Abigail was cute and cuddly and not too much of a drag, the way some little kids were, but from the very beginning Susanna had made life seem more fun, more exciting, *better*. When it came right down to it, Susanna was the big sister Tabitha had always wanted. When it came right down to it, Tabitha loved Susanna.

Hawke never came near Susanna again that evening, and Connie didn't say a word about her conversation with him until all the guests had gone and Bryan was escorting Lucy Battaglia and Abigail back to their hotel, before returning to take Connie, Tabitha and Susanna out to dinner.

"How do you think it went?" Connie was a little tired but glowing. The three of them were temporarily collapsed near the back of the gallery, while Max Groentken's staff began to clear up the debris.

"Fantastically," Susanna said, leaning against a clear piece of wall. "Everyone seemed to love it."

"I spent the whole time eavesdropping." Tabitha was cross-legged on the carpet. "There was a critic from the *New Yorker*— I think he was from the *New Yorker*—who said something about luminous sky and the clarity of your vision—I think he was talking about the North River shots—and there was this woman— the one wearing that weird snaky dress, you must have seen her —anyway, she said that your tulip was the most phallic thing she'd ever seen. Personally my vote goes to the lily." She looked at Susanna's shocked face. "There's nothing wrong with phallic symbols, Susanna."

"Don't push your luck, Tabbie," Connie said dryly, and looked up at Susanna. "How's my face? Anything need fixing before the restaurant?"

"You look gorgeous," Susanna said.

"Sexy as hell," Tabitha said.

"Really?" Connie looked pleased. She'd had her fair hair cut very short a few weeks back and had discovered not only how liberating it felt, but also that combining the cropped look with a little dramatic eye makeup seemed to draw other people's eyes to her face and away from the damned chair.

"You know I always say what I mean, Mom."

"How true." Connie paused, remembering something. "Tabbie, could you go and call the hotel to see if your dad is still there, and if he is, to bring my cream knit jacket?"

"Are you cold?"

"Not right now, but the restaurant may be freezing."

"If you're trying to get rid of me so you can talk to Susanna, I'll just go wait in a corner," Tabitha said, not moving.

"I don't want you to wait in a corner, I want you to call your father."

"So you can talk to Susanna about Hawke."

"Go make the call," Connie said.

With a heavy sigh, Tabitha got up.

"She told me exactly what Hawke had said to her," Susanna told Pete Strauss seven years later, sitting in the shade of an old oak tree in Central Park, a contented litter of eaten hot dogs and Coke cans beside them. "Connie was always great about being open with us all; she still is."

"What did Hawke say?"

"It was all very simple. Easy as pie, so far as he was concerned. Hawke's a little like Connie and Tabitha that way. Straightforward, with that same no-bullshit, clear-sighted, go-get-it attitude. Connie said he walked over to her, wheeled her chair away from the crowd, and told her that he wanted—no, actually, what he said was that he *needed* to photograph me. He said what he thought would happen if he started working with me, that he doubted it would end with just a few photographs. He said that his instincts were almost always right and that if Connie didn't approve, she'd better say so loud and clear there and then, and he'd try to get over it, and he supposed he would, in time, but it would be the world's loss, not only his." Susanna smiled wistfully at the memory.

"How did Connie react?" Pete asked curiously as a peacock blue rogue Frisbee skimmed low over their heads and whisked into the grass just yards away, pursued by a squealing red-haired girl.

"She laughed for about three seconds, and then she looked across the gallery at me, and back at Hawke, and she stopped laughing because she said she knew he was right."

"You were only seventeen. Didn't she want you to go to college?"

"I'd dropped out of school sometime before that. I think Connie and Bryan always hoped I might change my mind, but they said it was my choice."

She stopped talking. Pete watched her for a moment, observed the shadows darkening her eyes, and knew the present had returned. Susanna felt his gaze, knew he was aware, and nodded, still silent.

Pete tried to take her back again. "Did you have any idea, at the start, of what was going to happen?"

"None at all. The truth is, I fell for Hawke that evening, and I guess the knowledge that Connie knew and liked him just made it easier. I trusted him from the beginning, completely. He said he wanted to take a few pictures of me. Connie and Bryan said it was okay, and Tabbie thought it was a totally cool idea." She smiled. "So I went."

CHAPTER 4

~

The loft on Canal Street felt hollow without Hawke's physical presence. His things were all around her as usual, yet it felt empty as a shell. Susanna had lived with him for four years, and she was as much at home there as she thought she had ever been anywhere, but it still remained, in her psyche, "Hawke's place." She wondered, now, if perhaps a part of her had always guessed that she might just be passing through. If Hawke died—when Hawke died—Susanna knew that she would not remain there long. She loved the place, loved its rough redbrick walls and unreachable ceilings, its immense windows, the two spiral iron staircases, one leading to Hawke's darkroom, the other to their sleeping area with the early American dressing table Hawke had carried up so that he could lie on their futon and watch her make up and brush her hair. She loved the tiny but efficient kitchen space in which they had created hundreds of congenial dinners and fought countless trivial battles over ingredients in sauces and specks of food on washed-up dishes. And more than anything, she loved his studio, Hawke's immaculate kingdom, the only part of the loft about which he was intensely, sometimes savagely territorial.

Sometimes, when he was not home, Susanna sat cross-legged on the floor in the center of the studio, turning her head slowly from side to side, letting her gaze wander over every scrupulously maintained surface, every gleaming item of equipment, every neatly stacked prop, and it was almost as if Hawke were there, working, for Susanna could hear his voice in her head, talking and directing and cajoling and yelling, and she could hear his laughter, that deep, rough laugh of his. She sat there more often, now that he was back in the hospital, listening for him, drawing him back into the studio, back into his place, and she felt closer to him here than she ever did in the unreality of that sterile, clinical room.

Hawke had discovered his Canal Street loft on the old frontier, now grown hazy, between Chinatown and Little Italy, more than eleven years earlier, just two weeks after his arrival in New York from London. His colleagues and friends had pointed him toward SoHo, the artistic enclave, but Hawke knew what he wanted and where he wanted it to be. He was a foreigner, an Englishman, born and raised in a Northamptonshire village, reborn in London when he'd snapped his first pictures, and he had come to Manhattan to satisfy his soul. He had no urge to assimilate, no desire to become an American; he wished only to absorb, to observe, to grasp all the color and vibrancy of the culture around him. He photographed everything—mobile and petrified, living and dead, animal, vegetable, and mineral—and everyone he came across, for the world only came fully to life for Hawke when it was seen through a camera lens, and he liked talking to the strangers he photographed, and his thirst to greet them was so natural and so genuine that not a single individual, not Chinese ancient, or nervous tourist, or young gang member, had ever raised a violent objection.

It was a source of curiosity to some that an artist with an eye so voracious for everyman and everything in both their most humdrum and most unusual or rarefied forms, a man with such polymorphic tastes, should have chosen to limit himself, finally, almost exclusively to fashion photography. To Hawke, however, the decision to choose women and the garments in which they wrapped themselves as his preferred subject seemed natural enough, given that he had a great appreciation of beautiful women and the clothes that served to heighten that beauty, and given that he considered himself a self-indulgent man.

His entry into the big league had begun in 1976, when he had stepped in at the last minute for Polly Mellen at *Vogue* to take over a shoot for a Kenzo four-page spread. Always professional, Hawke had accepted the editor's story line and gone with her directives, but Mellen had been frustrated by Hawke's reluctance to bring what she had recognized as his spectacular talent for realistic drama into this new arena. The problem was that Hawke knew he was out of step with the mid-seventies industry, but the fact that controversial story lines and innuendo unquestionably tantalized and sold more magazines had no effect on him. A ravishingly lovely and intelligent woman wearing beautiful clothes was, so far as Hawke was concerned, a fantasy that ought to stand up all on its own. Sensuality was one thing, but Hawke believed that the current fad for bringing intimations of sex or violence into fashion photography only served to dilute the impact of what they were being paid to sell; Hawke didn't see the point of making the reader care more about what might be going on in a shot than what was being shot.

Hawke greatly admired Avedon and loathed Helmut Newton; he worshipped Irving Penn and avidly studied Arthur Elgort's brilliant techniques with models. Taking photographs out in the real world, Hawke was an adventurer, but where clothes and models were concerned, he was a purist. Alexander Liberman had said: "A fashion photograph is not a photograph of a dress; it is a photograph of a woman." Hawke believed that neither woman nor dress should eclipse the other. The more he worked with great models and clothes, the more dogmatic he became. If a photographer was not able, without resorting to cheap tricks, to pin the reader's eyes to a page upon which nothing but model and garment appeared, then, Hawke said, that photographer was not worth a damn. Hawke recognized the magnificent potential of bonding the best of both clothes and women; he had the talent to get 1,000 percent out of both garment *and* model. Before long *Vogue* had grown to love him, and then *Harper's Bazaar*, and designers began to clamor for him and models to pray for him.

By the time Hawke first saw Susanna, he had photographed Patti Hansen wearing Missoni, Lisa Taylor wearing Ralph Lauren, Cheryl Tiegs wearing Norma Kamali, and Lauren Hutton wearing Armani. They all loved Hawke; in the spring of 1980

Hawke was *it*. And yet from the instant he set eyes on Susanna Van Dusen, he gave up all the others.

She had never really understood why.

"There's a feeling," Pete Strauss told her during their second session, in his office, one week after the first, "among some of the staff in the hospital, that you seem to mistrust the treatment they're giving your husband."

"Really?" Susanna was surprised.

"That isn't the case?" Pete lit a cigarette.

"No, of course not." She paused. "Hospitals make me a little crazy, that's all. Which isn't helped by people like Nurse Himmler."

"Who the hell is Nurse Himmler?"

"I named her that first time we met, during Hawke's first bout of PCP. She's a hatchet-faced woman who makes a performance of putting on gloves just to take Hawke's temperature. They all wear protective clothing for certain procedures, and I hate that because I feel they're putting up a barrier around him, yet I know it makes sense, but this woman has all the sensitivity of a Nazi." She gave a small, wry grin.

"Why the smile?"

"I was thinking about the way I deal with her now."

"How's that?"

"It's a little eccentric, I guess." She smiled again. "I have a friend named Lulu Fiedlander—who also happens to be my aerobics coach—who's big on stress management. Lulu said it often helps to try visualizing a disease as something tangible, to help express your rage at it more easily. I chose Nurse Himmler as my symbol. Sometimes at night, when I can't sleep, I conjure her up and stick fantasy pins in her, like imaginary voodoo."

"Maybe you should go a little further," Pete suggested.

"Get a nurse doll, you mean, and use real pins," Susanna said ironically.

"If it would help."

"I doubt it." She shook her head. "I can't believe I told you that."

"Why wouldn't you?"

"Because it's private. And dark. Not the kind of thing I talk about."

"Have you talked about it to Hawke?"

"No."

"Why not?"

"Because I don't want him to know I feel that kind of anger."

"Hawke feels anger."

"I know. That's different."

"Why?"

"He's entitled."

"And you're not?"

"I don't have AIDS."

"You're not responsible for giving Hawke the virus."

"No." Susanna looked at Pete. "How do you know that?"

"Hawke told me."

"I see." She paused. "What else has he told you?"

Pete's green eyes were gentle. "He told me you'd tested negative."

"So far." She felt her stomach tightly clenched.

"You're entitled to your anger, Susanna."

"Maybe so, but it isn't important."

"I disagree with you."

"It doesn't help," she said. "All the rage in the world won't help Hawke stay alive, and it won't stop me from feeling the pain."

"That's true," Pete said. "But it's still a natural response. One that you shouldn't feel ashamed to admit to."

"I'm not ashamed."

Her time up, on her way out of Pete's apartment, Susanna stooped to pet his dog. He was a medium-size, shaggy gray creature with light brown, intelligent eyes and a thick, long tail that thumped the rug as she touched him.

"He's called Steinbeck." Pete watched her, cool and casual in jeans, white T-shirt, and navy blazer, and he knew again, as he had each time they had met, that she was the loveliest woman he would ever see.

"Great name."

"I didn't name him."

"How old is he?" Susanna still crouched, scratching the dog's chest. "You're a fine boy, aren't you?"

"He's eight, though he's only lived with me for just over a year."

"What happened to his owner?"

"She died."

Silence filled the hall.

"Were you close?" Susanna asked at last.

"Pretty close."

"You must have been for her to trust you with this one." The gray tail wagged harder. Susanna looked up at Pete and knew. "Was it AIDS?"

"It was."

"Was she a—I'm not sure what to call it—a patient? Client?"

"I was her counselor," Pete said softly. "She became a friend." He smiled wistfully. "I have a bird too—a cockatoo called Alice. She came to me the same way. Like Steinbeck, Alice's owner had no one else left to leave her with."

Susanna stood up. "Can I meet her? I like birds. I like all animals, except mice." She hesitated. "Or do you have someone waiting?"

"Not yet. And I'm sure Alice would love to meet you."

The cockatoo was on her perch in a domed, airy cage in the large living room in which Strauss ate, relaxed, and slept. Susanna spoke a few words to the bird, so softly and so low that Pete could not hear them. The cockatoo lifted her yellow crest, tilted her head to one side, and watched Susanna. They made, Pete thought, a wonderful picture. He understood Hawke.

"She's beautiful," Susanna said.

"Playful too," Pete said. "I close up all the windows for a while most days and let her out of the cage. She always checks out the whole room, the dining table, the bed, the bookshelves, you name it, and then the routine is she comes and nibbles at my feet, whether I'm wearing shoes or barefoot—she likes sneakers best, tugs at the laces—and then she hops up on the sofa and watches TV with me."

"Does she speak?"

"Never, but she has no trouble communicating."

"Not like me," Susanna said, and turned away from the cage toward the bookshelves.

"You communicate pretty well," Pete said. "I think it's just that you're selective about what and to whom you confide."

Susanna looked at his books. "You read detective novels." His Dashiell Hammett collection was bathed in sunlight from the open window.

"You seem surprised. What did you expect?"

She shrugged. "Freud, I guess."

"He's there too." Pete watched her for a moment. "You said something earlier about hospitals making you crazy."

"It wasn't important," Susanna said.

"If you're unhappy about anything to do with Hawke's treatment, I'd say that's pretty important."

"There's nothing wrong with Hawke's treatment. I mean, it's miserable and inadequate, but it's all they have." Susanna looked away from him. "I'm just uncomfortable around doctors."

"Any particular reason for that?"

Susanna did not answer.

"Okay," Pete said.

"I've always been that way," Susanna said softly. "Though for a while, a long time ago, I wished I could be a doctor myself."

"Why didn't that happen?"

"Many reasons." She paused. "My education was pretty screwed up."

"Was this before you and your sister went to live with the Van Dusens?"

Susanna nodded. "That's right."

"Is that something you'd like to talk about?" Pete asked.

"Maybe." She glanced at her watch. "I have to go."

"Sure," Pete said. "Will you come again?"

"You tell me."

"I don't want to put any pressure on you, Susanna. You didn't come to me for help; I approached you."

"Because of Hawke."

"Yes."

She looked back at him, right into his eyes. "If I keep coming back, it won't just be for Hawke, it'll be for me too."

"That'll be good," Pete said easily.

They fell silent. Outside on Eighth Street horns honked, voices hummed.

"There are things," Susanna said, "that have happened to me. In the past. Before Hawke." She paused. "I don't talk about them. I don't even think about them. But they're there."

"Would you like to talk about them?"

"Maybe."

"I'm here if you do."

"I'm not certain they're not better left buried."

"It's up to you."

They walked out of the room, back into the hallway, Steinbeck following slowly. Susanna reached into her blazer pocket and pulled out her Ray-Bans.

"I feel very much at ease here," Susanna said. "It's a good apartment."

"I think so."

She lifted her face and wrinkled her nose a little. "What's that smell?"

"Paint. Turpentine."

"You're an artist?"

"Dedicated and abysmal."

"You're probably wonderful."

"Don't count on it." Pete grinned.

"But you love it, right?"

"Right."

"I envy you that," Susanna said, by the front door.

"Don't you love your work?"

"No," she said. "Not really."

"So why do it?"

She slipped on the glasses. Her eyes vanished and her face became impenetrable. "Because of Hawke," she said.

"For him?"

"Not for him, no. Just because of him."

From Strauss's place, Susanna caught a cab to Lulu Fiedlander's exercise studio near Columbus Circle for an hour's private work-out with Lulu herself, and from there she went to the agency to take a look at a portfolio that had Andrea Marantz all revved up. Andrea valued Susanna's judgment more than most of her models, partly because her intuition was seldom wrong, but also because Andrea knew Susanna had no ax to grind, no hidden agenda, no covert jealousies. The Marantz Agency was small potatoes com-pared to Ford Models and the rest of the Top Four, but it was where Hawke had sent her at the beginning, and with nothing else to go on but Hawke's instincts and experience and the fact that she liked Andrea at first meeting, Susanna had gone with his recommendation and had never regretted it for a moment.

The agency's main office was noisy as always, the big central hexagonal table a frenzy of bookers juggling phones, marking calendars, selling, cajoling, organizing, hyping, smoothing, and soothing. Susanna greeted the bookers and walked straight on past the walls of photographs, through the mass of hopefuls waiting to be seen, saw the flash of excitement on some of their faces as they recognized her, noted with sympathy and a small touch of envy the desire and fear in their wide and lovely eyes. She had been so lucky, avoiding the nightmare of interviews and go-sees and castings, yet she was aware that in a way she lacked one of the most vital ingredients of the world she now lived in: ambition. All these women and men were desperate to make it, prepared to do almost anything to make it happen, and within the next hour or so most of them would be shot down in flames, but one or two would probably experience the mind-blowing high of knowing they had been at least halfway right about their own potential. Susanna had never, for a single moment, dreamed of becoming a model until Hawke had nailed her down, and she had let him talk her into it for only two reasons. One, her infatuation with him. And two, she had needed the money.

"I often wonder why none of those girls ever seems to resent me," she said to Andrea Marantz in the tranquillity of her office.

"Why should they?" Andrea, taller than most of her models and daunting as always in her mannish suit and horn-rimmed glasses, was genuinely surprised. "They may all secretly believe they're as beautiful as you, and one or two may be right about that, but you've made it, and you're the consummate professional so far as they're concerned. They admire you, my darling."

"But they're all struggling so hard just to get noticed."

"And seeing you among them gives them hope. You're real; you're flesh and blood; they feel privileged to be sharing your air."

"That's ridiculous."

"Of course it is, but it's still the truth."

Susanna sighed. "At least they all know exactly what they want."

Andrea smiled. "So did you. You wanted Hawke." One of the telephones on her big circular desk rang, and she picked it up, spoke briefly and succinctly for a few moments, then put down the receiver.

Susanna wasted no more time before asking the question she knew was uppermost in Andrea's mind as well as her own. "Are we going to lose the Grace contract?"

"I don't know," Andrea said.

"Do they know about Hawke?"

"They know he's sick," Andrea said, "and I imagine they have their suspicions, but if they do, they're keeping it to themselves."

The contract that Andrea Marantz had negotiated on behalf of Hawke and Susanna with Maison Grace for the forthcoming launch of its new international cosmetics line had been the talk of the industry for months. Marie Hueberlein, president of the Geneva-based corporation and granddaughter of the fashion empire's founder, had fought off considerable in-house opposition to the exclusive hiring of both model and photographer, but from the moment she had seen Hawke's first published shots of Susanna Van Dusen, Hueberlein had known she would settle for nothing else. Susanna alone was perfect for the Grace woman: fine cheekbones, straight nose, ideal skin, a mouth created for showing off lipstick, the glorious eyes, perfect neck, and strong shoulders. But Hawke had delved into that great but far from unique beauty, had sensed something rare behind those eyes, and had, without exposing or exploiting it, illuminated it. Hueberlein saw a woman physically youthful enough to maximize the high quality of her cosmetics, but over and above that, she saw a look that spoke of experience, of *living*, a look that would drag millions of older, life-damaged women to the Grace counters in stores all over America. Hueberlein recognized that it was Hawke who had elicited that look, and that any attempt to break up the partnership he and Van Dusen had so successfully created would probably fail, and that even if they could be split, the magic would be lost.

"How is Hawke?" Andrea asked Susanna.

"Much better. He should be home in a day or two."

"How long till he's well enough to work?"

"I don't know." Susanna shook her head. "Last time he recovered very quickly, but this time's been worse."

"You're scheduled to start for Grace in three weeks."

Susanna said nothing.

"Has he talked about it?"

"Hawke's determined to make it on time," Susanna said.

"That's great, but do you think he's being realistic?"

"You know Hawke."

"I guess he'll make it on time."

"He says he wants to launch the campaign, to get Grace and me up and running." Susanna stopped, looked away from Andrea's penetrating eyes. "He says that by the time he gets too sick to work, I'll be too well established for them to think of dumping me. That they'll have to find another photographer."

"He may be right."

Susanna swallowed hard. "I've never worked with anyone else. I'm not sure that I could."

"I'm sure you could," Andrea said. "The question is whether you'd want to work with another photographer."

"I can't even begin to imagine—I don't *want* to imagine it." Susanna struggled to find the words. "It's like I only joined the circus because I fell in love with a trapeze artist—if Hawke wasn't there to catch me, I don't think I'd want to jump again."

"Have you told Hawke how you feel?" Andrea asked gently.

"No."

"Don't you think you should?"

"No, I don't," Susanna said firmly. "He believes he can still take care of me, go on providing for me, by making me the Grace woman. Unless Marie Hueberlein pulls the plug, I'm not going to destroy that belief."

"If Hawke's fit to start on time, I don't think she will pull the plug," Andrea said. "Even if she'd like to."

The two women fell silent for a moment.

"What about me?" Susanna asked very quietly. "I've been tested. Do you think Marie Hueberlein knows that?"

"If she knows Hawke has AIDS, she'll take that as read." Andrea paused. "If she asked me about it, and if you gave me permission, I'd be able to tell her in all honesty that you'd tested negative."

"So far." Susanna's expression was wry. "Somehow I don't imagine that HIV testing, even when it's negative, goes hand in hand with Mrs. Hueberlein's image of the Grace woman, do you?"

"I don't imagine so."

"You know I'd like to walk away from the contract, don't you?" Susanna's voice was still soft. "Please don't be offended, but I wish I could walk away from the business altogether."

"I'm not offended. I've always known how you felt about it. But you're not going to walk away, are you." It was not a question. "Not while Hawke's still here."

Susanna shook her head.

"No," she said. "Of course not."

CHAPTER 5

~

"Tell me about life before Hawke."

"What would you like to know?"

"Anything. Everything. Whatever you want to talk about."

"That's easy. I don't want to talk about any of it."

"Is that really true?"

"Yes. No." Susanna smiled ruefully. "I'm not sure."

"What about the Van Dusens? Can you talk about your life with them?"

"Gladly."

"Was it a happy time for you?"

"Very. Most of it."

"Tell me?"

"We went to Cohasset to live with them in the spring of 1976."

"We? That's you and your sister?"

"And our father. Matthew Bodine."

Susanna sat on the sofa in Pete's office, shoes off, legs folded under her, Steinbeck beside her, his shaggy head resting on her left thigh, dribbling a little onto her denims. It was August, two days before the Grace shoot was due to begin, too hot to keep the windows open, and the air conditioner's buzz provided a low, dissonant accompaniment to the Vivaldi coming through the speakers to the left and right of Pete's big desk.

"I remember seeing the house for the first time," Susanna said, and saw it again in her mind's eye. "It was on this pretty stretch of road, and it all looked so clean and well kept and safe, and there were all these lovely trees just bursting with blossoms, and our father wasn't saying much, but he kept looking at me sideways, while he was driving along the road, and I knew he wanted a reaction, and I knew he wanted me to be impressed, and I remember I was relieved because I didn't need to act at all, because I *was* impressed. I loved it all right away, and that was before we saw the house itself, and then it was even better."

It was white clapboard with gray shutters and a gray front door with a brass knocker, and for just an instant it reminded Susanna of another house, long ago, but then that flash was gone, and she was climbing out of the car with the baby in her arms, and devouring the new house with hungry eyes. A low two-log fence divided the front garden from the road, a trellis of pink roses climbed up either side of the front door, and she thought it was the prettiest house she'd ever seen. There was a wooden porch, with a swing seat and a low pine table, and two bicycles leaned up against the side of the house, and a broad wooden ramp led up from the path to the house.

"Lady of the house is a cripple," Matthew Bodine said as he pulled their bags out of the trunk. "She needs you and me to help her; that's why they're taking us in."

He hadn't told her that before, but Susanna knew better than to say so, just held onto the baby and kept quiet, waiting as he tapped on the door. He tapped softly, too softly, not using the brass knocker, and Susanna thought for an instant how unlike him it was to be so tentative, and then she remembered he had been that way at the convent, moving gently and smoothly about the place, keeping himself to himself, going about his work and then, when it was done, slipping back into his own modest shadow.

No one came. He knocked again, harder this time.

The door opened.

"Well, hello there."

The man was big and friendly-looking, with red-brown hair and crinkles around his eyes and a large nose, curved like an old carving of an American Indian's nose. He put out his hand to take Bodine's and shook it warmly, all the time looking past the father to where Susanna stood, holding the baby.

"You must be Susanna," Bryan Van Dusen said.

"Yes, sir," Bodine said. "Say hello to Mr. Van Dusen, Susanna."

She stepped forward. "How do you do, sir."

"And this pretty little one must be Abigail." He peered down, all smiles, at the baby, and Abigail, opening her eyes, seemed to smile back, sealing the charm of the moment. Susanna heard a sound, thought for a second that it was just gulls, for they were wheeling overhead, a reminder that the ocean was less than a half mile away, but then she saw the big steel wheels of the chair, and Connie Van Dusen appeared in the doorway.

"Welcome," she said. "Come on in, all of you."

She reversed the chair, adeptly, swiftly, and Susanna saw that her slim, suntanned arms were strong, her fingers tough, though her legs, clad only in denim shorts, seemed immobile and useless.

"I'm glad to see you again, Mr. Bodine," Connie Van Dusen said, her smile as friendly as her husband's, and Susanna liked her right off, liked her small, sharp-featured, capable face with its clear, bright eyes. Her fair hair was shoulder-length and tied back off her face in a ponytail, and she wore a Save the Whale T-shirt.

"I want to thank you for your kindness, Mrs. Van Dusen," Bodine said with great humility. "Not too many people would take in a little baby; though like I told you, my Susanna's a great little mother."

"I can see that." Mrs. Van Dusen smiled up at Susanna. "I hope you and your sister will be very happy here, Susanna. We want you to think of our house as your home in every way."

"Thank you, ma'am." Susanna still gripped Abigail tightly, the warmth of her little body strengthening her. She was such a good baby, but it was getting close to her next feeding, and she hoped she wouldn't start to cry until they were safely up in their room.

"Where's Tabbie?" Van Dusen asked his wife.

"She's out back feeding Baskin."

"Our dog," Van Dusen explained. "He's a black Labrador and the dumbest, friendliest creature you'd ever hope to meet. Our daughter, Tabitha, named him that because he's so crazy about ice cream."

"Rocky Road's his number one." The young girl materialized from nowhere, holding onto the collar of an overweight dog. "Hi, I'm Tabbie and this is Baskin. I'm only holding him because he's so young and friendly and Mom said he mustn't jump up at the baby." The Labrador wagged his tail wildly, trying to get away. "I guess you're Susanna."

"Hi," Susanna said. "This is Abigail."

The girl was ten years old but tall for her age and with her father's looks. She came closer and took a look at the baby. "She's neat," she said.

"Thank you," Susanna said. "I think she's about to start crying."

"Can I hold her?" Tabitha asked.

"You hang on to Baskin," Connie said firmly. "Abigail must be tired from the trip. Susanna, why don't you come on into the kitchen and we can fix her a drink—I have some formula all ready—and Bryan can show your father where your rooms are?"

"You be good now, Susi," Bodine said.

"I will," Susanna said, and Connie Van Dusen wheeled ahead of her into the back of the house.

"Is Susi what you like being called?" Tabitha asked her while Baskin squirmed to be freed, his claws scratching on the parquet floor.

"Not really," Susanna said.

"So why does your dad call you that?"

"He doesn't, usually."

"I'll call you Susanna," Tabitha said.

"What happened to your mom?" Tabitha asked Susanna later, upstairs in the small square bedroom her parents had allocated to the fourteen-year-old and her tiny sister. Matthew Bodine and Bryan Van Dusen had adjourned to the garage so that Bodine could check out the failing motor of Bryan's old Dodge pickup. One of the reasons Van Dusen had decided to take on Bodine was his claim to "understand" engines and other inanimate objects; the other reasons were that the man was physically strong and hungry for work—both of which attributes would be of great assistance to Connie in her day-to-day striving for normality—and that he had looked so desperate.

"She died," Susanna answered Tabitha.

"I know that, but how?" They were both sitting on Susanna's bed, while the baby slept peacefully under a pink blanket in her new crib. Though Bryan Van Dusen had installed a Stairlift to give his wife more freedom of movement around the house, there was no way Connie Van Dusen could make it up the narrow steps to the third floor; but she had instructed Tabitha to prepare the bedroom, to show Susanna where to find towels and sheets and all the baby things that Connie had bought in readiness for their arrival, since Matthew Bodine had confessed to her husband that the shocking loss of his wife had left him ill prepared for their new daughter.

"She had a heart attack while Abigail was being born."

"That's terrible. Did you know she was sick?"

"No," Susanna said.

"You must miss her so much." Tabitha knew something about the fragility of life, having watched Connie's struggles to regain control of her own.

"Yes," Susanna said.

"If you want to cry, I don't mind," Tabitha said.

"Thank you."

Tabitha waited, but the other girl's eyes remained dry. "Don't you want to cry?"

"Not right now, thank you."

"Okay." Tabitha looked over at the crib. "How long will she sleep?"

"It's hard to say." Susanna smiled. "Sometimes she sleeps for hours; other times she's awake and wanting to play after just a little nap."

"She's too small to play, isn't she?"

"She likes to lie naked on the floor and kick her legs."

Tabitha stood up and went to look at Abigail. "She's quite cute. Some little babies are so wrinkled and red and ugly."

"I think she's beautiful," Susanna said softly.

"At least now you're all here, you won't have to play her mother the whole time."

"I don't mind," Susanna said. "I like doing things for her."

"Mom and Dad say we all have to pitch in."

"Your parents seem very nice," Susanna said.

"They are."

Curiosity overcame the restraint that Bodine had told Susanna to practice. "What happened to your mother?" she asked. "How come she can't walk?"

"She fell off a wall near our old house two years ago," Tabitha answered simply. "She broke her back. It was the worst time. The doctors thought she might not be able to do anything, that her arms were going to be paralyzed too, but Mom said right off that they were wrong." Her pride in her mother's courage glowed in her hazel eyes. "She can do most things for herself now, but Dad still said we had to move because our old house was right on the ocean and there were zillions of steps."

"I love the ocean," Susanna said.

"Me too. The old house was really neat. I'll show it to you if you like."

"Okay."

Susanna stood up and went to the open window. The Atlantic was two streets away, and the bedroom, at the top of the house, overlooked the backyard and some woods; but an unmistakable sea breeze ruffled the pretty blue and yellow drapes, and Susanna could smell the brine and hear the mewing of the gulls, and it was as comforting to her as a loving embrace.

"I've always lived near the sea," she said.

"I thought your Dad said you were from Vermont," Tabitha said.

"He is," Susanna said quickly. "But we've lived all over."

Tabitha sat down again on the bed. "Mom said you guys lived in a convent."

"That's right." Susanna did not turn from the window, kept her eyes fixed on the rosebushes in the backyard. Baskin was out there, rooting around for something buried or lost, his black nose plunging in and out of dark, rich soil, his foolish tail wagging crazily.

"How come?"

"My father worked there."

"That must have been weird, living with all those nuns."

"They were nice."

"Didn't they make you pray all the time?"

Susanna laughed and turned around. "Nuns are really normal. One of them, Sister Dominic, was almost like my best friend."

"Did your mom work there too?" Tabitha was still curious. "Yes."

"What did she do?"

Susanna moved restlessly back to the crib, looked down, patted the blanket with one hand, stroked the baby's head. "She cooked and cleaned, kept the place looking nice."

"I'm asking too many questions, aren't I?" Tabitha said.

Susanna flushed. "No, not really."

"Mom and Dad say I talk too much all the time. Dad said I shouldn't ask too many questions about your mother, in case you get upset."

"I don't mind," Susanna said.

"I think it's okay to talk about dead people." Tabitha went on. "After my grandmother died, almost everyone who came to the house talked about everything except her, but I thought that was dumb. If I died, I'd want everyone to talk about me."

When Abigail woke, her little face puckering before the first cry, Tabitha watched in fascination as Susanna changed her diaper and fed her some more of the formula she had carried up from the kitchen.

"You're really good at that," the younger girl said.

"I'm used to it now."

Tabitha stared at the rosebud mouth tightly clenched around the teat of the feeding bottle, at the intensity of the infant's eyes apparently focused on her big sister's face, at the tiny hands that clenched and unclenched repeatedly during the feeding, and then she watched as the older girl rested the baby against her shoulder and gently rubbed her back.

"Could I learn to do that?"

"I don't see why not." Susanna kissed the top of Abigail's head, felt the soft, tender fuzz of her golden hair against her lips. "It's easy, once you know how."

"Who taught you?"

"No one."

"Someone must have taught you."

"My father gave me a book. You can learn almost anything from books."

"I can't," Tabitha said. "I'm lousy at school."

"I bet you're not."

"I hate learning—except sports. I'm crazy about sports."

"What do you like most?"

"Swimming and tennis. And gymnastics."

Susanna looked away from Abigail at Tabitha. She was big for a ten-year-old, with strong legs and arms. Her red-brown, tightly curly hair formed a wild halo around her freckled face, and Susanna could picture her playing tennis or plunging through the waves.

"Could you teach me to play tennis?" she asked.

"Sure," Tabitha said easily. "And we can go swimming whenever you want."

"I'd like that," Susanna said.

"I'm going to like having you live here," Tabitha said abruptly.

Susanna felt warmth pass through her. "Thank you," she said.

Three weeks later, in the midst of the first warm snap of the season, Tabitha took Susanna and Abigail—in the old baby carriage that Bryan Van Dusen had dug out of the attic when they had moved house and that, unaccountably, he had felt unable to throw away—to White Moon Beach. There was a good sprinkling of people, some of them trying to get an early start on their tans, a handful of hardy types braving the cold waters, most just strolling or playing ball or building their first sand castle of the year.

" 'Roll on, thou deep and dark blue ocean—roll!' " Tabitha declaimed, flopping down on her knees in the cool sand and kicking off her sneakers. " 'Ten thousand fleets sweep over thee in vain'—"

"That's wonderful. What is it?" Susanna picked Abigail out of the carriage and laid her down on the big rubber sheet they'd brought with them. The baby stared up at the blue sky for a moment, startled, then gave a gurgle of pleasure and began to kick her legs.

"Lord Byron, I think," Tabitha said.

"I thought you said you were lousy at school."

"I am, but I like poetry, some of it anyway."

Susanna settled down beside Abigail, took hold of one of the tiny hands, and tickled the soft palm. The baby wriggled and gurgled some more, her happiness infectious, filling Susanna with warmth.

"Recite the rest of that poem, Tabbie."

"Can't remember any more. I found it in a book in the library, and I only remembered that bit because of the ocean."

Susanna gazed out to sea, drank in the waves, the unspeakable depths, the power and the throbbing, gentle menace of it. She closed her eyes.

"Are you okay?" Tabitha asked after a minute.

"Fine." Susanna opened her eyes and smiled at her. "Just listening."

"You looked weird. Sad."

Susanna shook her head. "I'm not sad. I was just listening to the ocean. To its voice. I used to lie awake sometimes at night, hearing it murmuring to me, letting it sing me back to sleep."

"Was your house right by the ocean then?"

"Uh-huh."

"As close as our old house?"

Tabitha had shown Susanna their old home, a large, curious-looking house built on stilts because of high tides and storms, and Susanna had seen how impossible it would have been for Connie to have gone on living there after her accident, and she had understood why Tabitha sounded so wistful when she spoke about it, because it was a house for growing up in, a place for fantasy and adventure and rummaging around and being at ease.

"Closer," Susanna said.

"Cool," Tabitha said.

They lay back for a while and were very relaxed and calm. They both wore denim shorts, and the sun grew warmer against their bare legs, the breeze softened, more people headed for the water, still more trickled onto the sand, mothers and fathers nagged by their children to bring them to the beach, impatient for summer's freedoms.

"Do you want to try the water?" Tabitha asked after a time.

"I can't leave Abigail."

"I'll stay with her."

"No, it's okay," Susanna said. "You go."

"You want to go, I know you do."

"I don't mind."

"Sure you do. Look at it. Can't you feel it lapping around your ankles?"

Susanna weakened. "Maybe just for a minute. But you have to watch Abigail; you can't leave her even for a second."

"I won't," Tabitha insisted. "Just go, Susanna."

Susanna walked, barefoot, down to the water's edge. She looked back, saw the ten-year-old planted firmly on the rubber sheet, Abigail like a doll beside her, and then she turned around and faced the Atlantic. A tremor, deep and intimidating, passed through her, and then was gone.

"Hello, old friend," she whispered, and the ocean responded to her, as it always had, its great voice familiar and soothing and awesome. Over to her right a herring gull came in to land, bold and unafraid, its own claim to the beach superseding hers and the other visitors'. The surf raced in, covered her feet, icy and vigorous, raising the gooseflesh on her arms and legs, but Susanna remained still for another moment, facing out to sea, watching, listening, breathing in the wild, timeless, unique fragrance of the deep, and then she turned to her left and began to walk along the shore. She took small steps at first, watching the imprints of her toes and heels forming in the damp sand, knowing they'd be gone with the next wave, smoothed away for all eternity. Her strides grew longer, and the breeze lifted and sharpened and stung her cheeks and blew her hair up and out into an aura, and her eyes were wet with tears of freedom and release. And the burden of her past seemed to melt further away with each step, swept into nothingness by the weight of the ocean as it pushed into America and drew back again, thrusting and receding, over and over, wiping away the past as it did each imprint of every visitor, all of them rendered less significant and lasting than a single grain of sand.

She heard the dog's bark long before she registered Tabitha's cry, both floating to her through the surf's roar and the sounds of laughter and gulls and bouncing balls. She turned around and saw that she was a long way away, had walked farther than she had realized, and it was another moment before she saw Tabitha, up and running, or trying to run, a bundle in her arms and a big brown dog leaping up at her as she kicked at it and twisted and turned in her efforts to keep the baby in her arms away from its open jaws.

"Abigail!" Susanna screamed, and began to run. Her heart pounded wildly; sand flew in all directions, spattering people. Getting closer, she saw the brown, square-jawed dog, sharp-fanged and agile and bullying, and she saw Tabitha's terrified face, and Susanna screamed again for someone to help, and a man turned around from his daughter's sand castle, and he was up on his feet and he had a stick in his hand and he ran toward the dog, yelling, and the animal stopped jumping and ran off, tail down, yelping and afraid, its terror spree ended.

"Give her to me!" Susanna snatched Abigail from Tabitha's arms.

"She's okay," the girl sobbed. "I think she's okay."

The baby was crying too now, her little face all screwed up, her mouth open wide, her skin reddened from fright and being held too tightly. Susanna got down on her knees, rested the infant on her thighs, checking her for signs of injury, scanning her face, body, arms, legs, her own breath coming harshly, and then she began again, eyes poring over every inch of baby flesh until she was satisfied that no physical harm, at least, had been done; and then she held her close, Abigail's little hot cheek to her own, whispering her name over and over into the warm skin, and the love in her was a torrent, so intense, so overwhelming it was almost terrifying, and nothing else mattered, and no one, not even poor Tabitha, standing beside her, distraught.

"Is she okay?" Tabitha asked. "Is she *okay?*"

"Yes." Susanna's voice was harsh, and she knew she was gripping Abigail too tightly because the baby was crying more loudly than ever, but she couldn't stop, couldn't let her go, and her eyes darted wildly around the beach, looking for the dog, looking for the enemy.

"I couldn't do anything," Tabitha said piteously.

"I shouldn't have left her with you." There was no forgiveness in Susanna's voice.

"The dog would have come just the same."

"I'd have seen it coming."

Tabitha kept silent while Susanna tucked Abigail back into the pram and packed away the rubber sheet. As they began their bumpy walk back toward the path, they passed the man who had chased away the dog, and Susanna stopped to thank him for saving her sister's life.

"Your friend did good," he said. "Big dog like that can be real scary."

Back on the road Susanna spoke without looking at Tabitha. "I'm sorry," she said.

"No, I'm sorry," Tabitha said.

"You heard what the man said. You saved her."

"I'm not sure it would have done anything," Tabitha said. "It just spooked me, going off like that."

"It would have spooked anyone," Susanna said. "You did the right thing."

"I guess I did," Tabitha acknowledged, and pride crept into her voice.

"Tabitha and I got closer from that day on," Susanna told Pete Strauss eleven years later. "We all settled into that house, and it began to feel like home. I went to school, and Abigail had her first birthday there, and the Van Dusens made it so nice for her, for us all. They wouldn't let my father do any work that day, and Connie and Tabbie made all the food, and I remember Baskin got up on a chair at the end of the table right opposite Abigail, and she giggled and got cake all over her face, and we were all very happy."

"What changed?" Pete asked. "I get the feeling there's a big but coming."

"A very big but," Susanna said. "And his name was Matthew Bodine. My father." She paused. "He left."

"What happened?" Pete's tone was gentle.

"The truth, or the original Van Dusen version?"

"Both, if you like."

Susanna nodded. "I went to school one morning without Tabbie, who had a cold. When I came home, Tabbie was in her room and the doctor was with her, and my father was gone. Bryan and Connie tried to persuade me that those two things weren't related, that my father had received a call and had told them he had to leave, but I could see in their faces that they were lying." Her voice was perfectly calm. "I didn't tell them I knew, I knew they were trying to be kind. I just went to pick up Abigail and took her out into the backyard, but Connie realized I needed to know more, so after a while she came to find me, and she told me— she was so gentle, so kind—that my father had got himself into some trouble, and that he'd had to leave, and that she wasn't certain when he was coming back."

Susanna paused, but Pete said nothing, just waited for her to go on.

"Two nights later, when Abigail was sound asleep and after

the light had gone out in Bryan and Connie's bedroom, I went in to see Tabitha. She was lying in the dark, but I knew right away she was awake and that she'd been crying. I asked her to tell me what had happened, and at first she wouldn't say anything, because her parents had made her promise not to tell me, but I told her that I needed to know the truth, and then she came out with it."

Beside Susanna, on the sofa, Steinbeck shifted his head from her thigh to her knee. Outside, on Eighth Street, people still came and went, the sun still burned its angry August heat through the polluted layers of Manhattan sky; inside, the air conditioner still throbbed, though Vivaldi had long since stopped playing. The clock on Pete's desk showed that Susanna had well overstayed her time, but there were no patients in the waiting room, and though Pete Strauss had long ago learned the psychologist's knack of driving a deadly pause through the heart of the deepest purging of the most troubled spirit, he had no wish or will to interrupt Susanna now.

"The truth was," Susanna went on, "that my father had sexually assaulted Tabitha." Her voice was still calm, almost a monotone. "He went to her room while Connie and Bryan were both out of the house, and while Tabbie was napping because of her cold. He pretended at first that he was checking out some wiring behind the bed. And then he tried to touch her." She paused again. "Tabbie told him not to, but he wouldn't stop. When she tried to get away from him, he made a grab for her, but Tabbie managed to escape." Susanna paused again. "She screamed at him as she ran out of the house that she was going to tell her father what he'd done. I guess that was enough to send him on his way."

"How old was Tabbie then?"

"She was twelve."

"Did you hear from your father again?"

"Never."

"I'm sorry."

"I'm not."

Pete lit a Marlboro and inhaled. "How did hearing that make you feel?"

"How do you think it made me feel?"

"I don't know. That's why I'm asking you."

"How was I supposed to feel? Disgusted? Ashamed? Guilty?"

"I wouldn't say you were supposed to feel anything in particular." Pete paused. "Why would you feel guilty?"

"Because we came as a package. Into that house."

"You came as a child. You were innocent."

Susanna said nothing.

"Don't you believe that, Susanna?"

"Sure I do." She gave a half smile. "You're really sounding like a shrink now."

"Sorry."

"I almost forgot, for a while, that you are." She made a small grimace, a gesture of grudging admiration, with her mouth. "You're good. I told you before, I don't usually share that much about myself."

"Does Hawke know about your father?"

"He knows about what he did to Tabbie."

"Is there more?"

"Yes, there's more," she said softly.

"Want to talk about it?"

"I don't think so." Susanna had the sense that she was coming to, almost as if she were wakening from a period of dream-laden sleep. She'd felt very relaxed while talking to Pete, very much at peace, but suddenly she felt tired, almost drained. She glanced at the clock on his desk, saw that it was after two o'clock and that she'd been there for almost an hour and a half. "I should go."

"There's no rush," Pete said. "I have no one until three."

"I need to get home to Hawke." Susanna stroked Steinbeck's head and straightened her legs, stiff from so long in one position.

"How's he doing?"

"Haven't you seen him?"

"Not since he left the hospital."

"He's doing great," Susanna said. "He has to be—we start work in two days."

Pete stubbed out his cigarette. "One more question, before you go?"

"Okay."

"What happened after your father left? I mean, I know the Van Dusens became your and Abigail's foster parents, but you must have had a difficult time."

"They made it easy," Susanna said. "Connie and Bryan, and Tabbie especially. I told them I thought that Abigail and I ought to leave too. They were genuinely appalled. Most parents would have wanted us out of their home, don't you think? But not Connie and Bryan. They didn't even let the police go after our father. Tabitha was okay, and they were afraid of the effect a trial might have on us all. They said that whatever Matthew Bodine had done had nothing whatever to do with his children, and they insisted that things should go on as before, though I refused to go back to school."

"Why did you do that?"

"I had to look after Abigail," Susanna replied simply. "I was almost sixteen, and as far as I was concerned, there was no alternative. She was my sister, my responsibility; it was different so long as my father was around the house to help, but it would have been impossible for Connie to manage alone."

"They could have employed someone else."

"I wanted to look after her myself." Susanna swung her feet to the floor, slipped them back into their loafers, then leaned back again. "They wanted to adopt us, you know, and I wanted that, too, very much. But my father wasn't dead, just missing, so the best they could do was become our foster family and let us use their name." She shook her head. "They're remarkable people, don't you think?"

"They sound wonderful," Pete said.

"We were very fortunate," Susanna said softly. "I knew how lucky I was to find them." She paused. "I guess my luck's run out now, though, hasn't it?"

"Do you believe in good and bad luck?"

"Don't you?"

"To a degree, but on the whole I tend to believe in destinies being shaped—too often not by ourselves. I like to think we can take a hand in the shaping, though." Pete paused. "What do you believe in, Susanna?"

"Is that a question about religion?"

"If you like."

"I have no religion."

Pete recognized another wall going up but persisted anyway. "Do you believe in God?"

"I tend not to think about God," she said.

He changed tack. "Did you miss your father after he left?"

"No."

"Two such major losses, though, so close to each other—"

"I didn't miss him." Susanna got to her feet. "You must think me very hard." Steinbeck, still on the sofa, gave a low groan, stretched, and closed his eyes.

"That's the last word I'd think of using to describe you," Pete said. "You may be strong. That doesn't make you hard."

"I'm not so sure," Susanna said. "I think I've grown a kind of hard shell around my heart over the years—at least around my memories." She bent down to pick up her purse.

"That's just self-preservation," Pete said.

"Isn't that what life's all about?" Susanna said.

CHAPTER 6

~

On the third day of the first Grace shoot, on location in the Monet room at the Museum of Modern Art, Hawke had a coughing fit that wouldn't let up, as a result of which a fragile blood vessel in his throat burst, and blood trickled from the corner of his mouth down his chin and onto his white T-shirt. It had occurred twice before, and it was always alarming, but both Hawke and Susanna were able to remain superficially calm while Angie Lopez, the hair and makeup expert Hawke had worked with for years, passed him wet Kleenex tissues and gave him a clean T-shirt. James Kline of UKA, the advertising agency, and Lori Underwood from Maison Grace, were, however, horrified and incapable of concealing their revulsion and fear. Susanna got Hawke home swiftly, and Saul Weinberg, their doctor, concerned about the possibility of PCP, recommended they go directly to the emergency room at the hospital. There was no sign of pneumonia; a crumb from a breadstick had caught in Hawke's throat, provoking the coughing fit which had in turn irritated the blood vessel. Within twenty-four hours Hawke was ready to go back to work, but neither Underwood nor Kline reappeared.

Five days later Marie Hueberlein flew in from Geneva and took Hawke and Susanna to lunch in the garden dining room at Lutèce. Well-trained, impeccable heads refrained from turning as they walked to their table, but Susanna felt eyes, admiring and judgmental, following her nonetheless.

"I won't beat around the bush," Hueberlein said, in her soft, husky, accented English, once they had ordered. "I am being encouraged to halt the campaign before it begins."

"Because of what happened last week," Hawke said. He looked well enough, his weight loss sufficiently pronounced to accentuate his strong, tough bone structure but not enough to make him drawn or gaunt.

"Exactly." Hueberlein's large dark eyes were perfectly candid, and her bobbed brunette hair gleamed in the sunlight.

"It was nothing." Susanna's stomach was taut with fear and anger.

"Of course it was something," Hawke said, quietly, looking at Marie. "I coughed up blood. James Kline was standing a few feet away from me. I saw him checking his face in one of Angie's makeup mirrors. He was petrified I'd sprayed some on him, and I didn't really blame the poor bastard."

"I do," Susanna said.

"So do I," Marie Hueberlein said. "But alas, I find that at Maison Grace I stand alone. The illness from which you are suffering, *mon cher*, is sending waves of fear through the whole fashion world."

"We weren't certain that you knew," Susanna said.

"Of course we were," Hawke contradicted. "Andrea Marantz just wasn't certain you knew officially, that's all."

"So what does this mean?" Susanna asked, point-blank, unable to contemplate eating the delicate scallop starter Marie had talked her into ordering unless she knew what they were up against. "Please, Marie. We need to know where we stand."

"I understand, Susanna," Marie said, gently. "But before I can answer your question, I have some of my own that I must ask, with your permission."

"Okay," Susanna said.

"And Hawke's." She spoke his name—'Awke—with respect and tenderness. "Most of all, Hawke's."

"You have it," Hawke said.

"Thank you." Marie paused. "How long do you think you will be able to work? As yourself, I mean, undiluted Hawke. Great Hawke."

"That's a little hard to answer," Hawke said honestly. "I can tell you what I've been aiming for, what I believe is a rational goal." He saw her nod. "I want to shoot the whole launch campaign, to create the Grace woman. I believe I can do that." He smiled his rough, disarming smile. "And since we're talking about Susanna, unless I thought I was going to be great Hawke, I wouldn't even take it on."

"Next question," Marie said, her voice confidential. "Is there some way you can prevent something as public as what happened last week from happening again?"

"I don't know," Hawke said.

"I don't ask for miracles," Marie told him. "I dislike asking you this more than I can say, *mon cher*—I despise the climate of fear and suspicion that makes it necessary, but the livelihood of many people depends upon my being a realist."

"You're asking Hawke to guarantee that he won't get sick in front of anyone else." Susanna's aggression level rose again. "You're asking him if he can schedule his next bout of pneumonia or toxoplasmosis—" She fought to keep her voice low. "You're asking him to bleed in private next time."

Hawke said nothing, just sat and sipped his white wine. Marie Hueberlein remained calm.

"I'm asking if such a thing is possible," she said. "Within reason, I'm asking you both if you can bring yourselves to share in my conspiracy, my unwilling conspiracy."

Hawke looked at Susanna. "She's doing this for us, gorgeous." He always called her that when they were working; it was his preferred photographer-model endearment, that or "sweetheart." At home, in private, even in bed, he called her by her proper name or just "love," English-style, never "darling," which he loathed. "She wants to know if we can play the game, or at least try to."

"*Exactement*," Marie said.

Susanna felt nauseated. "I can't treat this as a game."

"Wrong word, gorgeous," Hawke said quickly. "What Marie wants—needs to hear—is that when I start coughing next time, I leave the room before I start bleeding, that next time I start feeling like shit, I make a good, professional excuse to end the session before I start shaking or throw up or pass out."

Susanna looked away from him to Marie. "There's no reason

to believe that any of those things are going to happen. Hawke's well again now. He's probably going to be well for a long, long time."

"I'm happy to hear that," Marie said. "And looking at you"— she smiled at Hawke—"I do believe it. But—"

"But Lori Underwood was a witness to the ugly side," Hawke said starkly, "and let's face it, what happened to me that day didn't exactly enhance the image we're trying to create for the Grace woman."

"It did not," Marie said.

The starters arrived and were exquisitely served. None of them began.

"Fire me," Hawke said abruptly. "Keep Susanna and get shot of me."

"You go, I go," Susanna said.

"Susanna Van Dusen without Hawke is uncharted territory," Marie pointed out evenly. "And I am firing no one, if I can possibly avoid it." She paused. "I asked you a question. Is it possible, within limitations, to keep your sickness private?"

Hawke nodded, slowly. "For the moment."

"*Bien.* Then for the moment," Marie said, "leave it with me." She picked up her soup spoon.

"So what does this mean?" Susanna had to know, before she faced her scallops. "Do we go on?"

"We do," Marie said with conviction.

"I want to go on," Hawke said, and for the first time there was a hint of need in his voice. "I've got a lot of great Hawke in me yet, Marie."

Susanna felt her throat tighten.

Marie put down her soup spoon and picked up her wineglass. "To great Hawke," she said.

They drank.

When the spots first appeared on Hawke's chest and upper arms, just over a week after their lunch with Marie Hueberlein at Lutèce, they both were certain it was Kaposi's come to betray them once and for all. But Hawke felt so bad, and he was running a fever, and then the spots turned into blisters, and Saul Weinberg diagnosed chicken pox, and at first, though Hawke felt too sick to be really amused, they both laughed with relief. Within a few days, though, he was sick enough to be admitted back into the hospital, and the blisters were everywhere, in his mouth and trachea, and Lori Underwood sent flowers and a message that they were putting the campaign on hold until Hawke was better, and she trusted that Susanna had already had chicken pox. It was a kindly enough message, but neither Hawke nor Susanna needed to be geniuses to read between the lines: chicken pox was one of those opportunistic infections that everyone was hearing about, the kind of generally innocent disease that could kill an AIDS sufferer.

"And of course, the part of the message about me," Susanna said to Pete Strauss at the hospital after he'd come to visit with Hawke, "is just corporate code too." She was so angry she wanted to march into the Grace New York offices and spit in Lori Underwood's frightened eye. "Why doesn't she just come right out and ask me if I have it too?"

"She doesn't want to get sued," Pete said.

"I don't think we could sue if we wanted to."

They were sitting in the little used office on the floor below Hawke's room, the same room in which they'd had their first talk a few months earlier, Pete with his feet up on the old fake teak desk.

"Maybe they think you could sue them," he said.

Susanna shook her head. "There are about a dozen small-print clauses in our contract about health and morality and stuff like that."

"Relating to the Grace woman or to Hawke?"

"To me."

"You've done nothing immoral," Pete said. "Have you?"

"I sleep in the same bed as a man who has AIDS."

"Who happens to be your husband."

Susanna did not meet his eyes. "I'm unclean, Pete."

"That's absurd."

"It's what they think. It's what this will all come down to, ultimately. Marie Hueberlein may say, or even believe, that part of her reason for going with me was that I look as if I've had some tough times, so that older women can relate to the Grace image as well as young." She looked directly at Pete now, her expression hardening. "But when the chips are down, Grace will be no different from any of the other cosmetic houses. They may want a touch of smolder or experience with their purity, but they still want purity. The day Hawke coughed up blood in the Monet room, we both knew the writing was on the wall." Her smile was full of irony, and there were tears in her eyes. "And in the end it's chicken pox, goddamned *chicken pox*, that's going to finish it for Hawke."

"He'll get over this, Susanna." Pete was dismayed by her distress.

"I'm talking about his career." Susanna stood up and walked over to the filing cabinets, turned restlessly back to face him. "Work is Hawke's life, Pete. I mean, I know it is for a lot of people, but it's really true in his case." She shook her head. "I don't give a damn about losing this contract—I don't care if I never model again—but I think—I know—that the only thing that Hawke would mind more than his getting dumped by Grace is if I get dumped with him."

"Then you have to fight them."

She shrugged and came back to sit down again. "There's nothing to fight yet. That's part of the problem. They haven't done one wrong thing. All they've said is that they're putting the campaign on hold while Hawke is sick; they're full of concern and compassion."

"But you think that's bullshit?" Pete asked.

"Think, hell," Susanna said vehemently. "I don't know much about big corporations, but I do know there's no way they can possibly afford to put this on hold. The ads are booked; the features are probably all written—the TV spots too, probably."

"So you're saying the decision's already been made."

"That's what I'm saying."

"What about your agent? Your lawyer?"

Susanna shook her head again, tiredly. "I don't want to sue anyone, Pete. And even if Hawke does, he'll soon be too sick to consider it. So far as I'm concerned, I'll be glad to be rid of it. That way I can stay with him, every step of the way, be there for him when he needs me. The worst scenario, from my point of view, would be for Grace to keep me without Hawke, though it might be better from his."

"So what are you going to do?" Pete lit a Marlboro.

"Nothing. Stick around Hawke as much as he'll let me. You've seen him; you know how awful he looks with those damned blisters all over him. I've seen him look in the mirror and shudder at his own reflection—he can't even shave, and he says he feels hideous and dirty."

Pete was silent for a moment.

"Have you had chicken pox?" he asked.

"Yes," she said, and pointed to a tiny telltale scar close to the jawline on the left side of her face. "I guess I scratched."

Pete looked at it. "Wow," he said softly. "I'm surprised mirrors don't crack when you look into them."

"Me too." Susanna paused. "Pete, could I have one of your cigarettes?"

"You don't smoke."

"Maybe I should."

"No, you shouldn't. Why would you think you should?"

She shrugged again. "I need something. I don't want Valium, and I'm drinking more than I should."

"How much?"

"Not much, don't start worrying, but models are supposed to drink mineral water, especially when they're working with cosmetics." She smiled wryly. "I guess I won't have to worry about stuff like that much longer—then I can drink like a fish."

"I'd rather you didn't," Pete said evenly.

"Just kidding," she said. "And I guess I don't really want a cigarette either."

"More exercise?" he suggested.

"I do enough."

"How about yoga? I practice it most days. You could join me."

She smiled at him. "Maybe I will."

"We could combine your next appointment with a session if you'd like."

"Wouldn't that be unprofessional?" Susanna asked.

"I can't see why, if you don't mind. Might as well talk cross-legged as lying on a couch."

"I never lie on your couch."

"No one ever does," Pete said.

Susanna smiled at him again. "I like you."

"Thank you. I like you too."

"I'm glad," Susanna said.

* * *

On October 1, seven days before the museum shoot was scheduled to recommence, Andrea Marantz told Hawke and Susanna
that Maison Grace had pulled out but that Marie Hueberlein had
guaranteed to pay them both every last dime Grace had contracted to pay, plus a five-hundred-thousand-dollar penalty to
Susanna.

"Which is," Andrea said to them both in her office, "I guess
—to use one of Hawke's expressions—a hell of a lot better than
a poke in the eye with a sharp stick but is, in reality, as we all
know, hush money."

Susanna said nothing. She was very conscious of Hawke sitting
in the chair beside her, straight-backed, too straight, since Hawke
almost always slouched. There had been no reaction from him
when Andrea had broken the news to them, no significant change
in his expression or demeanor. Susanna wanted to reach out and
take his hand, but she sensed that he did not want to be touched,
that any hint of comfort might be taken by him as pity.

"What about keeping Susanna and using another photographer?" Hawke asked softly, though he already knew the answer.

"They won't consider it," Andrea replied.

"Great," he said, still softly.

Susanna had had enough. "I think it stinks," she said. "I think
it stinks to high heaven."

"You're right," Andrea said.

"I'd like to tell them to take their money and shove it," Susanna said.

"But you won't," Andrea said.

"No, she won't," Hawke said.

"I'd like to give the story to the *Times* or *Vanity Fair* or *60
Minutes*," Susanna said. "People should know."

"People wouldn't give a fuck," Hawke told her.

"If you take the money, you can't say a word to anyone," Andrea said. "And Hawke's almost right. Some people might give a
fuck, but a lot of them would side with Grace." She saw Susanna's
expression. "I'm as appalled as you are, Susanna, but I've always
been straight with you, and you've always been a realist too. We
know how scared people are of this. Sure, they know more than
they did—they know they can't catch it from a picture in a
magazine—but they don't want to be reminded of it when they

pick up *Vogue* or buy mascara." Andrea paused. "Grace isn't going with another model. They've decided to postpone the whole launch of the line in the U.S. for another year. Frankly, I'd say we're lucky they're not suing our asses. If they weren't terrified of negative publicity, you can bet they would be."

"I can't believe they're scrapping the whole launch," Susanna said.

"Postponing, not scrapping," Andrea said.

"They can't launch now," Hawke said, still quiet, "because people may associate the products with me."

"But the women who'd go out and buy their makeup don't even know you're sick," Susanna said.

"Not yet, but if the campaign were to get under way with another model and photographer, they'd get to know," Andrea pointed out. "The press knows you were going to be the Grace woman, and they know you're a team. Hawke's AIDS would be on every magazine cover so fast it would make your heads spin, and Marie Hueberlein knows that the cold hard truth is that every time anyone saw Grace lipstick on your lovely lips, Susanna, they'd turn around and buy Clinique or Lancôme instead."

"I have the plague, gorgeous," Hawke said, with a twist to his mouth, "and you're tainted with it."

"Shut up," Susanna said.

"It's the truth," he said.

"I don't want to hear it." Susanna stood up. She felt sick. "I have to go now, Hawke." She kept her voice steady. "Are you coming?"

"If you're going to a bar."

She looked down at him. The chicken pox marks on his face were nearly gone now, and there would be little scarring. He looked almost well, unless you looked at the stiffness of his jaw, or into his eyes.

"We could go home," she said, "get a drink there."

"I don't want a drink," Hawke replied. "I want to get drunk. As a lord," he added. "Stinking, roaring, out of it, drunk."

"Sounds good to me," Susanna said gently.

"Sounds dangerous," Andrea said.

Hawke stood up.

"Not half as dangerous as staying sober," he said.

CHAPTER 7

~

Pete and Susanna sat, in neat, erect half-lotus positions, on the worn Persian rug in Pete's living room. A painting, recently begun, of a snow-covered, early-morning Washington Square, stood on a paint-splashed easel near the window, brought in from the studio for inspection; it was, thus far, Pete thought and Susanna agreed, one of his more successful works, a tad better composed than most, a lot less gaudy and aggressive than many he had completed since Leigh had filed for divorce. The slow, expressive second movement of Bach's Sixth Brandenburg Concerto flowed from speakers concealed behind bookshelves about the room. In her big domed cage Alice, the cockatoo, crunched seed contentedly. Steinbeck lay, dozing, near the door.

It was eleven in the morning, a week before Christmas. Hawke had stayed well all through October, November, and the first half of December, and then an attack of toxoplasmosis, followed by another battle with pneumonia, had brought him to his knees. For the first time, two days ago, Susanna had looked at him and had faced what she had known for so long, known in her mind but not in her heart, that Hawke was truly going to die. His weight loss was now chillingly noticeable, and tufts of his lovely wavy hair were gone. His gray, intelligent eyes were couched in dark hollows, his clear English skin was parchmentlike, and because a brain abscess, successfully treated, had left him uncoordinated on one side, he was walking with a crutch. Hawke was thirty-five years old, but suddenly he looked fifty, and a dying fifty at that.

"I want to talk about Hawke and me today," Susanna said to Pete in the midst of their yoga peace.

"Okay," Pete said.

"About how it was. Before. About what happened."

Pete waited. They had plenty of time; his next patient wasn't due until two-thirty. The room was warm, the heat full on, the window open just a crack, letting winter air and life slip into the building. Susanna's arms were resting on her thighs, her hands open, palms up. She closed her eyes, took a cleansing breath, the way Pete had taught her, and began.

For the first few weeks after Connie Van Dusen's show at the Groentken Gallery in 1980, Hawke's only real communication with Susanna was through his camera lenses. Bryan arranged for Susanna to stay with an old friend of Connie's in Queens, and Hawke rented a car in which he collected her each morning and deposited her back each evening. He worked ceaselessly, tirelessly, sometimes in his studio in the loft on Canal Street, sometimes out on the streets. He photographed Susanna in Chinatown, in Little Italy, in Central Park, on the Upper and Lower East Sides, on Broadway, in Times Square, in singles bars on Second Avenue, emerging from the swankiest stores on Fifty-seventh Street, on street corners in Harlem and on the Staten Island ferry. Much of the time he worked silently, his visions in his head, unable and unwilling to share them; he gave Susanna physical directions and hints, clues to what he wanted from her; he tested her powers of imagination, her potential for performance.

"See the woman on that counter." He pointed on Saks's first floor. "See how good she looks, how great her hair and makeup are, but see how tired she is behind the mask. Look at the way she's slipped off one shoe and she's rubbing one foot against the other ankle and she thinks no one's noticed." He raised his camera. "Be her, Susanna, be that woman now. Don't think too much, just jump inside her mind, where she went last night, how long she's stood there, how bored she is—that's right, that's good, that's great." He clicked away. "Okay, now be you again, you're young and vital and the world's fresh and opening up and you're Susanna again and glad of it, and that's good. . . ."

Hawke kept it loose and easy most of the time, wanting her to enjoy herself, mindful not to scare her off, getting her to open up, to relax but to harness and maintain her own energy. He brought her forward and out, encouraged her to project her inner essence as well as her physical presence for his camera. And then, when he was done shooting pictures, he banished Susanna back to Queens while he developed and processed and experimented and examined and, ultimately, rejoiced in what he had found, for he knew by then, without the smallest glimmer of doubt, that what he had told Connie Van Dusen that evening on Madison Avenue had been true.

On June 24, three weeks after her eighteenth birthday, he picked Susanna up, drove her into Manhattan, took her to lunch at the Russian Tea Room, ordered for her, cold borscht, red caviar omelet, and strawberries Romanoff, and sat back to enjoy her bliss.

"Make the most of it," he told her while they waited.

"I am," she said, gazing around at the warm red leather and pink linen, drinking in the profusion of glittering samovars and pictures and flowers, and the magnificent clocks. "Is this a Russian holiday?" she asked, feasting her eyes on the festive baubles all around the restaurant.

Hawke grinned. "It's Christmas all year round in here. Do you like it?"

"It's wonderful. I've never seen anything like it."

"There is nothing like it," Hawke said. "But when I told you to make the most of it, I was talking about the food. You'll be on a permanent diet from now on."

"I never diet," Susanna told him.

"I'm glad to hear it," Hawke said. "But from now on, if you agree, you'll be watching your weight with the best of them."

"If I agree to what?"

"You have it," Hawke said.

"What do I have?" Susanna was confused.

"You have what I need."

She experienced a chill of pleasure.

"I told Connie before we started," Hawke said, "that I believed you had something special."

"You're talking about modeling," Susanna said.

Hawke shook his head. "The word *model* encompasses a lot

more, and a lot less, than I'm talking about. How much do you know about modeling?"

"Not much. I know about the big names, of course."

"Mostly runway or photographic models," Hawke said. "The clotheshorses who stalk up and down at the shows, and the beauties who stare out at you from *Vogue* and *Harper's*." He saw her nod. "Have you ever dreamed of doing that, Susanna?"

"Of course not."

"A lot of girls do. Millions worldwide."

"I don't," she said definitely.

"Yet you've modeled for me for the past few weeks, willingly, I thought."

"That's different. That wasn't modeling."

"Yes, it was." Hawke paused. "The girls who dream about it —who'd sell their souls and probably their grandmothers to break in—take every crumb they're lucky enough to get. Most of them get sent home, the majority of those who do crack it do catalog jobs, good, steady work that can take them all over the world and pay the bills."

"I'd hate that," Susanna said.

Their borscht arrived, Hawke's served with iced vodka, and for several moments they were both silent. Susanna was conscious that she was sitting with one of the most attractive and exciting men in the restaurant; he was wearing the same distinctively cut charcoal linen jacket that he'd worn the evening they'd first met, and she was aware again, as she had been most times they'd spent together, of the great force of the man, of that submerged intensity that contrasted with his relaxed exterior. She had already learned, during their working sessions, how swiftly Hawke's mood could change from easygoing to demanding, from laid-back to keyed-up. When Hawke was concentrating totally on her, he could make her feel rare, even unique, but when they were brought together in a social setting, as they were today, especially in this atmosphere of heightened New York City sophistication, Susanna felt—in spite of the new white linen trouser suit she'd bought herself in a First Avenue boutique—gauche, naive, and hopelessly out of her depth.

Hawke started to speak again. "I've worked with more gorgeous, successful women than I can count"—his voice was matter-of-fact—"and not one of them is just a pretty face.

Don't make the mistake of confusing models with bimbos, Susanna. Bimbos don't make it in this business, or not much past modeling undies in rag trade showrooms."

"I didn't mean—"

"Sure you did." He cut her short. "Don't worry about it, most people don't realize that models have brains." He saw the embarrassment on her face and relented. "I think you and I might just make a great team."

She felt another of those chills but said nothing.

"I know everyone there is to know in this business, Susanna. I know every decent agent, every fashion editor, every designer, the best makeup artists and hairdressers. They all want to work with me." He shook his head. "It wasn't always like that, of course. I was good, but a lot of photographers are good. I got lucky." He grinned. "And maybe I was better than good."

"Connie says that you're great," Susanna said softly.

"That's kind of her." Hawke paused again. "I think I got lucky again a few weeks ago. The minute I saw Connie's pictures of you, the hairs stood up on the back of my neck."

Susanna felt her skin burning.

"I want you to think about working with me exclusively," he said.

"What do you mean?" Suddenly every nerve and muscle in Susanna's body were on alert.

"Don't be scared," he said.

"I'm not," she said defensively, knowing that she was.

"What I want"—Hawke leaned across the table—"what I'd like to do, is to teach you everything about the business, about modeling."

"But why? Why me?" Her confusion was genuine. "I'm nothing special. I'm not beautiful. Tabbie thinks I'm pretty, but that's just because she wants to be blond. I'm just a regular girl. I'm *ordinary.*"

"We're all ordinary," Hawke said. "But we're all unique. And each of us sees others in a unique way too. Take Connie and the rest of your family. I'll bet you all see her in a slightly different, special way."

"Of course we do," Susanna said. "But that's because she's different things to each of us: mother to Tabbie, wife to Bryan—"

"I'm talking about the way you *see* her, literally, the visual impact she has on you and the effect of it." He scooped out the last morsels of dill and cucumber from the tall tea glass his cold borscht had been served in. "It's the stuff inside"—he touched the side of his head—"that creates the outside image, that conjures up that impact." He savored the final spoonful. "You're a very pretty girl, Susanna, but there are hundreds, if not thousands, as pretty as you. But behind those lovely eyes and that stunning mouth, behind every gesture you make and the way you walk and move and laugh and talk, is the stuff that makes you special." His gray eyes were fixed hard on hers now. "I'm talking about your impact and effect on me, Susanna. What sets me aside from the other people who may understand your uniqueness is that I possess the magic to transmit it to the rest of the world."

"Through your photographs." Susanna sat back against the leather banquette, trying to absorb what was happening to her. "You really, truly think I can be a model." She sounded and felt dazed.

"My model." Hawke too leaned back. "That's the deal." He watched a hint of suspicion flicker in the lilac eyes. "I teach you all I know. I turn you, at the very least, into a stunning professional, and in return you agree that for as long as the relationship works, you don't let any other photographer near you."

"At the very least," Susanna repeated softly.

"There's no doubt about that," Hawke said. He leaned forward again. "You have something about you, Susanna, something more. Something that doesn't normally figure in the face of a very young woman. You have all the advantages of your youth— the elasticity of your skin, your skin tones, the suppleness of your mouth, the sparkle of your eyes—all those things that older women have to struggle to pretend they still have." He went on watching her carefully. "But there's something else too. Behind your eyes."

Susanna didn't speak. Their borscht dishes were removed, and wine was poured. A group of diners came in from Fifty-seventh Street, and Susanna recognized one of them as an actress she'd seen often on television, but whose name she couldn't remember. Fame. She thought, through the haze of curious sensations that were buzzing around her head, that fame was one of the things that Hawke was offering her. It seemed too absurd to contemplate, yet she was here, in this wonderful place, with this undeniably famous man, and that, for Susanna, was almost as ridiculous in its way.

Hawke was talking again.

"I can't really fathom you out, Susanna."

"In what way?"

He smiled. Her question seemed so genuinely curious, and he couldn't be sure if the flicker in her eyes—so imperceptible that another man, less trained in the capture of each changing nuance of expression, might not have observed it at all—was one of confusion or of fear. He only knew that she was, either deliberately or subconsciously, evading him.

"You're a bit of an enigma," he answered her.

"Not really," she said, and flushed again.

"Enough of an enigma to make me ready to cast aside Tiegs and Hansen and Lisa Taylor and even Lauren Hutton, whom I consider the most wonderful creature on earth," Hawke told her. "This deal works both ways, you know. You use only one photographer; I use only one model."

Their red caviar omelet arrived, complete with sour cream, and they lapsed back into silence, and Susanna, who had thought herself unable to eat anything more, found herself hungry beyond description, and she wondered if perhaps this new appetite might be symbolic of her rising hunger for whatever it was that Hawke was offering her.

"I don't know if I want to be changed," she said when the omelet was gone. "That is, I don't want to be turned into something, someone, I'm not."

Hawke shook his head. "I'm no Pygmalion, Susanna. You don't have to be afraid of me. I don't want to change you at all. I just want to draw you out—to bring out the best in you."

She sat quietly for another moment.

"I don't think I want to be famous."

"What do you want?" he asked.

"I want to be happy," she replied unhesitatingly. "I want to stay with my family, with the Van Dusens." She paused. "With my sister."

"Tell me about Abigail."

"Abigail." Susanna paused again, and Hawke could feel her

warmth, could almost see the sun rising inside her. "Abigail is the most perfect thing in my life," she said.

"I'd like to meet her."

Susanna smiled. "I think she'd like you."

Hawke waited for more, but nothing came.

"Connie and Bryan seem like good people to me," he said at last.

"They're better than good," Susanna said. "They've been amazingly kind to Abigail and me."

"I know they're your foster parents, but I don't know the circumstances."

"No," she said. "Things were tough for them, financially, before we came. They never said a word about that to us. They still never have."

"So more money might help?" Hawke probed.

"Of course."

"Supermodels make a lot of money, Susanna."

She laughed. "You don't really believe I could be a supermodel."

Hawke shrugged. "It's possible. These things are unpredictable. You might not have any real success at all. Working exclusively with me might hamper you, might hold you back. You might learn more working with different photographers."

"I don't want to work with other photographers," she said.

"And me?" Hawke asked.

"I'm not sure," she said.

A waiter poured more wine for them both. A couple rose from the next booth, an old, silver-haired man with his dark-haired daughter. The girl lifted her right hand and touched the back of the old man's neck, caressing him. Not his daughter, Susanna thought.

"Think about it," Hawke said. "Talk to Connie and Bryan. And you should talk to an agent."

"Really?" Susanna's eyes left the departing couple. The word *agent* sounded practical and solid, not like *supermodel*.

"Definitely. Perhaps even a lawyer, though the right agent will probably do for the time being. I could recommend one, but Connie may prefer to choose someone herself." Hawke paused. "I'm not planning a takeover, Susanna. This is business."

Susanna looked right into the sharp, clever gray eyes.

"Is it?" she asked.

"What else?"

"My world began to grow," she told Pete. "Up until then I'd believed there could be nothing better, more fulfilling than what I had. A home with my new family. I thought there was nothing more important than that—that and taking care of my little sister. That's still true, of course. But Hawke showed me that there could be more, for me as an individual. He opened up the doors."

"He let you out," Pete said.

Susanna shook her head. "He let me in. To his world." She smiled wistfully. "Hawke's world."

He opened the doors gently, caringly, but he opened them wider than she'd ever dreamed possible. Right through that summer of 1980, while Susanna commuted between Cohasset on weekends and Connie's friend's home in Queens during the week, Hawke fulfilled all his promises. He sheltered her under his wings of experience and brilliance, taught her all that he knew, all the techniques and tricks that models either went to school or survived a hundred or more disasters to learn, introduced her to a choice handful of people who could help with her training: Tally de Kooning, designer and former dresser, who tugged Susanna around New York, showing her clothes, *real* clothes, and what to do with them, how to turn dross into treasure, how to change at the speed of light, how to know when to yell and when to shut up; Angie Lopez, hairdresser and makeup artist extraordinaire, who reintroduced Susanna to herself in a zillion new guises and a trick for every mood; Lulu Fiedlander, exercise coach and gifted ballet dancer, who taught her how to move, how to breathe, how to stalk, runway style, how to spin without getting dizzy, how to freeze at a microsecond's notice. Hawke asked them all not to talk about Susanna, to help him keep her under wraps, and because they all adored Hawke and thought he was a genius, Tally and Angie and Lulu agreed to do it his way.

"I'm doing this for purely selfish reasons," he said lightly whenever Susanna tried to thank him. "I'm teaching you my way," he added, big bad wolf–style, "all the better to shackle you to me."

They were, they had both agreed, to be a team for better or worse, but the more Susanna learned, the more she understood how much Hawke was sparing her: all the grind and anguish, the tedium and humiliation of fighting to sign on with a halfway decent agency, and doing the rounds of go-sees and castings, and clawing her way up and being bawled out by a long string of no-talent strangers who didn't give a rat's ass about her. Hawke steered Susanna away from the big New York agencies, and Connie, trusting him and respecting his judgment, gave him his head. The Marantz Agency had taken care of Hawke from his Manhattan beginnings, and now Andrea Marantz was glad to be charged with looking after this young woman who, it was plain to see, would never have considered modeling had it not been for Hawke. Andrea had seen so many girls desperate to succeed, so hungry that they were prepared to do virtually anything, from plastic surgery and hours of discomfort in a dentist's chair, to paying charlatans who claimed they could stretch their height the one precious missing inch that would bring them up to the almost statutory five feet nine. Susanna was five-ten and, as Andrea described her to her colleagues, unblemished fruit straight from the branch, and more vitally than anything in this game, the camera didn't just love her, it *lusted* after her.

When Connie had photographed her, it had always been family stuff, easygoing and effortless. Having Hawke endlessly studying her through his lenses, focusing on every aspect of her, was very different. Not always patient, he tried to be gentle with her, and when he couldn't be gentle, he tried never to be unkind. Hawke told himself that his sessions with Susanna were such a joy because she was intelligent, unaffected, and hardworking, and all those things were perfectly true. Susanna told herself that Hawke's ability to mesmerize her into feeling almost as beautiful as he could make her look in his photographs, to galvanize her into a level of performance that had almost nothing to do with the real Susanna Van Dusen, was entirely due to his experience and talent; and this too was true. The factor, however, which both underpinned and overlay their working relationship, but which neither Hawke nor Susanna was ready to recognize was that they were in love with each other. Neither wanted to acknowledge it;

neither, for vastly different reasons, believed it was right. And so they ignored it.

Summer ended, and Hawke sent Susanna home. She was happy to be there, it was wonderful being with Abigail and Connie and Bryan and Tabbie again, and just flying in and out at the weekends hadn't been the same at all, and she noticed now how much Abigail had grown, how she had changed in just a matter of a couple of months, and she told herself that some things were infinitely more important than modeling, *most* things were more important than that, she realized. Yet she knew, in her heart, that the moment Hawke had told her she was going back had been one of the most painful of her life.

"But why do I have to go?" she'd asked him.

"Because there's no reason for you to stay," he'd answered.

"What do you mean? I'm still learning. You said that I'll never stop learning."

"And that's true, but the crash course is over," Hawke said.

"Then why are you sending me home? Why don't we start working together, the way you said we would?" She was close to tears.

"Because we're not ready to start working yet."

"You mean I've flunked out."

"I don't mean that at all."

"If I've finished the course and you think I'm not ready to work, that must mean I've flunked out."

"Susanna, believe me"—Hawke grinned—"you have not flunked out. And it isn't just that you're not ready; it's that the time isn't right. You've been terrific, you are terrific—"

"When will the time be right?" she demanded.

"A month or two, probably."

"You're being evasive."

"You're being cheeky."

She flushed. "I'm sorry."

"Don't be. It just proves that you are almost ready after all."

"How come?"

"Because back in June you weren't hungry to work, and a couple of months on you're famished."

"So can I stay?" she asked hopefully.

"No," he said.

* * *

"I flunked out," she told Tabitha, in her bedroom, her first night back home.

"Is that what Hawke told you?" Tabitha looked dismayed. "I can't believe it—you're so gorgeous."

"Hawke says I didn't fail, but I don't believe him." Susanna looked miserably around the room at Tabitha's posters of her idol, Sting. She'd always loved hanging out with the girl she had grown to feel as close to as any blood sister, but tonight, after the incessant buzz of New York and the thrills of living in Hawke's world, what had seemed, before, to signify security and normality and warmth suddenly seemed simply flat.

"Why don't you believe him?" Tabitha asked.

"He says the time isn't right. He says that most photography models are in the middle of their hiatus now, whatever that means."

"I'm sure he's right," Tabitha said.

"You just think everything Hawke says must be right," Susanna said.

"No, I don't."

"Sure you do." Susanna teased her. "You have a crush on him."

"Of course I have a crush on him." Tabitha grinned. "He's the most terrific guy I've ever seen. Anyway, you're crazy about him too."

"I am not."

"Sure you are. I know it, and Mom and Dad know it too. Even Abigail knows it."

"Abigail's four years old," Susanna said crisply. "You talk such nonsense sometimes, Tabbie." Restlessly she got up from the bed and started to pace the room, fingering the curtains at the windows and the collection of stuffed bears on the dresser, looking at the photographs on the wall, all family snaps, herself and Abigail included in many of them.

Tabitha shrugged. "Okay, not Abigail, but I know you're in love with Hawke, and I'll bet you your favorite Levi's he's in love with you too."

"They wouldn't fit you, Tabbie."

"Don't be mean."

"Then don't talk garbage about me and Hawke."

"So it is you and Hawke." Tabitha looked triumphant.

"Sure it is. We've been working together all summer."

"I'll bet you're going to miss him."

Susanna sat down again, next to her foster sister. The brief mood of uncharacteristic snappishness was gone, and she felt only sad and quite tired.

"I am going to miss him, Tabbie," she admitted. "I'm going to miss a lot of things."

"Aren't you a little glad to be home?" Tabitha's eyes were searching.

"Of course I am." Susanna smiled, and a rush of love swept her. "I'm much more than a little glad. I've missed you so much. I kept thinking in New York, when things were really exciting, how much fun it would have been to have you there to share it with."

"Honestly?"

"Truly." Susanna shook her head. "It's Abigail I can't get over. She's changed so much in the last couple of months."

"But you've seen her every weekend."

"It's not the same. You don't look at things, or people, the same way when you're just flying in and out again." She tried to explain. "It was magic in New York, and with Hawke, meeting all those people, seeing all those places, pretending I really could be a model, but no place felt like home. The house in Queens was nice, and they were all kind, but it wasn't home. And when I came back here for the weekends, it all looked the same, *you* all looked the same, but it still wasn't right."

Tabitha reached out her left hand. "Then I guess you really are glad to be back."

"You bet I am." Susanna took the hand and squeezed it hard.

Abigail, at four, was an enchantress of a child, the image of Susanna aside from her eyes, which were large and dark, like Matthew Bodine's. Everyone who came upon her succumbed to her charms, and the little girl had become aware of her power over adults. If they weren't careful with her, Connie told Bryan from time to time, they'd be in danger of having a spoiled little kid, and they both agreed there was no room for that in their home. Life was easygoing in the Van Dusen household, but not undemanding; everyone was expected to pull their weight, do their share of chores, help out generally, and show respect. A four-year-old, naturally, was somewhat limited in what she could contribute to the smooth running of the house, but certainly no one was going to put up with tantrums, and no one—not even the youngest and cutest—was to be accorded favoritism. Abigail Van Dusen, however, pretty and fussed over as she still was, despite house rules, pulled few strokes, threw minimal tantrums, and had, for the most part, a most congenial spirit.

Susanna's adoration of her baby sister knew no bounds. It had been patently clear to the Van Dusens from the start, and even more plainly after Bodine had fled Cohasset, that Susanna was a veritable lioness and that Abigail was her most precious cub. Connie had remarked more than once to Bryan that her naked devotion was remarkable; she remembered how tempestuous her relationship with her own sister had been until they were in their twenties, how often sibling rivalry had gotten temporarily in the way of the love they had shared. Bryan told Connie that it was the age gap between Susanna and Abigail that made all the difference, that and the absence of their parents. Susanna wanted to be all things to Abigail: mother, father, sister, and closest friend.

"And yet she willingly spent most of the summer away from her," Connie said as they spoke about the sisters in bed late one night. "I was surprised that she agreed."

"She wouldn't have," Bryan said, "if anyone else had asked her."

"But you know she even applied for a passport while she was in New York just in case Hawke wanted her to travel. She wrote away for her birth certificate, got it all set up. He's got her really hooked."

"He's a powerful man."

With one hand under the bedclothes, Connie stroked her right thigh, focusing on the sensations in her fingers. It was something she liked to do each night, a kind of keeping in touch with the lifeless, numbed parts of her, as if she were reaching out and making contact, keeping faith, and Bryan, who understood her feelings well and who had always especially admired her legs, played his own role, still complimenting them when she wore shorts or a skirt and helping her paint her toenails during the summer months.

"I wonder what'll happen when he calls," Connie said.

"You think he will."

"I'm sure of it."

"He might be having second thoughts," Bryan suggested. "Out of sight and all that."

"He might be, but I doubt it."

"But it can't be right to have her just hanging on at the beck and call of a stranger." Bryan worried about Susanna's future. "I've been hoping that now she's grown used to leaving Abigail with us, she might go back to school."

"Hawke's not really a stranger, Bryan. And she's only been home a couple of weeks." Connie moved her hand under the sheets to Bryan's left leg, felt the muscle flex gently under her touch, thought with fleeting regret how wonderful it was to be able to respond that way. "If nothing comes of this modeling thing, there'll be plenty of time for Susanna to think about maybe going back to school. Though she's never exactly shown a lot of ambition in that direction, has she?"

Bryan closed his eyes, enjoying his wife's fingers. "I guess Matthew Bodine never instilled a lot of academic ambition in her. All that moving around."

"It's sad, in a way. She's such an intelligent girl."

"I think she wants more for Abigail."

"She wants the world for Abigail," Connie said.

Susanna had just begun to settle right back again, to feel that the time with Hawke had been some kind of dream, a fantasy, when the call came. It was a Tuesday evening in the third week of October. The whole family, except for Abigail, was sitting in the den on the first floor watching a TV movie and eating popcorn, with Tabitha feeding Baskin more than his fair or healthy share. Bryan went to answer the ring and, after a moment or two, called Susanna to the phone outside in the hall without telling her who it was.

"What would you say to five pages in *Vogue* wearing Kamali?" The voice was deep and clear and unmistakably English.

"Hawke!" Susanna's heart began to pound.

"You haven't answered me."

"Are you serious?"

"I never joke about things like that."

"But *Vogue*—you can't mean it."

"Where did you expect me to place you? The *Cohasset Examiner*?"

"No such paper," Susanna said.

"Do you want it or not?"

"Hawke, I couldn't."

"Why not?"

Her head was spinning. "I can't do *Vogue*. I haven't done anything."

"Of course you have."

"But not seriously, not professionally."

"What do you think I am?" Hawke's voice grew tougher. "Come on, Susanna, enough of the shrinking violet. You can do this if you want to, but it's up to you. It's a big step, but I guarantee it'll be fun."

"But Norma Kamali's clothes are so wonderful. I might ruin them."

"You'll make them even better." Hawke was patient again. "What's the worst that can happen? You screw up and no one ever uses you again. The world won't end, you won't die, and nor will I."

Susanna was gripping the telephone so tightly her knuckles were pure white. "When?"

"You come to New York tomorrow, and we fly to Paris Thursday."

"*Paris?*"

"That's where the shoot is."

Susanna looked around, saw that Connie had wheeled herself into the hall and that Bryan, Tabitha, and Baskin were right behind her. "Hawke wants me to go to Paris," she told them, her voice shaking.

"Fantastic," Tabitha said.

"What for?" Connie asked.

"For *Vogue*," Susanna managed to say. "Five pages, Norma Kamali."

"Why does it have to be Paris?" Bryan wanted to know.

"I don't know," Susanna said. "That's where it is."

"Let me talk to him." Bryan put out his hand.

"Let me," Connie said.

"Connie wants to talk to you," Susanna told Hawke, and handed over the phone.

"Someone has to go with her," Connie said crisply and clearly, then paused to listen to Hawke. "It may be 1980, and I know she's eighteen, but someone's still got to look after her." She paused again. "You don't count, Hawke." She listened again and smiled. "I'd love to, but I'd hold everyone up, and Bryan can't."

"I could go," Tabitha suggested, but no one even looked at her.

"I'll speak to Andrea Marantz in the morning."

"But he wants me to go to New York tomorrow," Susanna pointed out.

"Tough," Connie said, and let Hawke talk again. "He wants to know if you want to do it, Susanna."

"Of course she wants to do it," Tabitha said, her face burning with excitement. "I'd *kill* to do it if it were me."

"Shut up, Tabbie," Bryan said. "Susanna?"

Susanna nodded slowly. "Yes, please," she said.

"She says yes, please," Connie reported into the phone. "Hawke says that's okay then, and we'll work something out." She put the receiver down. "Looks like you're in business, darling." She was smiling, her eyes as well as her mouth. "How do you feel?"

"I don't know," Susanna said. "I don't believe it."

"You'd better go to bed," Connie said.

"I couldn't sleep."

"You have to," Tabitha told her. "Or you'll have circles under your eyes and *Vogue* will fire you."

"Are you okay with this?" Bryan asked, concerned. "I mean, there's no need to get swept away if you're not sure. There's no rush."

"If I don't go, they'll use someone else."

"That wouldn't be the end of the world, honey."

"That's what Hawke said." Susanna was still stunned. "He said if I screw up, the world won't end and no one would die."

"Wise man," Bryan said.

"So should I pack?" Susanna asked them. "What should I pack?"

"I'll help you," Tabitha volunteered.

"You can take Baskin for his walk," Connie told her. "I'll help Susanna with the packing."

"But you said you'd have to talk to the agency," Susanna said.

"And I will," Connie said calmly. "And we'll work it out."

"Are you sure?"

"Would you rather we said no?" Bryan asked.

Susanna shook her head.

"Then we're sure."

CHAPTER 8

~

"We went to Paris alone in the end. Andrea Marantz persuaded Connie that a trusted woman from the Paris agency would take care of me, make sure I'd come to no harm, lock my bedroom door at night, that kind of thing. And she did look after me, except that her idea of chaperoning was to delegate, and since I *was* eighteen and she thought Hawke was entirely responsible —once again he was *her* idea of responsible—she left me in his hands."

"How was it? Or don't I need to ask?"

"Magical. From start to finish. Oh, it was scary having to perform in front of so many accomplished professionals. I was terrified. But Hawke was in charge, and he's so great when he's working—he *is* a bit of a genius, you know—and he made me feel safe. He made me feel I could do it. And I did."

"What about the other side? The nonworking side."

"Nothing. Not a hint, not a touch, not a glance that wasn't professional. We had dinner together a few times, and you know how Paris is—a girl can feel she's in love even when she's walking down the street on her own."

"But nothing happened then?"

"Nothing. Not in Paris, or in Milan, or in Los Angeles, or in any of the places we went to over the next year."

"So when did things change?"

"In London," Susanna said.

*   *   *

Right after that first *Vogue* assignment the offers had started flooding in for the new package deal that was the gossip of the New York fashion business. By the spring of 1981 Hawke and Susanna were the hottest team around, and Andrea Marantz was regularly counseling Susanna on her rights and the wisdom of remaining Hawke's exclusive property when the biggest names in photography were asking about her.

"I could get you Arthur Elgort for Calvin Klein, for God's sake," Andrea told her. "I could probably even score Helmut Newton if I kissed enough ass."

"But I don't want to work with anyone else," Susanna said, as she had before more times than she could count.

"I understand you're grateful to Hawke, but you have to look at the future, you have to look beyond. I mean I love Hawke too, and God knows he's up there with the greats, but one day he's going to want to move on, Susanna, and I don't want to see you dumped."

"I'd rather worry about that when it happens."

"I'm your agent, I'd rather worry about it now. I'd rather make sure it can't ever happen."

"I know," Susanna said gently. "And I'm grateful, Andrea, but—"

"You spend altogether too much time being grateful, Susanna Van Dusen," Andrea scolded. "You're star material, and you're letting yourself get tied down like a wife."

"There's nothing like that between us," Susanna said.

"And the pope's Jewish," Andrea retorted.

Susanna smiled.

The only cloud on Susanna's horizon as the contracts for Hawke & Van Dusen fell thick and fast onto Andrea Marantz's desk was that back home in Cohasset Abigail was growing fast and, for the most part, Susanna wasn't there to see it. Hawke flew her back as often as possible, and Connie and the others reassured her regularly, mailed her photographs and cassette tapes so she could share in the little girl's progress, and Abigail herself drew pictures and sent them to the big sister she adored and missed, but it wasn't the same.

The offers kept on coming, even a movie with Polanski in

Paris, but Susanna stood firm. She was already making more money than she'd ever dreamed of, and Hawke and Andrea assured her it was only the beginning, and though the two *Vogue* covers she'd already been featured on had brought in a startlingly low fee, they'd been the springboard to major deals and cash to match. Every dollar Susanna earned went into the account she'd opened at a bank in Cohasset that she insisted was a family account. Bryan hadn't wanted to accept money from her, but Connie understood that aside from Susanna's patently obvious adoration of Hawke, her mentor, her only other real motivation for modeling was the financial contribution she could now make to her family; and eventually Bryan had come to understand too. And the money had already assured Abigail's education and meant they hadn't been forced to ask Lucy Battaglia, Connie's helpmate, to leave.

The work itself continued to be magical, but it was tiring too, and often grueling. Susanna's partnership with Hawke made it all worthwhile. He never talked over her head; he involved her in all aspects of every job. With Hawke beside her, she found she loved it all: the clothes themselves; the places they traveled to; the sometimes bizarre locations and even more bizarre situations they found themselves in; the people they met along the way, the tender egos, the modest talents, the tyrants, the nervous-breakdowns-in-the-making; the humor—sometimes hard to find —in the disasters that periodically threatened their shoots; the weather changes, equipment failures, temper tantrums, ripped seams, impossible sizes, union actions—usually in Europe—that stranded whole crews and even, once, wrecked an entire project. Had it not been for Hawke, there were many times when Susanna knew she would have wanted to run right back to Cohasset. But then again, had it not been for Hawke, she would not have been modeling in the first place.

They were in London, in late June 1983, staying at the Ritz in adjoining Belle Époque rooms overlooking Green Park, shooting for Ralph Lauren and *Vogue* at Wimbledon by day, going to the theater and Covent Garden and to Hawke's favorite restaurants by night—no nightclubs, of course, for shadows under Susanna's eyes meant Angie Lopez had to use tricks next day, and one of the reasons Hawke and Lauren loved Susanna's face was that it needed hardly any trickery.

Their seventh afternoon found them shooting Susanna in a white linen blouse and long, full skirt and eating strawberries and cream in the All England Club members' enclosure. Hawke, who liked working on his old home territory, was in an expansive, exhilarated frame of mind, more patient than ever with Susanna, who, though she'd never suffered from it in the United States, was suffering from a bad case of hay fever.

"Okay, gorgeous, let's have you on your feet now," he called to her, pausing to reload his Pentax. "Lean against the bar, watch the world go by, very laid-back, and contemplate those strawberries."

"Do you want me to eat?"

"Not yet. Just think how good they're going to taste." The loading was complete. "Someone get her a fresh bowl, and careful how you pour the cream, I want just a splash of it—no, let me do it."

Susanna sneezed.

"Bless you. Angie, fix her nose—and we need more Kleenex —you okay, gorgeous?"

"Fine." Susanna sneezed again, and her eyes watered. Angie handed her a wad of tissues, and she blew her nose carefully, mindful not to smudge her makeup. "I'm sorry."

"Not your fault," Hawke said. "Angie, her nose is pink."

Angie, always unflappable, used powder and blusher with gentle, economical brushstrokes. "I think she needs eyedrops, Hawke."

"Fine."

"I'm sorry," Susanna said, fighting to hold back another sneeze and forcing herself to ignore the itching in her ears and throat.

"Do you want a break?"

"No, I'm okay." She tilted her head back while Angie directed a single drop with perfect precision into each sore eye.

"Close them for a moment," Angie told her. "Don't squeeze, or your mascara'll run like hell. Okay, open, and I'll fix you up."

They were just getting back on track, Susanna holding a spoon with one perfect strawberry, cream meticulously arranged by Hawke, her eyes focused on the flow of the crowd outside the enclosure, when someone in the throng caught her attention. A man, his back to her, tall and dark, strolling slowly, shoulders broad and swaying slightly as he walked, triggering an old memory and blowing the shoot, her hay fever, and even Hawke right out of her mind.

"Gorgeous." Hawke's voice dragged her back.

Susanna blinked. "Excuse me," she said, standing up. She craned her head, struggling to keep the man in focus, but he was disappearing fast into the crowd.

"Susanna, you're not concentrating." For the first time Hawke sounded on the edge of irritation.

"I'm sorry," she said again, absently. "There's someone I have to—" Quickly she set down the spoon and bowl of strawberries on the bar, and leaving Hawke and the startled crew without another word, she ran to the entrance, light and easy in the season's new flat shoes. The man was there, about fifty yards ahead. Without thinking, without registering or rationalizing, Susanna followed, fixing her eyes on the dark hair glinting in the summer sunlight. She saw him turn toward Number One Court, and she turned after him. A storm of applause and wild cheering rose from inside the tennis court, and Susanna was walking quickly now, pursuing him, but then a woman and child stepped in front of her, blocking her view, and the child was complaining and pulling at her mother's hand, and Susanna had an almost violent urge to push them out of her way. And then they were gone, and she began to run, and there was a sick pain in her stomach, and suddenly, just as the man turned and she saw his face, Susanna tripped over a rough piece of paving and her ankle twisted beneath her, and she cried out and would have fallen if Hawke, catching up with her from behind, had not caught her by the arm.

"What *happened*?"

"Nothing." She was trembling and breathless, and her ankle hurt.

"Like hell. You ran out of there as if your knickers were on fire." His hand still gripped her arm, he stared into her face. "Are you okay?" He saw that she was not. "Let's get you somewhere you can sit down."

"Give me a minute. I don't want to go back for a minute."

"You don't have to. Let's just sit down, calm you down."

"I'm calm." She still quivered.

"No, you're not."

Hawke led her to the main public cafeteria, and Susanna

leaned against him, limping, and he sat her down and went to get her some hot tea. A woman in a floppy hat at the next table regarded her curiously for a moment, then looked away again. Susanna closed her eyes, a little dizzy, her pulses still racing, and when she opened them again, Hawke was there with her tea.

"Drink it. I put sugar in it."

"I don't like sugar." She sneezed.

"Drink the tea, the sugar's good for you."

"It's fattening."

"Don't be stupid."

She managed a sip, then put down the plastic cup.

"You saw someone you knew," Hawke said.

Susanna nodded. "I thought I did, but I was wrong; it wasn't him at all."

"Who did you think it was?"

"No one," she said softly.

"You chased after no one."

"In a way."

Hawke's gray eyes were very intent. "Tell me, Susanna."

She picked up the cup again, composing herself. "I thought, for just a moment, it was my father." She sipped some more tea. "Which was crazy. It couldn't have been him."

"Why not?"

"He wouldn't be here."

"In England or at Wimbledon?"

"Either."

"Why not?" Hawke repeated.

"He just wouldn't be, trust me."

"I do trust you," Hawke said gently.

Susanna glanced back toward the members' enclosure. "I'm sorry," she said, "about running off like that. We should get back."

"It's all right," Hawke said. "Take your time."

"No," she said, "it was unforgivable." She brushed at her hair with one hand. "I've probably wrecked my face and hair too. I'm sorry."

"No problem Angie can't fix in a minute."

She stood up. "Let's go then." She took a step and winced as hot pain shot through her ankle. "Damn."

"Sit down."

"No, I'm all right."

"Sit *down*. Okay, show me." He bent down and felt the ankle gently. "Does that hurt?"

"A little. I just twisted it. It's nothing."

"We should get it X-rayed."

She put her foot back down. "No need. There's nothing broken."

"You still have to rest it."

"No, I'm okay." She stood up again. "See? I'm fine. It's not as though you wanted to shoot me playing tennis."

"No, but I need you able to move freely."

"I can move." She took a few more steps, hardly limping now. "See? Mind over matter."

Hawke took her arm again, slowed her down. "That's the perfect way to aggravate an injury, Susanna."

"I'm not injured."

"Obstinate creature, aren't you?"

"I guess I am."

They finished the day's work, but by evening the ankle was badly swollen, and Hawke called a doctor to the Ritz who agreed with Susanna that nothing was fractured but that it was a nasty enough sprain to wreck at least the next day's work.

"I'm so ashamed," she told Hawke when the doctor had left.

"Why?"

"A whole day's shooting canceled, all the money wasted, all those people having to hang around—you having to hang around wasting your time." She was lying on the big bed, on the handsome spread, her freshly strapped ankle stretched out ahead of her.

"That is pretty awful," Hawke agreed.

"And it's all because of me."

"Because of your ankle."

"Which only happened because I went tearing off after a ghost."

"Your father's not dead."

"As good as," Susanna said.

Hawke sat down on the edge of the bed. "You want to talk about it?"

"What?"

"Your father."

"No," she said. "Thanks all the same."

Hawke took her hand. "I've known you for three years now," he said, "and I still know next to nothing about you."

"Sure you do."

"Not about the real you."

"This is the real me."

He shook his head. "No, it isn't. It's part of you, but not all of you."

"I'm sure I don't know everything about you either."

"You've never asked."

"It's not my business," Susanna said.

"Meaning I should mind my own too?" Hawke asked.

"No. Not really." She paused. "It's just there are things I don't especially want to talk about."

Hawke nodded. "I can understand that." He squeezed her hand, released it, and stood up. "I'll leave you to get some rest."

"Do you have to?" Susanna's disappointment was evident.

"No, but I assumed you'd like some peace and quiet."

"It's only my ankle," she pointed out. "I'm not sick."

"Okay." Hawke considered. "How about ordering dinner from room service? Could you face food?"

"I'm starved, but are you sure?"

"Why not?"

"I thought you might want to go out?"

"If I wanted to go out, I wouldn't have suggested room service."

"But you have so many friends here," Susanna said, "and there are all those wonderful restaurants."

"I've seen all my friends, and we've eaten out every night." Hawke hunted around and found the room service menu. "What do you fancy?"

"Steak," she said. "I hardly ever eat red meat these days."

"Chateaubriand," Hawke said, "with béarnaise sauce and a great bottle of wine, and crêpes suzette for dessert."

"I'll get fat," Susanna warned.

"Get fat and I'll dump you."

"Better order me a salad then," she said mournfully.

"Order a salad and I'll dump you even faster."

"I suppose I could pig out and then exercise like crazy."

"You have to rest your ankle."

"I can't win, can I?"

"Shut up and let me order."

"We ate and drank like kings," Susanna told Pete, "and Hawke even insisted they flame our crêpes in the room, and I remember I ate the whole feast propped up on pillows while Hawke sat at the table they'd wheeled in, and we talked and talked, so easily, the way we always did back then."

"What kind of things did you talk about?"

"About business, about our plans for the fall, about whatever was in the news, just stuff that was happening. And then the waiter came and cleared away and brought us coffee, but while Hawke was pouring, I fell asleep."

She fell silent. Pete waited.

"I woke up out of a nightmare. Hawke was still there in the room, and he soothed me, you know, told me it was okay now, that kind of thing. He asked me if I'd dreamed about my father, and I told him I had, and Hawke wanted to know why I was so adamant that it couldn't have been my father that afternoon at Wimbledon, and I told him that Matthew Bodine wouldn't have come to England because he'd have stuck out like a sore thumb and he was the kind of man who liked blending into the background so he could sneak about without anyone noticing him."

"Was that when you told Hawke about your father and Tabitha?" Pete asked.

"Yes."

Pete waited again. "And?"

"And it seemed to change everything. We'd become quite close before that, but it was just a close working relationship, or maybe a little more than that, more like the kind of intense warmth and respect a great teacher might develop with a student, but nothing more intimate than that. I guess my sharing that piece of my past with him forged another link in the chain." Susanna smiled wistfully. "Hawke told me more about himself that evening at the Ritz than he ever had before, tales of his childhood in Northamptonshire, of his father—he was a pig farmer, you know—and his mother, who painted portraits of her family and their pigs and exhibited them in the local village hall." She smiled again. "Hawke told me about his first love, a red-headed art teacher at his school, and about his first sexual experience, with a bus conductress in London—have you ever been to London, Pete?"

"Twice. I loved it."

"Me too. Anyway, the evening went on pretty much as you're assuming it did. I was a little drunk, and it had been such a strange day, with one thing and another, and finally Hawke said he ought to go, and I said I didn't want him to. And he stayed."

No man, Susanna knew, could have been gentler, more tender than Hawke that night. When he kissed her for the first time, it was so sweet, so right, that she felt herself melting against him, into the lean, hard, warm strength of him that she knew she'd longed for since the first summer they'd spent together in New York. There was no rush, no frantic tearing off of clothing; every stage felt considered yet at the same time mesmeric, as if they both knew they'd been sucked into a steady but forceful ocean current, as if this were now inevitable, something neither of them could stop, and neither wanted to stop it. They wanted the closeness; they wanted the rising desire, wanted the growing heat and hunger, needed desperately the linking, the union of their bodies.

"I need you, Susanna," Hawke said, just before he entered her, and he had hardly spoken a word since they had begun to make love; neither of them had wanted to talk, just to murmur softly, little breathless, infinitely eloquent expressions of how they felt, how they wanted each other.

"I need you too," Susanna said, tears of love and need in her eyes.

And then it all went wrong. They made light of it afterward, were just as tender, more tender, perhaps, than before, and neither thought to apportion blame, for it was just one of those things. And if they stopped to think about it logically, it had been bound to happen, given that they'd waited years, actual years, and what did it matter if Hawke's erection had failed at the crucial moment, and Susanna knew that had probably happened only because she'd suddenly become so *tense*, and she'd been too tight, too dry, and she couldn't really understand it because she'd thought she'd been so wet, so sure, so *ready* for him.

"It doesn't matter," Hawke said, his arms wrapped around her.

"I know," she said.

"Are you all right?" he whispered.

"I'm fine," she whispered back.

"You sure?"

"Better than fine." She smiled into his face. "Wonderful."

"You know I'm in love with you, don't you?" Hawke asked her.

"I think so."

"And you feel the same way." It was a statement, not a question.

"I do."

"That's why it didn't work. Too bloody important."

"I guess so."

Hawke drew back a little and looked at her. "Why do you think it didn't work?" His eyes were suddenly filled with alarm. "You did want us to make love, didn't you?"

"More than anything."

He relaxed again, held her closer. "I've never wanted anyone so much in my whole life, and that's the gospel truth."

Susanna shut her eyes. "I've never wanted anyone before you."

"I can't believe that." Hawke smiled.

"All the same, it's true."

"Poor Susanna," Hawke said softly. "Falling for me."

"Lucky Susanna," she said.

"He was your first?" Pete asked.

"My first lover?" Susanna nodded. "He was."

Over by the door Steinbeck groaned softly and rolled his eyes, deep in a dream. Alice, in her cage, was still now, her head to one side, listening. Pete, grown stiff in his yoga position, had transferred to the couch, but Susanna, still half wrapped in the past, remained cross-legged on the rug, her back perfectly straight, her head erect, her eyes half closed.

"My ankle got better"—she went on—"and we finished the shoot, and the rest of the crew flew home, and Hawke and I stayed on for some vacation. He hired a car, and we drove all over London, and if I wanted to see anything, Hawke just parked there and then, and he must have gotten twenty parking tickets, but he just smiled and threw them away. He seemed very happy."

"What about you?"

"I was in heaven," Susanna said simply. "Until he vanished."

"Vanished?"

She nodded. "The day before we were due to fly to Frankfurt. Hawke told me he had some friends he needed to spend time with before we left, and that was fine by me. I had a great day, went shopping, bought gifts to take home. When I got back to the Ritz, there was no sign of Hawke. It didn't worry me a bit. I took a long bath, washed my hair, started to pack for Germany. A little later I checked for messages, but there was nothing, so I ordered myself a sandwich and rested up. I still wasn't concerned. Hawke had spent just about every minute with me since we'd arrived in London, and I figured he deserved some time to himself."

"When did he get back?"

"He didn't. I woke up next morning, and his key was still in reception and he hadn't called."

"What did you do?" Pete asked.

"What do you think I did? I panicked."

Susanna abandoned the flight to Frankfurt, telephoned everyone she could think of who might know where Hawke was. Both Andrea Marantz and Angie Lopez agreed that the disappearance was totally out of character, that Hawke was more responsible than a lot of creative men they knew. Susanna contacted the police, but they told her that there was no record of an accident, that Hawke hadn't been arrested, and that he was an adult independent male and if he wanted to get lost, that was his right.

"What are you going to do?" Andrea asked her when Susanna reported back to her later that day.

"Try looking for him myself."

"How in hell are you going to find Hawke in London, Susanna? You don't even know the place."

"I know where he's taken me. I know the kinds of places he's talked about, recommended I go to."

"What kinds of places? Department stores? Harrods?" Andrea was scathing. "You think Hawke's gone shopping?"

"I don't know where he's gone." Susanna was suddenly close to tears. "For all I know, he's lying in some morgue with all his ID stolen."

"No one's mugged Hawke, Susanna." Andrea was gentler. "If I were you, I'd wait at the hotel. Have a good workout, read a book, rent a video, but don't waste your time pounding the streets."

Susanna put down the phone and went straight out. It was raining, making it even harder to see people's faces under their umbrellas. She knew how foolish she was being, that there was no chance she was going to see Hawke walking along Piccadilly or Knightsbridge or Beauchamp Place or Bond Street or Soho Square, but she couldn't stand being cooped up in the hotel any longer, and at least while she was outside among all those strangers, it stopped her from imagining the myriad horrors that might have befallen him.

She didn't find him, but when she returned to the Ritz later that afternoon, she learned that Hawke had called in to settle the bill with a credit card and that he'd left word that she was to fly to Germany ahead of him and he would join her there as soon as possible.

Relief came first, then anger, then the most intense disappointment. Obviously their relationship was nowhere near as close as she had believed, and it seemed suddenly likely that the escalation from partners to lovers had, when Hawke had stopped to consider, scared him off.

So be it, she thought, packing her things again. *I'll go to Frankfurt like the good little trouper I've become, and when he does deign to get there, he won't know I even batted an eyelid.* And if he ever tried to lay a finger on her again, she'd probably bite it off.

She'd been to Frankfurt once before and had hated its urban ugliness on sight, but this time Hawke had booked them into rooms at a beautiful hotel fifteen minutes out of the city, and her room overlooked a lake in the hotel's thirty-seven-acre park, and faced with the evidence, yet again, of the way Hawke had consistently cared for and protected her, much of Susanna's anger abated.

When Hawke checked in two days later, every last trace of resentment disappeared under a fresh wave of anxiety.

"You look *awful*," she blurted as he came into her room.

"Thanks." He was white-faced and drawn.

"You look as if you haven't slept for a month."

"Make that three nights, and you'll be right." He tried to kiss her, but she drew away. "You're angry," he said, and sank down in one of the armchairs.

"I was." She sat down opposite him. "What happened?"

"I can't tell you," Hawke said wearily.

"What do you mean you can't tell me?"

"Exactly that." He shook his head. "I wish I could, and I know I've let you down—"

"You scared me half to death."

"I'm sorry."

Susanna sat forward. "Hawke, you have to tell me."

"No, I don't."

It felt like a slap in the face. She stood up stiffly. "I guess you're right. You don't have to tell me anything."

"I told you, Susanna, I wish I could—"

"But you're not going to," she said coolly.

He looked up at her, too tired to stand. "It's not my story to tell."

"I see."

"No, you don't."

"No." She paused. "Hawke, was it because of us? Because of what happened between us? Are you regretting it, because if you are—"

"No!" He found the strength to get up, came over to her, put his arms around her, felt her start to pull away and then change her mind. "Not for a second. It had nothing at all to do with us. If it had, I'd tell you."

She drew away again. "Then why don't you?"

Hawke sighed. "I told you. It's not my story to share." He looked at her face, knew she was intensely disappointed. "Susanna, you have a past I still know very little about. I haven't pushed you, have I?"

"No," she admitted, a touch of guilt rising in her.

"There are things, sometimes, don't you agree, things that touch other people, that affect other people, that we can't share with the person we'd most like to?"

"I guess," Susanna said, and the guilt rose higher.

He put out his right hand. "So are we okay with this?"

"I guess," she said again.

"Then give me your hand."

She gave it.

"It's been a bad few days," Hawke said very quietly. "Worse than bad."

"For you?" she asked. "Or for this other person?"

"For them," he answered. "Not too good for me either." His eyes were very troubled as he looked into hers. "And I am sorry I can't share it with you, but it's not the time."

"Okay," she said, and all the anger was gone.

He still held onto her hand. "You're very special to me, Susanna."

"I know I am," she said.

They went to bed, Hawke almost too exhausted to sleep, and Susanna rubbed his back and his shoulders and stroked his hair, and gradually she felt the strain and tension melting out of him, until finally, his head resting in the crook of her right arm, they both slept.

In the middle of the night, sometime around four o'clock, Hawke woke with a start from a bad dream, and Susanna was up with him, soothing him again, gentling him, and suddenly Hawke was fully aroused, and his hands and mouth were on her breasts, wanting her, loving her, and she was responding eagerly, hungrily, all the fear and anger of the last days and nights translating into full-blown desire. And one moment he was hard against her, and she was ready for him, longing for him, and the next he'd pulled away, and was out of the bed and over at the window, naked and still.

"What's wrong?" Susanna asked, breathless, confused.

"Nothing."

She got out of bed too, went to him, reached out to him, and he let her touch him, gave a sigh and put his arms around her, drew her close.

"I'm sorry," he murmured against her hair. "I just couldn't."

"It's okay. It doesn't matter." She remembered he'd told her that their first time, in London, and he was so right, because the sex didn't matter at all, all that really mattered was that they were together, in each other's arms, their bodies close, and their minds, and she knew then, more than ever, how much she loved him.

"It was only a few weeks after Frankfurt that Hawke told me he wanted us to get married," Susanna told Pete at their next session, two days later.

"But you only got married a couple of years ago."

"I turned him down."

"Why?"

"All kinds of reasons. Fear, mostly."

"Of what?"

"Failing, I think." It was late afternoon, and they were in Pete's living room again, but Susanna was on the sofa—no yoga this time—and Steinbeck was sleeping again, at her side, snoring softly now and again. "I was very torn at that time. The life he'd given me was so all-consumingly different from everything I'd known before that I found myself scared of losing myself—the real me, whatever that was. And there was Abigail to consider. Mostly there was Abigail."

"How?" Pete lit a cigarette. Susanna said his smoking didn't bother her, but by the end of each session his ashtray was always overflowing, and Pete would have to open a window wide to let out a little of the fog.

"She was my little sister," Susanna said. "My responsibility. I'd been spending too much time apart from her already, but marriage would have made it permanent."

"Mightn't Hawke have agreed to have Abigail live with you?"

"He'd have had her with us in a second," Susanna said. "Hawke loves children, and he knew how much she meant to me. But I had to think about what was best for her, and there wasn't too much doubt that staying with the Van Dusens—with the only family she'd ever known—in her old familiar home, was going to be a whole lot better for her than running around the world with Hawke and me."

"Yet you went to live with Hawke anyway."

"That fall. And we got married eighteen months later. March twenty-second, 1985." She smiled. "I found I couldn't live without him. I tried for a while, but it was an impossible existence for us both, and Connie told me she didn't think I was doing Abigail any favors because being apart from Hawke was making me so grouchy."

"Still, leaving her must have been very painful."

"Yes."

Pete waited a moment. "Feel like talking about that?"

"Not really."

"Okay." Pete paused. "Was it easy living with Hawke?"

"It wasn't hard. We were both good at giving each other space, and he was so glad when I gave in that he never complained much about anything, which is pretty surprising if you consider that Hawke had lived on his own ever since leaving his parents' home."

"What about sex? Had things improved?"

"Yes." Susanna hesitated. "We had a few problems, from time to time, but sex was never the biggest thing for Hawke and me."

"Want to talk about that?"

"Nothing to talk about," she said lightly. "Sometimes it was wonderful, sometimes it wasn't so great. But it was always loving."

Her pain at living apart from Abigail intensified when, three months after their marriage, Hawke said he wanted to spend several months in Europe. It was a desire he'd often spoken of, and his aim was to take six weeks in Britain, spending at least a week or two with his parents, a further few weeks driving gently through France, and three whole months in Rome, the city that had loomed large in his fantasies for most of his life. He had visited several times, but always running, always working, always just passing through. This visit was to be slow, self-indulgent, and enriching, and he wanted Susanna with him.

Rome in late summer was, above all things, hot. Hawke adored the heat, but while he—sublime in the shade of a broad-brimmed, elegant white hat he'd bought in London's Jermyn Street—strolled happy as a clam through the Eternal City, seeking more culture, more ancient sights, more atmosphere, more and more Rome, Susanna spent much of each day damp, uncomfortable, and yearning for nightfall, when she could escape into the cool bliss of their suite at the Hassler-Medici.

"God knows I love Manhattan," Hawke exclaimed during their first week in the city, on their way to visit the Church of San Clemente in Laterano, "and I can't picture myself living anywhere else, but imagine this, Susanna, just *imagine*"—his eyes glittered with rapture—"a seventeenth-century façade with a twelfth-century basilica on top, a fourth-century church underneath —and beneath all that, there's an Augustan temple and a two-thousand-year-old alley. Isn't that bloody amazing?"

"Amazing." She halted for a moment, leaning on a sixteenth-century chunk of stone wall to rub one foot.

"Don't you want to go?" He looked surprised.

"Sure I want to go."

"Come on then."

Nothing tired Hawke, no amount of walking, no amount of standing or listening to Roman guides, or gazing at sculptures or mosaics or paintings, or tramping through ruins, or staring up at church ceilings, or passing through gates in ancient walls. It became a daily battle for Susanna to persuade her husband that ordinary mortals needed to sit or to eat lunch or to drink coffee, though in the evenings she had to admit they dined wondrously well in restaurants all over the city—fish served in a hundred different ways in the Piazza di Spagna, the greatest spaghetti alla carbonara in Trastevere, bistecca alla fiorentina in old Rome— and then Hawke became another man again, with no apparent need for sleep, content to drink wine and dance and talk and watch the world meander by into the early hours.

"I'm wearing you out," he observed one night, seeing Susanna's eyelids drooping in the taxi on their way back to the hotel.

"Are you ever."

Hawke looked suddenly dismayed. "You hate it here."

"Of course I don't hate it." Susanna struggled awake. "I love Rome. I wouldn't have missed it for the world, though I admit I wouldn't mind taking it a little more slowly."

"But we just spent four hours over a single dinner." Hawke's perplexity was real.

"And today we spent almost five hours in St. Peter's," Susanna pointed out, "and it was magnificent, but we could have paused after two hours and had an espresso, and then I would have gone back wanting more, but as it was, I almost—" She stopped.

"Almost what?"

"Nothing."

"You don't like churches, do you?" Hawke said.

"What do you mean?"

"I mean that I've noticed you're uncomfortable inside churches."

"The churches here are beautiful," she said.

"I'm not just talking about here. I noticed the same thing in Paris, and in England, when my parents took us to church that Sunday, you didn't really want to go."

"I didn't mind." The taxi swung too fast around a corner, and Susanna fell against Hawke's shoulder.

"We've never talked about religion," Hawke said.

"Since when are you religious?" she asked.

"I'm not. I just think it odd that we're married and never talked about it."

"There wasn't any reason to, since neither of us wanted a church wedding." She drew away from him again. "You didn't, did you? You didn't say you did."

"I wouldn't have minded," Hawke said. "But I remember asking you if you wanted it, and you were dead set against it."

"Why are you making a big deal about it now?" Susanna asked.

"I'm not," he said easily. "You're the one being defensive."

"I don't mean to be," she said. "It's just that I was talking about spending five hours in St. Peter's, and my objection had nothing to do with religion." She paused. "I don't want to spoil things for you, Hawke."

"No one could spoil Rome for me," he said.

Susanna believed him. "Overkill," she said.

"What?"

"That's what you're doing to Rome, for me." Instantly she regretted the disappointment on his face. "Hawke, we have so much time," she tried to explain. "We don't need to race through as if we were tourists on a five-day coach trip."

"You're right," he said flatly.

"I have spoiled it," she said.

"No, you haven't."

"I have. I can see it in your eyes."

Hawke shook his head. "You haven't spoiled anything, Susanna. I've been selfish."

"You're not selfish." She took his big, sensitive hand and held it against her cheek. "You're just in love with Rome."

"But you're not."

"Yes, I am. I just don't have as much energy as you."

"It's this city." Hawke pulled her hand away from his cheek and kissed her fingers. "Maybe it's something they put in the water; I feel as if I shouldn't waste a second." He shook his head. "I feel I just have to drain it to the last drop, you know?"

"I know."

"Do you?" He searched her eyes.

"I think so."

"We'll slow down," he said.

"Not too much." She still felt guilty. "Just a little."

"I promise," Hawke said. "From tomorrow we'll do it your way—a little taste at a time."

"I love you, Hawke," Susanna said.

"I love you too, Mrs. Hawke," he said.

The first shadow fell less than a week later. Hawke woke with a sore throat and a tickling cough that worsened as the day progressed until it was deep and resonant in his chest. By evening he was running a fever with chills and aching limbs. A doctor was called, a case of flu diagnosed and rest prescribed. Hawke protested but remained in bed, and Susanna hung the Do Not Disturb sign on the door of the suite and crept quietly around the living room, anxious for him to get as much sleep as possible, knowing that the instant Hawke felt any better, it would be tough going to persuade him to stay in the hotel.

At around three o'clock next morning something woke her. She lay, for a moment or two, in the dark, listening. Hawke's breathing sounded labored.

She sat up. "Hawke? Are you awake?"

He gave a low moan.

"Hawke, what's wrong?" She turned on the light and saw, with a jolt of alarm, that he was drenched with perspiration. "Do you feel worse?"

"Lousy." The word was a whisper.

Susanna felt his forehead. "Oh, Lord, you're burning up." She got quickly out of bed and put on her robe.

"Don't go," Hawke said, with an effort.

"I'm just going to call the doctor."

"Don't leave me," he said.

"Of course not." She came around to his side of the bed, knelt, and took his hand. "Your fever must be way up, sweetheart. I'm just going into the other room to speak to the doctor, and then I'll get you some water."

"Don't leave me," he said again.

Fear twisted in her chest.

"Never," she said.

"He must go to the hospital," the doctor told Susanna outside the hotel room.

"But it's just the flu," she said, shocked.

"Perhaps a little more, Signora Hawke."

"Surely you can treat him here at the hotel?" Susanna was white-faced.

The doctor shook his head. "I'm afraid not, signora. Your husband has some difficulty with his breathing, but with the right treatment he will improve quickly."

"But he won't want to go to hospital," she insisted.

"He's too sick to argue." The doctor picked up his bag. "I shall make the arrangements."

"Surely you could prescribe antibiotics?" she tried again.

The doctor looked at her intently. "You fear hospitals, signora?"

Susanna said nothing, still ashen-faced.

"Many people share your fear, Signora Hawke," the doctor said gently. "It's perfectly natural. But I promise you that in this case there's no cause to be afraid." He paused. "It is a fine hospital, believe me."

Still, she said nothing, fighting to control the panic that had soared, without warning, inside her. Hawke was sick, she told herself silently. The doctor was right; he was *right*.

"May I go and telephone now, signora?"

She took a breath, brought herself under control. "Of course," she said.

The hospital was on the east of the city near the university. Hawke's admission was gently, efficiently carried out, and before dawn, diagnosed with pneumonia, Hawke was neatly folded between cool white sheets, a crucifix on the wall over his head, an IV in his left arm, an oxygen mask at his disposal, and a pair of sweet-faced nursing nuns gliding calmly in and out of his private room at regular intervals.

"Do you feel any better?" Susanna asked him softly after a while.

"I feel bloody awful," Hawke told her.

"I feel better having you here," she lied, though in a sense it was the truth, for it was obvious he was better off here than in the hotel room, and her earlier panic had almost receded.

"Bully for you," he said, and reached for the mask.

Doctors came and went, blood was taken, and X rays and sputum samples, but the erythromycin already prescribed for Hawke improved his condition so swiftly that before the laboratory had even returned its findings, Hawke insisted on discharging himself.

"You can't just leave," Susanna told him, upon finding him dressed and waiting for her when she came into his room on the second evening. "You have pneumonia, for heaven's sake."

"I'm better."

"Better than you were, but not cured."

Hawke looked shaky and pale, but his jaw was set firm. "I need you to help me with my bag."

"Not until the doctors say it's okay," Susanna said, "which they won't."

"Which is why I'm not hanging around to talk to them." Hawke bent down to pick up the canvas bag. "I'll carry it myself if you won't help me."

"Hawke, don't." She snatched it away from him. "You're acting like a big kid."

"I'm just acting like a man. Everyone knows men make lousy patients."

"All I'm saying is that we wait for a doctor to say it's safe for you to go."

"Of course it's safe. I was sick; they gave me antibiotics; I'm better."

"You look awful."

"That's because I had pneumonia—*had*, okay? Give me the bag."

"No." Susanna sat down on the bed, the bag on her knees, her arms folded tightly around it, a part of her wryly amused that she, who so longed to be away from this place, was fighting to make Hawke stay.

"So I'll go without." Hawke opened the door.

"I can't believe how stupid you're being."

"Healthy people don't belong in hospitals." The door was open. "Are you coming with me or not?"

"Not." She stayed put, obstinately.

"Okay." He waved a hand, nonchalant in spite of its tremor, and walked out of the room.

"Hawke!"

The door swung slowly shut.
"Hawke!"

"I thought he'd want to stay on in Rome," Susanna told Pete. "Recuperate at the Hassler or maybe move out into the countryside, but of course it was so hot, and suddenly Hawke couldn't take the heat, and then I suggested going back to England for a while, but he was itching to get back home. It was as if he felt that Rome had let him down, that Europe had betrayed him in some way that I didn't understand. Not then at least."

"But now you do."

"Oh, yes." Susanna paused. "There was no more for a little while after Rome. He caught a bad cold at the end of September, and I remember feeling surprised that he let Saul Weinberg put him on a course of antibiotics before it had really gotten to his chest. That was so unlike Hawke. I should have known then that something was up."

"You had no suspicions at all?" Pete asked.

"None." She shook her head. "You know how it was then. It was still being called the gay plague—I had no reason to suspect. The Gay Men's Health Crisis people had been in touch from time to time, and Hawke was doing stuff for the AIDS charities, but everyone knew Hawke was straight and married to me, and I just didn't think. So there was Hawke sitting in purgatory, and me sailing around in Utopia." She paused. "Until one day in the middle of October—a week or two after poor Rock Hudson died and you couldn't read about anything else—Hawke broke a slab of glass in his studio and cut himself badly. There was a lot of blood, and I ran to get cotton and antiseptic. I wanted to clean it for him and bandage it, but Hawke pushed me away, really violently, and I was shocked because Hawke was never, ever violent." She stopped again.

"Go on," Pete said gently.

"Afterward he was so apologetic, so upset about the way he'd been, and I told myself it was the shock of all the blood, and I didn't say another word about it, and neither did Hawke, but I'd heard this deep, dark warning whisper inside my head, and after that day it never quite went away again."

"Were you exposed to his blood?" Pete's tone was very even.

"No. Hawke was very careful."

"And otherwise?"

"You mean sex."

"Yes."

"In the beginning, in London, Hawke used condoms," Susanna replied, "and for a while afterward. And then I got a prescription for the Pill. Hawke put up quite a fight, claimed he was concerned about its affecting my health, but I figured the Pill was a better bet—I really didn't want to risk a pregnancy—and in the end he gave in, stopped fighting."

Her voice tailed away, and she was silent for a while.

"What's the time?" she asked at last, seeing that it had grown dark.

"Almost five o'clock," Pete said. "I'm in no rush, Susanna."

"Are you sure?"

"I have no other appointments today."

"I should get back to Hawke. Angie's been with him today, but she'll need to get away soon."

"Awhile longer?" Pete asked. "It's up to you."

She nodded slowly.

"There's more," she said. "I need to tell you more."

"There's always tomorrow," Pete said.

"Is there?" she asked.

The day before Thanksgiving 1985, when Susanna got back to Hawke's loft at three minutes past six in the evening, she saw her husband stretched out in his hammock near the large plate glass window at the far end of the main, open-plan room.

"Sorry I'm late." She shut the great iron front door and headed over to kiss him. "Lulu worked me into the ground, so I went for a massage—Jean-Paul sends his love, by the way—and then I remembered that it's Lucy Battaglia's birthday next week and I hadn't bought her a gift, and I got her the loveliest hat and scarf from Henri Bendel—Lucy adores hats. And Connie called this morning while you were out to make sure we're on schedule for tomorrow—" She came to a stop.

"I didn't notice," Hawke said. "That you were late."

Susanna looked at him. He was holding a whiskey tumbler, and she thought he might have had quite a bit. Hawke seldom drank whiskey.

"What's up?" she asked.

Hawke did not look up at her. "I'd like to say nothing's up, but that never really works with you, does it?" His face was inclined toward the window and away from her, though he didn't appear to be looking at anything in particular.

"What is it?" Susanna's voice was very soft.

"I had the test."

Everything stopped, or seemed to. Heart, pulse, breathing. Feeling. She said nothing. Slowly, her hands already unsteady, she reached up to remove her favorite gray fedora, ran her fingers mechanically through her hair. She wished that she was able to extend this moment, this last moment of hope and comparative normality. She knew that she could, by asking him idiotic questions: *What test?* or *What do you mean?* But Hawke had not said "a" test, but "the" test. And so Susanna said not a word and tried instead to make time backpedal, willed it, in silence, to propel her backward, like the reversal of a videotape, back out of the loft, back down in the big old elevator, back onto Canal Street.

So that his next words would not have to be spoken at all.

Hawke's mouth, his lovely, firm mouth, was set very hard.

"I have the virus, Susanna," he said.

He found that he could not talk about it in the loft, so they took to the streets, moving deeper into Chinatown, heading for Mott Street, where the first Chinese merchant had taken residence more than a hundred and twenty years before, for Doyers Street, where, for the first three decades of the next century, rumors of opium dens and white slavery and bloody tong battles had abounded; for the heart of the triangle of streets where these days, with the old borders long since eroded and the modern New York Chinese expanding and assimilating and educating, the outside world came each day and night to share in the glories of the teahouses and restaurants and bakeries.

"I'm starved," Hawke said as they walked. "Ever since Saul told me, I've had food on the brain—must be my life force yelling for survival."

"Must be," Susanna said softly.

"Want to eat?"

"If you like."

"Only if you feel like it."

"Sure."

"Where shall we go?" He walked as he always did in China-town, taking on some of the character of the place, smoothly and easily and not too swiftly. "How about the Mayflower? Or maybe Hong Fat—at least it's noisy. I don't want anywhere too quiet; I'd like to go on drinking."

"I don't mind," Susanna said.

"You choose. You like the Peking Duck House, don't you?" He did not glance at her, had hardly looked into her face since she had come home.

"That's fine," she said. "Wherever you like is fine."

In the end they caught a cab over the Brooklyn Bridge and went to Crisci, an old favorite of Hawke's, where, in the reassurance of its plain old-fashioned dining room, he ate shrimp marinara and drank chianti while Susanna played with a bowl of pasta and focused most of her energies on not screaming.

"You're not drinking," Hawke said. "I can understand your not eating, but personally I'd say tonight was a good time to get drunk."

"Go right ahead."

"You're angry."

Susanna opened her mouth to speak, then closed it and shook her head.

"I can understand your being angry."

"You're very understanding," she said softly, wryly.

"I'm lost," Hawke said, and put down his fork. "Help me, Susanna."

"Oh, Hawke," she said, and she felt the tears that would soon be shed being born somewhere deep inside her. "Oh, dear God, Hawke, you have to talk to me, or how can I help you?" She reached over the table and took one of his big hands in both her own. The restaurant was warm, but his fingers were icy. "Talk to me," she said again.

"You mean tell you how."

"Do you know?"

"Yes, I know."

She waited, still holding his hand.

Hawke sighed. A long, sad sigh.

"Do you want to get out of here?" she asked. "Will it be easier outside?"

He shook his head. "It won't be easier anywhere." He glanced around. "No one's listening," he said.

"That wasn't what I meant," Susanna said.

"It has to be considered."

"I guess," she said.

He took his hand away, picked up his wineglass, drank some more.

"I had a lover," he said, "a while after I first came to New York. We lived together for almost a year, until it ended. Early in 1980. He was a designer, and he was one of my best friends in all the world." Hawke stared into his wineglass, did not raise his eyes to look at Susanna. "I'd known him back in London, and I'd always known that he was gay, just as he'd always accepted that I was straight. But here, in the early days, our friendship grew so deep, so intense, so loving, and for a while I think the parameters of our relationship got a little blurred." A sad, small smile touched his mouth and was gone. "I was younger, I had no prejudices, and I loved him. We'd always hugged, in friendship; it was natural, gentle, comforting. And somehow the comfort hugs got needier, became something else." For an instant Hawke's eyes darted to Susanna's face, then slid back to the warm ruby security of the wine. "It startled me a little, feeling that way, but it never shocked me. I let it happen. I wanted it to happen."

Susanna pushed back her chair and stood up. Her face was ashen.

"I'm sorry," she said, and her voice sounded hoarse. "You'll have to excuse me."

Hawke got up too. "Are you coming back?"

She saw the need in his eyes. "Of course," she said.

There was no one else in the rest room. She stood for a moment, staring at her reflection in the mirror, seeing nothing. Her stomach churned, and she thought again, as she had at the table, that she might throw up, but then the feeling passed. Slowly she walked into the toilet, locked the door, sat down, and buried her face in her hands, but could not weep. Her eyes were dry; she felt hollow and drained. She took her hands away from her face and watched their trembling. She could not imagine herself moving, could not conceive of herself returning to the table and sitting down and saying that she was all right and that he should continue. She did not want him to continue, did not want to hear any more.

I don't want to know, she thought.

And then she stood up and went outside and ran cool water over her wrists and put fresh lipstick on her mouth, walked back into the dining room, sat down, and looked at him.

"I'm okay," she said. "Go on."

He kept it plain and simple. He stopped eating but carried on drinking. Every now and again, through the story, he forced himself to look right at her, into her eyes, but most of the time he fixed either on his wineglass or on the wall behind her or away, somewhere, into the anonymous distance. His voice was hushed and so even that it was almost monotonous, and Susanna thought, as the tale flowed in a single, seamless piece, a tender, sorrowful episode sliced out of his past, that it sounded almost rehearsed, as if Hawke had always known that this moment would come, as if it were a chapter that ran and reran in his mind over and over again, waiting to be told.

The breakup and the final parting, when it came, instigated by Hawke, were painful for them both, the other man left wounded and with what Hawke saw as a justifiable sense of betrayal. Hawke's deepest regret, at that time, had been that he feared he might in some way have been using his lover, for he realized by then that part of him had surely always known that the affair was just a passing thing—not an experiment but a learning experience about himself and his own needs.

"I didn't know then what regret, or fear, really was," Hawke said bitterly. "But I know it now." He poured himself more wine from their second bottle. He was getting drunk, slowly, gradually. "Do you remember when I went missing in London two years ago?"

"I remember." It was about a half hour since Susanna had last spoken.

"He and I hadn't talked, hadn't even exchanged Christmas cards since the breakup; neither of us had any illusions about remaining friends after all that mess."

"Yet after Wimbledon—after us—you got in touch," Susanna said.

"No." Hawke shook his head vehemently. "No, Susanna, nothing like that. It was in the past, finished, a memory, and a damned important one, but nothing more." He drank more wine, then swirled it around his glass. "Oh, Christ, I was never ashamed of it, not of the affair itself, but I was monstrously ashamed of the way I handled it, the way I hurt him. After you and I finally got it together that night at the Ritz, I was so happy you can't imagine." He paused. "And then, on that last day in London, while you were out shopping, I bumped into a man I hadn't seen since those days, and he told me."

Susanna was very still. "That your friend was sick."

"He told me that he was in London, and that he was dying. He asked if I wanted to see him one last time." Hawke's eyes were very somber and distant. "I went with him. He was in hospital, a private place, in a room on his own. He was all alone, and when I saw how glad he was to see me, and when he asked me to stay with him, I knew I couldn't leave." He met her gaze. "I couldn't call you, Susanna; I couldn't explain to you, not then. Maybe if the timing had been different, but even then I don't think I'd have found the courage."

"You should have told me," she said.

"I know. I know a lot of things now."

"You knew that then too, Hawke. If you're honest, you'll admit that."

"Yes."

"Did you stay with him till the end?" she asked.

"Yes."

"Was it very terrible?"

"Yes. Until he gave in. Then it seemed a little easier."

"And then you came to Frankfurt."

"Yes."

"And you refused to tell me where you'd been." Her voice too was still hushed, but now it had a note of incredulity. "And then, just a few weeks later, you asked me to marry you."

"Yes," Hawke said again.

"How could you do that?"

"I loved you," he said simply. "I didn't want to lose you."

Susanna stirred a little and looked around the room. The restaurant was almost empty now, and only a handful of drinkers remained in the bar. She didn't glance at her watch. She knew without looking that it was late.

"I think we should go now," she said.

"Right." Hawke signaled the waiter, and the check came less than a minute later. He paid with cash, asked if they could call a cab, and leaned back in his seat again.

"You haven't used his name," she said.

"Do you want me to?"

"Do you want to?"

"It wouldn't help him, or us," he said.

"No," she said.

"What are you feeling, Susanna?"

"I'm not sure."

"Do you despise me?"

"I don't know what I feel, Hawke. Not yet." She rose again. "I'd like to go home now, please," she said.

Neither of them spoke a word on the journey home. Back in the loft, Susanna went up the spiral staircase to their sleeping area, undressed, tied back her hair, and removed her makeup, while Hawke, down below, brewed coffee in silence and, when it was ready, brought her up a cup.

"Thank you." She took it from him, set it on the antique dressing table.

"Shall I stay, or do you want to be alone?"

"I could use another minute or two," she said. "I'll come down soon." She paused. "Unless you want to go to bed."

"No," he said, and went back down.

Susanna stared into the mirror, as she had in the restaurant. A woman gazed back. Hawke's wife. Hawke's widow-to-be. She put the coffee cup to her lips and sipped at it, but swallowing seemed difficult. Her eyes were still dry. She closed them. Images flashed into her mind. Rock Hudson's body bag, being removed like shameful trash from his home. Police officers showing their masks and gloves in case of accidents involving AIDS carriers. Gay men and women demonstrating against the closure of the bathhouses.

From downstairs the sounds of Yehudi Menuhin's Elgar filtered through the newsreel playing in her head, wiping away the pictures and filling the fresh void with unbearable, melancholic beauty. *Now*, she thought, *now the tears will come*, but then she knew, after all, that they would not because she would not allow them to, would not permit herself such natural, easy release, not yet awhile.

She went down to join her husband.

Hawke was sitting in their deepest armchair, sunk low, his coffee cup clasped in his right hand. He looked up as she came close, and Susanna saw relief in his eyes, blending with fear. He looked, at the same time, older and much younger than before. Someplace between Brooklyn and Canal Street, she understood then, their roles had changed, subtly but devastatingly. The streetwise mentor and motivator had become vulnerable green-horn, and his new territory, *their* new territory, from now until the end, Susanna knew, would be sickness and fear. AIDS-land.

She knelt on the floor beside him.

"I'm not going to be gentle," she said. "There'll be time enough for that."

He said nothing.

"I'm feeling selfish." She went on. "Perhaps I should be think-ing only of you right now, but two things, above all the rest, keep going around and around in my head."

Hawke turned his head and forced himself to look right into her eyes. "Tell me."

"You kept it from me. That's the worst." Still, as in the res-taurant, she was very quiet. "And you put me at risk. Not only me. You put everyone I love at risk too." She paused. "How could you do that, Hawke?"

"I don't know."

"Not good enough." She saw his head turn away again, saw his eyes trying to escape hers. "Don't look away." She reached out and touched his face, and it was cold, the way his hands had been in the restaurant. "Look at me, Hawke. Answer me."

He turned back. His eyes were tortured.

"Fear," he said.

"Of what?" she asked, though she knew how many things he must have had to be afraid of. "Tell me. If you want me to try to understand, you have to tell me."

"I can't pretend—" His voice cracked. He took a sip of coffee, his hands unsteady, and cleared his throat. "There's no use pre-tending that I didn't tell you I'd had a love affair with a man

because I thought it was all in the past and so it didn't matter."
He paused. His jaw was very rigid, his body taut. "I didn't tell
you because I knew you'd be shocked, and probably repelled, and
even if you weren't, just knowing that about me would change
the way you felt about me, looked at me." He drank some more
coffee, grimaced at its coldness, then set the cup down on the
floor on the other side of his chair.

"Go on," Susanna said.

"That was before London, before you and I became lovers."

"Which didn't go exactly to plan, did it?" she said quietly.

Hawke looked at her. "You're wondering if our lovemaking
was sometimes difficult because I was bisexual?"

"You tell me."

"I don't think that was the reason. I can't be quite sure. I
thought then it was because you mattered so much to me, because
I was so much in love with you. I still think that." He paused. "I
did honestly believe it was all in the past. Not exactly an aber-
ration, because it was so much more than that, but entirely finished and done with." Hawke took a deep, shuddering breath.
"When I saw him again, and he was dying, and when I knew what
it was that was killing him, I knew that if I told you then, it would
be the end of us, and I couldn't contemplate that, so I kept it
from you."

"But you went on making love to me." The incredulity was
there again, in her voice, in her eyes.

"They hadn't even nailed down the virus then," Hawke said.
"And we were using condoms. I wanted to believe it was safe."

"But then I went on the Pill."

"I tried to stop you."

"I didn't know." She stared at him. "I didn't *know*."

"As soon as I knew they had a test, I thought I'd go for it, but
so many people were against testing because they were getting a
lot of false positive results, and anyway, they couldn't do anything
for you if you did have it. And I was healthy, I was perfectly
normal, and he and I had ended in 1980—I mean, it had been
years, for Christ's sake—"

"So you didn't take the test."

"I told myself there was no need. I calmed down, almost
stopped thinking about it." He paused. "And then I got sick the
first time, in Rome, and when we got back, I went to a place and

had them draw some blood; it was one of those places where they let you use any name you like."

"And?"

"And I never went back for the result. They said it would take about two weeks, and in those two weeks I talked myself out of it again. If the pneumonia had been AIDS-connected, I wouldn't have got over it so quickly; people get sick all the time, nothing to do with HIV. I had so many good reasons for not going back, Susanna, but all I was doing was the old ostrich thing. I was being a coward."

Susanna was silent for a while.

"I did wonder," she said, "when you cut yourself last month and you wouldn't let me touch you in case I got your blood on me."

"Yes."

"So you must still have thought you were putting me at risk."

"Yes." It was just a whisper.

"Were you feeling sick?"

"Not then."

"And now?" she asked. "What made you take the test?"

"I found a spot," he said, "just over two weeks ago. Just a little red thing, on my thigh. You didn't notice, but I was convinced it was a Kaposi's spot." His mouth quirked wryly. "The joke is it was nothing but a fucking spot, but I told Saul everything, and he drew the blood himself."

Susanna stood up. Her legs were cramped from kneeling.

"Where are you going?" Hawke asked.

"Nowhere." She walked over to the window, stared out unseeing into the night. "I'm just beginning to wonder where the hell I've been. All this time you were living a nightmare, and I didn't even notice."

"Why would you?" he said gently.

"The day you cut yourself, I had this flash about the virus, like suddenly I knew, but it seemed so unlikely, so impossible, and I pushed it away. I guess it was easier."

"It's hardly your fault, Susanna," Hawke said, still deep in the chair.

"I know that," she said. "But I'm supposed to be your wife."

"You are my wife." He got up, started toward her, then

stopped. Her back was to him. She still gazed out of the big window.

"You should have told me," she said again.

"Yes. God, yes."

They were both silent for a while.

"Are you going to leave me?" he asked at last.

"No." Still, she didn't turn around.

"I'll understand, if you change your mind."

"I won't change my mind."

He moved a foot closer and saw her reflection, mirrored in the dark glass beside his own. They looked like a pair of ghosts, somber and surreal.

At last, she was crying.

Her first HIV test result, two weeks later, was negative, and Hawke's relief was pitiful to see, but Saul Weinberg told them both that while the result was certainly good news, Susanna would need to go through the ordeal again in six months, and even then a negative test might not be a cast-iron guarantee.

When Hawke got sick again at the end of 1986, and they all knew it was full-blown AIDS for sure, Susanna's fears for her own health seemed to recede, to be pushed away, out of the picture. Hawke was the one to worry about; he was the one with pneumonia, being shot full of drugs, the one who was going to die. Susanna was the healthy one, the one who'd got away, whose second test had caused rejoicing in the Van Dusen household.

Yet in the back of her mind it was always there.

CHAPTER 9

A year later, shortly before Christmas 1987, Pete Strauss wrote in his journal for the first time in two weeks. He told himself he'd been too hard pressed, too dog tired at the end of each evening to make an entry, but the truth was that there were things on his mind he had been reluctant to admit to.

Hawke can't have too much longer. He's just come through a bad time, and he's feeling pretty great—by comparison— and he and Susanna are staying in Cohasset over the holidays. He's pitiful to look at and knows it, yet suddenly he seems filled with what he calls "dead man's optimism." It comes in part, I suppose, from being free, for a while at least, from the worst of the pain, and in part from the warmth and love and care of Susanna and the Van Dusens. But mostly I think it comes from a changed response to the knowledge that he has little time left to live. Carpe diem. Seizing each moment of every day Hawke feels even halfway normal seems to him right now to make more sense than all the drugs and psychobabble in the world.

I am deeply troubled for Susanna. Her husband is going to die soon, and for him the pain and fear will be over. But for her I fear it may only just be beginning. Susanna has invested so much of herself in Hawke; she focused every-thing on him, took on a career she never really wanted, then set it aside to take care of him when he got sick. All so simple, so clear. A woman in love. And when she becomes Hawke's widow, Susanna will be lost and empty and directionless, the way most bereaved people feel when the end has come and gone, and yet there's no end for them. Hawke will die, but Susanna will have to go on living.

Other things trouble me. The way I feel about her. I feel too much. I'm her counselor, a professional, but I dwell on her too much. Too often these days I catch myself having to struggle to maintain detachment. I manage it, but it's hard. She invades my mind at inopportune moments, day and night, and it isn't simply because of her beauty or her strength or her courage. I believe it's because of the pain, lying deep and suppressed inside her. The darkness she occasionally, fleetingly alludes to.

Susanna admits that there are things she feels unable to speak about. I have sometimes suspected that Hawke, in a way, has been a source of temporary escape for her, a refuge from that hidden pain, an excuse perhaps. I believe that she longs to speak about the past, that she needs to, desperately. Susanna was alive for eighteen years before meeting Hawke, years about which she has said so little, and she has a lifetime ahead of her. Yet if she doesn't find the strength to look back, to face herself, I'm afraid she may not be able to move forward, freely, into the future.

I came into her life as Hawke's counselor. When he dies, my role will be at an end. That of course is what I've been so reluctant to admit to, even to myself. My greatest fear.

Not seeing her again.

The first weekend in February, Tabitha, now a striking twenty-year-old at Brown University in Rhode Island, came to New York to visit Susanna, bringing Abigail with her. Abigail Van Dusen, at ten, had golden hair a few shades darker than her sister's, and eyes that seemed, to the Van Dusens, richer than Matthew Bodine's brown eyes had been. Abigail was tall and broad-shouldered like her sister, but otherwise fragile to look at, with a low, soft voice and a sweet, ready smile. She loved music and dance and books and animals; she loved the ocean with a passion that was even more intense than her sister's; she loved Connie and Bryan and Tabitha and Susanna and Hawke; she had no memory of either her mother or father and no true sense of loss or inadequacy relating to their loss. She knew that she and Susanna were foster children and that their real name was Bodine, but she seldom referred to that or asked questions about their roots. She was not incurious or even indifferent; she was simply a happy and complete person. Her brother-in-law's illness was the first real sorrow she had ever experienced, and she had begged Tabitha to bring her to New York so that she could spend time with Susanna and Hawke.

"No," Susanna told Abigail that Friday evening, when she said she wanted to visit Hawke in the hospital. They were sitting in the lobby of the Westbury Hotel, waiting for Tabitha, who'd gone to fetch a pair of gloves from their room before they went out to dinner.

"Why not?" Abigail asked.

"He's too sick for visitors." Hawke had been back in the hospital for more than a month, being freshly tormented with tubes and needles and drugs that made him throw up, and his hair was falling out again, and old friends like Polly Mellen and Lauren Hutton, who'd heard on the grapevine that Hawke was declining fast, were dropping by to see him, but Hawke was sending them away because he couldn't stand them to see him the way he was.

"You visit him," Abigail said.

"That's different, darling," Susanna said.

"Tabbie's going to visit him."

"Maybe."

"I want to see him." Abigail's face became set. She had a particularly beautiful mouth, even lovelier than Susanna's, but she had an ability to thin and tighten her lips when something displeased her that provided a warning signal to all who knew her well.

"I know you do, sweetheart."

"I want to see him before he dies," Abigail said.

"Abigail, for God's sake," Tabitha hissed, arriving in time to hear. "Hawke isn't going to die, not yet anyway, and don't you know yet that there's a time and place for talking about stuff like that?"

"Susanna won't let us visit with him," Abigail complained.

"Why not?" Tabitha turned to Susanna. "That's why we're here."

"I thought you were here to spend time with me," Susanna said calmly.

"We are." Tabitha sat down beside her. "Of course we are, but Hawke's important to us too."

"Both of us," Abigail pointed out.

Susanna felt the spurious calm deserting her. "I don't think either of you realize how sick Hawke is. It's getting hard for him to talk to people—"

"We're not people; we're family," Tabitha said.

Susanna reached for her hand. "I know you are." She paused. "Can't we talk about this later, after dinner?"

"She means she's going to talk to you behind my back," Abigail said.

"I didn't say that."

"And even if she does," Tabitha said, "it's only because you're ten."

"I'm not a baby. I know about dying, and I know about AIDS."

"Abigail, will you shut up?" Tabitha hissed again, though there was no one else around to hear.

"I thought we're supposed to be able to talk about it," Abigail protested. "Mom and Dad are always saying that it's wrong to sweep it under the rug, that it's not fair to people like Hawke."

"That doesn't mean you have to yell about it in a hotel lobby."

"I'm not yelling."

"No, she isn't." Susanna started to gather up her coat and bag.

"I want to see Hawke." Abigail was mutinous. "I'm going to get to see him whether you let me or not."

Susanna stood up. She could feel the trembling starting up deep inside, but she knew she had to control it, to breathe evenly, a few deep breaths, and shake it off. She'd been experiencing physical anxiety attacks for several months now; but the trembling had gotten worse over the past two or three weeks, and the very things that ought to make her feel better, calmer, more able to cope, like having Tabitha and Abigail with her, seemed instead to make her worse.

The girls had expected to stay at the loft with Susanna, but at the last minute she'd made reservations for the three of them at the Westbury instead. Tabitha and Abigail were both disappointed, loving the bohemianism of Hawke's place, but though Susanna told them she'd chosen a hotel because of lack of space in the loft, the truth was that in spite of all she'd learned about the disease and the ways in which the virus could or could not be transmitted, when it came to her adored Abigail, Susanna found that she couldn't bear for her to be inside their home just in case all the epidemiologists and doctors were wrong and it was proved that you could, after all, catch HIV from a towel or off a glass or a fork. Before their arrival she had confided her fears over lunch with Pete, who had, for once, lost patience with her, for how could she, who had fought battles with Nurse Himmler for almost two years, how *could* she now betray Hawke this way?

"I'm not betraying him," she had protested quietly, though they were eating in the noisy front room at Il Cantinori on Tenth Street.

"Of course you are. You know you are." Pete's anger was rare, and all the harsher for it. "Hawke and everyone like him, like you, Susanna."

"I can't help it." Susanna played with her pasta. Since the demise of the Grace contract, she had taken to ordering whatever she felt like, but the irony was that lately she had no appetite, so her figure was even more slender than before.

"Sure you can help it. You're an intelligent woman, you're informed, and you're strong."

"I don't feel strong."

"I didn't say you're not human." Pete had gentled. "Okay, so you overreacted a little about your sister; that isn't the end of the world. But it has to stop there. Cancel the hotel reservation."

"I can't."

"Sure you can."

"There isn't space for three people in the loft."

"Bullshit. The bedroom sleeps two, and you have a couch."

"I don't want to share Hawke's bed with anyone else."

"We're not talking about anyone else; we're talking about your sisters."

"It's Hawke's bed. Anyway, it's a futon; some people can't sleep on futons." Susanna flushed. "Okay, so that's not the real reason, but I can't help the way I feel. When it comes to Abigail,

I sometimes get a little crazy, a little overprotective. That's just the way I am about her."

"Not Tabitha, just Abigail."

"Tabbie's twenty. Abigail's only ten."

Pete watched her for a minute, saying nothing.

"What?" Susanna asked.

"Just thinking."

"What?" she repeated.

"That this is one time when I believe Hawke should come before Abigail."

"It isn't going to matter to Hawke where my sisters stay."

"But it'll matter when Abigail tries to hug him or, God forbid, kiss him, and you try to drag her off."

"I wouldn't," Susanna said, but she felt frost around her heart.

"Are you sure?" Pete asked.

"Perfectly."

She had made up her mind at that moment that although her two sisters were among the few people that Hawke would be happy to see, Abigail would neither get to hug nor to kiss Hawke. On the Sunday afternoon of their New York visit, when it had become clear that nothing short of a ball and chain would keep Abigail from her brother-in-law's bedside, Susanna took up a physical position between them that made it almost impossible for the ten-year-old to do anything more than take Hawke's hand. Susanna knew that everyone in the room was aware of what she was doing, and why, including Hawke, and she also knew that no one could possibly despise her more than she did herself, yet still she sat, like a shameful rock, between her gaunt, dying husband and Abigail, refusing to move, refusing to be moved.

"How could you do that?" Tabitha asked Susanna quietly while they waited for the elevator to take them back to the first floor.

"Do what?" Susanna asked, her throat aching.

Tabitha's hazel eyes met hers evenly. "Poor Hawke," she said.

Abigail did not refer to it, either when they left the hospital or later when she and Tabitha said their farewells at Penn Station, but it was in her eyes and drawn like a hard, unforgiving line on her mouth, and Susanna knew she would not swiftly, if ever, forget, yet she knew too that if she had the visit to live over, she would do the same, unpardonable thing again.

One week later, having rallied sufficiently for the doctors to allow him to leave, at least for the moment, Hawke came home to the loft. Susanna shopped for a celebratory dinner in Chinatown, bought fresh fish at the hectic market on Canal Street and vegetables at Lye Yan and everything necessary to make her own won ton at Canton Noodle on Mott Street, and miraculously, though for weeks now nothing had tasted right to Hawke and at times he'd found himself hardly able to swallow solid food at all, tonight he ate with a semblance of pleasure and sipped a little sake without ill effects.

"This is heaven," he told her in his poor, weak voice.

"It's the first time I've enjoyed cooking in a while," she said.

"You have to take good care of yourself."

"I know," she said. "I do."

"I worry about you."

"No need."

She helped him up the spiral staircase later, painfully aware that it might be for the last time, for he could hardly manage the steps anymore, and his legs were so thin and his muscles so wasted, but they made it, and it was worth it just to see the joy on his face when he lay down on the futon and she lay down beside him, snuggling close, no IVs or tubes to keep them apart.

"Will you ever forgive me?" he asked after a while.

"What for?"

"For this," he said. "For getting it, for exposing you to it. For dying of it."

"Hawke, there's nothing to forgive," she whispered in agony.

"Don't lie to me, Susanna, or to yourself."

"I'm not. I may have thought that way once, near the beginning, but not anymore."

"You never talk about it," he said.

"No."

"You made me afraid to talk to you."

"I know." The only lights on were their reading lights, but she wanted to turn them out, to keep her flaming face from him. "Pete told me."

"He's a wonderful man," Hawke said.

"Yes, he is. We're lucky to have him."

"He's probably in love with you."

"No, he isn't," Susanna said.

"He wouldn't do anything about it even if he was. Not yet."

"Hawke, don't." She kissed the bony shoulder that had been so strong. Hawke had been proud of his shoulders; she had caught him more than once checking out his muscles in the bathroom mirror and teased him about it, but she too had loved his strength, the power of him, never once abused, not with her. His face, with the fighter's nose and forceful chin, was all angles now, the cheeks sunken so that even the old scar had all but vanished into the gloom. It was hard for her to look at him for too long these days, for she felt his pain at her glance; he knew how bad he looked, how changed. And so Susanna waited, as a rule, until he was sleeping, and then she looked and looked, drinking her fill, for at least dying Hawke was still living Hawke, and besides, when he was sleeping, she didn't have to look into his eyes, frightened, condemned eyes.

He was not yet ready for sleep tonight.

"Do you want to talk?" he asked her.

"Of course I want to talk," she answered. "What do you want to talk about?"

"You. Me." He paused. "Dying."

For an instant she closed her eyes. "You talk about whatever you want."

"You always do that." He was gentle but accusing. "You won't accept that I need to talk."

"I do accept it," she whispered. "I just need you to start."

He waited a moment. His breathing seemed more of an effort than it had earlier in the evening.

"I'm scared," he said finally.

"I know."

"Don't say that. You don't know."

"Then tell me."

He smiled, wretchedly. "One thing about it, there's not much left to be scared of, in a way. The worst has already happened. I'm not going to die in a plane crash, I'm not going to drown, I'm not going to burn to death—I already have the worst disease I'm going to have." He paused. "I've already seen my wife refusing to let her sister kiss my cheek."

Susanna wanted to sit up, to escape, but she forced herself to stay.

"I didn't blame you," Hawke said. "I think you were right."

"No," she said. "I wasn't right."

He shrugged a little. "We'll never know."

"I hurt you," Susanna said.

"A little." Hawke agreed gently. "But it was the first and only time since I've known you, and that's not bad going, is it?"

"Bad enough."

"I only mention it because I know you've been giving yourself a hard time ever since it happened, and now you can forget it."

"Never," she said.

"I said forget it. Dying man's privileges and all that."

"Okay."

He shifted a little, painfully, on the futon. "How long have we known each other?"

"Eight years in May."

"Are you crying?" he asked.

"Yes."

"Me too."

She looked at him, and saw that he was. She'd never seen Hawke weep before, but his tears were flowing freely now, and she felt them fueling her own sorrow, yet they seemed, she thought, to bring him some relief.

"We've had a strange relationship, don't you think?" he asked.

"Strange how?" She wiped her eyes with the back of her hand.

"We started out kind of father and daughter, didn't we, in the early days. Me showing you the way." He spoke in short snatches now; it was growing harder for him to talk at length, to breathe easily. "And then it got turned on its head. Mother-son. You helping me through it."

"You helped me too, Hawke."

"Yeah, I know." A tear reached the left side of his mouth, and he licked it away. "We never had much time to be a regular husband and wife, did we?"

"I'm not sure if I know what that is," Susanna said.

"I think of Connie and Bryan that way."

"Yes," she murmured. "They're a good team."

"We've been a good team too," Hawke said. "Even if we have kept things from each other."

"Things?"

"Secrets."

She said nothing. Her heart thumped; her body stiffened.

"If you wanted," Hawke said, "you could tell me anything now, Susanna. I promise not to betray you. Even if I changed my mind, it would probably be too late."

"Hawke, shut up."

"I'm being serious, love." His right hand reached out to stroke her hair. "I don't mind if you don't want to, I've never minded that you kept things from me. If I hadn't got the damned plague, I expect I'd never have told you about the man who gave it to me." He stopped for breath. "I never did tell you his name, did I?"

"I don't care about his name," Susanna said almost violently.

"I don't blame you. What's in a name anyway?"

In the brief silence that followed, they watched each other, both remembering a moment years before, when they'd been starting out on their partnership, when they had reached a mutual understanding that they had a right to keep their pasts private. Hawke's secrets had been forced from him by his diagnosis. Susanna's, they both knew, remained locked inside her mind.

"So," Hawke said, his eyes still fixed on hers, "no deathbed confessions to spice up my last hours?"

A sudden longing, a vast yearning to unburden herself to him, swept Susanna, but then it was gone again, replaced by the old familiar tightening of self-control, the turning of the key.

She sighed, very softly. "No," she said.

"Okay."

"I'm sorry."

"No need." Hawke was very gentle. "I just wanted to help."

"I know."

"Will you be all right?" he asked.

"In time," she said.

Susanna had scheduled a meeting next morning with Andrea Marantz and an editor from Random House interested in publishing a collection of Hawke's work next year with proceeds going to AmFAR. Angie Lopez was due to sit with Hawke while Susanna was out, but when, at ten o'clock, Angie called to say she was running about a half hour late, Susanna started to dial the Marantz Agency.

"Who are you calling?" Hawke was lying on the couch, a mug of lemon tea beside him. When he picked it up, he used both hands, and both of them trembled.

"Andrea."

"Why?"

"I'm going to postpone our meeting."

"No," Hawke said.

Susanna held the cordless phone to her ear.

"Susanna, put the phone down." His voice was harsh.

Startled, she cut off the call. "What's up?"

"I don't want you to cancel."

"I'm not canceling, just postponing."

"Because Angie's running a half hour late?"

"Because I'd rather stay here with you," Susanna said defensively.

"Because you're scared to leave me without a sitter."

"Of course I'm not."

Hawke hadn't moved. "Listen to me, Susanna," he said. "It isn't nice to know that people are frightened to leave you on your own for thirty bloody minutes in case you fuck up their timetable and die on them."

"Hawke, that's an awful thing to say." Susanna put the phone down on the desk. "You just got out of the hospital yesterday. Of course I don't want to leave you alone in case you need anything."

"I won't, and if I do, I'll get it myself." He was half bitter, half patient. "This is my home, remember? I know my way around."

"I know you do."

"Now you're pissed off with me."

"No, I'm not."

"Prove it."

She went over to the couch, bent down, and kissed him on the mouth.

"Nice, but not what I meant," Hawke said.

"What did you mean?"

"I meant, go to your meeting." He paused. "My comfort and safety apart, this book deal's just what I could use—a little posthumous ego trip, not to mention the royalties to boost my estate or whatever's left of it after all the damned hospital bills."

"The royalties are going to charity," Susanna reminded him.

"I'd rather they went to you," Hawke said.

"You're the one who suggested AmFAR."

"I suppose I was. Part of the ego trip." Hawke handed her his tea mug. "Stick that in the sink before you go, love."

"Are you sure you'll be okay?"

"I'll be great," he said. "I'll probably nap till Angie comes."

"Are you tired?" Her anxiety mounted.

"I'm always tired, Susanna. Just do me a favor and go."

"I'm gone," she said.

There was no outward indication, when the cab dropped her back on Canal Street a little more than two hours later, that anything was wrong. Susanna went inside the building, called the big old freight elevator that led right into Hawke's place, and ascended to the loft.

Angie Lopez was waiting for her, her expression shocked.

"What's happened? Where's Hawke?" Susanna tried to pass Angie, but she stood in her way. "Where *is* he?"

"He isn't here."

"Oh, my God, what's happened to him? Angie, tell me!" She stared into the other woman's face, recognized the horror in her eyes, felt as if a sharp blade had pierced her heart. "*Tell* me."

"I had to call Saul Weinberg." Still, Angie stood right in front of Susanna, not letting her pass. "He's taking Hawke back to the hospital, but they only left a few minutes ago. You just missed them."

"But he was okay when I left—" Susanna attempted to step forward, but Angie sidestepped with her like a basketball defender. "Angie, what is going on?"

"I need to tell you, before you see—"

"See what?" Growing angry, Susanna pushed roughly past her. "See what, for Christ's sake?"

"His studio," Angie said faintly.

"What?" Susanna moved farther into the open-plan room, turned to the right, and stopped dead. She said nothing.

"He must have gone berserk." Angie was behind her.

"Hawke did this?" Susanna's voice was a disbelieving whisper.

"It was almost over when I got here—"

"I don't believe he did this."

Susanna stepped forward, into what she had always thought of as Hawke's beloved and immaculate kingdom. A place for everything and everything in its place. The place where he had taught her most of what he knew about modeling and about photography and about what brought paper images of fashion to vital, vibrant, breathing, effective life. Where inspiration had gone hand in hand with precision, fantasy with hard labor, glamour and beauty with sweat. Where Hawke's brilliant eyes and fingers and mind had shown his cameras how to tell its truths and its lies. All in ruins. Equipment smashed, lighting umbrellas slashed, backcloths ripped, blowups torn from walls and littering the floor. Hawke's favorite canvas and wood chair on its side, one leg broken off.

"I can't believe it," she whispered again.

"Nor could I." Angie was beside her, weeping now. "When I got here, he was all finished, slumped on the floor. There was red ink on his hands, and I thought it was blood, I thought he'd cut his wrists, but it was red ink." She looked at Susanna, saw that her whole body was shivering, put an arm around her. "Come and sit down."

"No." Susanna shook off her arm and took a step farther into the mayhem. She saw her face, black and white and as lovely as any man could have made her, a knife slash through her paper forehead, tossed in a corner like old garbage. "No," she said again.

Angie went away for a moment, came back with one of Hawke's Pentax cameras in her hands. "He was holding this when I found him. I think he was taking pictures of what he'd done. I'm not sure. He wasn't making any sense, Susanna." She held out the camera, and Susanna took it automatically. "I'm so sorry."

"Yes." Susanna held the Pentax against her stomach, pressed it hard into her flesh, wanting it to hurt.

"You'll want to go to him now," Angie said, softly.

Susanna said nothing.

"Hawke needs you, Susanna."

Susanna shut her eyes.

"Of course," she said.

* * *

Hawke hardly spoke to anyone again after that morning. The destruction of his studio had left him speechless, too deeply, profoundly depressed to talk, and it had also sapped the last of his physical strength. Within days of his being readmitted to the hospital, everything hit him at once. The catalog of his ailments grew like needlegrass on wasteland: his liver became enlarged, then his spleen; then his kidneys started to fail; he hemorrhaged, brought up blood, sending nurses of hardier stuff than Nurse Himmler running for their protective gloves and coveralls. They shot drug cocktails into his veins, and failing to persuade Hawke to sign new consent forms allowing them to do whatever was deemed necessary to prolong his life, they tried asking Susanna to sign on his behalf. She refused. Claiming that he was still responsible, they returned to Hawke, stuck the forms under his nose, badgered him gently but relentlessly until he scrawled, with pitiful, trembling fingers, a semblance of his old vigorous signature. With Susanna raging impotently on the sidelines, they pumped new blood into him, but only a matter of hours later Hawke lapsed into semiconsciousness and remained that way, mercifully oblivious of all that was being done for him in the name of medicine, for the next eight days.

Just after four in the afternoon on the last day of February, while Susanna was fetching coffee, Pete Strauss was sitting at the side of his bed when Hawke woke up for just long enough to say what Pete figured later had probably been bludgeoning hard enough at his unconscious mind to drag him up out of his twilight sleep.

Hawke's speech was slurred, but his words were urgent and clear enough.

"Tell Susanna I never meant to wreck her pictures." Hawke's right hand moved convulsively on top of the bedclothes. "All the rest maybe, but not her; tell her that."

"She'll be back in a minute," Pete said, tears rising in his throat.

"Tell her." His hand clenched and unclenched.

Pete took the fist and held it. "I'll tell her." The hand stilled.

"Look after her." Hawke's eyes had a sudden, fleeting clarity.

"I will," Pete told him.

"So much pain inside her," Hawke said. "She hides it, even from herself."

"She'll be okay." Pete kept hold of his hand.

"If you help her," Hawke said, and passed out again.

His heart stopped for the first time three hours later, but against Susanna's will they worked on him, hard and tenaciously and with all the professional love and skill they might have brought to bear on a five-year-old with the world ahead of him, forcing him back again.

"Find Saul Weinberg," Susanna begged Pete, while Hawke lay ticking over on life support. "Ask him to make them leave him alone next time it happens." The tears rolled down her cheeks, and she held onto Pete's hands, so tightly that her fingernails cut into his palms. "Can't they see what they're doing to him? Can't they see that he's had *enough*?"

Hawke's heart stopped again just after eleven. They worked on him again, for almost fifteen minutes.

And then they let him be.

Like so many other matters relating to his illness, Susanna had shied away from discussing Hawke's funeral wishes with him, and like many of those other matters, Hawke had chosen not to add to her misery and had talked his burial arrangements over with Pete Strauss.

"He told me cremation," Pete said, gentle as always, the morning after Hawke's death. "He didn't mind about a memorial or headstone or anything permanent. He told me he didn't want what he called one of those fashion requiems, with people feeling obligated to stand up and tell tales about how great and gifted he was. I asked him if there was any place special he wanted his ashes scattered, but he said he didn't care about that either—maybe back where he'd come from, but he said he couldn't picture you doing that anyhow." A smile touched Pete's lips. "To be exact, he said that if he couldn't be there to shoot a roll of film while you did it, there was no bloody point anyway."

Hawke had only told his parents about his illness in a letter written at Christmas, while they'd been staying at the Van Dusens', the last time he'd felt really well. In the letter he had begged them not to come over, to stay at home, where he could picture them as he always had, not bending over his sickbed with fear-ravaged faces. He knew that what he was asking of them was hard, but he said he was choosing the selfish way for himself; he could handle it better without having to worry about them.

When Susanna, supported by Bryan and Connie and Tabitha and Abigail, flew to England with Hawke's remains, his mother and father, both aged with shock and grief and confusion, greeted her with all the love and warmth and gratitude they might have accorded a daughter. Together, on a cold early March morning, they buried his ashes in the family plot in their village churchyard. It was raining, a chill east wind blowing through the trees, and in the naked branches of an old gnarled oak a pair of magpies cawed raucously throughout the brief service. Susanna, hearing few of the vicar's words, gazed at the rain-soaked grass around the exposed roots of the tree and thought about Hawke's early photographs, when he'd moved quietly and easily around the streets and parks of New York, capturing life in every form, tangible and incorporeal, solid and symbolic. And when the words had all been spoken, she took Hawke's Pentax, the same camera with which he had taken pictures of his destroyed studio, his final, long-overdue act of protest and resistance, and she photographed his grave, and the magpies in the ancient oak, and the faces of his mother and his father, and then she knelt and laid the camera in the cold, wet ground beside him.

She left the loft, Hawke's place, a month later, as she had known she would, for without Hawke's presence or any hope of his return to warm it and give it light, it was a shell, a skeleton, wholly without comfort.

"Back to Cohasset." Pete Strauss mused when she told him during what she said was to be their last session. "Think you'll be able to stand it for long?"

"Of course I will," Susanna said. "My family's there."

"They've been there for the last four or five years too," Pete observed, "and you've been in Manhattan. You've become a New Yorker, Susanna. I can't imagine you hanging around in a small town."

"I think I could use a little hanging around."

"Sure you could, a little. Go for a rest, take a month."

"Then what?"

"Come back."

"For what?"

"Get back to work," Pete said.

"Modeling?" Susanna shook her head. "Andrea's always saying she has inquiries for me, but she knows it's over for me. It was always Hawke or nothing so far as I was concerned."

"You've had a lot of experience, Susanna. You should use it."

"I never wanted to be a model."

"I'm not necessarily talking about modeling." Pete paused. "There are a lot of people who might benefit from what you've been through."

"Fund-raising?" Susanna nodded. "I've already told AmFAR I'll be available to do what I can."

"That's good," Pete said, "but I had something more direct in mind, more hands-on."

Her eyes widened. "You think I should work with AIDS patients?" She was shocked. "I couldn't do that, Pete."

"I think you'd do it wonderfully well," he said quietly.

"No."

"Not yet, of course."

"Not ever," she said. "I was useless to Hawke; you know I was. There were so many things he needed from me, and I failed him time and time again because I couldn't handle it."

"That's exactly what would make you more sensitive to the needs of another patient now, Susanna."

"You're wrong, Pete. I'm the last person to try to do that kind of work. I'm not like you."

"Maybe not."

"No maybe about it." She was adamant.

"I'll miss you," he said after a minute.

"I'll miss you too," she said, looking right into his green eyes. "You helped me so much."

"I'm glad." He paused. "Are we finished, Susanna? Professionally."

"I think so," she said. "What do you say?"

"It's not for me to say. You were never officially my patient."

"Wasn't I?" She smiled. "I thought we kind of slipped into it."

"I'd say we kind of slipped into being friends," Pete said softly.

"I couldn't have handled it without you."

"Yes, you could. You're tough, Susanna."

"No, I'm not," she said. "Not really."

"We'll see," Pete said.

PART TWO

CHAPTER 10

~

The blackmail threat came to her apartment on the last day of 1991, badly typed and imperfectly folded over twice, in a plain brown envelope with a Boston postmark. It was dated December 25, and in keeping with many letters of extortion, it was unsigned, but Susanna knew that the sender had no doubts that she would know who he was. She felt that he was secure about getting from her what he wanted. He was, perhaps, right.

You're so good, they all think you're Saint Fucking Susanna of the Fucking Sick, but I could tell them a thing or two that would blow their goddamned brains away. You're so good, maybe you wouldn't care too much what they knew about you. But what about Abigail? What about your precious little sister?

He wanted money. Fifty thousand dollars in cash. He gave her no instructions on how, where, or when he wanted it paid. That would come, she supposed, soon. She wondered if she would have to see him. The money part, somehow, she would cope with if she had to. The thought of seeing him was unbearable.

She had vomited after she had first read those words, made it to the bathroom just in time and been grateful that she was alone. She knew, as most people did, that she ought to take the letter to the police or, at the very least, show it to someone—Bryan, maybe, or else Pete. It would come as less of a shock to Pete than anyone else. But once one other person knew the truth, the whole truth, it was only a matter of time before it was out in the open, and though the blackmailer might not have his fifty thousand dollars, he would still, in another way, be the winner.

He was wrong about one thing. Protecting Abigail was only part of the reason why she might let him get away with it. Protecting herself, her serenity, her ability to go on, her sanity, was just as vital to her. She had been coming slowly apart in the almost four years since Hawke's death. Unraveling, both in private and in her therapy sessions with Pete Strauss. It was a painful, often anguished process, and one that she had approached with trepidation, but that she had known was necessary if she was to achieve what, after her initial months of grief, had become her aim. She had never had a real aim in life before, had never clearly known what she wanted, what she needed, to do. She knew now, and she had worked steadfastly toward it, beating all the odds.

She would not let him destroy that.

She had gone back to visit Pete Strauss a little over three years earlier, on one of her infrequent visits to New York. It was the second Sunday morning of November, nine months after Hawke's death, and she had gone to Eighth Street with a bag of Dunkin' Donuts without calling first, on the off chance he might be home. Just back from a morning jog, Pete was plainly pleased to find her at his front door.

"I want to open a respite house for AIDS patients," she'd told him almost immediately, and had been rewarded by the first genuinely startled expression she'd ever seen on his face.

They had sat in the living room, eating doughnuts and drinking coffee and talking things through, and everything had seemed as comfortingly unchanged as if she had never been away. Alice in her cage, crunching seed and listening keenly, Steinbeck, the passion of his greeting past, dozing by the fireplace, a new Strauss masterpiece on the wall, a vivid scene, in bright acrylic paint, of a summer street exhibition on University Place. Susanna had tried to explain to Pete what she had in mind; an escape hatch, as she put it, a warm, peaceful house in the countryside where sufferers and their loved ones could stay awhile to recover their senses between the shock of diagnosis and the bouts of sickness and the world that had turned its back on them. Pete, with unprecedented sharpness, had questioned her motives, had cautioned her thoroughly about the enormous difficulties and complexities of the type of project she had in mind, but Susanna had done her homework before coming to him and had stood her ground.

"Knowing you," she said at last, when they had talked for more than an hour, "you've already guessed that the house is only part of the reason I've come to see you."

"Tell me the other part," Pete said.

Susanna took a breath. "I want to come back into therapy," she said.

Pete said nothing.

"I know that I started mostly for Hawke's sake—" she went on slowly—"but I think maybe I always knew it was really for my own. I guess I didn't want to admit that, which was why I stopped coming after he died." She paused. "Or maybe I just lost my nerve."

"Why the change of heart?"

"I could say that I've decided that if I want to be of any real use to other people, maybe I should try to resolve some of my own problems first."

"But that isn't the real reason."

Susanna felt her cheeks flush. "No. Of course not." She turned her eyes on his, painfully but frankly. "I'm a mess, Pete. Grief was such a good front, such great camouflage, but I can't hide behind mourning forever. There's still so much old, bad stuff locked up inside me, and I started remembering how good it felt when we used to talk; I think maybe I almost became addicted to our talks. I really think I *need* to start again. And I don't know if I can really do it—face up to it all, I mean—but I think I'm ready to try."

Pete smiled. "Okay."

"You don't mind?"

"Why would I?"

The relief that filled Susanna was tinged with apprehension. She stood up, and Steinbeck, lifting his head, wagged his tail. "When can we start?"

"I'll have to check the calendar." Pete went ahead of her out into the hall. "I have a feeling I have a free space late tomorrow."

"That would be great."

Pete stopped. "Aren't you living in Cohasset?"

"I've taken an apartment on Beekman Place," she said.

"How come?"

"So I could be close by for our sessions."

Pete smiled. "Determined lady."

"I need to do this," Susanna said softly, simply. "It's taken me a long time to admit how much I do need it, but I've made up my mind now. I'm going to try."

"You're looking great," Pete said at the front door. "Your hair's different." He'd noticed the shorter cut right away, short enough to expose all of her lovely neck, still long and thick enough to swing as she moved.

"You're looking good too," Susanna said. "I like the beard."

"Honestly?" He stroked it. "I've been undecided."

"Honestly? I've always liked your chin."

"I'll shave tomorrow."

Susanna laughed.

"This is all going to be pretty rough on you," Pete said, one more time before she left. "Our sessions, getting the project under way. However hard you think it's going to be, I promise you it'll be harder."

"I know it will," she said quietly.

"You're sure you're ready?"

"I don't think I have a choice," Susanna said.

She began, at five the next afternoon, as she had known she must, with a leap into the dark. She was tenser than she could remember being for many years. It was hard to breathe.

"I was raped," she said, "when I was thirteen."

Pete saw the old locked window in her mind opening a little, saw the sliver of light, saw her wavering, uncertain whether to slam it shut again.

"Go on," he said.

"I'd first seen him about a year earlier. He worked in one of the places we used to live." Susanna paused. "In the convent."

"Where your parents both worked."

"Yes." She paused again. "I never really spoke to him. There was no need, and anyway, we were discouraged from speaking to strangers, especially men. It was just good mornings and greetings, just polite stuff, you know."

Pete didn't say anything, let her take her time.

"Is it stuffy in here or is it just me?" Susanna asked.

"I don't find it especially stuffy, but I can open a window if you like."

"No," she said. "It's okay."

He smiled at her. "I'll put out my cigarette." He took a quick last drag and stubbed it out, made sure it was quite dead and leaned over to tip the old butts out of the ashtray into the wastebasket.

"I don't mind you smoking. I never have."

"Don't worry about it. Just go on."

Susanna closed her eyes. It was such an effort, forcing herself back there, dragging herself down into those depths; it had been so much easier all these years just pretending it had never happened, keeping it all locked up, not permitting herself to think about it.

"I know it's hard," Pete said.

She opened her eyes again.

"Some of the other girls were excited about having him around. He was a gardener, and I guess he was good-looking. He never took off his shirt while he was working because the nuns wouldn't have liked it, but the girls used to say you could see the sweat glistening on him; they used to giggle about his big muscles, you know."

"What about you? Did you giggle too?"

"Sometimes, joining in with the others. I don't think I spent as much time thinking about him as some of the other girls did. He was the first real man I'd ever seen at close quarters, so I guess I was a little intrigued too."

"What about your father? Didn't you think about him as a real man?"

"No," she answered quickly. "Not that way, no."

"Go on."

"One of the girls tried flirting with him, really flirting, but though she claimed he liked her, I never saw him respond to her at all. Not a flicker."

"Did you ever flirt with him?" Pete asked.

"Never." She was definite. "He was old, about thirty. And I didn't even think that much about boys then, not the way some of the other girls did. I mean, I liked my share of rock singers and movie stars—" She smiled. "I was crazy about Jon Voight. I had his pictures hidden with my underwear because we weren't allowed posters on the walls."

They were in Pete's office. No Alice, no Steinbeck, no yoga positions to lighten the load. This was serious business, Susanna realized. Time to confront herself. A means to an end.

"About ten days before Christmas," she went on, "I was given the task of helping to decorate the big tree in the convent hall. A few of us had helped with it, and the sisters had been supervising us, but right that minute there was no one else in the hall but me, and the only thing left to do was to hang the angel at the top of the tree. I climbed up the stepladder, and I hung the angel, and then I heard a voice telling me to be careful, and it was him. He said he'd help me down, and I said I was okay, thank you, but he was holding the ladder steady anyhow, so I started down." Susanna took a breath, trying to remember her yoga breathing, but her heart was beating fast, and her hands were clammy with the memory. "I felt something between my legs, and for a moment I didn't know—I really didn't know what it was—but then I looked down, and I saw it was his hand, right between my thighs, not doing anything exactly, just there, touching me. And I froze right there, halfway down that ladder, and I didn't say anything. I didn't know what to say. And then he took his hand away, and I got back down on the stone floor, and he was just standing there, holding the ladder, nice as pie, smiling at me. And then Sister Michael was there beside us, and she thanked him for helping, and he went away."

"Did you say anything to Sister Michael?" Pete asked. "Or to your parents?"

"No." Susanna felt a trace of perspiration on her upper lip. "I didn't know what to say, and anyway, I wasn't sure what had really happened. I thought it might have been an accident or even my imagination. I know it sounds really foolish now, incredibly naive—"

"You were only thirteen," Pete said.

"That Christmas I was still twelve."

"You were a child. Children have a right to be innocent about sex. It has nothing to do with foolishness or naiveté."

"Maybe not."

"Did you feel guilty about what had happened? As if it had been your fault?"

"I didn't feel anything about it," Susanna answered. "I put it right out of my mind. I've always been good at doing that, burying stuff I didn't like or didn't want to think about."

"But it's still there."

"Oh, yes. All of it."

Christmas of 1974 passed, then New Year. Winter melted into spring, then blossomed into full-blown summer. By mid-July, one month after Susanna's thirteenth birthday, the incident on the stepladder was long forgotten.

The other girls were home with their families now, but the convent was home to Susanna, and she didn't mind its quietude, its tranquillity. Some of the time she read, or did a little work, or helped with chores. It was hot, and there were strangers outside the walls, summer tourists on the road, some speeding to their destinations, some slowly passing through, most in cars, some on bicycles, a few on foot.

There was a beach not far from the convent, and as often as possible Susanna walked there, usually late in the day, tying her sandals together and hanging them around her neck, letting her feet cool in the shallows, the sea breeze blow through her hair. The ocean soothed and stimulated Susanna; she fancied its ancient voice spoke poetry and sang songs to her in its gentler waves, told her tales, in its roaring surf, of other lands, other countries, of great ships and fishing boats, of sailors and smugglers, of its own depths, mysterious and unfathomable. Susanna was in awe of the sea, yet she was never more at home than close to its vastness. She wondered idly, sometimes, what it would be like to drown in it, to be sucked down, airless, into its frigid, infinite black belly, but it was no more than that, a fleeting fancy, accompanied by a tiny frisson of ice that stroked her spine, tickled the back of her neck, and was then gone. Susanna was not normally prey to morbid thoughts; it was only the ocean's magnitude and power that triggered them in her mind.

"You like the ocean?"

The voice close to her left ear made her spin around, startled. She had believed herself all alone but for the gulls. He was wearing cutoff denim shorts and a grass-stained white T-shirt. His feet, like her own, were bare. His dark, curling hair blew around his head. His eyes were friendly.

"I like the beach," she said.

"Me too."

She stepped to her right. He made no move to close the space between them.

"Would you mind a little company?" he asked.

"No," she said, and her heart beat faster. "Though I'll be heading back soon."

"Okay," he said easily. "How about a little stroll that way?" He nodded west, toward the point. "Just until you've had enough."

"All right," Susanna said.

They began to walk. He was a tall man as well as broad, his stride much longer than hers, though several times he slowed his pace to make it easier for her to keep up with him.

"I never went to a beach the whole time I was growing up," he told her. "We lived on a farm, and I went to school in a small town, and my father didn't hold with TV, and I had no time for books, so the only time I saw the ocean was in the movies, and that wasn't too often, I can tell you."

"I've always lived near a beach," she said, pitying him.

"It's the freest place I've ever been," he said.

The breeze blew up a little, caught Susanna's hair and tossed it back in her eyes. A sharp-ended strand scratched at her right eye, and she brushed the hair away and then rubbed at the eye.

"Got something in it?" he asked her. "Want me to look?"

She shook her head. "No, thank you."

"It's painful when that happens. Was it sand?"

"No, it's nothing," she said, and walked a little faster.

"Must be duller than watching grass grow," he commented.

"What must be?" she asked.

"Being here all alone in the summer, without your friends, I mean."

"No," she said. "It's okay. I don't mind it."

"Girl your age needs friends around." He glanced sideways at her. "How old are you anyhow? Fourteen?"

"Thirteen," she said.

"You look older," he said.

"Do I?" Pleased, she slowed down a little.

"Makes me feel younger just looking at you," he told her. "I like working around schools, keeps a man on his toes."

"Do you like being a gardener?" she asked curiously.

"Well enough," he said.

"I think it must be wonderful."

"How come?"

"Growing things," she said. "Flowers and vegetables. Your cabbages taste better than most."

"I thank you," he said. "Most youngsters hate cabbage."

"So do I." She flushed. "Yours are nice, though."

"You're very polite." He grinned at her. His face was darkly tanned from working out in the sun, and his teeth were strong and white. "Must be living around all those nuns."

"They're very nice," Susanna said.

"Like my cabbages." He was still smiling, his dark eyes narrowing to near slits of amusement. "All that prayer, though," he said. "Must be hard work."

"It's not so bad," she said.

"You religious?"

"No," she answered. "Not really."

"So how do you stand all that praying?"

"I daydream mostly," she said, and flushed again.

"That's okay," he said. "Fantasy's good for you, so they say."

"Really?"

"I fantasize all the time," he said.

"What about?" Susanna asked.

"Wouldn't you like to know?" he said.

She quickened her pace again.

Less than twenty yards farther on down the beach, stepping over a small outcrop of water-smoothed rock, he lost his footing and stumbled. Susanna stopped.

"Are you okay?"

"I think so." For a moment or two he stayed down on the sand, rubbing his left thigh, and then he got up, wincing when he put weight on the leg. "Hell," he said. "That's all I needed."

"What have you done?" Susanna kept her distance.

"Torn a muscle, I think." He took a breath. "Best start heading back." He put his foot back down, took a tentative step, and cried out sharply with the pain. "Shi-it," he swore, then caught her expression. "Sorry."

"That's okay."

"Guess I'm going to need some help."

Susanna looked around. There was no one else on the beach. She looked back at the gardener. "Should I go call somebody?"

"No," he said. "I don't need carrying. I just need someone to lean on." He looked her up and down. "You stronger than you look?"

"I don't know," she said. She felt awkward, uncertain. One part of her mind was sending out warning signals, telling her to go, to leave him, but the other part was reminding her about charity and helping neighbors and stuff like that, and what would the sisters think of her if she just left an injured man to fend for himself?

"Let's see," he said.

Susanna didn't move.

"You mind helping me?" he asked, his tone reasonable but laced just a little with accusation. "If I'm too heavy leaning, we can stop."

Susanna looked around again. Not a soul.

"All right," she said.

"Good girl," he said, and waited for her to come to him. "Come on then. Can't help me from there."

She moved toward him until there was less than a foot between them. He put his left arm around her, laid his big hand on her shoulder. She was wearing a light sleeveless dress, and the hand spanned all of the shoulder and a couple of inches of bare arm. The memory of the hand between her legs the previous Christmas came suddenly into her mind.

"Put your right arm about my waist," he said. "Got to get a firm grip so I can divide my weight between my right leg and you." Her arm went around his waist. "That's a girl."

They started back, slowly, uncomfortably. Susanna could smell him. She smelled sweat, though it wasn't a bad, dirty smell, and she thought she could smell soil and grass too. She focused on getting back to the convent and gritted her teeth, taking his weight. He was heavier than she'd anticipated he would be, but she could tell he was in bad pain from the way he grunted every few steps when, in the unevenness of the sand, his injured leg took too much pressure.

"Careful now," he said, breathing hard.

There were several dunes ahead between them and the road. Less than an hour earlier Susanna had come over those banks of sand as effortlessly as a goat, but now the first of them looked as daunting as a sheer cliff face.

"We should go around," she said, coming to a halt.

"It's too far," he said, reaching up to wipe his face with the back of his right hand. "Up and over may hurt more, but it'll be quicker."

"I don't know."

"I do."

She tried to inch away from his closeness, took her hand from around his waist, but he put it straight back. His big hand still clamped over her shoulder.

"Maybe I should go for help," she said. "There's still a long way to go."

The hand dropped from her shoulder.

"You want to leave me?" he asked, friendly and accusing again at the same time.

"It isn't that," she said.

"I don't mind," he said. "It's just that the pain is pretty bad, and what I'd like more than anything is to get back and rest up for a while in the cool."

"Okay," she said. "Let's go on."

The hand returned.

They managed two dunes, their feet sinking deep, and it was almost impossible for him to limp, and several times he yelped with pain, and his weight on her grew heavier each time.

"I got to stop," he gasped, letting go of Susanna and sinking down onto the sand. She stood for a moment, catching her breath. Glancing down, she saw that her dress was soaked with perspiration. Her pulse was racing, and her left shoulder throbbed.

"Sit down." He looked limp with exhaustion. "Take a break."

"I'm okay."

"Jesus, girl, sit down before you fall down."

She sat. A sudden breeze blew through the small valley between the dunes, blowing the beach grass and her hair and fanning her dress. Quickly she patted the damp fabric down, tucked her legs beneath her, though she longed to lie flat, sprawling. A pair of fork-tailed terns flew gracefully overhead and were gone. Susanna became aware that sitting as they were between two dunes, she could no longer see either the ocean or the road behind the beach, nor could anyone see them.

Their breathing quieted. The breeze blew once more, blessedly cooling the sweat on their faces and bodies. The air grew still again, still and hot.

With a swift, sudden movement, he pulled his T-shirt up and over his head. He noted her startled, anxious face and smiled. "I need a bandage."

She said nothing, just watched in silence as he located one of the side seams and tore it apart with his teeth. They were strong and sharp as well as white, Susanna realized, and without knowing quite why, she shivered. The first tear achieved, he ripped at the T-shirt with his hands.

"There you go," he said, still drained, but satisfied with the first length of cotton bandage. He held it out to her in his right hand. "You make a start with that, and I'll rip up some more."

"I don't know how," Susanna said.

"Just bind it around."

"I might hurt you."

"It hurts already."

"You'd better do it yourself."

He tore a second bandage and fell back against the sand. "Can't," he said, took a shaky breath, and blew it out. "You'll have to."

She didn't move. Close up, his injured thigh looked big as a tree trunk, glistening, like the rest of him, with sweat that trickled down through the short dark hairs onto the pale sand, wetting it in droplets. She couldn't bear the thought of touching him.

"Please," he said.

"I'd rather not," she said softly.

"Please," he said again, and there was a real plea in his voice. "I think I may have done more than tear a muscle. If it isn't strapped, I could make it a whole lot worse, and God knows if I can't work, I'll lose my job."

"The sisters would never fire you," Susanna said.

"Sure they would, if they had no choice. A gardener who can't garden's no more use than a hen that can't lay eggs."

Susanna shifted a little, increasingly uncomfortable.

"Strap it for me," he said, and suddenly there was a note of command in his tone. "Stop being such a scaredy-cat and do it." He thrust the second bandage at her and flopped back, closing his eyes. "Jeez, that hurts."

Reluctantly she picked up the bandage.

"You can't do it from over there," he said without opening his eyes.

She moved closer, on her knees. The thigh grew more immense. She felt a little nauseated. *Run*, a small voice in her head told her. She looked around. The dune walls were too high for an easy bolt. *If I try to climb up there, he'll grab my ankles*, a second voice said.

"What are you waiting for, girl? Fucking Florence Nightingale?"

Susanna scrambled to her feet.

He opened his eyes. "Going somewhere?"

"To get help." Her voice was strained, tight in her throat.

"No," he said. "You're going to strap my leg."

"I'll run all the way," she told him. "I'll have someone here in no time."

He put out his right hand and grasped her left ankle.

Told you.

"Get down here," he ordered her.

She wavered.

"Get *down* here."

Susanna, afraid, got down beside him.

He was staring up into her face, and the amusement was back in his eyes. "I'm not going to hurt you. I just want you to take care of my leg. Now stop fucking around and do it." He still had hold of her ankle.

"Could you let go of me, please?" she asked.

"No, I could not." He paused. "Are you going to strap my leg or not?"

"Yes." Her voice was little more than a whisper.

"Good girl."

She took the first strip of material and started to bind the thigh, about six inches above his knee.

"Too low," he said.

She moved up. His skin felt clammy, and at the touch of her

fingers, the muscles tightened up hard in a display of power. She looked at his face, saw the grin in his eyes again, and for the first time she wondered if he was really hurt at all.

"Go on." He still held her ankle, his grip firm. "Get the bandage right around. That's it, all the way—" He raised his leg a fraction, giving her a little more room for maneuver. She wound the bandage around twice, three times. "You'll have to knot the other one to it." He watched her do it. "Now wind it around a few more times, and higher."

Susanna did as she was told, felt a sense of relief as the bandage took shape around the leg, the distasteful task almost done.

"Tighter," he said.

She pulled it tighter, not caring if it hurt him or not, just wanting it to be finished. "Is that okay?" Her voice was still hushed, filled with fear.

"Once more around, and that'll be it," he said.

Her fingers were beneath his thigh when he pushed down hard, pinning her hand into the sand, trapping her.

"Please," she said, terror choking her. "Please."

"A kiss," he said softly.

"What?" she whispered.

"A kiss from my nurse," he said. "Kiss it."

Her eyes widened.

"*Kiss* it," he commanded. "Kiss my leg better."

"Please," she said again. "Let me go."

"Don't you want me to get better? Do you want me to lose my job?"

Yes, the voice in her head said. *Don't kiss him; kick him instead.* But the scared voice told her: *If you kick him, he'll hurt you.*

"Kiss my fucking leg," he said.

Susanna bent her head low over his thigh, made a kissing sound over it, not touching it, straightened up again.

"That wasn't very nice, was it?" he asked.

She stared down at him. He was lying almost flat, yet he still had her ankle, was still squeezing her hand between his leg and the sand. The size of him and the glint in his eyes terrified her. *He's going to kill you.*

"Kiss it properly."

She began to cry. Tears, soundless and smooth, rolled from her eyes down her cheeks.

"Kiss it properly, crybaby."

She bent her head again; her lips brushed the dirty, sweaty bandage.

"Higher," he said.

She started to straighten again, but his free hand came up and grabbed the back of her head, dragging her face back down.

"Do it," he said.

Her face was pushed against his skin, above the bandage, close to his shorts. She felt her ankle released, and her hand, but his fingers were in her hair, twisting it, tangling it, forcing her face closer into him. She felt him moving, felt him shifting, couldn't see what he was doing with his right hand, and then he dragged her head over a little, sideways, and she saw that he'd opened his shorts, and she'd never seen a man uncovered before, and she almost threw up with her terror, and she tried to scream—

"I tried to scream," she told Pete a dozen years later. "I wanted to scream, but I couldn't because he had other plans for me."

She stopped at last, too drained to go on.

"I can't," she said. "I'm sorry." Her voice was husky. "I know you want me to tell you everything, but I don't want to, not that. It's all there, all locked inside my head, and maybe it needs to be released, but I don't suppose it's anything much different from what you've heard before, often enough."

"May I ask a couple more questions?" Pete asked, very gently.

She nodded.

"He made you perform fellatio?"

"Yes."

"And then he raped you."

"Yes."

"Did he beat you?"

"No. I wished he had." Susanna paused. "So that people would have seen, and then they would have known."

"You didn't tell anyone."

"No."

"Not the sisters."

"No."

"Nor your parents."

"No one."

"Why not?" he asked.

"Because of what he said to me," she whispered.

"What did he say, Susanna?"

"He said—" She took a breath. "When he was all finished, all finished grunting and gasping and groaning, and he'd pushed it back inside his shorts, all shrunken now."

Pete waited patiently.

"He knelt on me, right on my stomach." Susanna's eyes were closed, thirteen-year-old tears spilling out again between the lids. "And he told me that I'd just committed the greatest sin in the universe short of murder. And if I ever told anyone, the sisters would throw me out of the convent, but he said that that wouldn't matter a hell of a lot because he would kill me."

"And you believed him?" Pete said when he was certain that she was finished, that she had no more to say.

"Yes, I believed him." Her eyes were still closed.

"I don't mean that he would kill you. You were thirteen. A thirty-year-old would probably believe that." He paused. "I meant, did you believe him when he talked about your sin?"

"Yes. I believed that, too."

"You've told me in the past that you don't believe in God," Pete said.

Her eyes opened.

"But I believe in sin," she said.

"What happened to him?" Pete asked later, out of nowhere, when they were almost out of time.

"Nothing happened to him."

"He went on working there?"

"Yes. Back to his gardens without a care in the world."

"Did he ever come near you again?"

"No. Not in that way." Susanna paused. "And then he left."

"And no one ever knew what he'd done," Pete said.

"No one except me," Susanna said.

CHAPTER 11

∼

Hawke's book was published in January 1989, carrying one of his all-time favorite shots on the dust jacket: Susanna, barefoot and suntanned in Ralph Lauren shorts and blue cotton sweater, feeding pink, shiny piglets on a farm in Connecticut. To boost sales, Susanna zigzagged the country, speaking at dinners and luncheons and talking to every journalist, TV and radio talk show host who would listen. By the time the tour was over, the book was ticking over adequately, and Susanna was exhausted.

She went home to Cohasset, seeking respite and comfort and, as always, finding it. The Van Dusen household was her foxhole, her sanctuary; it was that sense of safeness and calm, its very ordinariness, Susanna realized, that she hoped to bring to her project. The safety would, of course, be illusory, for no one knew more about danger than people with HIV or full-blown AIDS, those who simply waited, and those who were buffeted by one horror after another, recovering only to the grim certainty that there was more to come.

"There's so much to learn," she told Connie and Bryan one evening in February, while Abigail studied algebra in her room. "Only one year since Hawke's death, and already there's so much more information. I find myself wishing sometimes that I'd understood more when he was sick, but then I remember that my knowing more about T-cells and B-cells wouldn't really have made a scrap of difference to how he felt or whether he survived."

They were in the den, drinking hot chocolate laced with cognac. Connie was on the couch, feet up, covered with a tartan rug, Bryan in the armchair next to her, Baskin, grown white-muzzled and creaking, on the rug beside Susanna. She'd always liked sitting on the floor in that room, the snuggest, coziest in the house and one of Susanna's favorite rooms in the world. Bryan and Susanna both wore patched, faded jeans and navy fisherman's sweaters. The feeling among the three of them was intensely warm. Looking at her foster parents, Susanna supposed that they were middle-aged now. Bryan was still good-looking, craggier and a little heavier than he had been a decade before, but Connie, remarkable woman that she was, seemed to Susanna to look better than ever. She knew that Connie was often still frustrated by her disability, that she sometimes still yearned to fly off on a whim and ride elephants on safari in Africa or downhill race in Switzerland, but for the most part Susanna believed that Connie was happy.

"Do you really have to learn so much?" Bryan asked, concerned that she was growing more and more depressed by her work. "Medical stuff, I mean. I can understand most of the training—the counseling, that side of things—but you're not planning on doing any actual nursing, are you?"

"Of course not," Susanna replied. "But a lot of patients make a point of studying the virus and what's happening inside their bodies because it's one way they feel they can retain some tiny measure of control—even if it's only an ability to understand what their doctors are telling them, or to be better equipped to argue about a treatment they've decided they don't want."

"So the more you know," Connie said, understanding the reasoning, "the more likely you are to be helpful to them."

"That's the idea. One of the worst things for Hawke and me was how ignorant we were about what was happening to him."

"Where are you going to look for the house?" Bryan asked.

"Somewhere in the Northeast. Upstate New York, probably. We need a great big house with a lot of land. It has to be handsome"—Susanna smiled wryly—"and it has to have plenty of space between us and the neighbors."

"Who's we?" Connie asked.

"Pete's going to join me; he decided just this week."

"That's wonderful," Connie said. "Is it going to be private, like a hotel?" She was curious. "Or will it be more like a commune? I mean, just because people have AIDS doesn't mean they have anything else in common."

"The plan is to allow for both," Susanna replied. "For guests to feel absolutely free to do what they want, as they would in a good hotel, whether that's to laze around all day being pampered or to have some kind of activity. If they like, there'll be group therapy sessions or private counseling available, and obviously there'll always be medical staff on duty, but the main aim is to provide individuals with what *they* feel they need, whatever that is." She paused. "Except for a cure."

"I have another question," Connie said a moment later, "and it's an important one." She paused. "What about Abigail?"

"I don't understand the question," Susanna said.

"Okay," Connie said, and took a breath. "When Hawke was ill, dying, you wouldn't let Abigail near him. You were scared for her, you were protecting her, and I could understand that."

"She didn't," Susanna said.

"Not then, but she took a little time to think about it, and she realized that you'd been a little crazy because you loved her so much." Connie smiled. "Your baby sister's pretty wise for her age, you know."

"I know." Susanna paused. "What is it you're asking me, Connie?"

"I'm asking you if you're intending to keep Abigail at arm's length from now on." Connie held up one hand. "No, don't answer me yet." Her face was somber. "You're still doing it, Susanna. You're more subtle about it, and you get away with it some of the time; but I see it when you turn your face away when Abigail greets you with a kiss, to make sure she gets your cheek and not your mouth. I know that you never let her drink from your glass or touch your towels." Connie paused again. "And I know it's because you think there's still an outside chance you may test positive one day, and I know that you know you're being completely irrational, and I know too it's because Abigail's the most important person in the world to you."

"I can't help it," Susanna said. "I do know it's irrational, but I can't help it."

"Maybe not, but I think you at least have to be honest about it, face up to it. You've made a decision, a fine decision, to spend most of your life around HIV carriers. I'm asking you if you've thought this part of it through properly."

"I have talked to Pete about it," Susanna said slowly.

"And?"

"And I acknowledge that it's an area I'm guilty of being hypocritical about. But that doesn't mean I'm going to be able to change, at least not overnight."

"Okay," Connie said.

"How is that okay?" Susanna countered. "It's not the right answer, is it?"

"It's an honest answer," Connie told her.

Susanna looked around the room. Its timber-paneled walls and shelves laden as always with photographs and memorabilia were a reminder, if one were needed, of the warmth and closeness of their family. She had been away, off and on, for a number of years now, yet the instant she entered that familiar front door she felt embraced and secure.

"I know that this project, if it works out, will take me away from you all again," she said softly. "It may not be far geographically, but I know it's the kind of work that consumes you, if you do it right."

"You'll do it right," Connie said with conviction.

"I hope so," Susanna said. "I thought a lot about all the rights and wrongs of trying to make this work. More than anything, I thought about how it would affect Abigail."

"She may not thank you for cutting yourself off from her again," Bryan said, gentle but blunt at the same time.

"I will never cut myself off from Abigail, not emotionally at least." Susanna spoke evenly, remained calm. "I am afraid of spending too much time away from her if Pete and I achieve our aims, but one of the things I've had to face up to lately is that all I am to Abigail, all I really am, is a big sister who left home years ago. She's accustomed to being without me; you guys, you two and Tabbie, are as much or probably more family to her than I am."

"She may be used to being with us," Connie said, "but that's never stopped her from needing you."

"Emotionally, yes, just as I need her," Susanna said. "But not in the everyday, practical family sense. If Abigail gets in trouble or feels sick or has a problem at school, she has you to go to. I doubt she would even think of coming to me simply because I haven't been around." She gave a small, helpless shrug. "That's sadder for me than it is for her, but in a way it's what frees me to do what I so much want to do, what I feel I need to do."

They all fell silent again for a time. Their hot chocolate finished, Bryan took their cups out into the kitchen and returned to switch on the TV, sound muted, waiting for the ten o'clock news. Susanna stood up, stretched her legs, picked up the *Boston Globe*, sat down in an armchair, and leafed through it, not really reading anything. Connie, grown resigned, through the years, to ignoring brief impulses of restlessness, lay still, watching the other two and waiting.

"I'm going to take another test," Susanna said, breaking the silence at a minute before ten. "Next week."

"Why?" Connie's question was soft, the fear unmistakable.

"No special reason. Except I guess that bout of the flu the other week started me thinking again, and you know how I am: Once it's nagging at me, the best way I have of being normal again is to have the proof."

"Saul Weinberg's told you you're clear," Bryan said, quiet too and patient. "It's been more than three years since you were exposed."

"I know," Susanna said.

Bryan bit down on his sudden desire to yell at her. "If you insist on having another test, why not at least make up your mind that it's going to be the last? I mean, we know—we *know*—it's going to be negative, so doesn't it make sense to close the door on it after that, for keeps?"

"I don't know if I can do that."

"Because you'll always be afraid for Abigail?" Connie asked.

"That's right," Susanna said.

"It's going to make you crazy," Bryan said.

"What does Pete think about it?" Connie asked.

"Pete agrees with you. He's been trying to help me deal with it."

"You'll be too busy to worry," Connie said, "when you find the house."

"If we find the house," Susanna said. "If we can raise the money. If we can get the licenses and get past all the other authorities."

"You'll do it," Bryan said.

"With a fair wind," Susanna said.

The test, as expected, was negative, and Susanna found the house in April, a faded but still handsome nineteenth-century mansion a mile outside the town of Bearsville, just west of Woodstock in Greene County, New York.

"What shape's it in?" Pete asked when she called him.

"It'll need work," she said cagily.

"How much work?"

"Major surgery," she said. "But it's perfect, Pete. It's solid and beautiful, and it has the loveliest garden surrounded by pine forest, and there's a tiny lake close by, which means people could swim if they wanted to, and it's right in the Catskills, so they could ski too, and there's a fishing stream." She stopped for breath.

"Neighbors?"

"None that I noticed. It really is perfect."

"How many rooms?"

"Eight bedrooms on two floors, but they're all huge so we could easily double that, and there are five reception rooms on the first floor, and a wonderful old-fashioned kitchen."

"How much?"

"It's a bargain," Susanna said.

"A bargain at how much?"

"Two hundred thousand," she said proudly.

"For a house that size, with that much land?" Pete was disbelieving. "It must need more than major surgery; it must need a whole body transplant."

"Of course it does, but it would still come inside our budget."

"We don't have a budget."

"We talked about two-fifty."

"That was just talk," Pete said, "and if I'm reading between the lines correctly, it's going to cost more than fifty thousand to get it into shape. I presume it needs rewiring?"

"Yes."

"How's the plumbing?"

"It looked pretty ancient to me," Susanna admitted. "But then no one's lived there for years."

"How many years?"

"The agent wasn't sure."

"How many years?" Pete persisted.

"Fifteen."

"So we're probably looking at everything from rising damp to termites."

"I'm sure it doesn't have termites," Susanna said.

"So then we'll probably get dry rot instead."

"Probably."

"Are you still sure it's the perfect house?" Pete asked.

"Absolutely," she said.

Acting through Michael Frieman, Pete's lawyer, they managed to slice fifty thousand off the asking price and obtain the necessary permissions to renovate the house to legal standards. Both Frieman, who'd lost a friend to AIDS the previous summer, and Betty Thomas Clark, a millionaire socialite and prime mover in gay rights causes, wanted in on the project, and by the summer of 1989 Susanna was filled with optimism.

"Just you wait," Betty Thomas Clark told her over lunch at Rocco's in Boston. She was a petite woman in her fifties, her brown curls and pretty features at odds with her famed terrierlike disposition, and she was as much at home in the elaborately slick buzz of Rocco's as she was in the refinement of the Ritz-Carlton Dining Room.

"For what?"

"For the shit to hit." Clark paused. "When news gets out of what we want the house for."

"But everyone knows," Susanna said. "I told the agent at the outset. I said we wanted no secrecy in case it created trouble down the line."

"And she told you everything was going to be fine."

"That's right."

"She lied," Clark said bluntly, heartily enjoying her stuffed squid while Susanna played it safe with salmon. "Or at least she bent the truth." She saw the dismay on Susanna's face. "I'm sorry, darling, but she wanted the sale. The house was a white elephant to almost anyone else; you were the answer to a realtor's prayers."

"What do you think's going to go wrong?" Susanna asked, alarmed.

Clark shrugged. "Most things, a lot of it red tape, some of it

more serious. Local stuff, state stuff. You and Michael Frieman
are going to be spending heavy-duty time up in Albany, pulling
strings and pushing buttons and playing political games. You may
even end up in Washington."

"Why me?" Susanna looked anxious. "I don't have that kind
of experience."

"What kind? You mean you're not a politician? Sure you are;
we all are when we have a cause. You're not a lawyer, but you'll
have Frieman there for that." Clark smiled at her. "And I hate to
point it out, but there are a lot of men in Albany, or even D.C.,
who are going to find it harder saying no to you than, say, Pete."
Her smile widened as she saw Susanna's discomfort. "You know
what they say. If you've got it, use it. You did it for a living for
long enough, for God's sake."

Susanna used it and found she felt great about it; it was so *good*
to be doing something worthwhile, to be so stimulated by work,
to discover that she had gifts and inner resources that had nothing
whatever to do with her face or her body. Between September of
that year and May 1990, her life was spent shuttling among the
house, overseeing the renovations; Albany, addressing committees
and lunching with men and women of influence; Cohasset, checking in with the family; and Manhattan, working and training with
Pete Strauss.

Though Pete had never, before or since his divorce, let slip a
word about the troubling—to him—intensity of his admiration
for Susanna, he had raised the question, more than once, of
whether it was any longer entirely right and proper for her to
continue her counseling sessions with him now that they both
were involved in the new project; but each time Susanna had
made it clear that she could not stand to contemplate the emotional disruption of change.

"It's you or no one," she told him.

"You might do better with a more detached therapist," Pete
said. "I mean, aside from the house, I've known you for too long;
we've become friends as well as colleagues."

"Which is the reason I trust you so much," Susanna said softly.

"You feel safe with me now," Pete argued. "I sometimes have
a sense that I may be taking advantage of you—not deliberately,
perhaps, and not in an obvious sense—but that's just one of the

reasons why shrinks don't often treat friends." He shrugged help-lessly. "I don't want to exploit you, Susanna, ever, not profes-sionally or any other way."

"I don't think you ever would," she said, "not even subcon-sciously."

Pete's smile was uncertain. "All the same, promise me that if you ever do have any doubts in your own mind, you won't feel, even for a second, that you'd be letting me down if you wanted to end our professional relationship."

"How can I end it?" Susanna asked. "We're not finished, are we?"

"You never finish, Susanna," Pete said. "But you're a free agent. There aren't any hard-and-fast rules; you can quit anytime you like, or as I've said, you can switch counselors."

"And as I've told you, I don't want to switch," Susanna said. "Unless you really don't want to go on."

"No," he said. "That's not it."

"Do you think I should quit altogether? Am I ready to?"

Pete smiled again. "That's not my decision to make."

She shook her head. "You know it's hard for me, Pete. Every step we take feels like walking through quicksand."

"You knew it was going to be tough."

"That doesn't make it any less tempting to stop, to shut it all off again."

"I'd say," Pete said slowly, "that that would be a pity."

"I know," Susanna said.

With the project nearing completion, Susanna went solo with her first AIDS case in June, a young Cuban typist living in a run-down apartment on the Upper West Side who, it was believed, had contracted her HIV through a contaminated needle while getting a butterfly tattoo as a birthday present from her boyfriend. Maria Alonso was single and motherless, with a father in Jackson Heights who believed that AIDS was a curse visited on the cor-rupt. Her boyfriend had walked out on her; her boss, claiming she was inefficient, had fired her; she had already had PCP and toxoplasmosis, and her condition was poor. She had lost about fifty percent of her formerly beautiful dark hair; her skin looked prematurely aged; she felt discarded and alone. She was just nine-teen years old.

Maria was suspicious of everything about Susanna when Pete first introduced them: her motives, her fame, her beauty, and, most of all, her good health. Maria called her, predictably, a do-gooder, and she said, repeatedly, that she didn't want charity, and Susanna was careful to give her all the space she needed, told her that she was there to be called on anytime, day or night, and that her help could take whatever form Maria wanted, whether that was shopping or cleaning up or taking her places or talking or just making a long, sleepless night a little less lonely.

For the first two months they saw each other hardly at all, though Susanna, at her apartment on Beekman Place, would get calls from Maria at three or four in the morning; the calls were brief, often curt, but Susanna recognized them for what they were, a reluctant reaching out for human contact in the darkest hours.

"I will die before I'm twenty-one," Maria said one night on the phone.

"Maybe," Susanna said.

"Aren't you supposed to tell me how long I could live for?"

"You might live for years," Susanna said gently. "Or you might not."

"I don't want to die," Maria said.

"I know."

"You don't know anything."

"I don't know much," Susanna said.

"Then why say you do?" And the phone went down.

Gradually they began to spend more time together. Maria, feeling stronger for a time, introduced Susanna to a couple of Cuban restaurants, and when Susanna expressed an interest in learning how to cook ajiaco, a thick soup made with oxtail, pork, and root vegetables, Maria, without acrimony, said that Susanna would learn faster in her own kitchen, which she was certain was much bigger and more beautiful than her own tiny galley. Chopping vegetables, Maria cut herself and waited for the inevitable horrified reaction to come, but Susanna merely cleaned up with care, helped Maria to disinfect the cut, and handed her another knife.

"You're not frightened?" Maria asked.

"There was no danger," Susanna said. "There is no danger,

not if we're careful." She thought about Abigail, about her own hypocrisy, and inwardly cringed.

"What's wrong?" Maria wanted to know.

"Nothing."

"Is it me?"

"No, it's not you, Maria." Susanna turned to the sink.

"You told me we must have honesty," Maria persisted.

"I didn't say that you have to tell me everything you're thinking about," Susanna said.

"Okay." Aloof, Maria turned her back.

"You really want to know?" Susanna asked, regretting the wall that had gone back up between them.

"Only if you want to tell me." Maria kept her back turned.

Susanna talked for a while.

"I think you're crazy," Maria said when she'd finished.

"I know I'm irrational about Abigail."

"No, I think that's normal. It's the rest of what you do that's crazy."

"Why's that?"

Maria's dark eyes were round. "Your husband died, and you're really lucky, you escaped without HIV, and you spend your time around people like me. You're crazy, Susanna."

Susanna smiled. "I don't think so."

"Why do you do it?"

"Partly out of guilt." Susanna fought to remain honest. "Because I wasn't really there for my husband. Oh, I was there physically at his side, but I wasn't there in the ways he needed me to be. I was a coward, and I wouldn't let him talk about the things he wanted to talk about." Susanna shrugged. "I've been given a chance to use what I've learned, Maria. I just want to try to help if I can. There's nothing heroic about it."

"I never said you were heroic," Maria said. "I said you were crazy."

It became clear that Maria Alonso was unlikely to reach her twentieth birthday, let alone her twenty-first. In and out of the hospital, sick, isolated and terrified, she reached out increasingly to Susanna. Her death, in January 1991, was almost harder to cope with than Hawke's had been. Hawke, as Susanna tried to explain it to Pete, had had, for the most part, the life he wanted, and by the time the end had come, he'd been pretty much ready for it. Maria, in spite of all Susanna's efforts and those of a Cuban Catholic priest located by Pete, was no more prepared for death than she had been six months before.

"How are you?" Pete asked Susanna a few days later.

"Awful."

"Wondering why you're doing this work?"

"I didn't think of it as work," she said.

"It's hard to do that, isn't it?"

"Very."

"You become friends," Pete said simply. "Their pain hurts you, you miss them when they go, and you're left with bits of them, sometimes just memories, sometimes other things." He smiled. "Like Steinbeck and Alice."

"Maria didn't have anything to leave. She didn't have anyone."

"She had you."

"I don't think that counted for much," Susanna said.

"You were there for her day and night, and she knew that," Pete said. "That counted for a lot, I'd say."

"She asked me to hold her that last day," Susanna remembered. "Her mouth was sore, and it was bleeding a little, and she turned her face away, so that it wouldn't touch me."

"The way you would with Abigail," Pete said.

"I guess so."

Two weeks after Maria Alonso's death Susanna made the decision that she would have one more HIV test, but that this one would be her last, that this time she would, finally, close the door. It was again, as she had known it would be, negative. Wanting, after getting the result back from Saul Weinberg, to feel close to Hawke, Susanna went to Canal Street and walked from the site of the loft into Chinatown, their old routes, looking into the places he had loved. And later, with an hour or so of light left in the dull February afternoon, she took a cab to the cemetery in Jackson Heights where Maria had been laid to rest. There was a bunch of fresh flowers on the grave, and Susanna thought that her father, who had looked so haggard at the funeral, had probably been back again, and she hoped against hope that Maria knew about it.

Free at last came unbidden into her mind, and she wasn't certain if the thought was for Maria or for herself.

She looked around the overcrowded cemetery. It was bleak and cold, and the day was dying around her. She thought of the pleasure and warmth in Saul Weinberg's voice when he'd given her the news a few hours before, and she thought that no winter afternoon had ever looked lovelier.

Free at last.

A sudden desire for truth struck her with all the force of a bullet. Abruptly, moving more quickly than when she'd come, she left the cemetery and went looking for a pay phone.

She needed to see Pete.

CHAPTER 12

⁓

"When I told you, a long time ago, about the rape—you remember? Of course you remember."

"I do."

"You asked me what happened to him, and I told you that he went back to work and then, after a while, he left. And you asked me if he ever came near me again, and I think I said not in that way, or I said something like that."

"From memory, that's pretty much what you said."

"It wasn't true."

She shifted on the couch, trying to get comfortable. She thought about lying down, but she'd never done that before, and she didn't think it would make telling this any easier. Pete was sitting in his armchair, as he usually did, not too close or too remote. He'd agreed, without hesitation, to see her with minimal delay when she'd called from Jackson Heights. She thought he might have rescheduled another late-afternoon appointment to make the time for her, though he hadn't said anything. Pete never fussed, never made her feel she was too demanding, never made out his own time was valuable. He was like that with everyone, so far as she could tell. He was a remarkable man.

"Go on, Susanna," he said now.

He was good at that too, the gentle but firm nudge forward. *Don't stop now, get into it, move along, don't be scared.*

"He didn't leave," she said. "He stayed on at the convent, and he knew he was safe, knew I'd never tell anyone what he'd done because he knew I believed what he'd told me after he raped me. That I'd committed the sin, not him. And that if I told anyone, he'd kill me."

She stopped again. This time Pete said nothing, just waited. She always had the feeling with Pete that he'd wait forever if he had to. It was one of the many things she'd learned from him. She'd used it with Maria Alonso on the rare occasions when Maria had wanted to open up to her but had been slow getting started.

"I'd only had two periods before the rape," she said, "and there had been two months between them. So I didn't know I was pregnant until November. And I only found out then because he told me. He knew. He said he'd been watching me, he'd seen the signs. I was expecting a child for sure, he said one afternoon in the garden, when there was no one else around to hear. It was true I'd put on weight, and I'd been feeling out of sorts, but I didn't know why—I was only thirteen years old."

She paused again, and Pete waited again. She glanced for a moment at his face, but it was his professional face, kind and attentive but impassive, and she looked quickly away again.

"He said there was only one thing for me to do, and that was to leave. I said that I couldn't leave, that there was nowhere for me to go to, and he said that was true enough because I was evil now, full of sin, and no one decent in all the world would take me in, but so long as I kept my mouth shut, he would take care of me."

"What about your parents?"

She shook her head. "He told me it would destroy them if they found out, that the nuns would throw them out with me. He told me they'd never forgive me, no one would ever forgive me, no one would look after me."

"Except him," Pete said.

"Yes," she said. "He told me to be ready to leave a week from then. He'd arrange everything. He said that if I kept my side of the bargain, I had nothing to be scared of. He said that he knew I hadn't liked what he did—what *we* had done was how he put it—and that he was sorry about that and would never come near me that way again."

"And you believed him."

"Yes. He had this way about him. He was compelling some-how. And I didn't think back then that I had a choice."

Pete was silent for a moment.

"Where was the convent, Susanna?" he asked. "You've never said."

"Haven't I? It was near Brewster, on Cape Cod." She glanced at him, saw him nod. "What is it?"

"It's just that when you first came to me, I got the idea that the convent was back in Vermont. But then you told me about the rape, and you talked about the beach, and it didn't sound as if it could be around Lake Champlain."

"No," Susanna said softly. "It was a beach at Brewster, with pale sand and the prettiest views. I used to go there sometimes with one of the sisters who liked sketching there. On a clear day you could see the hook of the Cape, right to the tip."

"I visited the Cape once when I was a boy." Pete smiled. "My father took me one weekend in the summer." He nodded again. "It helps me picture it better, that's all."

It was a cold, damp November night when he came for her. He took her bag from her, put it in the trunk of his battered old Chevrolet, closed the lid quietly, easing it down until it clicked shut, and waited for her to get into the car.

"What are you waiting for, Christmas?" he whispered.

She hung back, afraid of being alone with him.

"Do you want me to put you in?" he asked.

She got in. The front seat was long, without a gap, and when he climbed in and closed his own door, she was terrifyingly conscious of his body less than two feet away from her own. He started the motor, and they began to move.

"You forgot to turn the lights on," she whispered.

"I didn't forget." He glanced at her. "We don't have to whisper any more, no one's going to hear us now." He checked the rearview mirror and then, apparently satisfied, hit the light switch on the dash.

Susanna sat motionless, her hands in her lap. It was starting to rain, and he switched on the windshield wipers. Back and forth, back and forth, the blade of the right-hand wiper dragging and squeaking on the misty glass.

"Here"—he reached down to his left and tossed her a cloth
—"clean the windshield."

She wiped her side.

"Well, that's a big help," he said. "How about doing my side
so I can see where I'm driving?"

"Sorry." Gingerly, she leaned across and wiped the other side.

"Thank you," he said.

"You're welcome." She held the damp cloth in her hands and
licked her dry lips. "Where are we going?"

"You'll see," he said.

She said nothing more. They got onto Route 6, the Mid Cape
Highway, heading east, so at least that meant they had to be
staying on the Cape itself, which meant in turn that they couldn't
be going all that far, unless they were taking a boat somewhere.
Susanna shivered.

"You cold?"

"No."

"Sure? I can put the heat up."

"No, thank you, I'm fine."

"You scared?"

"A little."

"No need," he said, and glanced her way again. "I told you I
won't hurt you so long as you behave yourself."

"I will," she said.

He stretched out his right hand and touched her stomach,
making her jump. He laughed and took away his hand.

"Just checking out the kid," he said.

She felt sick.

"How you been feeling?" he asked.

"Okay," she said.

"Throwing up a lot?"

"A bit."

"That's what sin does for you," he said.

The highway headed north, and they went with it, passing Fort
Hill and Eastham and Nauset and Wellfleet, the old Chevy devouring the wet black road, the rain growing heavier, lashing at
the windshield, spraying up from the wheels, and all the time the
wipers groaning back and forth, back and forth, like an unoiled,
aged metronome. The sound of those wipers and the growl of

the motor filled Susanna's mind, and she tried to give herself up to it, welcomed its mesmeric quality, for it stopped her from thinking too much about the man sitting beside her and about the fact that he was taking her somewhere, away from everyone and everything she knew, and that they were alone together, and that she was afraid of him.

"You ever been to P-Town?" he asked, halfway between Wellfleet and Truro.

"I'm sorry?" She stirred, aware that her eyelids had been drooping.

"Provincetown. I asked if you'd ever been there. P-Town, they call it."

"No," she said.

"That figures." He nodded. "The sisters wouldn't take you to a place like that."

"Why not?" she asked.

"Because it's no better than Sodom and Gomorrah. They did teach you about Sodom and Gomorrah, didn't they? The city God destroyed because it was full of perverts." He threw her another sideways glance. "P-Town's like that these days, full of homos and dykes."

Susanna said nothing. She didn't understand what he was talking about, but the tone in his voice scared her, the pally, confidential quality. It was the way he'd talked to her that day in July on the beach, before he'd stopped being polite and nice, before he'd grabbed her ankle. . . .

"What's up with you?" he asked.

She shook her head. "Nothing."

"You were breathing funny," he said. "Little gaspy breaths."

She hadn't known she was. "I'm fine." She forced herself to breathe normally, calmly, silently.

"I hate homos worse than anything," he said.

Again she said nothing.

"What about you? You ever met any?"

"I don't know," she said.

"You know what they are?" He grinned but kept his eyes on the greasy wet road. "You don't, do you? You're just an innocent little girl. Or you were." He paused. "Not any mo-ore," he said, the words a little singsong, teasing her. "You're a sinner now too. Guess you'd fit right in in P-Town."

"Is that where we're going?" Susanna asked softly.

"Nope."

She tried to remember the Cape Cod map tacked to the bulletin board in the classroom at the convent. There weren't that many places between Truro and Provincetown, at the tip of the Cape; she couldn't think of a single town, though she knew there had to be a lot of small places, villages maybe, little communities perhaps of just a few houses and maybe a church. Unless they were going to take a boat. Involuntarily she shivered again.

"You are cold," he said.

"No," she said. "I'm not."

"If you are, you could always snuggle up," he said.

She felt nauseated again.

"No, thank you," she said. "I'm fine."

"Then stop your damned shivering," he said, his tone still pleasant.

"I'm not," she said quickly.

"All right," he said. "Just behave yourself, like I told you."

"I will."

She sat very still, staring ahead through the streaming glass into the black night. She considered trying to pray, but she didn't think she could manage it. Oh, she'd done all the out-loud praying that the sisters had expected of her, but she hadn't believed in it, not for herself. It might have been nice, comforting maybe, to have been able to talk to God now, to believe in Him, to ask Him to get her out of this mess, but she knew that He wasn't there and that even if He was, He wasn't going to listen to the likes of her. He hadn't listened to her before she'd become a sinner, so what hope was there now?

He was talking again.

"You know what else they call Route Six?"

"The Mid Cape Highway," she said, trying to pay attention, not wanting to make him angry.

"Grand Army of the Republic Highway's its real name." His voice was wry. "I was in the army once—different army. More'n ten years ago now. I got discharged because I had trouble with my liver; I was real sick for a while. Army didn't seem so grand to me, I can tell you."

Just past North Truro they left the highway. It was so dark, even with his headlights on full beam, that he was peering hard through the windshield, and Susanna, who'd been getting sleepy again, felt her heartbeat increase, felt her palms grow moist, for she realized that wherever they were headed, they must surely be getting close now.

He spotted the turning at the very last minute, spun the wheels with a screech, braked hard, skidding a little but controlling it, and drove about a hundred yards on the narrow pitch-black side road before he stopped the car and turned off the ignition.

"Okay," he said. "All change."

Susanna sat frozen on the seat.

"Time to get out."

"Where are we?" she whispered.

"Nowhere much."

She swallowed hard. "Are we changing to another car?"

"Nope."

A boat. She was so afraid of a boat in the middle of this black, wet night, of sailing out with or without this man into all that ebony, roaring, impenetrable ocean.

"Are we taking a boat?" she whispered.

"No way," he said, grinning again. "I hate boats."

The relief was wonderful.

"Feet," he said.

"Excuse me?"

"That's what we're changing to. We're walking from here."

They got out of the car. He opened the trunk, took out her bag and gave it to her, took out a flashlight and a zipped-up knapsack, shut and locked the trunk. The lid closed with a loud, echoing, hollow sound that did not appear to trouble him. Susanna knew, from the quality of the night silence, its totality, from the feel of the air, the curiously tranquil desolation of it, that they were too far off the beaten track for it to matter whether anyone heard them or not. Her fear, which had subsided a little with her relief about the boat, began to mount again.

Without another word he began to walk. More terrified of being left alone in the dark than of going with him, she followed.

He turned the flashlight off every now and then, kept it on long enough to check out the straight path ahead of him for a dozen or so yards, then clicked it back off again.

"Can't we keep the light on?" Susanna dared to ask once.

"Don't want to drain the battery," he said. "Else we'll be in the dark for keeps."

So long as they stayed on the road, Susanna felt able to keep some small grip on her fear. *We're on a road,* her inner voice told her. *While we're on a road, there could be cars, people; he won't do anything bad to you where people could see.* But there might have been people on the beach at Brewster that July afternoon, and it hadn't stopped him. *But if we're staying on the road, we might come to a town, or a village, or someone's house, and maybe someone else is going to look after you, not just him.* He'd told her he would look after her. *Did he say he'd look after you or he'd take care of you?*

Suppressing another shudder, Susanna silenced the voice in her head and walked on behind him. It was tempting to hold onto him, to his coat or to his sleeve. If it had been anyone else, she would have done that; it would have been so comforting to feel another human being's solidness, the confirmation that she was not all alone, but not with this man, who could change moods in the flicker of an eye, who could walk softly in the presence of nuns, who could joke and tease, who could rape a girl, who could threaten to kill her.

She felt the change in the air first, even before she heard the sound of the ocean, heard its unmistakable, perpetual voice, even before she felt the hard road give way first to sandy path and then, at last, to the soft, powdery, shifting instability of the beach itself.

"We're on our way," he said, and she heard a note of excitement in his voice. "We'll have to keep the damned flashlight on now or one of us'll bust a leg or something." The light revealed smooth, pale sand as far as its limited beam could reach. "It'd be easier if there was any kind of a moon. Better pray we make it before the battery dies."

Walking became difficult. Susanna asked, after a time, if they could stop so that she could remove her sneakers and socks, and he followed suit. The rain had eased, but the sand was cold and damp, and as they went on walking, Indian file, Susanna walking in an endless void, a nightmare mystery tour whose ending might be better than the journey—might, more probably, be worse— she let her mind fill up with images of the imprints her feet were making as they walked, small prints trekking behind large, evidence of their promenade through this unidentified, wet, dark Cape Cod desert. *Except that no one will be looking for evidence*, her inner voice pointed out with its comfortless logic, *and anyway, everyone knows that the prints will be wiped away by daybreak, washed away, blown away, gone, gone, like you from the convent.*

Their feet sank deep, past their ankles, and it was hard work dragging them back up and out for the next step. Every few yards seemed to take an eternity, and they were in the dunes now, and they were steeply banked and slowed their progress even more. It was tough going for him too in spite of his strength, she could hear it in his grunts, in his labored breathing, and she'd figured out by now, letting her mind's eye wander back again to the map on the schoolroom wall, roughly where they were, and she screwed up her eyes, concentrating, trying to remember some of the names of the beaches, but only one returned to her, Head of the Meadow Beach, and she found it a curious name; the beaches around Brewster had all had straightforward names, Breakwater Beach, Paines Creek Beach, Robbins Hill Beach, you knew where you were with names like that. *But you don't know where you are, that's the whole point, and you don't know where you're going, and he doesn't want you to know.*

It might have been an hour or more or less since they had left the car; it might have been a lifetime, it felt that way to her, and maybe to him too, though she didn't care about him at all. He seldom spoke a word, just a curse every now and again as he slipped and slithered in the treacherous sands, and the occasional rebuke to her to keep up or to hurry. Once, when she stumbled and fell, he asked if she was all right, but she knew he cared only that he should not have to carry her, and she felt his hand on her arm and got up quickly, drew away, walked on, weaving only a little, knowing instinctively by now which way they were heading, following her nose until he again took the lead, the fading light of his flashlight pointing the way forward.

The light died.

"Shi-it," he said, stopping dead.

The darkness clamped down on them. They might have been

blind. Panic rose in Susanna, like the flapping of a bat's wings in her heart, in her chest, in her throat, and she wanted to scream or to run or to drop down on all fours and to pin herself to the sand, eyes tightly closed, only letting herself open them again when it was day, when she could see again.

"Keep calm," he told her.

Keep calm, her voice warned, *or he'll do something, hurt you, take care of you, or leave you.*

"I'm okay," she said shakily.

"Good girl." He was almost kind. "We'll just stand awhile, and let our eyes get used to it. I think there's a little bit of moon now. The clouds are thinning out some, see? All that wind, chasing them on through. We'll just wait awhile."

They waited, and he was right, and gradually their eyes grew less blind, and the strange, moonlike landscape began to form about them, little dune mountains and crater dips, and wildly blowing beach grass like madman's hair, waving back and forth as her own hair blew, tugging at the roots, and there was sand in her eyes, gritty and painful, and her face was sore, but the small pain was real, down to earth, anchoring her, lessening the extremity of her panic.

"Okay," he said at last. "We can go on now."

"Is it much farther?" She had not spoken for the longest time.

"Hope not," he said.

And suddenly they saw the ocean.

It was far off still, but now, with the thinning of the rain clouds, it was possible to define the lines where beach became water and, way, way beyond, somewhere on the infinite horizon, where ocean met sky. Susanna stared out to sea and experienced an inexplicable thrill of what seemed like hope, yet at the same time she realized that all that her fleetingly upturned spirit was registering was the lessening of her blindness, the awareness that this night would in time die away and that nothing, however terrible, would seem quite as bad in the light.

"That way," he said.

They turned northwest. More dunes lay ahead of them, separating them from their destination, an undulating series, large and small, some as daunting as little Alps, others, from a distance, looking like stranded dead great gray whales. They went on walking, and Susanna hardly felt her legs anymore, hardly recognized her numbed, trudging feet as her own, dismissed the gnawing pain in her thigh and calf muscles as something outside herself; and they were getting nearer now to wherever it was they were going. She saw it in his renewed strength, his longer strides, and she had quit groping around in the befuddled recesses of her mind for where or what their destination was. It would be a stopping place, and that was all she cared about now. He would let her stop, put down her bag, sit or lie down, and that was enough.

Even if he does it to you again? the voice asked. *Or worse?* But Susanna had an answer to that one: *Why bring me all this way to do that?*

Awhile later they came to it.

Buried in the soft underbelly of the vast, empty Atlantic desert, out of sight of the ocean, tucked between two mounds of wind-pleated sand, both around fifteen feet high, both winter barren but for their fuzzy heads of night gray beach grass hair.

It was an old tar paper shack, lit just enough by the watery moon for Susanna to see that it was windowless, with a cracked chimney and a rusting door. The roof was on a slant, broken, with missing shingles on the edge facing them. Somewhere, unseen, something banged, a piece of wood, maybe, slamming in the wind.

"This is it," he said.

Susanna felt his eyes on her face, waiting. She could not tell if he hoped for dismay or pleasure. She gave him neither. It was a shack, just that, no more or less. She had no response to give; she was too confused for that; she was way past anything except the desire to stop walking.

"What do you say?" he asked, easing his knapsack to the ground.

"Can we go inside?" Her voice was hoarse from the cold and damp and the wind and the sand blown into her mouth through the long hike.

"Do you like it? I want to know if you like it."

She shrugged wearily. "Sure."

"Just as well." He picked up his bag again. "Seeing as it's going to be your home."

Disbelief almost roused her, almost managed to struggle its way up through the layers of fatigue that were suddenly rolling over her, weighing down on her head and her shoulders like a too-heavy blanket. It was his little joke, she knew it had to be. This wasn't home; it was just a tar paper shack.

"Go on in," he told her.

An old screen door hung, half off its hinges, creaking as she went past, gripped the handle of the main door and stepped inside.

It was dark as pitch.

The door creaked as he entered behind her. New panic flew up inside her chest again, clearing away the fog of fatigue like a whistle blast. *He is going to do it to me again.* Her body and mind cringed away from the sound and smell of him.

He struck a match.

"There's a kerosene heater," he said, "and a two-burner stove."

He bent to light the heater on the far side of the shack, and as the flame caught, giving a little pale light, Susanna stared around. There was a mattress, old and a little torn but clean enough, and a blanket, folded up on the center of the mattress. There were two big cardboard boxes, and when Susanna, gathering courage and strength to move again, peered down into them, she saw six bottles of water, cartons, cans, and jars.

"Take a closer look," he told her.

Four cartons of graham crackers, a dozen cans of Heinz beans and a dozen more of Campbell's mushroom soup, a carton of tea bags, a jar of instant coffee, two cartons of long-life milk, three rolls of toilet tissue, a bar of Dove soap, and a bottle of vitamin capsules.

"Ought to hold you till I can bring more," he said. "Take a look in the other box."

She stared wordlessly. Old magazines, paper towels, a copy of *Gone with the Wind*, a photograph of Vivien Leigh and Clark Gable on the stained, torn jacket.

"I found that one day in the trash at the convent," he said. "Figured it was long enough to keep you going for a while."

She picked out the book. Beneath, at the bottom of the box, lay an immaculate black-jacketed Holy Bible. She wondered if it was his own or if he had stolen it from one of the nuns.

"I know you said you weren't religious," he said. "But I thought you might like it here anyway."

She tried to speak, but her throat was dry. She cleared it. "How long are we going to be here?"

"You. Not me."

She nodded. "How long?"

"Till I tell you different."

"But there's no lamp. There's nowhere to wash, or—"

"There's a bowl, and a bucket—" He nodded back toward the mattress. "I couldn't let you have a light, or someone might see. I wasn't too happy about giving you the heater or the stove because of that, but I don't want you getting sick, so you have to be warm and you have to eat, and I guess with no windows and only that little flicker when you light the kerosene, there should be no real problem, even if someone does come close." He paused. "Which they won't, not at night anyhow."

His eyes were on hers, measuring the level of her dismay.

"I've been watching this place for a while now," he went on. "In the summer it crawls with visitors. In the winter there's no one but the odd national park ranger, but they won't come at night, and you won't go out in the day."

"But I have to go out," she said softly.

"You will not," he said.

Her shock, a deeper, less frenzied creature than the panic had been, was nonetheless mounting steadily. He was going to leave her here entirely alone; he expected her to stay here, in this damp, cold wooden shack, with nothing, with no one.

"I can't do it," she said.

"Sure you can."

She shook her head, her eyes grew wilder. "But there's nothing here. It isn't a house, it isn't even a proper *room*, there isn't a—" She stopped, not wanting to say the obvious, not to him.

"I told you, there's a bucket." He was unmoved. "At night you can take it out, wash it out, bury what has to be buried." He nodded, as if she'd given him a thought. "You're right, though. I ought to bring you some Lysol or something next time I come."

"Next time?" Her voice was back down to a whisper.

"Soon as I can." He was still studying her face. "What did you expect, girlie, the Ritz? This'll be fine. You have food, you have water, you have a bed, you have things to read, you even have fucking vitamins, for Christ's sake—what did you *expect*?"

She shrank from the rising anger in his voice.

"You're pregnant, girlie, you're having a goddamned *bastard*, you're a sinner, remember?" He stepped closer. "Remember?"

"Yes," she whispered.

"I told you I'll take care of you. Look around you—" He made a sweeping gesture with his right arm. "I thought of everything, didn't I? I got you a roof over your head. I got you someplace no one can find you to punish you or take away your baby." He was so close now he was almost touching her. "Did you think they'd have let you keep your baby if you'd stayed? No, they'd have thrown you out, but first they'd have taken your baby out of you."

"They wouldn't," Susanna whispered. "They're not allowed."

"They'd have called it natural, but they'd have made it happen, take my word for it."

His words, and the gruesome pictures they conjured up, swam in her brain. She felt sick, felt faint; she longed for him, suddenly, to leave, even if it meant she would be alone in this awful place.

He laid his right hand on her shoulder, and she almost screamed.

"Shut up," he said, and she nodded her head wildly. "Keep your mouth shut, or I'll kill you right here and now. No one will ever know, never find you, and you and your baby will both be dead and gone. So you keep quiet, right?"

She nodded again.

"Right?"

"Yes," she said.

His hand was still on her shoulder. "Now you have to promise me some things, okay?"

"Okay."

"Get the Bible."

She went to get it from the box, glad to be free of his grasp.

"Bring it here." He took it, rested it in his big left hand. "Place your right hand on top of it. Now you have to swear, and it's sacred, right? Even if you're not religious, swearing on the Bible means the Lord is witnessing it, and the devil'll come and get you if you break your promise. Okay?"

"Yes."

"You have to swear you won't ever go outside during the daytime and only at night if you really, really have to go." His eyes bored down into her face. "Say it. I could lock you in, I got a padlock in my bag, I could do that, and then you couldn't even open the door."

"I won't go," she said.

"Say, 'I swear I won't ever go outside during the daytime, and only if I really have to at night.' Say it."

She said it.

"Now that's what they call a sworn oath; that's what they make you say in a court of law, and they put you in jail if you break it, okay?"

"Yes," she said.

"Keep your hand on the Bible. There's one more."

She was afraid she was going to throw up, but she didn't like to think of what he'd do if she did that, so she gritted her teeth and tried to steady the trembling in her legs.

"Now you swear that even if you do see someone—and you won't, not if you do what you swore—but if someone does happen by, you swear you won't say nothing to them about living here, or about me, or about the kid. Swear it."

She swore it, and even in the dim, flickering light from the heater she could see his dark eyes glittering.

"And if you break that oath, you won't just have the devil or jail to worry about, Susanna, you'll have me, and I'll kill you for sure, and I'll swear to that on this Bible too."

He showed her how to light the stove, warned her of the dangers of knocking it or the heater over, gave her a can opener out of his knapsack and a metal spoon, and a big red apple which he said was a special treat and she should save it for when she really needed it, but not to wait too long in case it went bad, and then he asked her if there was anything special she needed next time he came.

"I don't know," she said, longing for him to go, terrified of being left.

"Speak now or forever hold your peace," he said, all jokey again.

"I can't think—" She tried, but her mind was all jumbled up. "When are you coming back?"

"I told you before: when I can."

"What if I get sick? What if something happens?"

"It won't, not if you do what I told you." He grinned. "And you won't get sick; you're a strong girl."

She didn't feel strong; she felt ready to fall down.

"Last chance," he said.

She stared at the apple in her hand. She was pregnant. Fruit was healthful.

"Could I have some more apples?" she asked.

He nodded slowly, as if weighing the request. "Don't see why not, if you behave yourself."

"I will," she said, her voice back down to a whisper.

He zipped his bag back up. Susanna wondered what else was in it, it still looked laden. *Maybe a gun,* her inner voice hazarded, *or a knife, or a rope to tie you up or a shovel to bury you with.*

"You better get some sleep," he said. "You look beat."

She said nothing.

He went to the door, pulled at the handle. It stuck a little, at the top, and he had to yank it harder to open it.

"Remember your oaths," he said.

And he went.

"You'll never know how many noises there are in a place like that in the night," Susanna told Pete. "While he was with me, it seemed like there was nothing else about, and then suddenly, once he was gone, I realized that what I'd thought was silence was filled with sound, birds, other creatures maybe, the wind in the grass on the dunes outside, creaking the timbers on the walls, shifting the loose shingles on the roof, flapping the torn old tar paper. I spent the rest of that first night huddled on the mattress under the blanket, facing the door, knees bent, my arms wrapped around them, my chin tucked right down, and my eyes squeezed shut against the dark."

"Did you sleep?" Pete asked, his voice hushed.

She shook her head. "I'd thought I was so sleepy—I know I was exhausted—but when it came down to being left there all alone, I was too scared to sleep. I just sat there, all hunched up, not daring to let myself go, I suppose. And then dawn came. I'll never forget that first dawn. I remember I went to the door, started to open it. I wanted to breathe the fresh air; I wanted to see the sun rise. And then I remembered what I'd sworn, and though part of me knew he wasn't there to see me, and whatever he said, if God did happen to be watching, He wasn't likely to share what He saw with a man like that, the rest of me was just too afraid to go against him." She half smiled at the memory, a little pitying twitch of her lips for the terrified girl she had been back then. "But I did see the dawn. There were a few cracked timbers on two of the walls, and they became my spy holes. On one side there wasn't anything to see but sand, but one on the other side was at an angle where I could crane my neck and see a patch of sky."

"Was it a beautiful dawn?"

"It was still cloudy, but yes, it was incredibly beautiful to me." Susanna paused. "After all, I'd survived the night. I'd ridden and walked with the devil, I'd been alone with him in the midst of nowhere, and then I'd been alone without him, but I was still alive."

They went out for a while. Susanna had talked for almost two hours, and Pete knew it was another of those times when maybe he ought to have ended the session and scheduled another, but though she was drained, there was more to come, and she didn't want to stop, and it was a judgment call, and he made it knowing full well that friend, rather than counselor, was making it, but he made it anyway.

They strolled over to the Coach House on Waverly Place, sat on red leather banquettes, and ordered pepper steak, sautéed potatoes, and a bottle of Beaujolais. It was an evening for anchoring themselves with fine, solid food in snug, safe, attractive surroundings. They talked for a while about the house project, about the final go-ahead, which Michael Frieman seemed to believe was at long last just around the corner, about Susanna's plans to live in the house itself, in a private suite on the top floor—plans that Pete thought she would be wise to reconsider, but that Susanna believed were necessary if she was to give her total commitment to the project.

"I want to go on now," she said, suddenly, between steak and deep-dish apple pie.

"Are you sure?" Pete asked.

"If I don't go on tonight, I may never get it out."

"You want to leave? Go back to my place?"

She shook her head. "It's lovely here, and no one's close enough to hear. We can take our time, then head on back." She stopped. "Oh, Pete, I'm being so selfish; you must have had more than enough by now."

"No," he said. "I want you to go on."

"Are you sure?"

"I never lie to you, Susanna, you know that."

She smiled at him. "I know."

"It was two weeks before he came back the first time," she told him. "I guess you want to know how I coped, but sitting here, now, years later, I'm not sure I have the answer. I was very afraid, I know that, and I remember the fear coming in waves, great surges of panic, and then a kind of calm."

"But you did cope," Pete said.

"I didn't see that I had any choice. I mean I know, in hindsight, that of course I did. I should have left the shack that first morning and gone to get help. But the thing was I believed every word he said to me. I believed that if I went outside, somehow he would know, that if I told anyone what he'd done, he would come to get me."

"Two weeks must have seemed forever," Pete said. "Did you stay inside the whole time? Were you brave enough to go out after dark? It must have been terrifying."

"It was, especially the first time." She nodded. "I remember that part of it very clearly, trying to open that stiff door, frightened at first when it wouldn't open, feeling I was trapped, and then jumping half out of my skin when it did open, suddenly, and there was all this cold black air, and though God knows the walls of the shack were thin, the sound of the ocean was so much *louder* outside. I think I took a couple of deep breaths and banged the door shut again. It was a long while before I really went outside. Long after he came back that first time."

"Did he say why he'd been gone for so long?"

She shook her head. "He wasn't about to give me explanations for anything. That was part of his power over me, keeping me guessing, keeping me hoping and scared at the same time, the way they probably used to train circus animals, tidbits and terror."

Their apple pie came, and for a moment or two they busied themselves, and then Susanna, no longer able to eat, put down her spoon.

"By the time he came, I knew for sure that he was right about my pregnancy. My stomach was growing, and my breasts, which have never been much but had been tiny back then, seemed fuller. I didn't know anything about having babies, except that what he'd done to me was what made them happen. I hadn't even seen a birth in a movie; by the time a girl's thirteen these days, she's probably seen ten kinds of births and deaths on her TV at home, but I'd hardly ever watched TV. I was totally ignorant, and he knew that, and he used it."

Coffee came.

"I think, you know, that he was a little surprised to find me still there. He seemed kind of relieved. Looking back now, I guess it might have been a relief if I'd gone too, because at least he wouldn't have had to keep looking after me, though then he'd have had to run in case I'd told someone; he could never have been certain of me."

She stirred a little sugar into her coffee. In her days with Hawke she wouldn't have allowed herself either the potatoes or the apple pie, let alone the added sugar, but those days were long gone now.

"He brought the Lysol, as he'd said he would, and a bag of apples, and some oranges too, with a little pocketknife so I could peel them. And he brought more cans of soup and beans." She shook her head. "To this day the sight and smell of baked beans and canned mushroom soup make me feel queasy." She drank a little coffee. "It wasn't a bad visit. He was in a fine mood, and the sun was poking its head out, and he said we could take a little walk because there was no one around, and just before he left, I plucked up the courage to ask him if he could bring something else for me to eat the next time, and he made some crack about me being in no position to order room service, but I didn't think he really minded my asking. I didn't feel as scared of him that time as the last."

It was sleeting as they walked back to Pete's. For the duration of the stroll Susanna did not talk at all. The story could not, she felt, be told on New York City streets, was not a Washington

Square tale, but neither could she bring herself to make small talk while the past was still in there, bursting to get out, to be shared at last.

They didn't return to Pete's office but adjourned instead to his living room, with good old Steinbeck content to snuggle close in his familiar place beside her on the sofa, and dozing Alice in her cage. Pete offered more coffee and brought cognac at the same time. Before she began again, he got out a new pack of Marlboro and settled down to wait.

"He came twice a month after that," Susanna went on. "He seemed to be growing into a different kind of role, a combination of master, protector, and father-in-waiting. I think it must have been like keeping a subservient dog, only better, more satisfying. And looking back, I think maybe he found it compelling watching my belly grow while the rest of me was still so young and skinny." She paused, remembering. "As time went on, he brought me all kinds of things I'll bet he hadn't reckoned he would in the beginning. He brought me shampoo, and one night he brought one of those big round water dispensers. It must have been incredibly hard for him to get it to the shack; he might have rolled it some of the way, but he'd have had to carry it a long way too. He said it was so I could keep myself clean and nice as well as have enough to drink; I guess I wasn't too fragrant."

"So he really was looking after you," Pete said.

"Yes." Susanna nodded. "That's how it felt. He saw how uncomfortable I was, with my two skirts half undone, and he brought me a blue maternity dress. He told me he'd started reading up on having babies, and he brought me a book on exercising during pregnancy, and he started bringing me fresh milk, and once—and this sounds really bizarre now—he brought some lotion, which he said I was to rub into my stomach to keep me from getting stretch marks."

"He said you were to do it."

"Oh, yes, he didn't want to. He never made any attempt to touch me, not once during that whole time." She shook her head. "I still can't imagine why he cared about my getting stretch marks. It might have made some sense if he was planning on having me as a lover or whatever after the baby, but as it turned out, that wasn't the case, so I don't know."

"Sounds like he was fascinated," Pete said thoughtfully. "Like you were fulfilling some fantasy for him. The child having a child. His child."

"I think what he may have liked best," Susanna said slowly, "was that I was becoming more grateful every visit. Oh, I was still scared of him, but the longer he was kind, the more time that passed without him hurting me, the more my fear became focused on other things rather than him—childbirth mostly." She paused. "I was becoming dependent on him. He was becoming my protector, my benefactor."

"He was a terrorist," Pete said, and stubbed out a cigarette violently.

"I know he was," Susanna said softly. "But he was also doing what he'd promised he would. He was taking care of me and my baby."

Her time came closer. She had spoken to no one, seen no one else but him for four months. She had endured three severe winter storms, during which she had seen fork and sheet and chain lightning, had felt and heard great winds that she'd feared might blow the shack away and her with it. She had seen snow, had been blanketed and almost smothered by fog, had learned, until her mind screamed against it, the mournful voice of the foghorn from the lighthouse at Race Point. She had seen the dunes shift, the landscape alter overnight. Yet she had not frozen to death, had not miscarried, had not lost her mind.

She never considered her age at that time; it seemed an irrelevance, yet she was conscious of maturing in more ways than physical. She knew now that she was a strong person; she was aware of her strength. She had grown used to the tar paper shack, accustomed to the isolation and the elements, had found the courage to go outside after darkness had fallen, had learned to make the cover of night her friend. She finished reading *Gone with the Wind* and most of the magazines, and then she began them all again. She did not touch the Bible. She read the book on pregnancy and exercising, and late at night she left the shack and walked up and down the dunes closest to home until the sweat ran down her back and she was breathless but stronger, in better shape. She thought a lot about the past, about her family, about the convent, but mostly she thought about the future, about her unborn baby. She knew she could never go back to the convent.

She had done wrong, she'd done evil, just as he'd told her, and now she and her child had to be alone. Apart.

Her child. It moved and kicked, and sometimes it just stirred softly, like a whisper, and she had a sense at those times that this child was her friend, that perhaps the baby had always been there, deep inside her, waiting to be conceived, waiting to be born. She was still afraid, of pain, of dying, of living, but she no longer felt alone. She loved her child, and she knew, with absolute conviction, that it would love her.

She was infinitely grateful to him for that.

The days began to lengthen. With the great beach still icy, barren, and deserted, Susanna ventured out some days a little before dark. Daylight, weak as it was at that time of day, washed through her like purest sunshine, soothing her spirit, and she clambered over the dunes and down to the shore, her hands resting on her swollen belly, speaking softly to her child. She spoke to it constantly now, felt its response within her, loved it more with every passing day. Her back ached badly, her ankles were swollen, and several times lately, on getting up from the mattress in the tar paper shack, she had felt dizzy and almost fainted, yet still she rejoiced, felt optimism and excitement rush through her after each surge of fear. He had brought her another book some weeks back, and she had read about the changes that were occurring in her own body and the baby's, had devoured those chapters hungrily over and over again, but every time she had come to the chapter on birth she had closed the book. So much of what was written in that book revolved around doctors and hospitals and midwives and prenatal checks, and none of it seemed to apply to her or her baby, and sometimes that awareness made Susanna intensely afraid; but those moments were mercifully brief, swiftly replaced by her inexplicable conviction that all would be well when her time came. *He'll come before then*, she told herself and the child. *He'll take care of us, the way he has since he brought us here.*

She had asked him a few times what he planned for the birth. Not in so many words, of course. She'd framed the questions cautiously, the way she always did in case she angered him, though these days he grew angry less and less often.

"How will it be?" she asked.

"What?"

"When it comes."

"It'll be," he said.

"Will you be here?" she'd dared ask.

"If I can."

He'd never promised, but then he never promised anything, yet he did always return, always brought her what she needed, what she'd asked for and a little more.

He'll come, she told the baby. *Don't be afraid.*

One evening in late March, two days after one of his visits, Susanna went outside and on hearing a curious sound, she looked up and saw a flock of geese flying north in exquisite formation. Their wings, gold-tipped by the pale sunset, beat strongly, slowly, rhythmically, and their wild, haunting cries tore the air, bringing a new life force to the late-winter landscape. Susanna stood, face upturned, gazing at the sky, drinking in every last magnificent sight and sound, and then, when the travelers were gone, she sat down, slow and heavy and cumbersome with the baby, on the cold sand, and she closed her eyes and the picture was still there in her mind, and a few tears rolled down her cheeks for the wondrous, unblemished perfection of what she had seen.

She stayed outside longer than usual that night. No one came. She heard, but did not see, a fishing boat, chugging somewhere out to sea, and later she saw, a long, long way out, a great ship, its outline black on the dark blue horizon. The gulls called their night calls; the great dark voice of the Atlantic rolled back and forth, peaceful this evening. She walked for a while, never far from the shack, always mindful that a patrol might pass and see her, though none ever had; she had heard voices a few times during the day, but she had kept silent as he had commanded her to, had kept faith with him, as he had kept faith with her and the child.

About to turn around and head back to the shack, she passed a rock pool, filled by the last heavy rainfall a few days earlier. Behind her the moon was rising between two banks of cloud, and as Susanna looked down into the water, she saw her own reflection mirrored in the pool. She had not seen herself for many months. Fascinated, she stared. Pale silver hair, grown longer, framing her face. She peered harder, trying to make out the features, but it was like gazing through gauze, like seeing a ghost, distorted by water and the breeze and the beguiling moonlight. She was a stranger, tall, with long legs and arms and a round belly. With an effort, still yearning to see her face, to see into her own eyes, she got down onto her knees, and there she was, or at least a likeness of her, and it was so curious, in its inky black-and-silver wash, and she saw her long, straight nose and her wide mouth, and it was all so familiar, yet it was not quite her at all, not Susanna the way she had been. *I'm different*, she told the baby. *Look at me*, she said, *I've changed.*

With April, the ninth month of her pregnancy, came spring. The ocean itself remained winter frigid though the sun grew warmer, drawing the chill from the land. Fresh green points thrust up from the dunes; new birds, ringnecks and gannets, swooped down to feed on their journey north. *On their way to breed*, Susanna remembered one of the nuns telling her on the beach near Brewster long, long ago, a year, a lifetime. The nights grew clearer. Susanna sat outside the shack, gazing up into the multitudes of stars and planets, trying to soothe her soul with their brilliant peace, drinking in the salt purity of the air, aware that she was marking time now, waiting for him to come back so that her baby could be born, and she was growing restless and tired and impatient, and he had not come to them for three weeks now, and she missed him.

It began with a dull cramp, in the deepest, darkest hour of night, waking her out of a dream. She lay still for a few moments on the mattress, waiting for it to go. She'd had such cramps before, often, had read about them in the book he had brought her, but they had mostly been in her lower abdomen, and they had always passed. This one was in her lower back, and it did not pass. It spread, instead, through her, radiated into her stomach, into her legs, and it ceased to be a cramp and became a pain, so fierce and so startling that Susanna forgot the rule of silence to which she had adhered for almost five months and cried out, her voice echoing in the stillness.

The pain went away. Susanna lay still again, her eyes wide

open in the dark, half afraid that someone might have heard her, half afraid that they had not. She remembered Melanie in *Gone with the Wind*, recalled her long and agonizing confinement, and she wished now she had never read the book, for suddenly that account seemed all too monstrously real: little Prissy's terror, Scarlett O'Hara's grudging courage, the laboring mother's narrow survival. At least Melanie, for all the accompanying horrors of her wartime nightmare, had had help, but there was no one to help Susanna, and she wondered now, for the first time in months, if she would, in the end, die alone, all alone in the tar paper shack, with no one, no one, not even him.

Her waters broke, soaking the mattress. Weeping with confusion and shame, Susanna mopped at it with tissue, smelled a strange, never-before-smelled sweetness, and knew that she had not, after all, urinated, as she had thought, and for a minute or two, sitting up, she felt comforted, for if he came now, he might be less angry with her than if she had peed in her bed. But the moment she lay back down to rest, the fluid began to leak out of her again, and now her tears were of fear, for she had not read the chapter on labor in the book, and it was too dark to see the pages now, and she thought perhaps that her baby had drowned or that her womb had been somehow pierced, and she could not feel the child move, and she thought it had died or was, at that very instant, dying, needing help, needing her.

The pain returned, grew more intense, and at first Susanna was filled with joyous relief, for it meant, it surely meant that the baby was alive, was on its way, would soon be with her, in her arms. But as it went on and on, grinding through her, tearing at her, with no sign of birth, no sign of him coming to help her, she became increasingly afraid again. Unbidden, like an illustrated prophecy of worse, infinitely worse, to come, Melanie came back into her mind again, the unending agony of her labor. Susanna remembered her gripping Scarlett's hand so hard the bones almost broke, remembered Scarlett knotting towels into a rope for Melanie to hold on to, to wrench at when the pains came, and Susanna struggled up off the mattress and looked for a way to do that for herself, but there were no towels, no sheets, and the blanket was too heavy to tie, and anyway, she hadn't the strength to do it. She got water from the dispenser, soaked paper towels with it, mopped her own face and body, and then thirstily drank some, vomiting just a minute later, and she wept then for a while, cleaned herself again and rinsed her mouth, and lay down again, exhausted, just in time for the next contraction.

The pains seized her, took her over, consumed her, hot poker fingers dragging, tearing at her insides. She began to think about dying again, felt that neither her body nor her mind could bear much more of it, that she would go mad before she died. *But if I die and if the baby lives*—oh, how desperately she wanted the baby to live—*will he come to find it? Will he look after it?* He had talked about the child, but he'd never spoken of it as his own, only as the evidence of her sin, yet more than once he had laid his big hand on her swollen stomach and felt its kick, and Susanna had seen something then in his dark eyes, meeting her own for just an instant, a spark of something new and different, of complicity, of sharing perhaps, she had never been sure. . . .

It went on, and he did not come. Daylight came, its tiny rays flowing through the small cracks in the timber walls, and Susanna found the chapter in the book on childbirth that she had not read, held it up to one of the little spears of light, found a page on delivering in an emergency, read about panting and washing the vaginal area and clean towels, and trying to keep the baby's head safe when it appeared, but it was all useless, *useless*, without anyone else to help her, and how could he have done this to her and his baby? How could he have left her to give birth all alone in this awful, dirty place? And the light grew dimmer, and she threw the book across the floor, slamming it against the wall and breaking its spine, and the wind blew up, and she pictured the landscape shifting again, the sand flying, beach grass whipping, and rain beat down hard on the roof, and the pain went on and on, and it grew dark again.

Be brave, the voice in her head told her, *be calm and breathe, and help the baby; the baby needs your help,* and Susanna writhed on the mattress and bit on a corner of the blanket to muffle her cries and moans, and she was drenched with perspiration, and she had soiled herself, and the stench offended and repelled her, and even in the midst of the worst of it, she was afraid of what he would say when he came.

If he comes, the voice said.

"He *has* to come," Susanna whispered back.

The last contraction was so strong, so agonizing, silencing the voice in her head, ripping her apart so completely, so mercilessly, that she screamed out loud, unmuffled and uncaring, mindless now, beyond fear, beyond everything. And suddenly she saw a light, brilliant and fierce, and it was there even when she shut her eyes. It seemed to be inside her, invading her mind, illuminating her whole being, and she wondered for a moment if she might be on the point of death, and a part of her welcomed it, longed for it. But then she was pushing with all her might, knew that she had to push, that the baby was coming now, and she was half sitting, half squatting, grunting, her hands clawed around a loose timber in the wall beside the mattress, and she felt that half the world was being born rather than one small baby; and then its head came through, and Susanna bent double, screaming with agony and determination, and she cradled its bloody head and half eased, half tugged its tiny shoulders into the hard, cold, but welcoming world.

And there was her baby, her daughter, her beloved, and Susanna clasped the infant to her stomach, felt her slithery with blood and mucus, felt her fragile and strong and warm and alive. The first wail came, thin and protesting and growing stronger, and Susanna laughed and wept with her child. And with the last of her strength, she wiped the tiny open mouth clean with moist paper towel, and then she wrapped the rest of the roll around the baby and covered them both with the soiled blanket. And then suddenly she needed to push again, and the placenta was delivered, but her daughter was with her, and they were both alive, and Susanna sobbed and sobbed with love and joy and relief and exhaustion. And slept.

He came before dawn. Silently he cut the cord with his pocket-knife, warmed water on the stove, took the infant and washed her and dried her, and then he washed Susanna, very gently and carefully, and it was all done without words on either side, and Susanna, only half awake, watched him through sleep-slitted eyes, saw him take care of their child, let him take care of her, and he was like a father now, and there was no threat in him, no darkness, and she realized then that in spite of all his planning, he had not anticipated this moment.

He cares, she thought. *He did not expect to care.* Maybe he had expected her to die, perhaps both of them, maybe he had planned to bury them both out there, beneath the wild beach grass, forgotten and unmourned. But now here they were, facing him. Mother and daughter. Child and infant. Both his creatures.

Weak and drained as she was, Susanna observed that the baby had changed everything between them. She did not really understand, but then she had understood nothing for so long; she had just lived, survived, gone on with it all as best she could. Yet still she sensed now—she could not have described it in words—but she sensed that the infant had given her something she had never possessed before. A measure of power. This day at least, this moment, she could see it in his face. He was linked to the scrap in her arms, he *wanted* it, and the warm, beloved scrap was hers; it needed her, for love, for survival, for existence. They were all linked now. Family, of a kind.

"He stayed longer than usual that day," Susanna told Pete. "He'd hardly ever come during daylight hours, had almost always come and gone in the night. He heated a can of soup and fed it to me, and he combed my hair, kept the heater alight. He didn't say much, but I watched him, and I could see his mind ticking over, and I knew he was making plans, and I felt they were surprising him a little somehow."

"What were the plans?" Pete asked.

"He didn't tell me, not that day anyway. He was too busy coming to terms with the fact that I'd just had his baby. He put her to my breast, and for a while nothing happened, and then a little milk came, enough for her anyway, though I didn't know that at the time. I thought she was going to starve, and I panicked a little. He calmed me down, he was really okay about it, though I thought he might be angry with me, but I guess he'd been reading and knew it was all right, the way it was meant to be."

"And was it?" Pete asked softly.

"Oh, yes, it was. It was a miracle, I suppose, a miracle that either of us survived, though I took it for granted then. I was too young to know any different; we'd made it, and that was that so far as I was concerned." Susanna paused. "He left that night, told me he'd be back in a day or two at the outside, that he'd bring stuff that the baby might need, and he'd never made promises like that before, and I believed him."

"He just left you?"

"Yes."

"Dear God," Pete murmured.

"But not before we'd named the baby. It was my choice; I'd had it all ready, a girl's name. You know, I can't remember what name I was going to choose if it had been a boy." She looked into Pete's face. "You've guessed it, haven't you?"

"I think so," he said.

There were tears in Susanna's eyes.

"My baby sister," she said. "Abigail."

CHAPTER 13

~

Susanna stopped talking about the past again after that evening. She cut her next three appointments with Pete, changed the subject whenever he attempted to bring it up, ignored every attempt, gentle or firm, by him to encourage her to go on. She buried herself in work, saw less of her family, even Abigail, than before. The truth that had emerged with almost as much agony as the birth itself now seemed too painful to face up to. The old wound closed up again, sealed by the fragile membrane of her renewed determination to forget.

Hawke House, now the project's official name, opened its doors. Within a few weeks Susanna—who was keeping her Beekman Place apartment but living most of the time on the top floor of the house—knew that perhaps her greatest contribution to its hoped-for success had been the finding of Joe Zacharias, its resident manager. Zacharias, a trained nurse, chiropractor, and passionate believer in holistic medicine, had for some time wanted to play a part in the battle against AIDS, but his many qualifications and talents alone were not what made him so uniquely right for Hawke House. Joe was a local, born, raised, and educated in Phoenicia, a few miles west of Bearsville, and his mother was a churchgoer and a member of the Women's Guild. If Jane Zacharias thought it was okay for her only son to work at "that place," while certain people might never share her opinions, her approval made it harder for them to voice their objections too vociferously.

They began with just three guests: one on his own; one with a partner and his mother; the third with her husband and son, all escaping different aspects of the disease. They came not only for the temporary escape that the project offered but also to try to find a means of looking ahead, of moving forward, no matter how much or how little time they had left. They liked the fact that Hawke House was not a sanatorium, or a health farm, or a hotel; they liked the fact that they could feel safe there yet be unfettered by even the mildest regimen. The finest thing about staying there, the first three all agreed, was the absolute freedom of choice that was being offered. If they got sick while they were there, they would be taken care of; if they wanted to declare a moratorium on AIDS, to pretend, for a while, that it simply was not happening to them, no one at Hawke House would heap guilt on them; if they wished, on the other hand, to use their time there to let it all out, all their anguish, fear, rage, whatever, and if they wished to do that either in private or before a select group of fellow sufferers or specialists, that was okay too.

It worked. It was what Susanna had hoped it would be: an oasis, a place apart, but tethered to the real world by humanity and practicality. They came and went, sometimes returned, sometimes recommended. Some called it refreshment, others remission, some a vacation or simply breathing space; one even referred to it as a cease-fire.

"I think that's the best description I've heard," Pete said one evening over a prime rib dinner with Susanna and Betty Thomas Clark in the main dining room, a large but not-too-large room with high ceilings, two old lead glass chandeliers, oak-paneled walls, and soft pale rose linen on the tables. "This is a war, I guess, and if people feel this is where they can come to lick their wounds for a while, I'd say it was doing its job."

"What do you say, Betty?" Susanna asked the tough, pretty woman who'd come up for a weekend visit to check them out.

"I say so far so good." Clark smiled. "I knew you could do it, Susanna. You had a few doubts about your ability to fight, but you pulled it off."

"She sure did," Pete said warmly.

"Well, I hardly did it alone," Susanna protested.

"It was your concept, your brainchild," Clark said.

"But none of it would have happened without you and Pete and Michael—not to mention Joe Zacharias."

"Yeah, yeah, yeah." Clark shook her head. "What's with you, Susanna? It isn't taboo these days to sing your own praises, you know. You've done a good thing here, a fine thing, and you'll be wise to remember that when the next battle comes along."

"Oh, no," Susanna said. "This is it for me. No more projects."

"I wasn't thinking of more. This baby'll give you trouble enough all on its own, believe me."

"I hoped we'd had most of our troubles."

"You don't really believe that, do you?" Clark's smile was ironic.

"Susanna's an optimist," Pete said.

"Aren't you?" Susanna asked, a touch defensively.

"We all are," Clark assured her. "There's no way anyone but an optimist and an idealist could have got Hawke House up and running. Just don't make the mistake of thinking that your work's all done, either of you." She looked around. "This is a lovely house, but even with all the improvements, it's still old, and old houses will always give you problems." She paused. "Though I'd guess that most of your troubles won't have anything much to do with plumbing or the roof."

"I'd guess you're right," Pete said.

Susanna looked at them both. "What?"

"Hysteria," Clark said.

"I think we're over that," Susanna said.

"No," Clark said. "Not if I'm any judge of horseflesh."

"I agree," Pete said.

"The people around here have been fine," Susanna protested. "They were concerned when they first heard about our plans, but they're used to the idea now, and we all know how much help Joe and his mother have been in that direction."

"People are people," Clark argued. "Some are good, a few are bad; most are just normal. All people get scared, especially when they think their loved ones may be at risk."

"But we've been through all that," Susanna said. "They know there is no risk."

"That's the theory," Clark said. "It's much too early to be sure about how it's all going to work in practice."

"I may be an optimist," Susanna said, "but I think you guys are being overly pessimistic. You have to have faith in people."

"Oh, I have faith." Clark grinned. "But I also have lawyers."

Over the next six months, three incidents occurred that bore out Betty Thomas Clark's pessimism. In May a Hawke House guest and his lover, picnicking in the woods on the perimeter of their land, were observed in a close embrace by a twelve-year-old schoolgirl from Wittenburg, who told her father, who demanded that police officers be dispatched to Hawke House to press charges of public indecency against those responsible.

"They were just kissing, for crying out loud," Joe Zacharias told the policemen, one of whom he knew from school in Phoenicia.

"Were they naked?" the other officer asked.

"Of course they weren't naked."

"The father seems to think they were."

"Then either his daughter has a vivid imagination or he's a liar."

"Take it easy, Zacharias," the old school pal said, eager to cool things down. "We've had a complaint; you know we have a duty to act on it."

"Well, you've acted," Joe said, "and I've put you straight."

"I still think we should talk to the gentlemen concerned," the second officer said, although Susanna and Joe had already agreed that their guests would under no circumstances be questioned.

"No," Joe said.

"We have a duty."

"You already said that," Joe pointed out. "And I have a duty to see that our guests are allowed the peace and quiet they're paying for." He paused. "Look, guys, if I thought there was the slightest possibility that this man and his daughter were right, I'd be the first to draw the line."

"You're saying there's no possibility, Zacharias?" the Phoenicia man asked.

"That's what I'm saying," Joe said steadily.

"Okay."

"I still think we ought to question the gentlemen," number two persisted.

"If I were you, I'd go back and question the girl's father some more," Joe suggested. "Get him to ask her for a few details about what she saw, what the men looked like."

"He won't care to do that, Zacharias."

"I imagine he won't, but you might point out to him that if he wants to take this any further, someone else'll be asking her questions."

The matter was dropped, but two months later, after a group of Hawke House guests had gone out for the afternoon and gone swimming in a lake a few miles from Bearsville, the same two police officers, visibly embarrassed, were back, this time in Susanna's office.

"What's the problem, gentlemen?" she asked. "Has someone complained about nude swimming? Because if they have, I happen to know it's not true—"

"No, ma'am," the man from Phoenicia said. "Nothing like that."

"Well, what then?" She tried to be patient. "Would you like to take a seat, have some coffee, perhaps?" Her office was a welcoming place, simple but comfortable, with oak ceiling rafters, a warm red rug on the polished wood floor, and family photographs, all taken either by Hawke or by Connie, every place she'd been able to put them.

"No, thank you, ma'am," the second officer said.

"You have to understand, ma'am," Joe's school pal said, shifting awkwardly, "that this has nothing to do with us. We've just been asked to pass on some comments; it isn't even really an official complaint, not yet at least."

"What isn't?"

"They were swimming in a public lake, ma'am."

"Yes." Susanna paused. "There's no law against that, is there?"

"No, ma'am."

"So what's the problem?" Even as she asked the question, she knew, with a sick chill of disgust, what was coming.

"Contamination, ma'am," the second man said.

She felt her whole body tighten with anger, forced herself to remain calm.

"Would you explain that, please?"

"I'd say it was pretty clear."

"Not to me."

The first officer had red cheeks. "The local force told us they've had a bunch of people worrying that there's AIDS in the water."

Susanna took a breath to steady herself. "You can tell them they're wrong."

"Are you sure?"

"Yes, I'm sure."

"Didn't the people who went swimming have it, ma'am?"

"I'm not prepared to discuss that with you, officer."

"It might be helpful if you did, ma'am."

"It would not be helpful to my guests," Susanna said. "And in any case, I can assure you that it's irrelevant."

"They're worried about their kids, ma'am."

"Yes," Susanna said. "I see they might be, which is why I suggest you put them straight."

"And the fish."

"Fish?"

"There are fish in that lake, ma'am."

"Are there?"

"Yes, ma'am, and the people are worried that the fish might catch AIDS."

"They don't have to worry." Susanna paused. "And it's HIV, not AIDS."

"Whatever. They don't like the idea of the fish carrying it."

"I'm sure they don't," Susanna said. "And they aren't."

"Can you be sure of that, ma'am?" the Phoenicia man asked.

Susanna shook her head. "I have to admit it's something I've never been asked about before."

"You mean it is possible the water might be contaminated?" The other man came in sharply.

"If a carrier were cut and bled into the water," she answered slowly, coolly, "then yes, theoretically, I suppose there's a tiny chance that a passing trout might run a risk."

"Is that supposed to be a joke, ma'am?" the sharp one asked.

"I don't see anything funny about it," Susanna answered.

"No, ma'am," Phoenicia said. "Nor do we."

The water and the trout were declared perfectly safe, and that incident too did no lasting damage, but new questions were raised at the state level about the precautions that Hawke House management was taking with regard to public health, and Susanna, Joe Zacharias, and Pete all noticed a slight cooling in the attitude of some local residents toward the house.

It was the dog incident the following October that caused Susanna the most anguish and that brought her most forcibly back into the public eye. Guests were allowed, even encouraged, to bring their most beloved pets to Hawke House if it would help them to relax more completely, and rules relating to animals were as easygoing as possible. Until the day that a schnauzer named Billy, belonging to a writer of children's books, escaped from the grounds and was found mounting a pedigree collie bitch in a backyard two miles away. Three days later, at the insistence of her owner, the collie was put to sleep by a reluctant veterinarian, and a demand was made that Billy share the same fate.

When the writer refused, backed up by Susanna, a letter appeared in the *Greene County Examiner* in which the collie's owner claimed that his dog had been not only valuable but also the apple of his little boy's eye. It had broken his heart to have the collie destroyed, the man said, but he'd had to put the safety of his child first. If Hawke House was to be allowed to continue operating, he suggested, it had to be forced to take its responsibilities to the public more seriously. As it was, there was a potentially dangerous animal still at large in the area, and this was one more symptom of the risks the community had feared it might be taking if an ex-model was allowed to run an establishment that ought, if it was going to exist at all, to be state-controlled.

Outraged, Susanna was determined to set the record straight. Within days the *Greene County Examiner* had given Hawke House the right of reply, with a center-page spread complete with photographs of the writer and her blameless dog and of Susanna hard at work at her desk. Letters came flooding in, to the paper and to Hawke House, eighty percent of them in full support. Word got around, and journalists from the *Boston Globe*, the *New York Times*, and *People* magazine came looking for interviews with Susanna.

"Is this right?" she asked Pete one evening on the phone. "I mean, should I be doing this? I'm not qualified."

"You're entirely qualified," Pete told her.

"To talk about Hawke House, perhaps, but not the wider issues."

"Talk about what you know and nothing more." Pete paused. "Trust your instincts, Susanna. They haven't let you down yet."

The interest engendered by the articles in the *Boston Globe* and *New York Times* and especially by the two-page spread in *People* had both a good and bad side. Hawke House was declared a respectable and well-meaning, nonprofit-making venture run by men and women who cared and it was hailed by many as the right way forward in the battle against AIDS. The writer's children's books leaped off the alphabetically arranged bookstore shelves onto the bestselling tables, and Billy, the lusty schnauzer, was off the hook. The downside was the risk of the end of anonymity for both the project and those who came to stay there; anyone hoping to check quietly in to Hawke House encountered photographers with zoom lenses hovering close to the big electric gates Joe Zacharias had advised Susanna to install. Many of the easygoing aspects of the project had to be sacrificed for the sake of acceptance; it was no longer practical for guests to picnic in the woods or go off on day trips, at least not if they set great store by their right to privacy. For a time bookings dipped, then gradually they rose again, but Susanna and Pete both knew that the simplicity they had sought was lost forever.

Two weeks before Christmas, when Susanna returned from three days in the city, Joe told her that Abigail had arrived unexpectedly a couple of hours earlier.

"Where is she?"

"I saw her awhile back up on the second floor, giving housekeeping a helping hand."

Susanna stopped in her tracks. "Doing what?"

"Cleaning up one of the checkouts," Joe said.

Susanna flew up the staircase, located Abigail, and whisked her, with hardly a word of greeting, up to her office.

"Where's the fire?" Abigail, now fifteen, still tall, still fragile, and lovelier than ever, was bemused.

"No fire." Susanna, unloading her bags, was flustered. "What are you doing here?"

"I thought you'd be glad to see me."

"Oh, sweetheart, I'm sorry." Susanna dumped the last bag and came over to give her a hug. "I'm thrilled to see you. I was just so surprised when Joe told me you were here. I had no idea you were coming."

"It was a spur-of-the-moment thing," Abigail said. "Connie said I should call ahead, but I thought that would spoil it."

Susanna held her at arm's length. "Let me look at you." She checked out the gorgeous big brown eyes, the lovely, expressive mouth, the dark gold hair cascading over her shoulders. "Still the most beautiful sister in the world." They embraced again, until Susanna pulled away. "So how long are you here for?"

"A couple of days."

"Really?"

"You don't look exactly overjoyed." Abigail was perplexed.

"I am, sweetheart, believe me." Susanna dragged herself together. "I'm just tired from driving and the city, and I want to make some plans, so we can have the best possible time." She glanced at the clock on the mantelpiece, gathering her thoughts. "Okay, so while you take a shower, I can put my feet up for a half hour, and then we can organize ourselves."

"I don't need a shower."

"Yes, you do."

"No, I don't. I had a shower before I left home."

"And now you can have another one."

Abigail stared at Susanna, anger flaring swiftly. "I don't believe you."

"What do you mean?"

"You know perfectly well."

"No, I don't." Susanna turned around, avoiding Abigail's accusing eyes, busying herself with some papers on her desk.

"It's because I was cleaning that bathroom, isn't it?"

"I'm sorry?" Susanna kept on sorting folders.

"You heard me." Abigail's voice was tight. "It's because I was touching towels and soap and stuff that someone with the virus had used."

"Wouldn't you say that was a sensible precaution?" Susanna didn't turn around.

"Is it one you take?" Abigail demanded. "Do you tell the maids to shower between rooms?"

"You're overreacting." Susanna turned now, registered the real anger on Abigail's face.

"It's hardly me doing that," Abigail retorted. "Ever since Hawke House opened, you've all but forbidden me from coming anywhere near the place."

"I have not," Susanna said indignantly.

"Yes, you have, you know you have. It's been one excuse after another, every time I even *thought* of coming." Abigail was in full flow now. "I told Connie and Bryan that's what you were doing, and they said I was wrong, but about thirty seconds after you see me here you want me to take a stupid shower. I'm surprised you don't just pour a bottle of Lysol over my head."

Susanna's cheeks were flushed. "You're being ridiculous."

"Not me, Susanna."

Susanna took off her coat and hung it in the oak closet. "So don't take a shower," she said, with forced lightness. "I don't care either way. You're making a big deal over a tiny little suggestion."

"But you do care, don't you?" Abigail wasn't about to let up, had waited too long to have her say. "If I don't scrub myself clean, I'll bet that you'll sit over dinner this evening and then lie awake all night worrying in case I had an open scratch on a finger and the virus took a nosedive right into it."

"You are talking absolute nonsense, Abigail." Susanna was starting to get angry herself now. "You know better than that, and we both know that I certainly do."

"Yes, you do. That's the whole point." Abigail grew a little gentler. "You've given interviews to national papers, for God's sake, putting people straight on all the dumb things they're still scared about, and I've been so proud of my big sister, telling them how it is and actually making them listen to you. But the instant it's me, all the rules seem to change." She paused. "Just the way they did when Hawke was sick and everyone else was allowed to hug him except me."

"Oh, not that again," Susanna sighed.

"Yes, that again," Abigail insisted. "I was only ten then, so there wasn't much I could do, but I'm not a little girl anymore." Her face was tight with intensity. "I know you were only scared for me because you loved me so much, and I know that's why you hardly let me near you for so long after Hawke died, because you were still afraid you might get it."

"That's all over now," Susanna said softly.

"Yes, it is, thank God," Abigail said, "and at least when you come home, you're halfway normal with me; you at least let me *near* you again, the way you used to, before, when I was little."

Susanna sank down onto her sofa. Suddenly she felt very weary.

"I'm sorry," she said. "I know everything you're saying is true."

"But you can't help it, right?" Abigail sat down beside her.

Susanna shrugged. "I guess so."

"Well, it's time you started trying to help it, sis." The fifteen-year-old was gentler now, but still standing firm. "For one thing, how do you think it makes Tabbie feel? She's our sister too, but you've never been this irrational around her."

"Tabbie's twenty-five years old," Susanna said, reasonably.

"That's not the point," Abigail argued.

"I think it is."

Abigail shook her head. "I give up." She stood up.

"Where are you going?" Susanna was anxious.

"To take a shower."

"You don't have to."

"I know I don't, but I'm going to because I know otherwise you're so dumb it'll drive you crazy, and that's not what I'm trying to do to you." Abigail stopped halfway to the door. "You really do have a problem with this, you know, sis."

"I know I do."

"Maybe you should talk to Pete about it."

"I have."

"Maybe you should talk some more."

"Maybe."

It was Abigail herself, two days later, before she left Hawke House, who raised the subject with Pete, just up from the city for a few hours. Pete listened to what she had to say, was quiet and patient until she'd finished, then as noncommittal as he felt obliged to be.

"This isn't something I can really speak with you about, Abigail." They were strolling outside near the barren vegetable garden, both warmly wrapped up in down jackets and scarves against the cold December wind.

"Why not?"

"It would be unethical, for one thing."

"What's the other thing?" she asked.

"Nothing. It was just a figure of speech, you know. Unethical is what I meant, and maybe disloyal too."

"Because you're partners in Hawke House," Abigail said.

"Yes."

"And because you're Susanna's shrink."

Pete's green eyes gave nothing away. "We have been professionally involved in the past," he said, walking a little more briskly.

"What about love?" Abigail asked, her long legs easily keeping pace.

"I beg your pardon?"

"What about the fact that you're in love with Susanna?"

Pete blinked, turned his face quickly away, and went on walking.

"I knew it." Abigail was triumphant. "I told Connie ages ago that you guys were in love with each other, and she told me I was just being romantic."

"Who says you're not?"

"You didn't deny it. If there'd been nothing in it, you'd have laughed in my face right away."

"I tend not to laugh in people's faces," Pete said.

"No, I know that," Abigail said. "But you know what I mean." She grinned. "Anyway, I am right, and I think it's great."

Pete stopped walking. "Do you?"

"Of course I do." Abigail stopped too and put out one gloved hand to touch his arm. "We all love you, Pete. If it hadn't been for Hawke, I think you and Susanna would have gotten together ages ago."

"If it hadn't been for Hawke," Pete reminded her quietly, "we would never have met."

"That's true." Abigail's eyes grew somber for an instant. "Poor Hawke."

Pete said nothing. For a few moments they both stood still beside one of the empty vegetable beds, its soil well turned but dusted with frost. Their breaths steamed from their lips and noses, and their minds ticked.

"Susanna doesn't feel the same way about me, you know," Pete said finally.

"I think she does."

"You're wrong."

"Maybe." Abigail shrugged. "I don't think so, though."

"You have to promise me you won't say a word about this to her," Pete said, suddenly urgent. "Not a single word."

"I wouldn't. Not yet anyway." She grinned again. "Not until I thought there'd be any real point."

"What point could there be?"

"Susanna sometimes needs people to show her things that are right under her nose."

"I don't want you showing her this, Abigail, okay?"

"Okay," she said lightly.

Pete moved a step closer, a mock threat. "Not a single word, or else."

"Or else what?" She laughed into his eyes.

"Just or else." Pete paused, became serious. "Mostly, I think if you said something, you might blow my chances for keeps."

"I wouldn't want to do that."

"Good."

"I mean it," she said. "I want you to be my next brother-in-law."

"Really?" Pete smiled.

"Sure." Abigail paused. "Imagine how neat it would be when I have my first nervous breakdown."

"I didn't know you were planning one."

"I wasn't, but I may have one pretty soon, unless you stop Susanna from making me shower every time I breathe in Hawke House."

Late that night, back home on Eighth Street, Pete wrote in his journal.

She's such a great kid. Almost grown up, but still Susanna's little sister. If she only knew. Lord knows I hear more than most about complicated lives, but this one, so full of pain, past and present, is almost more than I can bear. And how much more lies ahead for Susanna, and for Abigail too, when she finds out the truth. To her, life still seems so simple, all straight, clear, clean paths. If Susanna and I love each other, Abigail says, then go right ahead and love. Simple as that.

If she only knew.

It got harder for him as time went on. Four and a half years had passed since they'd first met that day in the hospital. Hawke's wife was all she had been to him then, at the beginning, and later, Hawke's widow. Friends now, and associates, and he was still her shrink, as Abigail had reminded him, and if Susanna had ever thought of him in any other way, he would have known it, would have read it in her eyes, those eyes that touched him so, that made him a boy again, besotted and vulnerable. He would have known it. Yet would he, when he had never even begun to imagine the secrets she held in her head?

I talked about professional ethics to Abigail today, like a pompous ass. I still think of myself as a halfway decent therapist, striving to help my patients, when the truth is I'm just a lying coward hiding behind my professional mask, not man enough to face my own truths. She needs me, I tell myself, that's why I can't quit on her—she *needs* me.

Who the hell am I kidding?

PART THREE

CHAPTER 14

The fact that the anonymous letter containing the blackmail threat and dated Christmas Day had been mailed to Susanna's Beekman Place address chilled her as much as anything. Hawke House was where the public in general believed that she lived. Putting the city address on the envelope was an added threat in itself; he knew where she lived, what she did, where she went.

Her first response, once the immediate shock had subsided a little, was to get over to her bank on Third Avenue, to make arrangements to get the fifty thousand dollars he had demanded. *Give him the money; get rid of him; get it over with.* She was almost out of the door when a semblance of common sense halted her. In the first place, she didn't have that kind of money hanging around in her bank account. Hawke House had proved, as she had known it would be, a huge drain on her resources. Oh, she could probably put the cash together given time, she was still lucky enough to know she had that option, but it wouldn't be easy, and in any case he hadn't given her detailed instructions yet, so she had no choice but to sit and wait.

He likes making you wait for him. Didn't he always?

Her second response was to call Pete. Since it was New Year's Eve, his appointment book was full until lunchtime, and after that he was visiting at two hospitals, but he had time, he told her, at three o'clock.

"Something's happened," she said at five minutes past three, safe in his office. "And suddenly I don't seem to have too many choices left. I shouldn't have stopped talking to you when I did, and now I have no alternative. I have to stop hiding. I have to face up to the truth so that I can see how to deal with this thing."

"What is this thing?"

She shook her head. "Later, I'll tell you that later."

"All right." Pete lit a Marlboro, leaned back in his chair, saw her smile in spite of her obvious distress. "What?" he asked.

"Just you," she said. "That little gesture you make with your cigarette, the way you settle back to wait, always patient, always gentle."

"Not much else I can do."

"No." Susanna paused. "I think you guessed, back when I told you about Abigail—you guessed who he was, the man, didn't you?"

Pete shook his head. "No guessing games, Susanna, not now."

"Okay," she said. "It was Matthew Bodine. Who raped me. Who kept me in the tar paper shack on the dunes. Abigail's father."

"And yours." His green eyes sharpened.

"No," she said. "Not my father." She watched Pete's dismay clear a little. *One trauma less.* "But all the stories I told you about my parents living with me in the convent near Brewster—none of them was true."

"What happened to them, to your parents?"

"I don't remember my father. He died when I was two years old."

"And your mother?"

"Dead too." Susanna paused again. "But that's another story."

Pete inhaled deeply. "I thought you were going all the way with this now. Facing up to the truth. Your words."

"Yes," she said. "But not that. Not yet anyway."

He nodded, saying nothing.

"Matthew Bodine came to work for the sisters just after my twelfth birthday." She went on. "He was the gardener, mainly, as I told you, though he drove, too, took care of things around the place. I guess he was good at his work. He got on with it; he was quiet and strong and respectful to the nuns." She paused. "I'm sure they trusted him."

For the first three weeks of Abigail's life Bodine came to the shack twice each week, sometimes three times. Susanna didn't have enough milk for the baby, so he brought formula with him, and disposable diapers. Each time he came, he asked questions about how Susanna was feeling, and she guessed that he was afraid she might get sick because there'd been some bleeding for the first few days after the birth, but that had stopped, and now she was growing stronger every day, and Bodine had begun to look less wary, more like his old self, but Susanna couldn't help feeling touched that he cared. He had told her that he would look after her and the baby, and he had kept his word. She had long since ceased expecting more.

"I'm making plans," he told her when Abigail was eighteen days old. "For her, for you, for all of us." He paused. "Spring's here; days are getting longer; before we know it, there'll be people all over the place."

"Where will we go?" Susanna asked, cradling the baby in her arms.

"I'm not sure yet, but I've worked some of it out. I figure we'll have to tell folks I'm your father as well as hers." He scratched his dark head. "The story is your ma died giving birth to the kid."

"But I'm her mother." Susanna looked at him blankly.

"I know that, you know that, but no one else is going to, you got that?" The old harshness was back in his voice, in his eyes. "Don't interrupt me, girl, okay?" He saw her nod. "Okay. The story we'll tell everyone—and I mean *everyone*—is that your ma just died, back in Vermont, we'll say, where we came from." He fixed her with another stare. "Vermont, right? Not Brewster, or anywhere else. Vermont."

"Vermont," she said softly.

"Now here I am, widower with two daughters, needing work and a home for my kids. I'm a hard worker, and I'll get myself some good references, and one look at you and the kid—"

"Abigail," Susanna said.

"One look at you and Abigail"—he went on, his temper improving again with his inventing—"and any decent person's bound to want to bend over backward to help us." He nodded. "One of those big houses near Boston would suit me, I guess. And my kids."

In her arms Abigail stirred, eyes tightly shut, tiny rosebud lips pursing up a little, then relaxing again. Susanna gazed down at her daughter and felt love rock her, fill her, warm her.

"You like the idea?" Bodine asked her.

"I don't know."

"Get used to it, whether you like it or not." He was not especially unkind, just matter-of-fact. "And get used to calling yourself Bodine. You're my daughter now, and she's your baby sister. Got that?"

Susanna looked away from the infant, up into his face.

"I asked you if you got all that," he said. "Remember all I've done for you and her. Remember you're a sinner. Remember what happens if you tell anyone the truth."

"I remember," she whispered.

"And that's forever," he said. "You got it?"

Susanna nodded. "I got it."

"You know most of what happened after that. We arrived at the Van Dusens as Susanna and Abigail Bodine, Matthew Bodine's daughters. I played my role as well as I could, almost slipped up once or twice, but got away with it. He worked for Bryan and Connie as well and as convincingly as he'd worked for the sisters at the convent. He could be very smooth."

"Until he assaulted Tabitha," Pete said.

Susanna nodded slowly. "Twelve years old seems to be a weak spot for him, doesn't it? I was twelve that Christmas when he first touched me." She stopped, waited for Pete to speak. "Aren't you going to ask me why I kept quiet after that happened? How I could *stand* to keep quiet?"

"You were still afraid of him."

"Oh, yes. I was desperately afraid. He was gone, and I knew —some of me knew—that he couldn't come back because he'd blown it all the instant he'd laid a finger on Tabbie. But a greater part of me didn't quite believe that, the part that made me lie awake most of every night waiting in case he did come, break in downstairs or just creep through our window." Susanna paused.

"And then there was the other fear. Of what might happen if the Van Dusens found out the truth."

"What did you think might happen?" Pete asked.

"I thought they might throw us out," Susanna replied. "Oh, I don't mean that I thought they'd *actually* throw us out, not onto the street. But I knew that if they found out what he'd done to me, there'd have to be an investigation, and the police would get involved, and I was afraid that Abigail and I would be put in some institution, maybe even separated. It had been more than a year since we'd come to live in Cohasset, time enough for me to have grown accustomed to pretending that Abigail was my sister rather than my daughter." She paused. "They were such a wonderful family, Pete. I guess that going on with that charade seemed a small price to pay for staying with them, staying a part of that family."

"And the longer it went on," Pete said, "the harder it became to tell the truth."

"It became impossible," Susanna said. "And to be honest, once I'd made that initial decision, after he'd run away, it never even occurred to me to think of telling the truth." She paused. "I was lying to myself too, as much as to anyone, you see. I know that now. I guess I've always known it. It would have been too painful to face up to. It was so much easier to bury it."

They were quiet for a while.

"You say you were lying to yourself," Pete said. "How close do you think you came to actually forgetting the things that had happened?"

"Pretty close. When you have a past you'd sooner had never happened, it can be surprisingly easy to pretend to forget. Of course, it is only pretense, and you know damned well that's what you're doing, faking, but it works, on an everyday level at least." She winced a little. "I'm a fake, Pete. When you get right down to it, that's what I am."

"Hawke never knew?"

"Never. He knew my real name wasn't Bodine; he found that out before we were married, when he saw my passport. But he knew I didn't want to explain, and he didn't push. Hawke never pushed. Later, when we were married and I found out his first name, which he hated, we made a deal: he wouldn't ask me about my name if I didn't tell a living soul his." She smiled, one of her sad, rueful little smiles. "So he stayed just plain Hawke, and my husband, my foster parents, and my foster sister never knew who I really was. Not even my own child."

Another brief silence flowed between them, stifling, without peace.

"So who are you, Susanna?" Pete asked softly.

"That's a good question."

Pete waited another moment, watching her. "What about your mother?" he asked.

"Bodine told me she was dead," Susanna said, "just before he came to take us from the shack. He told me she'd died of cancer."

"Was that true?"

"Yes."

"Won't you tell me about her?"

"No."

"Why not?"

"Because this is not the time."

Pete lit a fresh cigarette, the last in the pack.

"So tell me about the thing that's happened. The thing that brought you here today."

"All right."

Susanna took the envelope out of her bag and handed it to him. Pete opened it, unfolded the single sheet of paper, and read. His face, impeccably trained over the years, remained impassive, but his eyes grew darker with anger.

"Bodine," he said.

Susanna nodded. "Bodine."

"What are you going to do?"

"I thought, for a moment, that I was going to pay. That I'd do anything to keep Abigail from finding out the truth. Other people, all that nasty stuff about what learning the truth about me would do to my reputation, all that Saint Susanna stuff—that doesn't matter, it really doesn't matter to me. Abigail matters. That's all."

"You said 'for a moment.' You thought you were going to pay."

"That's right."

"And now?"

"Now I know that there's no point, that paying him would

never be the answer." Susanna's jaw felt stiff, and her eyes ached. "It's blackmail—isn't it?—plain old blackmail, and everyone knows that blackmailers never stop, that you can never feed them enough."

"I'm sure that's true," Pete said.

Susanna got up from the couch and walked over to the window. "What would you have me do, Pete? Go to the police?" She shook her head violently. "I won't do that. That would be too much; I'm not strong enough for that."

"I think you're strong enough."

"No." She shook her head again. "Anyway, I'll need my strength for what I do have to do. I no longer have a choice."

"You're going to tell Abigail," he said.

Susanna felt dead inside.

"God help me," she said.

"When will you do it?"

"I'm driving up for New Year's now, right after I leave you. Tabbie's home for the holidays, and we're going to have a family dinner—nothing too wild, Bryan says that Connie's worn out from her last shoot." Susanna paused. "I won't tell them tonight. Tomorrow's soon enough. First day of 1992."

"Fresh start," Pete said.

"That's one way of putting it."

She found Abigail on White Moon Beach shortly after ten o'clock next morning, New Year's morning. It was bitterly cold, with a stiff wind blowing, and though the pale, watery sun was fighting to get through, the heavy clouds scudding westward promised rain or worse within the hour.

Abigail was sitting on a rock not far from the shore, gazing out to sea. She wore a heavy sweater, denims and boots, no hat. Slowly, her hands deep in the pockets of her parka, Susanna walked toward her.

"You'll catch your death."

Abigail looked up at her and smiled, a sweet, contented smile. "I feel great."

"This always was one of your favorite places," Susanna said.

"I can't think of anywhere I'd rather start the year." Abigail patted the rock beside her. "Join me?"

Susanna stayed on her feet, drinking in Abigail's upturned face, so open and welcoming, so blissfully unaware of what was to come. "I have something to tell you," she said, and her voice caught in her throat.

"What?" Abigail caught her sister's tension. "Have a seat. Tell me what's up."

Susanna got down on the wet sand, on her knees.

"Not on the ground," Abigail said. "You'll freeze."

Susanna said nothing and stayed where she was. Abigail looked down at her, and something in her face changed. Susanna observed the change, saw the swift ripple of fear, and she realized abruptly that Abigail was afraid she was going to tell her that she was sick. A reminder, if she needed one, of how much Abigail loved her. But though she knew that she could, with a few words, at least dispel that fear, Susanna still waited another long moment, wanting to absorb the way this beloved girl felt about her now— *now*, before she changed everything forever.

"I'm not sick," she said at last. "In case that's what you were thinking."

She felt Abigail's relief almost tangibly. For one more instant she savored it.

And then she began.

Abigail was silent when Susanna finished. Motionless, apart from her long hair blowing in the stiff ocean wind. Her face was a snow white mask. She looked as if she were about to faint. But she did not faint. She just sat perfectly still, at one with the rock, looking into Susanna's eyes for what seemed an eternity. And then she stood up, without a word, and began to walk away.

"Abigail." Susanna, still on her knees, could not move, could only watch as her daughter walked, like a stiff-legged doll, away from her. "Abigail, wait." She struggled to her feet, but her legs, ankles, and feet were numb from kneeling too long in the cold, wet sand.

Abigail went on walking.

"Abigail!" Susanna called, but her voice seemed to carry out to sea on the wind, and she couldn't be sure if her daughter heard her. "*Abigail!*" she yelled with all her strength.

Abigail began to run.

Susanna did not follow. She longed to, more than anything,

but she knew that Abigail did not want her to follow, that she wanted, needed to be alone for a while. When she was ready, she would come back. If she was ever ready.

She did come back a little less than an hour later. Susanna, sitting on the rock, noted even from a distance the aggressive hunch of her daughter's shoulders, the determination of her stride, and felt her stomach shrivel with apprehension. And then Abigail was right in front of her, and her face was more stony now than ashen.

"Do the others know?" Abigail asked.

"No. Not yet. I thought I should tell you first."

"Because you got the letter. If you hadn't, you wouldn't have told me at all, would you?"

"I don't know." Susanna remained sitting, not certain if her legs would hold her if she rose.

"If it weren't for him trying to blackmail you, you'd have gone on lying."

"Perhaps, for the time being." Susanna was determined now to be as honest as possible, however painful it might be. *Too little too late.* Yet it was the only way to try to move now, forward, out of the darkness. "I think I always knew I'd have to tell you some-day, but I would be lying if I said I'd really worked out when that day would be."

"When I was eighteen, maybe?" Abigail's big expressive mouth was drawn tight with disdain. "Or twenty-one? Perhaps when I got married, though that doesn't seem to make any difference to you; you didn't even tell Hawke, did you?"

"No," Susanna said. "I didn't tell him."

Abigail stared down at her, her hair blowing like an aura. "What kind of person are you? How could you let someone marry you and keep all that from him? I mean, it's such"—she sought the right word—"such an *insult* to Hawke."

"I don't think he would have felt that way if he'd known."

"Well, he didn't, and he's dead, so we'll never know either."

Susanna looked up at her daughter. In all the years of her life she had never seen Abigail do or say anything wantonly cruel or even nasty. She could be difficult, be demanding, sometimes churlish, but she'd always hated hurting anyone. Like all the Van Dusens. *But she's a Bodine,* her inner voice taunted her. *Learned characteristics, not inherited ones.* No, Susanna answered back. This reaction had nothing to do with Matthew Bodine's genes; it had to do with the shock of betrayal.

"Won't you sit down?" she asked after a moment, and moved over to make some space on the rock. "Or we could go back to the house. It's very cold here."

"I'm sorry you're uncomfortable." Abigail knelt on the sand as Susanna had an hour earlier.

Susanna closed her eyes for an instant. They were just feet apart, yet the emotional distance between them seemed as agonizing in its way as the greatest of the labor pains she remembered all those years before.

"I love you, Abigail," she said softly. "I loved you from the moment you were born." She shook her head. "I loved you way before that, from the very first second I felt you stir inside me."

"You loved me so much," Abigail said, "that you gave me to another mother."

"What would you have had me do? I was fourteen years old, and Bodine was calling all the shots." Susanna was trying to put herself into Abigail's place, into that torn part of her heart. "And the moment I met Connie, and she was so kind and warm, so special, I knew we'd fallen on our feet." She shook her head. "That sounds almost calculating, doesn't it?"

"Yes," Abigail said, "it does."

"Maybe it was, in a way, though looking back to that time, I find it hard to imagine that there was anything calculating in me. I was a mess, Abigail." The unrelenting coldness on her daughter's face weakened her, but Susanna steeled herself to continue. "You have to try to picture what it was like for me—not all of it, I don't want you ever even to *imagine* what came before. But the time he kept me captive—"

"You weren't locked in."

"But I felt as though I was. Bodine told me he'd know if I so much as stepped outside in daylight. He said that if I told anyone, he would kill me and you. I believed him."

"You're too smart for that."

"I wasn't too smart then. Unless you count not wanting to die. Not wanting my baby to die."

Abigail shook her head. "That doesn't really matter anymore, does it? It's all in the past, all finished." She stood up, walked restlessly a few yards down the beach, closer to the ocean, then turned back as Susanna got up to follow her. "Maybe you couldn't have done anything then," she said, raising her voice against the wind and waves, "but you could have told Mom and Dad the truth, you should have told—" She broke off, and Susanna saw tears glistening in her dark eyes. "What am I supposed to call them now? Do you expect me to call you *Mom?*" There was mockery in the last word, and the tears were brushed angrily away with the back of one gloved hand.

"Of course not," Susanna answered quietly. "Connie is your mother, Abigail. She's been the most wonderful mother to us all." She paused again. "I'll be happy if you just go on thinking of me as your sister."

"My sister who's lied to me my whole life." Abigail turned away again, began to walk again, bigger strides, and Susanna went after her, and this time Abigail did not, at least, run away, and they were walking together, and the hood of Susanna's parka was obscuring her view of her daughter's face, so she pushed it back, and the wind, already bearing the first of the rain, lashed at her cheeks and eyes like needles.

"I can't deny that I lied to you."

"Some mother," Abigail said with spite. "Not to mention my rapist father."

"Bryan's your father."

"Not really."

"Not biologically, no"—Matthew Bodine flashed back before Susanna's mind's eye with a greater clarity than he had for many years—"but I don't think I believe much in biology."

"That's a dumb thing to say."

"Maybe, but when I look at you and remember him, I can't believe in inheritance. You have my hair and my nose. You have his color eyes more or less, though not their expression; your eyes are so warm, so beautiful, and his were brown but very cold. You're a thousand times smarter than I am and far more straightforward. You would not, I daresay, have allowed those things to happen to you, and I doubt you'd have kept them shut up inside you if they had."

"You're right," Abigail said. "I wouldn't."

They went on walking, facing into the wind. Down on the shore a small brown and white bird that Susanna could not identify stood looking out to sea, beating its wings but going nowhere.

"Your so-called biological father is a beast"—Susanna went on in quiet desperation—"whereas you are a kind, warm, intelligent, gentle person. Some of those traits have been learned from Connie and Bryan and Tabbie, but most of them were just born inside you. You are your own person, Abigail."

A flicker of cruelty passed over Abigail's eyes. "I used to be so proud of being the famous Susanna Van Dusen's sister."

A little more sorrow flowed into Susanna, a little more fear. With her hair flying, broad-shouldered and tall, Abigail seemed suddenly as intimidating as one of the Furies.

"Until today"—Abigail continued—"I never stopped being proud of being your sister—not even when I got really mad at you when Hawke was dying and, later, all those times you wouldn't let me get close to you in case I got HIV."

"Does that make any more sense to you now than it did?" Susanna looked at her intently. "I mean, I knew it wasn't right or even rational, but there were so few things I'd been able to do to protect you through your life—"

"So you thought you'd start by trying not to give me AIDS."

"I think," Susanna said, "I started by letting Connie and Bryan be your parents."

"You said you had no choice."

"That was true, in the beginning, anyway. Later on I guess I did have choices, and I think I made them for the best. At least that's what I thought then." Susanna paused. "They were still decisions made out of fear, but I do know that if it hadn't been this family he brought us to, I might have chosen differently."

"Is that supposed to make me grateful?"

"No, not grateful. Maybe a little more understanding."

"It doesn't."

Too numbed by the cold and wet, too drained to go on, they left the beach and returned to the house. Abigail walked a little ahead of Susanna, as if stressing by their physical separation that this conversation at least was at an end, that she had no more to say, that she did not wish, could not bear perhaps, to hear any more, and once inside the house, she went directly upstairs to her bedroom and closed the door.

Susanna found the others in the kitchen. Tabitha and Bryan were putting together the first lunch of the year, while Connie was sitting in her wheelchair at the big oak table, doing a crossword puzzle in the newspaper, a cup of coffee in front of her.

She told them right away. It was the third time in less than twenty-four hours she had recounted the tale, and it came more easily this time, slipped from her lips almost mechanically, and it was all right so long as she didn't look at their faces while she was speaking, for she knew that if she looked into their eyes, she would be unable to continue, to reach the end. And when she did at last arrive at that moment, Susanna found she could go no farther, could endure no more questions, and she told them it was Abigail who needed them now, and all she wanted, all that mattered was that they should see to her, take care of her, as they had always done.

Later that long, long day Connie came to Susanna's room.

"How is she?" Susanna asked.

"Quiet," Connie answered, just inside the door. "How are you?"

Susanna shook her head. "I'm so sorry," she said.

"What in the name of heaven do you have to be sorry about?" Connie wheeled herself farther into the room and pushed the door shut behind her. "I'm the one who's sorry—mostly, right this moment, because I can't just do what I really want to do. I can't jump out of this damned chair and put my arms around you." Her blue eyes were full of angry tears.

"Is she still in her room?" Susanna asked very softly.

"She is." Connie saw the despair in Susanna's eyes. "She'll come around, you know."

"Will she?"

"Of course she will."

"When her whole world's been ripped apart?"

"Her world's still intact," Connie said. "All the people who love her, whom Abigail loves, are still alive, still here for her. She'll realize that soon enough." She looked at Susanna, in the armchair near the window, looked intently at the beautiful woman she had loved as her daughter for so many years. "I'm still reeling about what you've been through."

"It was a long time ago," Susanna said.

"And you've been suffering from it ever since." Connie was deeply troubled. "Abigail's had a shock, but she's also had fifteen contented years, while you had to give up your child, to stand back and watch while someone else—while I—took her over, stole her from you."

"You loved her for me," Susanna said. "You took care of her in a way I couldn't have done, not at that age."

Connie looked at her as if she were really seeing her for the first time. "I always knew you were an extraordinary person. You were so quiet, so adult when you first came to us. Bryan and I guessed that some bad things had maybe happened to you in the past, but neither of us ever, for a single *instant*, conjured up anything like this."

"Why would you?" Susanna said. "How could anyone?"

"I can't let myself off the hook that easily. I should have known. Your love for Abigail was so powerful, so overwhelming. I just assumed it was especially intense because you'd lost both your parents."

"It was a reasonable assumption."

"Was it?" Connie shook her head. "I was a woman in my thirties with a ten-year-old child of my own. It's *outrageous* to think I saw no sign of what you'd just been through."

"I was okay by the time I came here," Susanna said gently. "I was strong and healthy and very, very lucky."

"Which is nothing more than a miracle." Connie gave a shudder.

"I don't believe in miracles," Susanna said.

Connie took a moment before she spoke again. "When Bodine assaulted Tabbie and ran out on you and Abigail, Bryan and I began to wonder if he'd ever laid a hand on you. But then I think we both put it out of our minds, partly because you seemed so content but mostly, I guess, because it was too unbearable to contemplate." She paused. "We used to think about your mother. We wondered if she'd had a very hard time with Bodine, and we talked about the kind of effect that might have had on you." Connie paused again. "Did she have a hard time?"

"I don't know," Susanna said.

"You always said so little about your mother."

"There wasn't much to say," Susanna said, and turned her face away.

Bryan came a little later, brought her a bowl of beef broth, held her in his arms for a while, then watched and waited, as if she were a small child, while she lifted the spoon to her lips and drank the soup until a little color had returned to her cheeks.

"I'm going to call the police," he said at last.

"No," Susanna said, her eyes horrified.

"Are you kidding? Why not?"

"Because of Abigail."

Bryan's eyes narrowed. "You're not thinking of paying him."

"No," she said.

"Thank God for that, at least."

"I did think of paying when I first read the letter." Susanna shook her head in wonder. "Was that only yesterday morning? It seems such a long time ago."

"Susanna"—Bryan fought to stay calm, to keep his rage against Bodine under control—"we have to bring in the police. If he doesn't get the money, there's no telling what he may do."

"What can he do?" Susanna, setting the empty bowl down on the floor, was matter-of-fact. "He needs cash, that's all he wants. It's been thirteen years; he doesn't give a damn about me or Abigail."

"He's threatening to expose you, baby."

"What can he possibly say to hurt me now that Abigail knows the truth?"

"I think we're missing the biggest point here," Bryan said. "Matthew Bodine isn't just a blackmailer. He's a child rapist and a kidnapper. He's been out there, free as air, for more than a dozen years. For all we know, he may have done it again, maybe even to more than one little girl."

Susanna felt ill. Her daughter's face, chalky white, bobbed in her mind. "You're forgetting Abigail," she said. "Her reaction to this, what a nightmare it must be for her, and now you're talking about setting the police on Bodine—on her *father*—about getting him into court—"

"Which is where he belongs."

"—where the whole world will hear every tiny detail about

how her father raped her mother when she was thirteen years old, about how she was born in a tar paper shack on the beach."

"Abigail would cope if it came to that," Bryan said. "We'd all be with her; it would be all right."

"And Bodine's defense attorney"—Susanna went on as if he hadn't spoken—"will say I wasn't really his prisoner at all, that Bodine was just looking after me, that there was no lock on the door of the shack. That's what Abigail said when I told her, that I could have escaped any time I wanted—" She paused for a quick, shaky breath. "Just as I could have told the truth to the family who took me and my child into their home." Susanna's eyes were haunted; she could see Bryan's dismay, see his anguish. "They'll say that I'm a liar, and no one, not even you, will be able to deny it, and I don't mind it for myself, but Abigail will mind—"

"Susanna, stop it."

"I can't stop. I have to make you see what could happen."

"It wouldn't be that way, and even if it were, we'd all be there together." Bryan got up from the bed, came and crouched beside the armchair, took her still-cold hands in his, tried to warm her. "And for the moment, my darling, I just want Bodine stopped, so that he can't threaten you anymore, can't torment you anymore."

Susanna sat still and limp.

"Sweetheart?" Bryan watched her anxiously. "Let me call the police."

"No," she said. "Not with Abigail the way she is."

"But it's for Abigail as much as anyone."

Susanna shook her head.

"No," she said again. "No."

Tabitha, coming last, was loving, forgiving, and outspoken, the way Tabitha always had been.

"Why don't you hate me?" Susanna asked her.

"Why should I?" Tabitha was startled.

"Because of what he did to you."

"You're not responsible for what that pervert did."

"If I'd told the truth, it wouldn't have happened."

"If you'd told the truth at the start, neither of you would have come to live with us, and I'd have been an only child." Tabitha shook her head. "Anyway, he did me no real harm. I got away, didn't I, before he could do anything. And I had my parents to run to. And you to comfort me."

Susanna said nothing.

"Promise me something," Tabitha said.

"If I can."

"Promise you won't pay the son of a bitch."

"I won't pay him."

"And you'll let Dad call the cops."

"No. I've already told him. I don't want that. Not yet anyway."

"I think you're wrong," Tabitha said.

"I know you do."

They were silent for a while, thinking, being still, Susanna in the armchair, Tabitha on the bed, feet drawn up under her.

"How did Pete take it?" Tabitha broke the silence.

"He was shocked," Susanna replied. "I mean, he seemed calm about it, professional, the way Pete always is, but I knew he was very shocked."

"But yours isn't just a professional relationship anymore, is it?"

"No, it isn't," Susanna said. "We're partners in Hawke House, and we're very good friends."

"Still just good friends?"

"Of course. What else?"

"Abigail says Pete's in love with you."

"She says what?" Susanna was startled.

Tabitha smiled. "She told me after she went up to see you at Hawke House a couple of weeks ago. She said that she'd talked to Pete about it."

"Abigail told you that?" Surprise gave way to alarm.

"And according to her, Pete didn't deny it, thought he said he was sure you didn't feel the same way, and when Abigail told him she thought you did, he made her swear not to mention it to you." Tabitha smiled again. "She told him she wanted him to be her next brother-in-law."

"God." Susanna was mortified.

"Doesn't sound all that awful to me. I think Pete Strauss is a really good guy." Tabitha paused. "What do you think, Susanna?"

"You know what I think about Pete."

"Not really."

"Sure you do."

"Yeah, yeah," Tabitha said, "we all know you think he's nice and kind and a great shrink and a wonderful all-around human being, but the question is, do you love him?" She stopped, observed the lingering wretchedness in Susanna's face. "This is not the moment."

"No."

"You look exhausted."

"I think I am," Susanna admitted. "I might try to catch some sleep now." A raw flicker of hope touched her eyes. "Unless you think Abigail might be ready to talk to me."

"I don't think so," Tabitha said gently. "Not yet."

"No." Susanna felt tears threatening.

"Give her tonight," Tabitha suggested. "Let her get some rest too. You can both start again in the morning."

"Yes." Suddenly Susanna felt a desperate need to be alone, to lie down and close her eyes and shut it all out for a while.

Tabitha got up from the bed. "Connie wanted to know if you needed anything."

"No," Susanna said. "Thank you."

"She suggested a hot-water bottle?"

"No. I'm okay."

"If you change your mind, just holler."

"I will."

"And if you can't sleep, come into my room."

"I think I'll sleep."

At the door Tabitha turned once more. "Abigail loves you, Susanna. You're her heroine. You always have been."

"Not anymore," Susanna said.

She found Abigail at seven next morning on the porch, sitting on the swing seat, knees bent, feet up on the seat, arms around her legs, hugging them. It was another cold day, and the swing groaned as it moved in the wind.

"Mind if I join you?" Susanna asked softly.

Abigail shrugged. "It's not my porch." She waited as Susanna sat down beside her, moving carefully, leaving plenty of space between them. "I figured you'd be out."

"You don't mind?"

"I didn't say that."

Susanna looked around at the old familiar deck, at the land-marks she knew so well. The porch, the rose trellis around the front door, the low two-log fence, and the wooden ramp for Connie's wheelchair had been the first things she'd seen when Bodine had brought them here all those years before. There had been a few coats of paint since then, and there were no roses today, but otherwise nothing significant had altered.

"I am so, so sorry," she said after a few moments, her voice low, catching with the tears she had not let herself shed since last night, feeling she had no right to the release, to the temporary relief of tears. "I don't know what else to say to you. I don't know what I can do to make things right between us again."

"Things can never be the same again," Abigail said.

"Not the same as they were." Susanna longed to put out her hand, but held it back. "But maybe they can still be right again."

Abigail said nothing. Susanna studied her profile. She looked so strong, yet she was still so young, mature perhaps for her years, yet still so vulnerable.

"I thought—" She groped for the right words. "I honestly believed I was doing the right thing, keeping it from you, from the family."

"I know that."

"Do you?"

"Sure." Abigail's voice was huskier than usual. "That doesn't mean I think you *were* right."

"No. I can see that."

"Tell me something."

"Anything. If I can."

Abigail looked right at her for an instant, then turned her face away again, as if looking into Susanna's eyes might make her weaken. "I've been sitting here thinking," she said. "I spent a lot of last night doing that, just rolling it over and over in my mind."

"Me too."

"You've had fifteen years to think about it." Briefly Abigail turned accusing eyes on her. "I've only had one night."

Susanna flushed. "I know. I'm sorry."

Abigail looked away again, back toward the road. "So what I want to know is this." She took a breath. "If you loved me so much, why did you leave me?"

"I didn't leave you."

"Sure you did. The minute Hawke came along and told you how gorgeous you were, you were off like a rocket."

Susanna was silent for a moment. "I thought you liked Hawke."

Abigail's chin went up. "I adored him."

"Then what are you saying exactly? That I shouldn't have married him?"

Abigail shook her head, and her hair blew in the wind. "No, that's not what I'm saying." She paused. "You didn't leave home to get married. You didn't marry Hawke for years after that." She looked at Susanna again. "You gave me—the daughter you claim you loved so much—exactly four years of your life."

"I didn't leave you, Abigail," Susanna said, her voice strained. "I did what most sisters put in that position would probably do."

"Only you weren't my sister, were you?"

They fell silent. From nowhere in particular a piece of bright, shiny yellow paper came skimming through the air between the porch and the road, trapped for a moment or two by the wind, spinning like a manic paper canary until, released again, it was carried on, eastward and away.

"It hurt me, Abigail. Leaving home, going with Hawke. Leaving you."

"It can't have hurt all that much," Abigail countered, "or you wouldn't have gone."

"You're wrong," Susanna said.

Abigail shrugged. "Maybe." The swing seat groaned, and her hair blew into her eyes and she brushed it away. "What are you going to do about the letter?" she asked abruptly.

"I'm not sure."

"Are you going to pay?"

"No. I don't think so." Susanna paused. "Bryan wants to tell the police."

"Oh."

"If they catch him—if he goes to trial—it could be a very tough time."

"I guess it could," Abigail said. "For you."

"For us all." Susanna took a breath. "That's why I think you should be part of the decision process."

"A little late to start considering my feelings, isn't it?"

Susanna's fingers gripped the edge of the wooden seat, her

nails digging in, once perfectly manicured nails, blunt nowadays and workmanlike. "I've always considered your feelings. You may not believe that, but you've always come first."

"I don't believe it."

"That's your prerogative. I still think it's important you give this police idea some thought." Susanna paused. "You don't have to talk to me about it. Talk to the others—talk to Tabbie. A trial would drag us all through it, Abigail, you most of all. For myself, I don't mind—I really, really don't mind, and a part of me would love to see him punished for what he did to me—"

"You must really hate him," Abigail said thoughtfully.

"In some ways."

"He made you have a baby, at fourteen."

Susanna looked up, her eyes intent on her daughter's face. "If you're trying to get me to say that I've ever regretted having you, you're out of luck, Abigail." Emotion strengthened her voice. "You were his greatest gift to me. Even back then, while I was alone and scared for all those months, I felt grateful to him for that. Which is why I don't think I ever have been able to really hate him. He raped me. He terrorized me. But he also gave you to me."

Abigail was silent for a long moment. "I'd like to stop talking about this now."

"But we need to talk," Susanna said.

"We've talked."

"There's still so much more to say."

"Not now." Abigail's face was set and unreadable. "Please."

In despair, very slowly, Susanna stood up.

"Try to understand what I did," she said. "What I felt I had to do."

Abigail said nothing.

"Please."

"You're asking a lot," Abigail said.

"I know I am."

CHAPTER 15

～

The decision made not to bring the police into the situation, at least for the time being, Susanna left Cohasset and returned to Hawke House. Two weeks of January had passed, communication with Abigail had remained stiff and fruitless, and so finally, heartsick and frustrated, Susanna had gone.

"Leaving," Abigail said to Tabitha in the kitchen minutes after she'd driven away. "I guess that's what she's best at."

"Did you give her any real choice?" Tabitha had originally planned to stay home for only a week, but after Susanna's bombshell she'd hung in, still hoping to help in some way.

"Don't misunderstand me." Abigail tossed her hair. "I'm glad she's gone. I was beginning to feel suffocated, knowing she was always there, waiting for me to forgive her, like some pathetic puppy."

"You know something?" Tabitha said. "I'm beginning to feel really pissed off with you, Abigail. Why don't you stop being such a selfish little jerk, for crying out loud, and start thinking about other people for a change?"

"Like sweet Susanna, you mean." Abigail sat down hard at the table, scraping her chair over the tiles.

"Yes, I do mean." Tabitha spooned instant coffee into her mug and waited for the kettle to boil. "We've all told you—you *know* what she went through to have you, to keep you safe, the danger Bodine put her in."

"She might have died," Abigail said flatly. "I might have died. What about the danger she put you in by coming here with him?"

"She was fourteen, and she was in shock."

"That's only a year younger than me, and how long is shock meant to last anyway?"

Gritting her teeth, Tabitha poured boiling water into her mug and set the kettle back on the stove before coming to sit at the table. "You think you're so grown-up, Abigail, but I've got to say you're really showing your immaturity. Worse than that, I never dreamed you were this insensitive."

"I probably take after my father," Abigail said, flushing.

"Perhaps you do," Tabitha said steadily. "Though I can't say I'd ever noticed it before, so I doubt it." She spooned sugar into her coffee, took a sip, and put the mug down again, watched her foster sister for a moment, thought she caught a glimpse of the struggle she knew must be happening behind the obstinate exterior.

"You disagree with her and Mom about not bringing in the cops, don't you?" Abigail asked after a few moments.

"I'd like to see him locked away, yes."

"So would Dad."

"Yes. But it isn't his call any more than it is mine."

"He hurt you."

"He tried to." Tabitha paused. "You do realize that Susanna and Mom are both trying to protect you, don't you?"

"Because he's my real father." Her tone was ironic.

"Don't you believe they want to protect you?"

Abigail looked steadily back at her. "If it were just Susanna saying it, I'm not sure I'd believe her, but I don't think Mom's ever lied to me."

Slowly Tabitha shook her head. "You still don't get it, do you?"

"I guess not."

"You honestly don't understand how lucky you are."

"To have two mothers, you mean."

"That's it." Tabitha got up. "I give up."

"You haven't finished your coffee," Abigail said, startled.

"To hell with my coffee."

"I'm sorry," Abigail said abruptly.

Tabitha picked up her mug and took it over to the sink.

"I mean it," Abigail said. "I hate it when we fight."

"We're not fighting. I just don't like you very much right now."

The fifteen-year-old stayed at the table, one hand clenched furiously in her lap, battling suddenly to suppress unwanted, treacherous tears. "Don't you understand how I feel, Tabbie?" she asked, half plaintive, half raging. "Don't my feelings count at all anymore?"

"Sure they count." Tabitha turned around, exasperated. "But they're so *misplaced*, don't you see that? Can't you see that all Susanna ever wanted, from the very beginning, was to have you healthy and happy? And she achieved that, didn't she?"

"By lying to Mom and Dad and you."

"Yes, if you like, by lying—and later she lied to you too, but it was a means to an end, don't you *see* that, Abigail? Survival, first and foremost, and then the best darned quality of life she could have for you."

"She had a good life too," Abigail said, softly, knowing she was losing but still clinging to her stubbornness with the remains of her strength.

"Do you begrudge her that?" Tabitha asked. "Don't you have to admit she might have earned a little peace, a little ease, though Lord knows she didn't have it for long, did she?"

"She didn't even tell Hawke the truth."

"And don't you think that cost her?"

"I guess it must have." Abigail's voice was scarcely above a whisper.

Tabitha returned to the table and sat down. "Well, thank Christ for small mercies," she said.

On Friday morning, two days after Susanna had returned to Hawke House, the telephone in her office rang. It was a soft, bleating sound and one to which she was well accustomed, yet on this occasion Susanna, filling her Waterman fountain pen with blue ink, was so startled that she knocked over the bottle.

"Hello?" she said into the phone, abstractedly, as she tried with an inadequate Kleenex to stem the flow of royal blue liquid swiftly spreading itself over her desk, down the side and onto the red rug below.

"It's me."

It had been more than thirteen years since she'd heard his voice, but she knew it immediately. Her legs turned to jelly, and she sat down quickly, the ink-wet tissue falling from her fingers, the stain forgotten.

"Hi, Saint Susanna," he said, amiably. "How're you doing?"

"What do you want?" Her own voice sounded cracked, faint.

"I know you got my letter," he said. "I know you went right on over to see your shrink, and then you went home to dear old Connie and Bryan. How are they, by the way? How's little Tabbie? Not so little now, is she?"

"What do you want?" she said again.

"Don't play games," he said. "You didn't answer my questions; you didn't tell me how the family is. Not that I care. There's only one person I care about in that house."

Susanna watched the ink sinking comfortably into the rug. She said nothing. Her body was clenched tight; she felt as if a steel rod had been forced through her from head to toes.

"How is our daughter?" he asked. "How is Abigail?"

Susanna sat up even straighter, gripped the receiver harder, coming to.

"No," she said.

"That isn't the answer to my question."

"No, you're not getting the money."

"If that's a joke, it isn't very funny."

"No joke," Susanna said, gathering strength.

"Maybe you didn't understand my meaning, in the letter, that is."

"I believe I understood it well enough. If I don't give you fifty thousand dollars, you're going to expose my past. It's called blackmail."

"That's an ugly word, Susanna."

"What would you call it?"

"I'd call it sharing. With the father of your child. People do that." There was a smile in his voice, the old, sneering smile that she remembered had always preceded some special cruelty. "I'm sure our daughter's important to you."

"There's no one more important."

"And who gave her to you?"

"Abigail isn't a possession or a package," Susanna said, struggling to stay on top of the conversation. "No one *gave* her to me."

The voice grew more belligerent. "Are you denying she's my daughter?"

"In a purely biological sense, no, of course I'm not denying that."

"Are you denying that I took care of you when you needed it?"

Susanna's laugh was short and very bitter. "That may have worked fifteen years ago, but I know better now, believe me." She took a breath. "No money."

"Fifty thousand's nothing to a rich woman like you—Susanna Van Dusen, supermodel, faggot champion."

"No fifty thousand," she rapped. "Not one thousand. Not a single dollar. And if you ever, *ever*, try anything like this again, I swear to you I'll see you in jail."

"You're making a big mistake if you think I'm just going to melt—"

"I don't think so," Susanna interrupted him. "You see, there's nothing you can do to me anymore. Abigail knows everything, the whole sordid truth. So you do see, don't you, that even if you do try to sell your version of the story—and I don't doubt it would be juicier and smuttier than my own—and even if it does get printed in some rag all over America, I don't honestly give a damn."

There was a long pause, so long that for a moment she thought they might have been disconnected, but then she heard his breathing and realized he was probably too angry to speak.

"You're going to regret this, Susanna," he said very quietly. "There are so many ways I can still hurt you."

"No. I'm never going to regret it." She was right on top now, in command, and she was startled by how good that felt. "You're a child rapist, Matthew Bodine. You're a kidnapper. You're a blackmailer. You're not the kind of man decent people pay much heed to." She took one last deep, purifying breath. "And as far as I'm concerned, you can go straight to hell."

She put down the telephone and looked down at her still-trembling hands. They were smeared with ink, and the blue stains were everywhere, on the phone, on her papers, on the rug, on her skirt. They didn't matter; at this moment they would not have mattered if they'd spread right over the ceiling or onto her favorite Dior white silk blouse.

The words that had flown into her mind the day, almost a year earlier, when she had visited poor Maria Alonso's grave at the Jackson Heights cemetery, came back to her now. *Free at last.* Free of Matthew Bodine.

It felt better than good.

Verging on euphoria, she called Pete in New York and told him what had transpired. Eager to know exactly what Bodine had said, anxious that Susanna was on some temporary and perhaps unrealistic high, Pete made plans to come up to Hawke House that Sunday. He arrived, with Steinbeck, in time for brunch. They ate alone in Susanna's sitting room, omelets with crab meat and bagels and cream cheese bought by Pete in Manhattan that morning.

"I don't like the sound of his threats," he said, his omelet eaten—with Steinbeck's help—and embarking on a second bagel. "I think maybe you should still contact the police."

"No need," Susanna said, drinking orange juice.

"I disagree." Pete paused. "And so does Bryan."

"Has Bryan enlisted your help then?"

"Don't be angry."

"I'm not." She wasn't. Tabitha had called her the previous evening to tell her that she thought Abigail was starting to come to terms with her shock, so her spirits were still too high to be seriously dented.

"Bryan's worried about you."

"I know he is."

"So am I."

"There's no need," she repeated.

"Just for protection," Pete persisted. "Even if you don't want to press charges against the son of a bitch, a man like that, watching you, threatening you—what if he tries something?"

"Like what?" Susanna's calm was genuine. "He's all bluff, Pete. He wanted the money. Finding out that he wasn't going to get it and that he has no real hold over me made him mad. He knows how lucky he is that the police haven't been brought in; he knows he'd be crazy to try anything else now." She shook her head decisively. "Matthew Bodine may be warped, but he doesn't want to go to jail."

Pete drained the last drops of coffee from his cup.

"Shall I make some more?" Susanna asked.

He shook his head. "Not for me." He grimaced as he lit a cigarette. "I'm trying to cut down."

"It'd be better if you cut down on those instead," she commented.

"Tell me about it." He was wry. He inhaled deeply. "Susanna, you seem to be overlooking the fact that the man's dangerous."

"But only a certain kind of dangerous," she said. "He goes after young girls."

Pete hesitated only briefly. "What about Abigail?"

Susanna shook her head. "She's fifteen, going on twenty. Abigail's smart, and pretty mature—not Bodine's scene at all." Her cheeks colored a little. "He likes them at twelve, thirteen, tops. He likes children." She paused. "And he likes to con people, to lull them into a false sense of trust; that's when he pounces. If he is going to get up to his old tricks, he won't get up to them around us."

"Doesn't that trouble you?" Pete asked. "Some twelve-year-old someplace being put at risk because he's roaming free as a bird."

"Of course it troubles me, a great deal," Susanna answered. "But Abigail has to be more important to me. I've thought it all through very carefully, Pete, believe me, and I may not be right to feel that way, but more than anything at this moment, I need to get her back on track, with herself as well as with me."

Pete shrugged. "So no police."

"No police."

They put on down jackets and went for a walk in the woods. Steinbeck snuffled around in the undergrowth and caught a couple of sticks Susanna threw for him, but he'd never gotten the hang of bringing them back, seemed happy just trotting around their feet holding the stick in his mouth, so Susanna stopped tossing them.

"Can we talk serious stuff for a moment?" Pete asked her.

"So long as it has nothing to do with calling the police."

"Not a thing."

"Okay."

It was cold and damp, the dead leaves, moss, and bracken underfoot squelching from the rain that had fallen the previous night, but the winter sun was shining this afternoon, and the scent filling their nostrils was pungent but invigorating.

"Some things have been bothering me since we last talked," Pete said. "I've done some reading about adolescent mothers and the risks pregnancy presents to them, and frankly, I'm staggered to think how remarkably easily—physically at least—you came through it all."

"I know," Susanna said. "I've done my own reading."

"So you know how close you came to so many problems."

"I do." She kicked at a branch, and Steinbeck skittered away like a pup. "I can give you the whole list if you like. Toxemia, anemia, urinary tract infections." She rattled them off like meaningless statistics. "He might have given me gonorrhea, or syphilis, or Lord knows what. I had an inadequate pelvis, so I might have had a fistula, which would probably have made the rest of my life a misery." She stopped walking. "But I didn't get any of those things. I didn't even get any stretch marks to speak of."

"Abigail might have died," Pete said.

"Yes, she might."

"And so might you."

"Yes. But I didn't."

They began walking again, very slowly, their breath steaming in the cold air. Steinbeck, sensing a dip in their moods, ceased fooling around and walked sedately at his master's heel. Susanna looked around, at the trees, up through their barren branches into the blue sky, and she was aware that while she always loved walking in these woods, as she had grown to love Hawke House itself, she often experienced pangs of loneliness. When Pete Strauss was around, the place had a different feel, warmer, perhaps safer. She felt different; she felt safer with Pete than she thought she had ever felt with anyone. Hawke had made her happy, but her love for him had always been edged with excitement and perhaps a tinge of something approaching fear. Not of Hawke, of course— she had never, for a single instant, had cause to be afraid of him—but she did realize now, looking back, even to the most secure period of their early marriage, before he'd fallen sick, that she had always been afraid that it might not last, that she might somehow lose him.

"I have to ask you something," she said after a while.

"Go ahead."

"Tabitha says Abigail told you that you're in love with me." She threw him a swift glance, saw the fleeting, unguarded shock in his face, watched him quickly recover as they walked. "I've been wondering," she said, "if maybe that means you ought not to be my shrink anymore."

Pete did not look at her. "Maybe."

"Does that mean Abigail was right?"

Pete slowed to pick up a stick, held it out to Steinbeck, teasing him, giving himself time before he answered. "If she was," he said, "how would that make you feel?"

"Can't you give me a straight answer?"

"I'd rather not, not while I'm still your counselor."

She smiled. "You're tap dancing."

"We both are."

"I know."

Pete stopped walking, put out his free hand to halt her, let it rest briefly on her left arm, then dropped it back by his side. His eyes were on her face, searching, the usually cool, calm, practiced eyes alight suddenly with a hope that he had never, through the five or so years that he'd known her, dared entertain.

"Do you think we're finished yet, professionally?" His heart was beating faster than it ought; he commanded himself to steady, to simmer down, but failed.

"You mean, do I think I need to go on being counseled?" Susanna asked.

"That's what I mean."

"Probably," she said.

He waited an instant. "I could always recommend you to someone else."

"Could you?" she asked lightly.

"If you wanted me to." He paused. "Do you want me to, Susanna?" He observed laughter in her face, somewhere behind her eyes, yet he felt sure there was no mockery there, that she was not laughing at him.

"I think—"

"Yes?"

"I think I should give the matter some thought."

"Of course," he said.

"There's no hurry, after all, is there?" Susanna asked.

Pete thought, abruptly, that his heart might burst with impatience.

"No hurry at all," he said.

And they walked on.

CHAPTER 16

~

Matthew Bodine was not a happy man. He was only forty-eight years old, and Jesus knew he'd tried to keep himself in shape all his life. He'd always prided himself on his strength, his muscular build, his arms and thighs and pecs and the stomach muscles he could tighten at will and wet a woman's cunt at twenty paces. But now he had arthritis. Goddamned *arthritis*, for fuck's sake, slowing him down, swelling his joints, turning him into an old man before his time.

And the bitch wasn't going to pay him.

He'd never asked her for anything before. Not a dime, not even a look at his daughter. She'd had the kind of life women all over the world dreamed of: happy family, secure home, a kid, a career that had made her rich and famous. And all of it had come about through him. *He'd* given it to her, all of it. He'd seen her safely through her pregnancy; he'd found the big house, the people; he'd transformed her into Susanna Van Dusen. It was because of him that she'd gotten the chance to make something of herself. She'd even met her pervert husband because of him. The faggot photographer, Connie Van Dusen's buddy and Susanna's leg up into the big time.

If he hadn't taken her out of that convent, she'd have done some typing course or some other dull old thing, ended up a secretary or a maid or a cook or a salesclerk or whatever. She'd have been a nothing, a nobody.

And she'd never have had the one person who seemed to mean more to her than anyone else in the universe. Abigail. Her daughter.

Their daughter.

He'd never asked for *anything* till now. He'd left her and the kid behind in that beautiful, safe house when he might just as easily have dragged them with him when the Van Dusen brat had forced him to run. It rankled still. He knew he'd made a mistake with Tabitha, choosing a spoiled rich bitch with her daddy on tap to come to her aid. He'd learned his lesson that day, had gone back after that to picking on the poorer, the vulnerable, less sophisticated ones, and some of them pretended they didn't like it, but some of them made no pretense at all, just lay back and wriggled their sweet, untouched little fannies, and let him teach them what he knew so well.

Susanna had pretended she hadn't liked it, and he'd never been a fool; he'd realized the fear was real enough, and what a turn-on that had been, what a power kick. And she was the only one he'd made pregnant. All these years of fucking around, and only one kid that he knew of in the whole goddamned country.

Abigail.

He had been watching her for a while now too, as well as her mother. She was very like Susanna to look at, though she had his brown eyes, which made him feel kind of good. But there was a lot of Tabitha there too, more of the rich bitch, in the way she held herself, that cocksure, youthful confidence, that come-on swing of the hips and shoulders, that idle tossing back off the face of the shining golden hair. Not his kind at all. Not in that way at least.

Besides, she was his own flesh and blood, and in his book that was the one thing a man didn't do, whatever his appetites. She was his kid, and it pissed hell out of him that he couldn't even get to pass the time of day with her, but he'd screwed that up, and he recognized that had been his own failure, and he'd never sought to blame Susanna for that; he wasn't an unfair man.

All he wanted was some money. He needed hard cash. He'd worked like a dog all his life, he'd never been choosy, he'd done what he was able, what was available, all of it menial, often back-breaking, sometimes demeaning work, and he'd never griped about it. He'd gotten by. The way Susanna would probably have gotten by if he hadn't given her her break. The way most ordinary folk in this drab old world always got by, or didn't, depending on whether they were strong or weak. He'd always been strong, but now his body—the one thing he'd always been able to depend on—was betraying him.

He'd only asked her for fifty thousand bucks, for Christ's sake, not a goddamned million! Everyone knew about supermodels, the big bucks they could earn in a single day. He'd read all about Susanna and about the money she'd made; okay, they'd said she might have made a lot more if she hadn't tied herself to Hawke, but he still had the cuttings about some megabucks cosmetics deal she'd signed up for a few years back, and he remembered his eyes had practically popped right out of his head when he'd read the figures, and even if it was true what he'd read since then about her putting a lot of her own dough into Hawke House, she still had to be rolling in it.

She'd called him names. He felt a sick rage rising up in his gullet when he thought about them. Rapist. Kidnapper. Blackmailer. Not once had she chosen to remember what he'd done for her, all those months when he'd kept her and Abigail alive, when he'd seen her eyes light up as he'd come through the door of the shack with some new thing she needed.

There's nothing you can do to me anymore, she'd said. So uppity, so sure of herself. Not a morsel of gratitude left in her. Not an ounce of fear. Well, he was going to show her who was still boss. His joints might be sore and creaking, and all the docs said it was going to get worse, but he still had what it took, was still stronger than the average guy, and he still had it up top, too. He had plans.

He was watching. Susanna thought she was safe now, he knew she'd believed her own words, that there was nothing more he could do to hurt her. But he was watching them, all of them, biding his time. Waiting for the right moment.

He knew it would come.

CHAPTER 17

~

Connie called Susanna the following weekend.

"She's really coming around. Tabbie's worked a small miracle, I'd say."

Susanna felt her heart rate quicken. "You think I should come back?"

"Maybe not just yet, but soon."

"I don't want to wait too long." Susanna was anxious.

"You won't," Connie said. "But I think Abigail needs a little more time away from you, a little more space."

"Meaning I might blow it." A touch of hurt colored Susanna's tone.

"No, that's not what I mean." Connie was patient. "But if you come too soon, I do think you might set things a pace back instead of forward. Think of it from her point of view, sweetheart: so much new information to absorb, about you, about your past and all that it means to her and to the two of you as a unit. Until she's ready to talk to you some more about it all, I'd say she needs to be away from you."

"When do you think she will be ready?"

"My guess is that it won't be all that long, and that when she is, she'll be the first to tell you."

"What if she feels too awkward?" Susanna asked. "The last time we saw each other, she wasn't exactly warmly disposed to me."

"Abigail's not an especially stiff-necked girl." Connie reassured her. "I'd be surprised if she let pride get in her way."

"So what do I do? It's driving me crazy doing nothing."

"Just be patient a little longer."

"That's easier said than done," Susanna said.

"Believe me, I know something about patience." Connie was a little wry.

Susanna winced at her foster mother's rare reference to her own restricted lifestyle. "I'm sorry, Connie. I'm being very selfish."

"You're just being human." Connie paused. "You're being a mother."

Three days later, on the last Tuesday in January, Abigail called Susanna at a quarter past seven in the morning, as Susanna was about to go down to the Hawke House gym for a workout.

"Could we meet?" There was no preamble.

"Sure." Susanna was startled, had dropped her towel and sweater on the floor by the telephone. "Shall I come home?"

"No." Abigail answered swiftly. "And I'd rather not come to the house, if you don't mind. Could we meet somewhere else— Woodstock maybe?"

"But that's so far for you to come."

"It's no big deal. I'll come by bus."

Susanna was about to argue, to suggest she come to pick her up, but bit her tongue in time. This was Abigail working out her own terms, and she was entitled to do it her way.

"When will you come?" she asked softly.

"Tomorrow?"

"What about school?"

"I want to take a day off," Abigail said, not asking permission. "Is tomorrow too soon for you?"

"Not a bit." *An hour from now wouldn't be too soon*, she thought. "If you're staying over, we could have dinner at Christy's."

"I'd prefer lunch," Abigail said. "Something easy, like the Corner Cupboard."

"Okay," Susanna said, staying calm. "You want to call me or set a time now?" It was like fixing a business appointment. "I'll be in no rush tomorrow, so it doesn't matter if I have to hang around."

"Let's say one-thirty, depending on the bus."

"One-thirty it is." Susanna paused. "Thank you."

"No problem," Abigail said lightly, and put down the phone.

If Susanna had been a believer, she thought she might have fallen right down on her knees and given thanks.

At twelve-thirty next afternoon Susanna called Pete.

"How should I handle this?"

"You don't need me to tell you that."

"I think I do, or I wouldn't be calling."

"You're calling so I can tell you you'll know exactly how to handle it."

"I wish that were true." Susanna was nervous as a kitten. "It was like talking to a stranger on the phone yesterday."

"You said she was fine."

"Well, she was, but she was so grown up. I felt like the child and she was my big sister."

"That's because she was laying the ground rules."

"Which is good," Susanna said. "It's just that I feel she's about to pass sentence on me."

"I doubt that's true," Pete said.

"I don't know how to treat her, Pete."

"Treat her like Abigail," he replied simply. "Above all, be honest. That's what she wants from you now, more than anything. Whether it hurts either or both of you, the truth is what's going to get you through this."

"Wish me luck," she said, feeling nauseated.

"Break a leg," he said.

"I wish you could be here too."

"Next time," he said.

Susanna called home, and Connie answered.

"She left on time, and she seemed fine."

"Happy fine, or cool fine?"

"Just fine." Connie paused. "Don't make yourself crazy, sweetheart."

"I can't help it."

"Nerves are catching. Try to be natural with her. She'll be feeling scared too, remember."

"But she'll be in the driver's seat," Susanna pointed out.

"I doubt she sees it that way," Connie said. "No matter how much power you know she has over you, Susanna, don't forget that she's half your age; you're still the one with all the experience. She's going to need you to guide her."

"She has you for that, Connie."

"But she wants you too."

"I wish I had your confidence," Susanna said.

The bus got in twenty minutes late, by which time Susanna's crazed mind had zigzagged through sixteen variations of traffic wrecks and Abigail's decision not to get on the bus in the first place or to get off somewhere before Woodstock.

In that brief, precious moment between Abigail's walking into the Corner Cupboard and locating Susanna, her mother-sister's eager, hungry eyes devoured her, the beauty of her slim young body only semidisguised by ski pants, baggy sweater, denim jacket, and hideous Doc Martens. Her hair swung; her face was pale, with two spots of high color on her cheeks; her eyes were narrow in concentration, searching.

She found Susanna, who rose, not knowing whether she was permitted a hug or perhaps just a light kiss.

"Hi." Abigail accepted a hasty clutching of one arm about her shoulders, then quickly sat down to face her. "Sorry I'm late."

"Were you?"

Abigail's swift grin was balm to Susanna's terrified soul. "Don't give me that—you've always been paranoid if I was more than a minute late anywhere."

"Okay," Susanna admitted. "So I did have you in the hospital at one point."

"We started out on schedule, but the traffic was heavy—"

"It doesn't matter," Susanna stopped her. "I told you I'm in no rush today. I have all the time in the world."

Abigail looked a little cornered. "I was planning on getting back before evening, so—"

"Will you stop," Susanna told her. "I don't expect you to stay. I'm just so happy to see you again. Am I allowed to tell you that?"

"I'm happy too."

"Then everything's fine."

"Not quite," Abigail said carefully.

"Not yet," Susanna said. "But as long as we can talk, can go on communicating . . ." She ground to a halt, uncertain whether or not she was on the right track.

"That's what I want," Abigail agreed. "We need to talk."

"How about food?" Susanna asked.

"Sure." She paused. "I'd like a hot dog, please, with everything." She thought about it. "Or maybe a Reuben—"

Susanna ordered hot dogs for them both with fries and Cokes. They ate slowly, chatting rather than talking the way they knew they both intended and needed: small talk like the way Hawke House was going, the new show Connie was planning, the passion with which Bryan was flinging himself into golf, a sport he had always, for some unknown reason, jeered at, and Tabitha's latest boyfriend, a student dentist by whom Abigail was appalled.

"What about you?" Susanna asked. "Any boys on the scene?"

"No one special," Abigail said.

In those three words the altered, still-alien footing of their new relationship was transparently and, to Susanna, painfully clear. Until New Year's Day Abigail would have talked freely to her big sister about boys, whereas this afternoon she was veiled in caution more suited to an estranged mother.

They ordered dessert, but their hunger was gone now, and they spooned at it with small, halfhearted motions, their thought processes too disturbed, too fraught to allow their insides to relax fully. People came and went, called out greetings to one another, laughed and joked and gossiped, or read quietly, and were gone again, but Susanna and Abigail still sat, ice cream melting away, their words and fears and curiosities and desires unspoken, trapped inside their minds.

"What I need," Abigail said, at last, giving up on food and other defenses, "is to start over with you, but I don't know if you'll go for that."

"Why wouldn't I?" Susanna asked, relieved it had finally begun.

"Because I want to know all about you. Everything, from the beginning, and you may not want to tell me everything."

Susanna took a moment before she answered. "There are some things, Abigail"—her voice was very low—"I've spent a long time not letting myself think about." She paused. "Can we just see how it goes?"

Abigail nodded slowly. "One condition."

"Which is?"

"You promise to be honest with me. I mean, if you really don't want to tell me something—if you're maybe just not ready to tell me—you say so, but you don't make up something else to cover it."

"Sounds fair," Susanna said. She felt the hot flush of old shame creeping up over her cheeks. *My daughter has to ask me not to tell her fairy tales about my own life.*

Abigail was watching her carefully. "First question."

"Go for it."

"What's your real name? I mean, what was it before Bodine?"

"My name," Susanna said, "was King."

"King?"

"Yes."

"King," Abigail said again, testing its sound. "It's a good name."

"I suppose it is," Susanna agreed. "I had to leave it behind in the shack when Bodine told me to. I haven't even spoken it to myself in the dead of night since the day he ordered me to forget it." She paused. "Hawke knew I'd changed my surname, but he didn't know any more than that. He knew I didn't want to talk about it, and that was okay with him."

The waitress poured Susanna some coffee, and Abigail asked for a glass of water. They sat for a few more moments in silence.

"Mom said you told Bodine to take a hike," Abigail said suddenly, "that you weren't going to pay him."

"I told you that's what I was going to do."

"What did he say?"

"He was upset."

"Tell me what he said." Abigail was impatient again. "You promised to be honest with me, Susanna. I'm not a little child. If he threatened you, I'm entitled to know."

"He made a couple of vague, veiled threats," Susanna said. "They were just bluffs, nothing real."

"How can you be sure?"

"Because the whole point of this for him was the money, and the real threat, so far as he was concerned, was exposing me. Once I told him that you knew and that no one else mattered to me, he knew it was over."

"And you're really not scared of him anymore?" For the first time in weeks Abigail seemed almost impressed.

"No," Susanna said. "I really don't think I am." A sense of well-being swept her, a similar sensation to the high that had blown through her after she had told Bodine to go to hell, but there was a new, additional warmth to this feeling, and she realized it was because suddenly she had the chance to share it with her daughter. "I feel free, Abigail. Truly free. I used to believe I was free once he was out of our lives, when you and I had been living in Cohasset for a year or so without him. But I guess I was always kidding myself. He still had his hooks in me; I just didn't want to think about it."

"And now you really think that's over?" Abigail asked.

"I really do."

Abigail smiled, the warm, generous smile Susanna had always loved.

"I'm glad for you."

"For us," Susanna said.

"Yeah, in a way, I guess. But I didn't have to live with it all those years. You did." She paused. "I am glad, for you."

"Thank you," Susanna said, and feeling the words inadequate, she laid her right hand on the table, yearning for her daughter to take it, hoping, at the same time, that she would have the strength not to let her sorrow show too visibly if she did not. *No pressure*, her inner, wiser voice reminded her. *Ask too much of her and you may lose her altogether.*

Abigail's hesitation was infinitesimal. But she did not take Susanna's hand. Rather she laid her own on top of it, rested it there for a long moment, long enough for the gesture to be complete and understood, before she took it away again.

"Thank you," Susanna said again, whispering the words. She felt warmed, renewed with optimism and joy, yet already, in her heart, she knew that she wanted more, longed for an embrace, to feel Abigail's arms about her, to feel again her child's closeness in her own arms. *Such greed*, she thought, chastising herself, aware that she had gone from famine to feast in little more than an hour. *This has to be enough for now; it must be enough.*

Yet it was not.

* * *

Abigail too wanted more than Susanna could give her. They left the café and went for a drive around the beautiful Ashokan Reservoir. Susanna drove slowly so that they could both absorb the loveliness of the views, saying little, scared of blocking any natural impulse that Abigail might have to go on talking. And she did go on, and it was mostly questions, about her marriage to Hawke, about the way Susanna had felt keeping her great secret from him, from all of them, about her time in the tar paper shack, about her pregnancy, about her captivity—nothing about the rape itself; Susanna suspected that Abigail didn't want to know, could not bear to know too much about the pain and fear that had brought her into existence. They covered old ground, things that Abigail had already known everything about, and Susanna felt that she was being checked now, as if her one great lie had brought everything else she had ever told her family into doubt, but she did not mind that, could understand that, and she answered Abigail's questions as they came, as well and as thoroughly as she could.

Until it came to her life before Bodine.

"You've talked so little about that," Abigail said.

"That's because I hardly remember a time before." Susanna kept her eyes on the road, but her hands gripped the wheel more tightly.

"You must remember."

"No, Abigail, I'm not sure I do." She tried to explain. "I don't mean amnesia, or that my memory's really blank, but you want to know—I think you want to know what I was like before, if I was any different before, and of course I must have been very different, but I can't seem to get a grip on that part of my life. It's as if what happened with Bodine, and then having you, made the past so insignificant that it isn't worth remembering."

"But everything's worth remembering." Abigail persisted. "I need to know who you are. I need to know who I am. Most people's lives are ordinary, compared to what happened to you, but that doesn't mean they're not important." She paused. "I want to know what you did when you were a little girl, where you lived, the things you liked doing, what your parents were like—my grandparents."

"I don't remember my father at all. He died when I was so young."

"Do you have any pictures of him or your mom?"

"Just one," Susanna said, still gripping the wheel harder than she needed to. "It's their wedding photograph, but I'm afraid it won't tell you much." She had kept it hidden away for so many years, ever since Matthew Bodine had commanded her to forget her true identity, but that picture, at least, was clear in her mind's eye. "It's rather distant; you can hardly see their faces; they both look very austere and formal."

"Will you show it to me?"

"Of course I will."

"How come you only have one photograph?" A note of disbelief colored Abigail's voice. It was almost impossible for her, product of the picture-crazy Van Dusens, to conceive of a home not liberally coated with images of family and friends.

"That's all I have." A flash of her mother's house came to Susanna, then was gone again. "I don't remember ever seeing any others."

"That's weird."

"Yes, it is a little," Susanna said, "yet I can't alter the facts."

Seeing a small blue sports car in her rearview mirror, its driver growing impatient at her slow speed, Susanna put her foot down a little harder on the accelerator and concentrated for a few minutes on getting to the next clear stretch, where they could be safely passed.

"You have to try to understand something, Abigail," she said after a while. "Having you changed everything, *everything*, about me. It really does seem to me that I didn't exist before or that whatever or whoever was there before you just doesn't matter anymore."

Abigail shifted in her seat. "You're the one not understanding," she said, irritation returning, her terms no longer being perfectly, unquestioningly, complied with. "I need to know about myself, my roots."

"And I do understand that need," Susanna said. The blue sports car passed them and disappeared around the next bend. "But what I think I'm asking you, what I'm hoping you'll learn to accept is that because of what happened to me, your roots are just a little shorter than some."

"But that isn't really true."

"Not literally, no, of course not. But the way I see it, Abigail, is that the family you've always known is the one you need to know about. The Van Dusens are all you need to know. They're who you are: they formed you; they helped make you; they stood behind you."

"This is bull, Susanna." Abigail's voice was harsh, and Susanna felt the harshness of her glare. "You're hiding something."

"I'm not hiding anything."

"So let's forget your father—maybe he did die when you were a baby—"

"He did."

"But your mother didn't, did she?"

"No."

"So how come you don't remember her either? That is what you were trying to tell me, wasn't it?"

Susanna was driving now without concentration, her mind darting a hundred different ways, seeking escape. "I didn't say that I didn't remember her. I said that everything before you doesn't seem significant anymore."

"Including your mother."

"That's right."

"And I'm supposed to buy that? From you, who's been trying to make me believe how much being a mother means to you."

"I know it sounds odd—"

"It's bull," Abigail said again.

"Abigail, please."

Abigail changed her position, turned her head so that she faced the side of the road, away from Susanna. "You're still lying to me." She was incredulous. "After all this you're still keeping stuff from me."

"I'm very tired," Susanna said limply.

"Sure you are." Abigail was sarcastic. "It's been an exhausting lunch."

"Maybe it has, for me."

"You know something?"

"What?"

"I don't think I'm ever going to believe anything you tell me again."

For a split second Susanna shut her eyes, then opened them again quickly as she felt the car swerve a little. Forcibly she brought herself under control.

"I'm sorry," she said to her daughter. "You're right of course to be angry. And you're right to say that I'm keeping things from you." Her mouth started to quiver a little, and she bit her lower lip hard to stop it. "But what I am asking you to believe is that maybe I've been keeping those things from myself too over the years."

"But why?" Abigail gave her another chance. "Were things so bad back then too? Even before Bodine?"

"No, of course not."

"I think they were."

Susanna's throat and chest felt constricted; she was having trouble breathing normally. "I'm sorry," she said again. "I guess I'm still not ready to talk about that yet."

"When do you plan to be ready?"

Susanna shook her head. "It isn't the kind of thing you can plan."

"Okay," Abigail said.

Susanna glanced at her uncertainly. "Is that really okay, or is that an 'I hate you more than ever' okay?"

"I'm not the one playing games," Abigail said coolly. "I'm just accepting, as you put it, that you're not ready yet."

"Thank you," Susanna said.

"You're welcome," Abigail said.

They drove on, almost strangers again. *Back to square one.* Susanna knew that she had disappointed Abigail grievously, that she had failed her. But there were limits. There would always be limits. She had known that for years now, ever since she had begun to open up her past to Pete Strauss. She'd always stopped short of talking about her mother with him too.

She glanced at her daughter again.

You'll lose her, her inner voice warned.

The car moved along, the scenery still spectacular, but neither of them saw any of it. Abigail felt trapped in her seat, had the curious sensation that she was growing smaller and smaller, like Alice in Wonderland; she felt detached, in a way that seemed somehow menacing, from the woman beside her, the sister-mother she had, until the first day of this still-new year, loved and trusted with her life. Susanna went on driving, registered dimly that it was time to turn around and go back, that Abigail had said she wanted to catch a bus that would return her to Cohasset by evening.

Something's gotta give, the voice said.

But there are some things I just don't want to talk about, she answered back. Some things I just can't face.

Face them or lose her.

And Susanna, stopped in a turnout waiting to turn the car around, arrived at the same decision she always arrived at when things got really rough: first thing tomorrow morning, no matter how many reasons she found to put it off, she was going to drive down to New York to see Pete. If he was with patients, she would wait. If he was loath to go on counseling her because of their last meeting, or if he was impatient with waiting for her to make up her mind, she would talk him around.

And this time, no matter how much it hurt, no matter how much her subconscious begged her to stop, she would not. She would go on; she would go all the way back.

All the way.

CHAPTER 18

~

If Susanna had been able to see Pete the next day, as she had hoped, events back home in Cohasset might have unfolded differently. As it was, when Susanna returned from Woodstock that Wednesday afternoon, she found Hawke House in a state of barely controlled uproar. Joe Zacharias had, just after lunch, come across one of the guests in someone else's room, rifling through his private possessions. Since then Joe had discovered not only that the intruder was not sick, as they had been led to believe, but also that she was a reporter for a gutter magazine, and there was no question that now was not a good time for Susanna to leave for New York.

It was a big mistake.

Abigail received the first letter on Thursday morning. She collected it from the mailbox with the rest of the family's mail, an ordinary-looking white envelope, poorly typed and postmarked Boston, and took it, together with a postcard from her friend Amy, who was visiting Europe with her parents, to her bedroom. Had she opened the letter in the kitchen in Connie's or Bryan's presence, her expression would very likely have given her away even before she had read the first line. She was glad, by the time she reached the last, that she had brought it upstairs, into privacy.

My dear Abigail,

I can imagine how surprised you are hearing from me like this but *please* don't just rip up this letter and please don't show it to your folks. Not anyhow until you've finished reading and taken some time to think about it. I guess I'm asking a lot Abigail, but all I'm really asking is that you give me—your father—a chance.

Your mother says she's told you the truth. About her and me and who your real Daddy is and what she feels I did to her. I've been thinking about you hearing all that now and I can imagine you must be real confused so I'm writing you this letter to try and set you right about one thing.

When I left you and your mama it was because I wanted the best for you. No other reason. I made some bad mistakes in my life back then, I know that now and believe me I have lived to regret them. But one thing I was clear on even back then was that if I'd taken you with me when I left you'd have lost out on your best chance of a good life. That was why I left you, Abigail. That was the only reason. I want you to believe that.

I'm a lonely man these days, getting older, not as fit as I once was and suddenly it seems I need to tell my little girl —because that's how I've always thought of you—my little girl. Anyhow, I want to tell you that I miss you so much. God knows I've always missed you.

I expect your mama and the others speak of me badly, about the mistakes I made and then some. And your mama's maybe told you too that I asked her for money, but that was only because I need it so badly now because of my poor health and I can understand her not wanting to give me anything and I forgive her for that even though I know she has so much and I have nothing.

Having nothing makes you think about the really important things, I guess. Which is why I'm writing you now asking you to forgive me for leaving you when I did. You were such a pretty little thing back then. You still are. Just like your mama.

If you can keep this our secret you'll be helping me a lot. All I want now is to be quiet and work hard for as long as my health holds up. But I will understand if you can't keep it quiet. Don't worry your head. If they come after me I guess I'll get by. I always have.

Can you forgive me Abigail, do you think? We all make mistakes. I'm still paying for mine. I guess I'll go on paying till I die.

Your loving father Matthew Bodine

Abigail knew, even before she reached the halfway point of the letter—the part about his being lonely and growing older—that she would neither show it nor mention it to anyone. There was something symbolic somehow—or maybe *fatalistic* was a better word for it—in the letter's arriving that very morning, just when she had made up her mind that no matter what Susanna said, she was going to find out everything she could about her roots. Except that up until this minute she had only really thought about those roots relating to Susanna and her faceless, nameless grandmother, and now, suddenly, from one moment to the next, she saw that her father, lousy as he might be, was an important part of the picture too. And Matthew Bodine probably was as lousy as Susanna had painted him, but at least this letter proved one thing: that he cared for her, always had done, still did.

The next day, while Susanna was still heavily involved in the mess at Hawke House, the second letter arrived.

Dear Abigail,

I suddenly had this great big hope that you might, just might want to speak with me. Only on the phone of course. You needn't be afraid I'm going to hassle you to see me. (Though nothing in this whole world—not even getting my health and strength back—would make me happier.)

There's a phone booth on Seagull Road. If you do want to talk with me—just so I can hear your voice one more time—please get yourself to that booth this Saturday afternoon at two o'clock. I'll call then and I'll keep on calling (in case someone else is using the booth) till three. If you don't come, I'll know for sure you don't want to know me and I will understand.

Your ever loving father

At five minutes to two o'clock on Saturday afternoon, Abigail was outside the booth, waiting for the woman using the phone to finish her conversation. Her heart was racing, her palms were damp, and she was praying that the woman didn't have fifteen more calls to make and that neither Bryan nor Connie nor Lucy Battaglia would happen along Seagull Road and ask her what she was doing.

The woman was talking long distance; she kept putting quarters into the slot. It seemed to Abigail that she'd been talking forever, and she knew that Bodine had promised to keep trying until three, and it wasn't even five after two yet, but the waiting was driving her crazy, and the worst part of it was that she had this nasty little wriggle of doubt in the pit of her stomach that she knew was caused by feeling disloyal to Susanna and to Tabbie too.

I have a right to talk to my own father, she told herself three, four times, but the woman kept on talking and feeding quarters to AT&T, and the feeling of guilt kept on wriggling deep inside Abigail.

And then, finally, the woman was through. She put the receiver back on the hook, picked up her wallet, dropped it on the floor, bent to retrieve it, fumbled to put it into her purse, turned to leave the booth, then changed her mind, turning around again to check that she'd left nothing behind, while Abigail jiggled the keys in her jacket pocket and stomped from foot to foot in an agony of suspense.

"All done," the woman said with a pleasant smile.

"Thank you."

Abigail slid quickly in behind her in case anyone else had any ideas about getting in first. For a moment she stood still; then, seeing a man approaching, hand in his pocket, maybe fishing for coins, she picked up the receiver with her right hand and pressed the index finger of her left hand on the hook so that it could still ring if it was going to.

A minute passed, and then another. The man who she'd thought wanted to make a call had walked on by, but now a couple of girls, a year or so younger than she was, were hanging around, waiting, while Abigail kept her finger on the hook and talked to no one about the movies she wanted to see and the new jeans she wanted to buy.

Another minute passed.

The phone rang, jolting her heart.

"Hello?"

It rang again. Jerkily, foolishly, she took her finger from the hook.

"Hello?"

"Abigail?"

"Yes."

"It's me."

He sounded so normal, was her first thought. His voice was deep, but not overly so, just a regular, ordinary kind of voice.

"You called," she said, not knowing what else to say.

"I said I would."

"I know."

"But you weren't sure."

"I thought you probably would," she said, still awkwardly.

"Thank you," he said.

"What for?"

"For being there. For letting me talk to you."

"That's okay," Abigail said.

"It means a lot."

She said nothing.

"You sound pretty," he said. "So grown-up."

"Thank you."

"I wish I could see you." Bodine stopped. "I'm sorry. I promised myself I wouldn't say that; it just slipped out. I know you wouldn't want to see me."

"It would be hard," Abigail said. "Without, you know, telling anyone."

"I know." He paused. "Does that mean you'd want to if you could?"

"I don't know. I'm not sure."

"Okay. That's okay. I understand."

She heard the sadness in his voice. "Maybe one day. Just not yet."

"That's okay," he said again.

"You said in your letter that your health was poor," Abigail said. "Are you sick?"

"No, not really sick, just not as strong as I used to be, you know."

"Oh." Again Abigail didn't know what else to say.

"Nothing for you to worry about."

"I'm not," she said. "I mean—"

He laughed. "I know what you mean. It's hard, isn't it, talking like this?"

"It is a little weird," she said.

"But better than nothing."

"I guess."

"Still, beggars can't be choosers, can they?"

She didn't answer.

"I guess you'd better be going now," Bodine said.

"I guess," Abigail said again.

"Just one thing."

"Yes?"

"I was thinking—" He stopped.

"What?"

"If there was anything I could do for you. I guess that sounds strange, coming from a no-hoper like me. I mean, you must have most things you need."

"Yes," Abigail said. "I don't need anything."

"What about questions?" he said carefully. "About me or about your mama maybe. Anything I can tell you, help you understand what happened back then."

Behind Abigail, on the sidewalk, the two girls, bored with waiting, began to cough, trying to attract her attention, to irritate her into finishing. Fighting to ignore them, Abigail focused on what Bodine had asked her, on what questions, if any, she could put to him.

"Do you know stuff about my mother before—" She didn't know how to put it. *Before you raped her and shut her up in a shack on the beach*—she couldn't very well say that, and anyhow, something inside her had begun, since his first letter, to question the story Susanna had told them. Susanna admitted she was screwed up about it, and Bodine had said that he'd made bad mistakes and that he regretted them, and a long time had passed since then, more than fifteen years, a lifetime, her lifetime—

"You want to know about your mama's past, before you came along?" Bodine put it perfectly. "Is that what you mean? Didn't she tell you all about that?"

"Not everything," Abigail said, suddenly needing to defend Susanna.

He was quiet for a moment or two.

"It's hard on the phone," he said. "But I know you don't want to meet me, do you?"

"I can't," she said.

"No." He paused. "You could probably find out some things yourself. If you knew the right places to look."

"But I don't know the right places," Abigail said.

"I do," Bodine said.

"I can't meet you," she said again, nervously.

"I know. I told you I understand." He paused again. "But maybe if I told you where to look—"

"Would you do that?"

"Sure I would. If that's what you want. I want so much to do something for you, Abigail." Bodine paused. "I guess it might help you a whole lot"—he went on slowly, thinking it over, taking his time—"if you could go someplace your mama used to live."

"I guess it would." Abigail's pulses were flying again.

"Like the convent maybe."

"Yes," she said, openly eager now.

"She didn't ever tell you where it was?"

"Just that it was on the Cape somewhere."

"You could go there maybe. Pay a visit, talk to someone who used to know her. Those nuns don't move around a heck of a lot. I guess there'll be someone there who still remembers your mama."

Abigail thought a moment. "Should I write a letter or call, do you think?"

"I wouldn't if I were you," Bodine said. "I'd just show up. That way they wouldn't be able to call up your mama first or the Van Dusens. If you're there, they've got to talk to you."

"Right," she said, trying to take it in.

"But you can't just go anytime, not to a place like that. They have a lot of rules, you know, times of day when they pray, when they don't like to talk to people."

"So when is a good time to go?"

"Midmorning, before noon," Bodine answered decisively.

"And not on a Sunday." He paused again. "You want to know where this place is?"

"Yes. Please."

"Got a pen?"

"No, it's okay." Abigail glanced around, saw that the two girls had gone. "Go ahead, I'll remember."

"It's on the bay side, just off Six A," he said, "a few miles east of Brewster, close to what they call the Cranberry Highway. Name of St. Catherine's Convent. If you get past Nickerson State Park, you've gone too far."

"St. Catherine's," Abigail repeated. "East of Brewster."

"Sure you don't need to write that down?"

"I've got a good memory."

"Me too."

Abigail did not respond.

"So when are you going to go? You're in school now, aren't you?"

"I'll make the time," Abigail said.

"How will you get there?"

"On the bus, I guess."

"Unh-unh. The only bus to the Cape goes to Hyannis."

"Oh." Abigail thought about it. "I could hitch from there, couldn't I?"

"So long as you're real careful."

"I'll be careful."

"When you get there, you might try asking for Sister Dominic," Bodine suggested. "I remember she and your mama spent more time together than most. She was young then. I guess she could still be there."

"Thank you," Abigail said.

"That's okay." Bodine had a little smile in his voice. "Get them to show you the gardens, where I used to work. They were real pretty. Guess I did a good job, if I say so myself."

"I'll take a look," Abigail said. "And thank you. Really."

"I hope it helps."

"Could I write you somewhere, after I've been?"

"I'll be moving around," Bodine said. "But I'll write you again if you want me to."

"Sure," Abigail said. "Why not?"

"I am your daddy, after all."

Bryan's face came forcefully into Abigail's mind, brought back that ache of guilt she'd had before the call.

"Anyway," she said, "it's been good talking to you."

"And to you, Abigail."

"I hope you feel better."

"I hope so too."

In the phone booth on Seagull Road, Abigail put the receiver back on the hook and stepped out onto the sidewalk. Her hands were quivering; most of her was quivering. *St. Catherine's Convent.* Bodine was right: if Susanna wouldn't tell her the facts about herself, she could find them out on her own, though she wished she could get rid of that niggling sense of guilt. If she told either Mom or Dad, they'd certainly stop her from going, and they'd probably set the cops on to Bodine too. And she thought he probably had paid for his mistakes, and it was obvious he was sick now, whatever he said; and just hearing that longing in his voice on the phone now made her sure he'd meant it when he'd said how much he'd missed seeing her all these years.

In the room he'd rented on the second floor, three doors from the post office on Seagull Road, Matthew Bodine stared out of the window at the young woman just walking away from the phone booth. He loved the way their conversation had led back to that place. He liked the ironies of life when they went his way. Helping her with the one thing the Van Dusens couldn't do for her, the one thing her mother still hadn't shared with her, was a nice touch. Watching her find her way to the place from where he'd plucked her mama would be even better.

He'd watched a rerun of *The A-Team* a few afternoons back, and the George Peppard character came back to him now. *"I love it when a plan comes together,"* George had said, beaming and chomping a cigar.

His own plan had been too vague till now, too half assed to get excited about, but all that had changed; he could feel it in his poor, sore bones. And if Bodine had been a cigar-smoking type, he'd have lit one up right now.

CHAPTER 19

~

Abigail went on Monday morning, left the house just as if she were going to school as usual, then rerouted by bus to Rockland to wait for the P&B bus to Hyannis. From there she hitched her first ride in a Chevrolet with a friendly housewife en route to visit with her father in Dennis, and after that she rode in the back of a pickup truck as far as Brewster.

The guilt was with her again in the early part of the journey, riding tandem with her excitement and nervousness, for though much of Abigail believed she was doing the right thing for herself, part of her recognized that given enough time, Susanna might come through for her anyway. But Susanna had said she was going to be straight with her in Woodstock, and then, at the last minute, she'd balked, reneged on her promise. And in any case this was something a little different; this was Abigail Van Dusen out on her own on a personal voyage of self-discovery, and if Susanna had been more up front with her from the beginning, it would never have been necessary.

It was a gorgeous winter's morning, the kind that made Abigail glad to be alive and on the move. Even in its February starkness Cape Cod sparkled, and its people, in the towns, on the roads, appeared vital and contented to Abigail, gazing out at it all, calmer now than at the beginning, for there was something consoling about doing rather than thinking; and whatever he had done in the past, whatever kind of man her father still might be, Matthew

Bodine had done her a favor by encouraging her to quit moping around and *do* something for a change.

Nearing Dennis, between fielding bouts of amiable questions from the good-natured Hyannis housewife, Abigail was trying to reassemble in her mind what little she already knew about her mother's early life. *Mother*, she thought. How strange that she should find herself, so soon after discovering the truth, able to think of Susanna that way. She supposed it was different from someone's finding out, after years of living with one family, that her birth mother and father were strangers in some distant place. In her case, of course, Abigail had always known that Connie and Bryan were only foster parents, and Susanna had always been her closest living relative, so maybe the step between older sister and mother was not the steepest to climb. Yet until lately Connie and Bryan had still been all the parents Abigail had ever wanted, and Tabbie had been as much sister to her as Susanna. *Mother*.

By the time she was approaching Brewster, sitting among boxes of canned goods in the pickup, with the convent only a few miles east, Abigail had reaffirmed how pathetically little she knew about Susanna's early life. She knew that her real name had been King, that her father had died when she was just two, that Susanna possessed only one old photograph of her parents, and that she had lived for a time in a convent. She knew that Susanna said that she had been raped by Matthew Bodine, that he had taken her away from the convent to a shack somewhere on the dunes up around Provincetown, and that a few weeks after Abigail's birth, they had all come to Cohasset to start a new life. And she knew that somewhere before all that, before the convent, Susanna had had a mother about whom she found it even harder to speak than the rape.

And climbing out of the truck at Brewster, contemplating that last fact, Abigail shivered.

St. Catherine's Convent and School stood in the northeast corner of its own grounds, a substantial old brick house with a pitched roof, one ivy-clad wall, and an adjoining chapel. It was surrounded by lawns on every side, with hedge-divided gardens and vegetable patches and hothouses and, beyond, within the high stone wall that encompassed its land, an attractive strip of wild forest. It was the most peaceful place Abigail had ever seen, more tranquil, even, than Hawke House. It was impossible for her, standing on the gravel path that linked the main building with the outside world, the only tangible sounds the creaking of barren branches and the winter-thin strands of birdsong, to imagine such an environment spawning the kind of violence that Susanna had described.

She began to walk again, toward the house. On the far side, traveling in the opposite direction, three black-robed nuns moved across a lawn, appearing almost to glide, the motion of their veiled heads scarcely discernible, three perfect, matching models of deportment. On the near side, untroubled by Abigail's approach, a pair of magpies perused the grass for an early lunch, their occasional raucous cries wafting away on the air.

The door was tall and solid oak, unornamented, without knocker or handle. A polished brass plaque to the right, fastened to the brickwork, read ST. CATHERINE'S CONVENT, and beside the plaque Abigail saw a bell push.

"Here goes nothing," she said.

And taking a deep breath, she pressed it.

Sister Dominic was, Abigail guessed, about fifty years old, with fine, pale skin, a firm, wide mouth, the clearest, sharpest green eyes Abigail had ever seen, and strong, capable hands, blunt-nailed and startlingly weathered for female hands.

"Yes," she said, her voice warm and bell-like, the kind of voice Abigail could imagine soaring to the peak of a beautiful hymn. "I remember your mother. I would have remembered Susanna King even without the mystery of her departure." She paused, looking very directly at Abigail. "I gather that you are seeking information of some kind about her?"

"Anything you can tell me."

"Do you mind if I ask you why you need me for that?" The nun was gentle enough but candid nonetheless. "Are you separated from your mother?"

"Not exactly."

"Wouldn't it be better, simpler to ask her?"

"She won't tell me." Abigail knew that this woman, with her penetrating gaze, would see right through anything less than honesty. "She never talks about her childhood at all."

"I see." Sister Dominic paused. "I can't imagine that I have anything of special significance to share with you. Nothing that would be very meaningful to you."

"I was told," Abigail said tentatively, "that you and she spent quite a bit of time together."

"Were you?" The nun did not ask who had told Abigail that. "That's true." She smiled. "You would like to know about that?"

"If you don't mind."

"I don't mind at all. It's a happy memory of mine, and there's nothing confidential about it." Sister Dominic smiled again, more wistfully. "I was something of an artist in my time, a poor one, I'm sure, but the other sisters were generous enough to allow me to hang an occasional work in the public rooms."

"You were probably very good," Abigail ventured to say politely.

"Maybe less poor sometimes than others." The nun paused. "But if I did paint a few tolerable portraits, then your mother was probably responsible."

"Why?" Abigail asked, surprised.

"Because she was my model."

"Really?"

The older woman smiled again. "Even at the age of nine or ten, your mother was unusually lovely. And there was a rare quality about her that made her more than simply pretty." She closed her eyes for an instant, remembering. "She had poise, for one thing, which is uncommon in itself in a child, don't you think?" The eyes opened again, regarded Abigail. "You have something of that too. You're very like your mother, you know." She nodded. "Of course you know."

Sister Dominic had come into the visitor's room, a simple, rugless room with plain white walls, bearing a pine tea tray. Now she began to pour from the porcelain pot, and the atmosphere between them became more companionable.

"If you liked," she offered, "I think I might be able to find one of those portraits."

"I'd love it," Abigail said, fascinated.

"I used to sketch Susanna on the beach. She would sit on a rock, and the wind would blow her lovely hair around her face. She had an ability to sit still for long periods. Most children of my acquaintance hate to sit still, but Susanna was a very disciplined girl, and she loved being close to the ocean, never complained when I took too long."

"You do know," Abigail said, "that she became a model?"

"Yes, I know who she became."

Abigail was curious. "How could you know?"

Sister Dominic laughed. "You mean, how could a nun keep up with fashion? The very fact that we are a teaching order opens us up to worldly things, Abigail. We go out, we see newspapers, even magazines, and the girls bring them in with them too. I recognized your mother the first time I saw her photograph. It was in *Vogue*. The other sisters argued with me, and the name of course had changed. But I knew her. I clipped the photograph. I still have it somewhere. She was astonishingly beautiful then."

"She still is," Abigail said softly.

The nun smiled at her again. "You're very proud of her, aren't you?"

"Yes. Very."

"That's good." Sister Dominic paused. "Is your mother well?"

"Yes," Abigail answered. "She's very well."

"I'm glad."

They drank their tea. Sister Dominic handled her cup and saucer, Abigail thought, as if she might have grown up in some distinguished old Bostonian residence. She supposed that women from all kinds of backgrounds became nuns. She had never thought much about nuns before.

"Would you mind," the sister said, "if I asked you a personal question?"

"Not at all."

"How old are you, Abigail?"

"I'm fifteen." Abigail looked directly at her. "My mother was very young when she had me."

"I see." An expression of great sorrow passed briefly across Sister Dominic's eyes. "I thought that might have been the case." She paused. "I was so afraid for your mother when she vanished. For all the years between her disappearance and the first photograph I saw of her in the magazine, I remained afraid. But then, a little later, when I saw a picture of her with her husband, Mr. Hawke, I saw how happy they both looked, and how much in love, and at last the fear went away."

"They were very happy."

"I know that he passed away," Sister Dominic said.

"He was very sick for a long time," Abigail said. "I liked him a lot."

"That's a blessing."

Abigail waited for a moment, expecting the nun to cross herself or perhaps to say something about Hawke's soul, but Sister Dominic seemed so down-to-earth, was so normal, so easy to be with, and it was harder than ever to imagine evil of the kind Susanna had described emanating from this place.

She set down her cup and saucer. "What happened," she asked, "when my mother disappeared?"

"What happened here in the convent, you mean?"

Abigail nodded.

"We searched for her. She left in the middle of the night, while everyone was sleeping." Sister Dominic hesitated. "Has your mother told you what happened to her at that time?"

"Yes." Abigail offered nothing further.

"It was November, I remember. November 1975. It was cold and wet. An unlikely night for a girl to choose to run away, I thought, but as the police pointed out to us, if a runaway wanted to wait for the weather to improve on Cape Cod at that time of year, she'd have a pretty long wait." Sister Dominic too put down her teacup. "There isn't much to tell. One morning Susanna was gone, with most of her things. We looked everywhere for her, searched every inch of the grounds, sent people outside the convent to see if they could find anyone who might have seen her."

"There were no clues?"

"Nothing." The nun paused. "Everyone was very helpful; they all cared a great deal. All our outside helpers, the merchants who delivered goods to us and the shopkeepers in Brewster offered to keep their eyes open. Our gardener and handyman was especially helpful, I remember. For months after she vanished, he went on checking the neighborhood, even went off on day trips and promised to keep his eyes open in case he saw Susanna. But of course he never did."

Abigail was silent. She was remembering what Susanna had said about Bodine's regular visits to the shack. It had never occurred to her—she thought it had probably never occurred to Susanna either—that Bodine had remained in his post at the convent, had just gone on with his work and helped in the search for the missing girl. But of course, if the gardener had left on the same night as Susanna, the police would have known who else to look for.

"*Bad mistakes*," he'd said in his first letter to her. But the things he had done had not been mistakes. Abigail knew that now. They had been calculated acts, devised by a cunning mind.

Her stomach turned, and she felt suddenly nauseated.

"Are you all right, Abigail?" Sister Dominic was looking at her anxiously.

"Yes," Abigail said. "Thank you."

"Are you sure? You've turned quite pale."

"I'm fine."

"Did something I said upset you?"

"No. I'm all right, really. I just felt a little queasy, but it's gone."

"Did you have a long journey to get here today?"

"Not too long. I came from Cohasset, on the South Shore."

"Are you hungry perhaps?" the nun asked. "I could get you something from our kitchen."

"No, I couldn't eat. Anyway, I'm okay now."

"How about some fresh air?" Sister Dominic, who knew young people well, was not giving up. "I could use a walk myself."

Get them to show you the gardens, where I used to work.

Slowly Abigail nodded. "A walk might be good."

They both got up.

In a shrubbery, partway between the forest strip and the stone wall, on the southwest side of the convent house, Bodine was watching the back door and waiting. He'd watched Abigail from the time she'd caught her first bus that morning in Cohasset right up until she'd entered the building an hour or so before. There had been nothing difficult in the surveillance. A target as innocent, as naive as this girl was easy to follow. And now that she was here, now that they both were here, he had known the best place to wait; few people knew the grounds of St. Catherine's as well as he did.

It was getting colder and damper, and his left knee was acting up today, and crouching on the ground was making it worse; but it was nothing he couldn't handle, and it was worth a little discomfort to try to get this right first time. There was always a chance that Abigail would leave by the front door, perhaps accompanied, and head right back to Cohasset, and then he might have to abort, but he had a strong notion that the girl would want to take a look around her daddy's gardens, and if that was the case, the door he had in his sights right now was the one that she would come out of.

In spite of the pain that he knew was going to keep getting worse, knotting him up, crippling him maybe, Bodine knew that for the first time in a long while things were going his way. He crouched in the shrubbery, gazing out over the grounds that had once been his domain, and waited for his daughter to appear. He wondered if she had asked the nuns about him, wondered what they would have said. *"He was a good worker,"* they'd probably tell her. They'd always liked him, the sisters. He'd known how to treat them with respect, and yet he'd always talked to them like women, which he supposed they were, under the getup. Women liked Bodine. Except Susanna, and if she'd only be honest with herself, she'd have to admit she'd liked him too. When it came to it, most females were pretty much the same.

He glanced down at his gloveless left hand, saw a little bug crawling on the back of it, and squished it with his right thumb, wiping the small mess off on the grass at his feet. He looked at his wristwatch, felt the cellular phone in his coat pocket, wondered if he'd get to use it as he'd planned today. Oh, he had it all worked out, if luck was with him. And if not today, then soon; he knew it would be soon.

All his instincts, though, told him it would be today.

Sister Dominic and Abigail came out of the house by the rear door, stepped out onto a gravel path matching exactly the one at the front, and stood, for just a moment, not moving.

"It's really beautiful," Abigail said softly. "I thought it was lovely from the front, but from here it's so—"

Sister Dominic nodded. "It is difficult to describe, I agree. Symmetrical sounds too much like geometry, and yet it is. Orderly sounds too soulless, and yet it's that too."

"It's a world of its own," Abigail said, grasping it. "It's so separate from the outside."

"And yet we're not a strictly cloistered order," the nun said.

"I like the atmosphere." Abigail realized that she felt surprised by that, just as Sister Dominic had surprised her, that she had anticipated that both the convent and its inhabitants would be far more oppressive and unnatural. "It's so calm, but it feels free, somehow."

"Susanna liked the gardens too."

They started to walk.

"Which did she prefer, the gardens or the beach?" Abigail asked.

"The gardens perhaps. She told me once that she felt in awe of the ocean, but I think most of us feel that way some of the time." Sister Dominic paused. "I never had much of a sense that she felt captive here, the way a young girl might. Most of them, you see, had homes and families to go back to in vacation time, but Susanna of course had neither."

Abigail almost stopped walking but pushed herself on. At last here was something important, a clue to what she sought, but if she made her interest too obvious, the nun might clam up and refuse to say any more.

"I gather that was news to you." Disconcertingly Sister Dominic read her mind. "Of course, you said your mother never speaks of her childhood. Forgive me, I'd forgotten for a moment."

They continued walking side by side, Abigail striding out in her denims and boots, the older woman moving easily in her calf-length habit.

"I wish," Abigail said, her breath steaming in the cold air, "that you would go on. I really need to know what happened to her, why she finds it so hard to talk about it."

"Why do you need to know?" Sister Dominic asked.

"Because I need to know about myself." Abigail paused, reflecting. Honesty was, she supposed, a two-way street. She looked down at her feet. "I only found out a few weeks ago that Susanna was my mother."

"Oh. I see."

"No, you don't." Abigail went on. "For a whole bunch of reasons, which I don't think she'd want me talking about— though maybe she wouldn't mind if it was you—"

"I'd rather respect her privacy," Sister Dominic said quickly.

"Yes." Abigail paused. "But the fact is, I grew up believing that Susanna was my sister. She only told me the truth this January first, and it's been kind of hard taking it in."

"I can imagine."

"And the thing is," Abigail went on, "in one way she has told me a lot, about the bad things that happened to her here"—she felt the nun's sideways glance, sensed her dismay—"and after she left. Yet she still won't talk about what came before, and I can't imagine it could be worse than she's already told me, but I guess it must be, or else it wouldn't make any sense at all."

"Perhaps," Sister Dominic said, "she's afraid of causing you pain."

"What could cause me more pain than knowing she chose not to be my mother for fifteen years?"

They had entered a bloomless rose garden, row upon row of savagely cut-back bushes, but even now, in its dormant period, Abigail imagined she could smell the garden as it would be in spring and summer, could hear the droning of bees and wasps and the pure, sweet songs of scores of birds.

"The Susanna I knew," the nun said, "was unlikely to have made such a choice unless she felt she had no alternative."

"I know that," Abigail said. "Or I'm beginning to believe that. But it hurt terribly when she first told me, which is why I can't imagine what she's keeping from me that could hurt me more."

"I can't answer that," Sister Dominic said. "I know too little myself." She stopped walking and gestured to Abigail to do the same. "Look," she said quietly. A finch, hopping on one of the grassy borders, was coming closer to where they stood. "I never tire of watching the birds," she whispered. "Some of them here are quite tame. If we're still, it might come right to us."

In the forest, several hundred yards away to their right, something stirred, and the bird flew away. Sister Dominic began to walk again, and Abigail followed her. They left the rose garden and entered, almost immediately, what was clearly a vegetable garden, the soil well turned, all neat and tidy.

"When your mother came to us, she was a very grave, sad child. At times it was hard even to think of her as a child. She was only seven years old, yet she seemed so grown up." Sister Dominic glanced at Abigail's face. "Not precocious, that's not at all what I mean. Susanna was mature. Adult. Everything a child ought not to be." She paused, giving the teenager time to absorb what she was being told. "She did get better as time passed. The other girls helped a great deal, normalized Susanna, taught her to play, how to enjoy life. I remember being concerned that they might poke fun at her, the way children often do when someone is different, but they didn't. Everyone liked Susanna."

"Most people still do," Abigail said.

"That doesn't surprise me. I found her a very interesting person. There was no question that sad things had happened to her, though I didn't know precisely what they were. It was not for me to know, Abigail," she added quickly. "I guess the details were known to the mother superior, and they're probably in her records, but I never knew, and if I did, I would not be in a position to share them with you."

"You said you found her interesting." Having stirred the nun's memories this far, Abigail was not about to let the conversation end now.

"Because in spite of her troubles," Sister Dominic went on, "there never seemed to be any bitterness emanating from Susanna, at least none that I could sense."

"Why should there have been bitterness?"

"You're fishing, Abigail." The nun smiled.

"I need to know."

"And I can't tell you."

They moved out of one vegetable garden directly into another. Beyond a band of hedges Abigail saw a row of glass houses, gleaming in the morning sunlight.

"I'd like to show you something, Abigail."

"The portrait?"

"No, not that. I'll dig one out for you, but this is something else." Sister Dominic turned to her left and began walking, more briskly than before. "Coming?"

"Sure."

Abigail followed. They left the ordered gardens, entered the strip of forest, and suddenly there was no path and they were picking their way around tree stumps and across sodden carpets of bracken and dead leaves, and the sunlight had been left behind and only thin shafts of brilliance illuminated the dimness. Abigail always liked forests, liked the strange purity of the air that rose from a forest floor, the mixed scents of mosses and rotting leaves and trampled weeds and wildflowers.

"Where are we going?" she asked, a little breathlessly, still following the nun's lead. She heard the sounds of invisible creatures scampering in the undergrowth, heard the sudden flapping of anonymous wings, gazed around at the gnarled tree trunks and twisting branches, each one unique, as singular as any human fingerprint.

"Almost there." Sister Dominic hoisted her skirt a little higher with her left hand, pushed aside low-hanging branches with her right. She turned her head a moment. "Ready?"

"I don't know what—"

And suddenly they were there. It was just a clearing, one of those unexpected patches of open space that are generally found in any forest. Yet instantly Abigail saw why Sister Dominic had brought her to it. This was more than just an ordinary clearing; it was an oasis of tranquillity, a forest glade of wondrous beauty, verging on the enchanted.

"It's a perfect circle," Abigail said softly.

"Isn't it?"

There was a rough bench in the center, carved out of two aged tree trunks, the area in the middle of the exposed trunk smoothed down by years of visitors sitting on it.

"Why don't you sit?" Sister Dominic asked.

"You first," Abigail said.

She shook her head. "I can sit here anytime. This is for you. You've come a long way, and you've learned so little. I thought you might like to spend a few minutes in your mother's favorite place."

Abigail sat down. Directly ahead of her, unfurling like a theatrical scene, a group of pine trees leaned in toward one another, appearing to defy the laws of wind and nature, branches touching, brushing in the breeze, forming an exquisite and magical natural arch. She knew now why Susanna had picked Hawke House, wondered if she had a favorite spot in the woods there too. *Susanna used to sit here*, she thought, closing her eyes. *My mother watched these same trees.*

"I think I'll go find that painting now."

Sister Dominic's voice made Abigail open her eyes. She knew she ought to stand, ought to walk back with the nun, but some curious, almost magnetic power was making her remain seated on the log bench.

"You stay," Sister Dominic told her gently. "It'll do you good."

"You don't mind?"

"I'll mind if you don't."

The nun turned and walked away, moved back through the cluster of closed branches, and was gone, only the soft tread of her feet still audible.

Abigail shut her eyes again.

He watched for a few minutes more. He wanted to be sure that the nun had gone and that they were alone. He could scarcely believe his luck. She was there, just yards away, in his grasp, and they had plenty of time, for it would take Sister Dominic more than ten minutes just to reach the convent house, let alone make it back with the painting.

He studied Abigail's profile. His daughter's nose was straight and fine, like her mother's. There was little of himself to be seen in her, at least not from where he squatted. The eyes, of course, the pretty eyes he'd seen turn from baby blue to his own brown during the first months of her life. The life he had given her.

My daughter, Abigail.

He wondered, not for the first time, if his plan, the plan that had come together so perfectly, could perhaps still be refined. He'd done and been many things, but never since boyhood had he had a family. Except for those special days in the shack when he'd realized what it meant.

The pain in his knee grew suddenly worse, screamed out for him to change position, to stand up or to lie down. Cautiously he moved just a little, just enough to ease it.

Abigail heard the sound and opened her eyes.

"Sister Dominic?"

There was no reply. For a moment she listened, and then, hearing nothing more, she yawned and stretched out her arms above her head and closed her eyes again.

She had never felt such peace.

"I knew she'd bring you here."

She opened her eyes again, whirled her head around.

"Hello, Abigail."

The man was tall and broad, Bryan Van Dusen's height but tougher, harder-looking, with curly hair, dark mixed with gray, and brown eyes the same shade as her own. He wore a hunter's jacket with a lot of pockets for knives and bullets and stuff like that. He was smiling at her, but it was the strangest, most discomfiting smile.

"Hello," she said, staying put, too afraid to move.

"You know who I am, don't you?"

She knew. She recognized the voice from the telephone. And the eyes. She remembered what Susanna had once said about their sharing the same color eyes. *His color, more or less, though not their expression.*

"What are you doing here?" she asked.

"What do you think?" He moved closer, so that he stood less than four feet away. "I'm here to see you."

"How did you know I'd be here today?"

"I knew."

He's been watching me. The realization, striking hard, increased the fear. She tried to hide it, tried to keep her face calm, her hands steady.

"There's no need to be frightened," he said. "I just want to spend a little time with you."

"That's not possible. I'll be leaving any minute now. Sister Dominic's coming back."

"I know she is," he said. "But we'll be gone by then."

Abigail stood up.

"That's good," he said. "Ready to go. We don't have too much time."

"No," she said. "I can't go anywhere." Her eyes darted this way and that, seeking the best escape.

"Forget it, Abigail. No one knows these grounds better than I do."

Adrenaline fired her up, and she bolted to her right, but he was fast for such a big man and caught her, grabbed her left arm, halted her, dragged her close to him. Gasping, she kicked at him with one boot, caught his shin, heard him yelp, but his strength didn't falter. Up in the trees, some big bird, startled by the disruption of the forest's tranquillity, flew off with a flapping of wings. Abigail opened her mouth to scream, but he covered it with his spare hand before any sound emerged.

"Shut up," he said roughly. "You're making a big deal out of nothing. I don't want to hurt you. Don't make me hurt you."

She stopped struggling, stared at him, wide-eyed.

"That's better." He kept his big hand over her mouth. "I don't blame you for being scared, not with all the garbage they've fed you about me. But I promise I'm not going to hurt you unless you make me." His eyes, inches away from her own, were wounded. "You're my daughter, Abigail. You're my little girl."

A cold breeze blew suddenly through the forest, and the arched pines rustled and groaned.

"Can I take my hand away? Can I trust you?"

She nodded, still wide-eyed.

"If you scream, I'll gag you." She shook her head. "Okay, then." He took his hand away but still held her tightly with the other.

Abigail sucked in a deep breath. "What do you *want*?"

"I told you," he said with exaggerated patience. "I want to be with you. And your mother too. I want us to be a family again."

"My mother?" She still stared. "My mother's hundreds of miles away."

"I know where she is," Bodine said. "I know exactly where she is."

Abigail's fear intensified.

He checked his watch. "Now then, we're running out of time. Are you going to behave, so you can walk with me?" He observed the wildness in her eyes, the fright. "I guess not. Guess I'll have to carry you, or else the nun'll be back—"

"She'll know," Abigail said quickly.

"No, she won't."

"She will. She'll know you've taken me."

"She doesn't know a damned thing about me," Bodine said.

"She does. I told her."

"What did you tell her?" he asked, mocking. "That I'm your father? So what?"

"I said that you told me to come here and ask for her," Abigail said, playing for time, praying for Sister Dominic to walk faster, willing her to start running. "She'll know you've taken me."

"No, she won't," Bodine said with conviction. "She'll just think you left, the way your mama did all those years ago. That's what they thought, you know, that she just upped and ran away."

He made his move then, gripped her more firmly about the waist, and as Abigail, frantic with shock, cried out and began to struggle again, he took a broad strip of adhesive tape from one of his jacket pockets and slapped it right across her mouth.

"I'm sorry, daughter, real sorry, but you leave me no choice."

He got her down on the ground, moving rapidly now, aware that they were running out of time. She kicked out again, flailing with both feet, caught him on one hip, but Bodine took no notice, ignored her struggling and kicking as if she were no more nuisance than one more little bug. He pinned her down with his good knee, and come to think of it, he hardly felt the pain in the other leg now, and it felt so good to be doing this, to be doing the right thing at last, to be taking what was his. Moving easily, smoothly, he took cord from another pocket, tied her hands behind her back, checked the knot, making sure it was tight enough but not too tight, then did the same with her legs, just above her ankle-height boots.

"Ready now?" he asked, breathing hard but amiable. "Good girl."

And he picked Abigail up and slung her over his left shoulder, and Christ, she was heavier than he'd imagined, but he could handle it, arthritis or not, and the first phase was over and it was time to get going, to get the hell out of this place, and to get on with phase two.

He looked around one more time, and a chuckle, a laugh of sheer triumph, long overdue, years overdue, rose from deep inside him.

"Don't you just love it," he said to no one in particular, "when a plan comes together?"

CHAPTER 20

~

Just before half past two that afternoon Susanna was working alone in her sitting room when the telephone rang. Idly, her mind still on other things, she picked up the receiver, continuing at the same time to scribble down notes on a yellow legal pad.

"Yes?"

"I have our daughter."

The pen fell from her nerveless fingers. "What did you say?"

"You heard me," Bodine said. "Are you alone?"

Susanna's mind felt as if it were in free fall. She tried to speak, but her jaw seemed rigid, her tongue suddenly heavy.

"I said are you alone?"

"Yes." She got the word out, but her mouth was very dry. There was a coffee cup on her desk, and she reached out her hand to pick it up, but its trembling was too great. "What have you done with her?"

"No questions," Bodine rapped. "You just listen to me, and listen good."

"I'm listening." Susanna stared at a photograph on the wall of Abigail at twelve, laughing out at her. She closed her eyes for an instant.

"Abigail's with me, and she's fine." The telephone line crackled with static for a moment, and she knew he was calling from a mobile. "If you don't believe I have her, you'll be getting a call from Mom and Pop Van Dusen soon enough, when they realize

Abigail isn't coming back tonight, but you are not—I repeat, you
are *not* to call them. Is that clear?"

"Yes," she whispered, terror and bewilderment like a numbing
cocktail in her bloodstream.

"I want money. No more than when I asked you before. Fifty
thousand dollars. Cash."

"I can't get that much." Susanna's thoughts raced wildly. She
never kept more than a few hundred in cash. "No bank will give
me more than a few thousand, not without prior arrangement."

"They'll give you more than that," Bodine insisted. "You get
as much as you can, but you better make it real money, *serious*
money, or you'll never see Abigail again, and that's a promise."

"I'll get it," Susanna said, struggling desperately to sharpen
up. "Tell me where and when."

"You leave now, right after we finish speaking, and you get
straight over to the bank. There's time enough before they close."

"And then?"

"Then you bring it to me."

"Where?"

"You get in your car and you make sure no one's following
you, and you drive to where we are."

"Where?" She was suddenly terrified that he might be toying
with her, that he'd cut her off without saying where he'd taken
Abigail. "You haven't told me *where*?"

"You don't need me to tell you that, do you now?"

"Of course I do. How can I—" And she stopped dead. Because
Bodine was right, she didn't need him to tell her that. Because
where else would he, warped son of a bitch that he was, go with
their daughter?

"You got it," Bodine said.

"Yes," she said, her voice a whisper again. Fresh panic rose in
her. "I won't find it. I'll never *find* you—"

"Take it easy." He interrupted her. "I know you won't find it,
which is why I'm going to meet you on the road and take you
there myself."

"With Abigail?" Hope leaped in her.

"Abigail will be waiting for us, don't you worry about that,
Susanna. Abigail won't be going anywhere."

Sudden, blinding fury seared through her, stripping her mo-
mentarily of caution. "If you've hurt her, Bodine, I swear I'll—"

"What will you do?" He remained maddeningly calm. "And haven't I already told you that she's fine? I haven't harmed a hair on her head." He paused. "Now, we're running out of time. Do you want to know where I'm going to meet you or not?"

"Yes." She was quiet again, keeping the rage down. "Please."

"Okay," he said. "You ready?"

"Yes."

"Take Route Six past Truro, go on till you get into North Truro; then watch out for some little turnings. You'll see a sign or two for Head of the Meadow Beach. Ignore that; you're looking for Small Swamp Trail. Got that?"

"Small Swamp Trail," Susanna repeated.

"It'll be on your right. If you get to Pilgrim Lake, you've missed it, so you'll have to turn back. Got it?"

"Yes," she said urgently, aware of time ticking past, but staying calm now, not daring to risk angering him. "And that's where you'll be?"

"Uh-huh," he said. "Now let's check our watches, okay? I have two thirty-seven. Check?"

"Check."

"You'll need till around half past three at the bank."

"It might take longer," Susanna said quickly. "You know how banks are."

"I know your daughter's life's in danger," Bodine said, "so I know you'll find a way to hurry them up, right?"

"Right." She wasn't going to argue.

"It's around a five-hour drive from Hawke House to P-Town, so I guess you should make it by nine."

"So you'll be there at nine?"

"I'll be there when I'm there," he said. "You get there and you wait."

"What if I'm delayed?"

"You won't be."

"What if the roads are busy?"

"It's February," Bodine said. "No one goes to P-Town in February."

"I'll do my best," Susanna said.

"You'd better do more than that," he said, harsher again. "And you better understand that if you tell anyone, and I mean *anyone*, I swear on Abigail's sweet head that you will never, *ever* see her again." Bodine took a breath. "And if I so much as smell a cop within five miles of Small Swamp Trail, I swear to you on my own life—and it may not be much, but it's all I have—I swear to you I will kill Abigail before they get one foot closer."

"I won't tell anyone," Susanna said. "I swear it."

"You'd better not."

"Please," she said quickly before he hung up. "Please don't hurt her. You wouldn't really hurt your own child, would you?"

"I'd rather not," Bodine answered.

And she didn't need to hear him say any more than that, because her old familiar inner voice said it for him.

He will if he has to, it said. *You know that.*

CHAPTER 21

~

Connie was working in her darkroom and Lucy Battaglia was seasoning a rack of lamb ahead of time for that evening's dinner and had rosemary and pepper all over her hands when the telephone rang. Bryan, in bed with the flu, his head full of cold and his body aching with fever, picked up and spoke to the caller. An instant after hanging up, he was out of bed and running down the stairs.

"Is Abigail home?" The question was shouted for whoever was in earshot.

Lucy came out of the kitchen, wiping her hands.

"Is Abigail home from school yet?"

Lucy shook her head. "I haven't seen her."

"Where's Connie?" Bryan asked. "Connie!"

Connie came wheeling herself from the direction of the dark-room. "What's the commotion?" She saw Bryan's face and stopped. "For heaven's sake, Bryan, what's happened?"

"I don't know." His voice was hoarse.

"I heard the phone. Who was it?" She blanched. "Is it an accident?"

"No." Bryan shook his head. "Nothing like that."

"Who was it?"

"It was a nun, a Sister Dominic, calling from a convent—St. Catherine's, I think she said—near Brewster." Suddenly weakened by his dash from bed, Bryan leaned against the wall. "I can't figure it out, Connie, but she said that Abigail was there this morning—"

"Our Abigail?" Connie asked stupidly.

"That's what she said."

"But she was at school."

"Was she?" Bryan paused. "According to this Sister Dominic, Abigail went there to talk to her about Susanna, looking for information about her past."

"Susanna's convent," Connie said, trying to take it in. "It must be."

"Apparently," Bryan said. "But that's not the reason she was calling." He shook his head, confused. "Sister Dominic said that she left Abigail alone for a few moments in some garden, while she went to fetch something, an old painting of Susanna, from the convent house, but when she came back, Abigail had gone."

"And?" Connie looked up at her husband, trying to make sense of what he was telling her. "So she left."

"That was what Sister Dominic thought at first. She said she had no reason to think differently, and she admits she still has no particular reason, but she said it's been troubling her all afternoon because she found Abigail such a courteous young woman, and she was sure she really wanted the painting, and it worried her that she left so abruptly. She thinks Abigail might have been upset because she couldn't help her with the information she wanted. She wanted to check that she'd gotten home okay."

Connie looked at her wristwatch. It was just after five.

"I'm going to make some calls," she said, already heading for the den. "And you get yourself back to bed," she called over her shoulder. "If we've got trouble, I need you fit."

By the time Connie had called Abigail's teacher at home and the various homes of all her friends, it was half past five, and there was still no news of her. She lifted the intercom and buzzed her husband upstairs.

"Should I call Susanna? I hate to worry her."

"Of course you should call her. Abigail might have gone there."

"I doubt that. Susanna would have let us know, for one thing."

"Abigail could still be traveling; it's quite a hike from Brewster up to Hawke House."

Connie called the house but found that Susanna too was on the missing list. According to Joe Zacharias, shortly after a call had been put through to her, a staff member had seen Susanna hurrying out of the building, looking anxious.

"Apparently she jumped right in her car and drove off without a word."

"And this was at what time?" Connie asked.

"Around a quarter to three," Joe replied.

"Thanks, Joe." Connie had an afterthought. "Do we know who the call was from?"

"No idea. Just some guy."

"Not from Abigail?"

"Definitely not."

Connie hung up, then dialed Susanna's New York apartment and left a message, and then, after another moment, she dialed Pete Strauss's number.

"Do you have any idea where Susanna is?"

"Hawke House, I think," Pete said.

"Not anymore."

"Then I can't help you, Connie. Sorry." Pete paused. "What's up?"

She told him. "And it's one thing for Abigail to go off by herself like that, but it's really not like her not to call to let us know she's okay."

"She's probably on a bus, stuck in traffic somewhere," Pete said.

"I guess."

"Or maybe she and Susanna are together."

"Then why hasn't Susanna called us?" Connie asked.

"I don't know," Pete said. "What does Bryan think?"

"Bryan has the flu really badly, and I think he's having trouble deciding whether he's mad as hell at Abigail or scared to death."

"What can I do?"

"Nothing. I don't think."

"Abigail's probably going to walk through the front door any moment," Pete said. "Try not to make yourselves too crazy." He gave a wry laugh. "Who am I kidding? You're both going to make yourselves completely bananas by the time she does get home."

* * *

Pete checked in with Connie twice in the next hour.

"I think I'm going to come up."

"What for?" Connie asked.

"Moral support, I guess. And maybe, if we all put our heads together, we can figure out where Abigail's gotten to."

"You stay home, Pete. Bryan's already called the police."

"What do they say?"

"All the usual stuff about the unpredictability of teenagers, you know."

"I know." Pete paused. "I'm coming."

"Oh, Pete, I don't like to ask you to do this."

"Am I butting in?" he asked. "Tell me, Connie, I won't be offended."

"You know better than that," Connie said.

"You're sure?"

"Pete, you're almost family."

"Then I'm on my way."

While Pete was en route to La Guardia to catch the shuttle to Boston, Susanna was heading east on the Mass Turnpike, ten thousand dollars—all the cash she'd been able to sweet-talk the recently appointed branch manager of her bank into—stuffed into her shoulder bag. Her route was worked out—she would make a right off the turnpike about ten miles past Millbury onto Route 495, then take Exit 2, pass the old Hudson River tugboat, now high and dry on restaurant property, cross the Cape Cod Canal over Bourne Bridge—and she was making sure she drove fast but safely, but her mind was focused on an old tar paper shack someplace in the dunes, and she couldn't believe it was still there after so many years, and then she thought about meeting Bodine on Small Swamp Trail, and what if she was late, or what if she couldn't find it, what would happen to Abigail then, and if anything did happen to her—

Cut that out, her inner voice commanded her. *Nothing's going to happen to Abigail as long as you keep your mind on getting there in one piece.*

But she had only ten thousand dollars. Ten thousand, when he'd wanted fifty, and who was to say what he would do when he found out that was all she'd brought him?

You'll tell him it's just a start. Tell him you'll get him more. He'll buy that: he needs money, so he won't throw ten grand in your face.

She wondered if he was armed, whether he had a gun or a knife. He'd always carried a knife in the old days, though he hadn't ever used it against her or even as a threat. He hadn't needed to because she'd been so weak and afraid of him, and then, as time had passed, he'd developed power of a different kind as she'd grown dependent on him and his visits and his gifts of red apples and cans of soup and—

That's it, the voice said. *That's the best idea you've had all day, Susanna. That could just be your ticket out of this mess, yours and Abigail's.*

Exit 6 for Springfield loomed up ahead.

Susanna signaled right and got ready to leave the turnpike. She had some shopping to do and one call to make.

Arriving at Logan Airport, Pete went straight to a bank of pay phones. About to call the Van Dusens, to let them know he would be with them soon and to check if there'd been any news, he called his own voice mail service first. Just one message had come in, logged at 6:45 P.M., approximately fifteen minutes after he had left his apartment.

"Pete, don't, whatever you do, tell anyone about this call." Susanna sounded clipped and strained. "I'm only calling you because I want someone to know in case things go badly." She paused, clearly struggling to find the right words. "Bodine has Abigail. I'm on my way to meet them now. I have money for him, and I'm going to get her back. Pete, no matter how hard this is for you, you must *not* tell anyone, especially not the police. He says if he so much as smells a cop, he'll kill Abigail, and I believe him." She paused again. Pete could hear the noise of speeding traffic behind her voice, as if she were calling from somewhere close to a highway. "Pete, if no one hears from me by morning —and I mean real morning, like eight or nine, not dawn, okay? —this is to let you know I'm heading for the Cape. He's taken Abigail to the shack, and I know that I'm the only person who can get her back safely. Pete, I know this is tough on you and the others, but you have to swear you'll do nothing until morning. Okay? Swear it, Pete." Another pause, while she deliberated whether to tell him more. "He's meeting me on Route Six just past North Truro. At Small Swamp Trail, Pete, but you use that only in the morning—right?—and only if you haven't heard from me." There was one last pause. "Swear you won't tell anyone, Pete. If you love me, *swear* it."

Pete heard the click, then the recording that told him there were no other messages. He replaced the receiver. Anger was surging in him, rage against Bodine, frustration toward Susanna for making him impotent. And fear. He had never known such fear.

For a full minute he stood at the pay phone, oblivious of the airport buzz. He checked his watch. Almost eight forty-five. If Susanna had left Hawke House at a quarter to three, that meant she could have reached the tip of the Cape by now. She could be with him now.

He made his decision. Fishing in his pocket for some more quarters, he stuck two in the slot and punched out the Van Dusens' number.

"Connie, it's Pete. Any news?" He knew the answer before it came.

"Nothing yet. Where are you?"

"Still in New York," he lied. "Listen, Connie, I'm sorry, but I've hit some problems, which means I may not be able to make it to you tonight after all."

"Oh." Connie covered her disappointment quickly. "That's okay, Pete. One of your patients?"

"Something like that." He felt bad. "How're you all holding up?"

"We're all right. Don't worry about us. We got in touch with Tabbie, and she's coming home, so we'll have a houseful."

Only not the houseful you need, Pete thought.

"I'm sorry," he said again.

"Pete, it's not your fault," Connie said.

"No," he said. "Still, I'd like to be with you."

"We know," she said.

There were no flights available that night to the Cape, so Pete went to the Hertz desk and rented himself a compact, then changed his mind and switched to a four-wheel drive.

"How long do you reckon it'll take me to drive to Province-town?" he asked the man at the desk.

"Two hours on a normal winter's night," the man said. "But I heard they're forecasting a big storm, so the roads might get a little jammed up—could slow you down a bit."

Pete finished the paperwork, got the keys and a Cape Cod map, located his Jeep Cherokee, checked his best route, and lit the Marlboro he'd been craving for the past couple of hours. He wished, suddenly, that he'd thought of bringing the dog along on the trip, but then again he couldn't imagine Steinbeck taking too well to being dumped in the hold at thirty-three thousand feet, not even for the man he loved.

Christ, he felt lonely. He couldn't recall ever feeling so lonely before in his whole goddamned life.

In her lighter moments, if one could call them that, Susanna felt like a character in *The Twilight Zone*, being sucked back into the past, into some surrealist nightmare from which, as soon as the closing credits began, she would awaken. In her darker moments—most of her moments now that she was nearing the last sector of Route 6 between Truro and Provincetown—she knew she was not going to awaken, that this was not some program she could switch off with a flick of a button. Yet there was never any doubt in her mind that she was doing the right thing—not so much perhaps the right thing, but the *only* thing—because he had Abigail, and all that mattered was finding her child and bringing her away from there, safe and well.

The rain had started a little way before Middleboro, and they'd been forecasting a storm for the Cape since she'd first switched on the radio, and each time there was an update, the predictions seemed to grow gloomier, and it was obvious it was going to be a big one when it hit, and Susanna remembered those winter storms, remembered the tumultuous lightning and the howling winds, how the little shack had only barely seemed to withstand the force of those nights, and they had always struck at night, or maybe that was just the way her memory played them back to her now. And it was night again now, and the rain was pounding harder against the windshield and the roof of the car, and great puddles were turning into pools in the dips of the road, and from the far side of the central strip, where there was one, the water thrown up by the speeding cars and trucks cascaded down on her side like waterfalls, and it was hard to see, what with the defroster and the wipers working overtime. And Susanna remembered from that other time that even Bodine had almost missed his turning, and most people agreed that Cape Cod nights were darker than most, and how was she ever going to find a little side road in all that rain and darkness?

The Cohasset police were being kindness personified, but there wasn't too much to be done, since all the evidence still pointed to Abigail's no-show being a spinning out of an apparently well-planned day's truancy from school. No one was ruling out the awful possibility that she might, along the way, have got herself into some kind of jam, but then again, her older sister's parallel disappearance gave the officers additional grounds to hope that both Abigail and Susanna would reappear, unscathed, sometime tonight.

"You don't believe them, do you?" Connie asked Bryan, dressed now and sitting with his feet up on the couch in the den.

"Do you?"

"I don't know. I want to, but—" She stopped.

"You have a bad feeling." Bryan shook his head. "I keep trying to tell myself that my bad feeling's coming from this damned flu, but I know that's not true." He mopped his runny nose. "I'm scared, Connie. I'm sorry, I'd much rather be able to lie to you and tell you not to worry, but I've never been able to keep secrets from you."

"Me neither." She took his hand.

"Tabbie should be here soon."

"Yes."

"I'm glad."

"Me too. She'll probably agree with the police."

"Yup." He took away his hand and blew his nose.

"Lucy said she's kept Abigail a serving of lamb, but she'll only give it to her if she has a damned good excuse."

Bryan looked into his wife's eyes.

"She's in trouble, isn't she?"

Connie didn't trust herself to answer.

At nine-thirty Pete was still crawling along behind a rain-created pileup on the John Fitzgerald Expressway, cursing the other drivers, cursing the weather, cursing just about every little thing that was at this moment preventing him from getting to Susanna and Abigail. At the rate he was traveling, he'd be lucky to get anywhere near Provincetown by midnight, and by that time Christ only knew what might have happened between them and Bodine. Maybe, just maybe, Susanna might have already handed over the cash and gotten Abigail back, in which case maybe they were already on their way back home. But Pete had a nasty feeling in his gut that told him it wasn't going to be as straightforward as that. A man like Matthew Bodine, a man with his perverse history, was unlikely, Pete figured, to make an honorable blackmailer, if such a creature existed.

He thought about the way Susanna had described the shack, thought about the storm they kept trumpeting about on the radio. He wondered if maybe Susanna was stuck in traffic too, somewhere on the Cape, in which case she'd be going nuts about Abigail, thinking about her all on her own with Bodine. He wondered if Bodine still had a thing about Susanna after all this time or if he was sufficiently warped to stoop as low as incest.

The mess up ahead was clearing just a little, and they were beginning to speed up from a crawl to a gentle low-gear saunter. Peering through the gloom at the drivers to the left and right of him, Pete saw resigned faces, irritated faces, angry faces, placid faces, and he wondered what kind of journey's end awaited them, whether there would be anxious families, or impatient wives, or dogs with full bladders, or lovers left jilted in restaurants, and he envied every one of them. And he didn't know if he felt like some gung ho hero chasing after his beloved in danger or a damned fool poking his nose into something he had been beseeched to keep out of.

And if I do get there sometime tonight and if I do find them, what the hell do I do about it? He couldn't call the police or Susanna would never forgive him. He didn't have any kind of weapon; he'd never even touched a gun, wouldn't know what to do with it if one was stuck in his hand. *What if Bodine has a gun?* What if that bastard had one—or a knife, maybe?—and if Pete went barging in on them, maybe he'd only be creating mayhem when Susanna might just have been calming things down.

And all that was presupposing that he was going to locate them in the first place, and he'd never even been so much as a Boy Scout, and map reading had never been his strongest point; he was a psychologist, for Christ's sake, not James fucking Bond. He shook his head at the lunacy of his mission. *I listen to people*, he thought, *I let them tell me things, I enjoy trying to make them feel better about themselves.*

The last thing he was interested in doing was making Matthew Bodine feel better about himself. He'd like to see the man behind bars, or dead maybe. He didn't think he'd ever wished a human being dead before.

It just went to prove there was a first time for everything.

Susanna found Small Swamp Trail at the third attempt, and only then by using the big flashlight she'd bought in the mall near Springfield. She saw in the funnel of light close to her face that the ribbon of steam that was her breath in the cold, wet night air was erratic as the whistle of an old steam locomotive, realized that she was panting with fear, with the sense of terror that he might be lurking close by, watching her, that he might be right behind her. But the minutes ticked away, and he wasn't there. No one was there on this awful, miserable night, with the trees bending almost double, groaning like rheumatic old men, whipped into distorted shapes by the angry, ever-rising wind and drenching rain.

For the dozenth time she checked her watch, and it was thirty-five minutes after nine, and she, who hardly ever prayed, was praying like a fervent priest that she had not come too late, that Bodine had not been and gone, and she knew now, with absolute certainty, that she would never find the shack without his guidance, not at least tonight, not till morning, when it might be too late, when Abigail, her beloved Abigail, would have been forced to spend a whole night with him. And no one in the world knew better than Susanna what that might mean, of what Matthew Bodine was capable, and the thought made her sick to her stomach, and she hurried back to the car and got into the driver's seat and locked the doors and wrapped her arms around herself, struggling to control her shivering, to control her terror.

"You made it."

The voice behind her made her scream. Susanna had never believed that people did that when they were shocked, had always thought that movie screams belonged to the realms of fantasy and fiction. But now, tonight, hearing his voice, seeing his face loom

290 / *Hilary Norman*

suddenly above her own in the rearview mirror, smelling him, his cologne, his sweat, his heat, she screamed so loudly she thought half of Truro would hear her.

"Better now?" he asked when the scream had ended.

Susanna, fighting to catch her breath, was twisted around in her seat, looking for Abigail, knowing she would not be there, hoping against hope in spite of that.

"Where is she?" she gasped.

"You know where."

"Is she okay?"

"Of course she's okay."

"Take me to her." She heard her voice, hoarse and quivering, wrecked by the screaming. "Please take me to her."

"Do you have the cash?"

"Yes. In my bag."

"How much?" He reached over to the passenger seat, grabbed the shoulder bag, and started to open it.

"All I could get."

"How *much*?"

"Ten thousand. It's all they would give me. I did everything I could—"

"Are you *kidding* me?" he bellowed in her face. "Are you serious? I told you fifty and you get me *ten*? Ten thousand miserable fucking dollars instead of *fifty*?"

"If I'd been able to tell them why, they might have given me more." Frantically Susanna fumbled for the right words to calm him, remembered what her inner voice had told her hours before. "It's just a start," she said. "I'll get you more later, I swear it. No matter where you are, I'll get it to you."

Bodine shook his head. "Ten thousand dollars—*Jesus*!"

With his right hand clenched into a fist, he pounded the back of her seat twice, then three times, and the whole car shook, and Susanna thought, for an instant, of trying to unlock the doors and making a run for it, but she knew he'd stop her, and besides, if she did that, who knew what would happen to Abigail?

"My God," he said, still shaking his head in that same disbelieving fashion. "My God, Susanna, I've got to hand it to you, you've learned to fight dirty over the years, haven't you?"

"No," she said, quickly. "Don't think I didn't try my hardest.

I begged them to give me more, but you didn't give me long enough. Oh, I know you probably thought that was best, no one having any time to react, and I guess you were right about that, because probably if I'd had all day, I might have had too much time to think about telling someone else—"

"But you didn't, did you?" Bodine asked. "I mean, you're too smart for that, aren't you? Because you know if you lied to me about that, I'd kill Abigail. You believe that, don't you?"

"Yes," Susanna said, thinking fast now, trying to plan ahead. "That is, no, I didn't tell anyone, because I promised you I wouldn't. But no, I'm not sure I believe you really would kill your own daughter, and maybe I'm wrong about that, but—"

"You're wrong," he said decisively. "Like I said on the phone, one whiff of a cop, and I would most definitely kill her, and perhaps I'd take you out into the bargain."

They were silent for a moment. Outside the car the wind subsided for a moment, then picked up again, rocking them just a little and sending a snapped off piece of a branch flying into the windshield.

"Can we go to her now, please?" Susanna asked. "She's alone in the middle of this, and she must be terribly afraid."

"I guess you'd know how she feels."

"Oh, yes," she said.

"That's good." He began to shift in the backseat. "Okay," he said suddenly, "time to go."

Susanna unlocked the doors.

"I have some stuff in the trunk," she said.

"You don't need anything."

"It's not for me," she said. "It's some things I bought for you and Abigail. You can take a look if you like."

They got out of the car and went around to the back. Susanna opened the trunk lid and shone her flashlight inside. Bodine bent a little—not too far, as if he were afraid she might whack him over the head with the flashlight—and peered inside.

"You remembered," he said, and his voice grew less harsh.

"Of course I remembered," Susanna said. "Can we take it?"

"I guess."

She leaned in and hauled out the box.

"I'll take it," Bodine said.

"It's okay. I can manage."

"You'll fall down or something." He slung her bag over his left shoulder and took the box from her arms. "We'll make better time this way."

Susanna looked at him. "Are we walking again?"

Bodine turned and started away from the car.

"Don't ask damned fool questions," he said over his shoulder.

Pete was moving now, getting used to the four-wheel drive, smoking his way too fast through his pack of cigarettes, trying not to think too much now, just to focus on the road, on the lousy driving conditions, on getting there safely.

Bypassing Cohasset on Route 3, he did think about the Van Dusens, about what they must be going through. Bryan, hampered by his flu and the dark, must be going nuts if there was nothing he could do, though maybe he was out there anyway in his car, checking the neighborhood, and maybe Tabitha was the one out on the roads, and given that their only clue had come from the Brewster area, perhaps Tabbie was on this same highway heading for Cape Cod right now. *Lord, I hope not*, Pete thought in a new wave of guilt, his eyes narrowed in concentration as the rain and wind lashed the Jeep. He hoped she was safe at home with Connie, who must be the most frustrated of all, Connie, the driving force of the family yet the one most likely to be expected to sit in her wheelchair by the phone, waiting for news.

Near Manomet, Pete stopped at a gas station to buy more cigarettes and to make two calls, the first to the Van Dusens, and he had been right, Connie was the one who snatched the phone up first, and Bryan and Tabbie had both been out on the road for a time, but they were home now, and no, there was no news. And when he called his own voice mail service, there were three messages to listen to, but nothing more from Susanna, and it was past ten-thirty now, and that meant whatever was going on near the tip of the Cape, Susanna had not been able simply to hand over the cash to Bodine and walk away with Abigail, or surely she'd have made it to a phone by now.

And Pete ran back to the Jeep, slipping on a slick patch and almost falling, but then he was back behind the wheel and back on the highway and there were about ten miles to go before he would reach the Sagamore Bridge, and soon after that he'd be on Route 6, the Mid Cape Highway, all the way, and he wasn't going to stop again, not for anything, not until he'd found Small Swamp Trail or that old tar paper shack where the woman he loved was probably right now reliving her childhood nightmares.

CHAPTER 22

He'd left Abigail in the dark; there'd been one candle, stuck in its own wax to the lid of a rusty tin, but the wind, whistling through the old timber walls, had blown it out almost as soon as he'd gone. She was huddled over in the far left-hand corner of the shack, her mouth no longer stuck with tape, but her hands and feet still bound with cord. When the door had opened again, and she'd seen the flashlight, she'd cried out in fear, but then she'd heard Susanna's voice, and when Susanna had knelt beside her, arms around her, embracing her, kissing her, holding her, checking that she hadn't been hurt, Abigail had begun to cry, whimpering like a small child.

"I was so scared."

"It's all right now, I'm here."

"I thought you wouldn't come—"

"Of course I came. I'm here now."

Bodine stood watching them for a while, until Susanna began unfastening the knots that tied her wrists.

"Stop that."

"Why?" Susanna stayed where she was.

"Because I say so."

Susanna took both Abigail's icy hands in her own, trying to warm her, to reassure her. She looked up at Bodine. "You said we could go. When you had the money."

"Except you didn't bring me what I asked for."

Susanna felt a tremor pass through Abigail and kept hold of her hands. "You know why, and you know I've said I'll send you more."

"And you know I don't believe that," Bodine said.

"I'm not a liar," Susanna told him quietly.

"Aren't you?"

"Whether we're going now or not, why does Abigail have to stay tied up?" Susanna fought to remain calm. "Now that I'm here, she's not going to run away, and I'm not going anywhere."

"Damn right," Bodine said.

"So may I?"

Abigail was quiet now, no longer weeping but her shoulders still shaking. She sensed it was wise to be silent now, knew that this was Susanna's territory, that their survival was in her mother's hands.

"Can I untie her, please?" Susanna asked him. "Please."

Bodine shrugged. "I guess."

Susanna got the first knots undone, and Abigail, still shivering, flexed her sore wrists while her mother attended to her ankles.

"Okay." Susanna rubbed the skin above the boots where the cord had bitten in. "Better move them about a bit before you try to stand up."

"No need to stand," Bodine said.

They turned and saw, in the beam from the flashlight, the knife in his hand. It was a hunting knife, the kind that could double for killing and skinning, with ugly jags in the blade. He held it in his right hand and stroked the blade with three fingers of his left.

"I know I won't need to use this," he said.

"No," Susanna said, scared but definite. "You won't."

She straightened up, took a step forward.

"Where you going?"

"Just to get something from the box." She'd known, long before she'd asked Bodine if they could leave, what his answer would be. She'd known it as far back as Springfield, when she'd gone shopping. She'd heard about what they called Stockholm syndrome; everyone who'd ever watched a news bulletin about a hostage situation knew something about Stockholm syndrome, which had something to do with captives befriending their captors against all the odds. This cardboard box, containing about as many of the same things Bodine had brought to the shack for her all those years ago, was Susanna's own Stockholm tool, her only weapon, she guessed.

"Okay," he said.

Abigail was still silent, following Susanna's movements with her eyes, flicking over to Bodine every now and again and then, quickly, averting her gaze in case he returned it. Glad to be occupied, aware that doing something, anything, would help keep her own fears damped down, Susanna took out the little gas-burning heater she'd bought from the camping equipment store in the mall and started setting it up. She caught Abigail's expression, read the confusion in her eyes, saw that she wondered at Susanna's apparent acceptance of their situation and that she resented it.

"I figured you'd both be cold and hungry by the time I got here," Susanna said quietly. "I brought some soup."

"Mushroom," Bodine said, looking down into the box.

"Of course. And graham crackers."

"No marshmallows?" Abigail's first words, out of her mouth before she could help herself, were ironic.

"Afraid not," Susanna said lightly.

"That's the trouble with kids these days," Bodine said. "Spoiled rotten."

"Abigail's not really spoiled," Susanna said.

"Gee, thanks," Abigail said.

Bodine took a step closer to her. "Don't sass your mama, girl."

"It's okay." Susanna saw the flash of fear returning to Abigail's eyes.

"No, it isn't," Bodine said.

No one said another word. Susanna got the stove working, opened a can of soup, emptied it into a small pot, and squatted on the floor to wait for it to heat. She remembered it all so well, the roar of the ocean and the weather from outside, the flickering from the little stove she'd had back then, and nothing seemed altered at all, except that the mattress was gone and someone, some time, had given the walls a lick of paint that looked yellowish cream in the faint light, and one of the cracks she'd used as a spy hole on the far wall had been sealed up with another small slab of timber nailed over it; and there was a covering on the floor that hadn't been there back then, and she figured that it had once been a decent enough rug, but sand and damp and bugs had been at it for a long while now, and the place would probably be better off, healthier, anyway, without it.

You won't be here that long. Her inner voice brought her to. *And if you're going to start thinking about those days, at least use the memories to help get you both out of here.*

Susanna looked at the soup, just starting to simmer, then glanced over at Abigail, saw her eyes fixed on her, saw that still her daughter didn't understand what she was up to, sitting down on the floor in the middle of a kidnapping and cooking supper, and how could she understand when Susanna didn't really know for sure what she was doing herself?

"You must be exhausted," she said softly to Abigail.

"I'm okay," Abigail said.

"You just have some of this soup"—Susanna spoke clearly, evenly, in a calm, low voice, willing Abigail to cooperate—"and then you can take a nap, now that you're more comfortable."

Abigail started to open her mouth to speak, then shut it again. Bodine was staring down at her, she could feel his eyes boring into her, and suddenly she thought that maybe she comprehended just a little of what was going on here now, that there was some kind of a bond happening between her mother and Bodine and that Susanna was planning to use that in some way for their sake, for her sake.

"I am kind of hungry," she said very quietly.

"Smells good, doesn't it?" Susanna said, relieved.

"Yes," Abigail said.

And Matthew Bodine sat down.

They drank their soup and ate some crackers, and Susanna offered Abigail and Bodine a red apple each.

"Not right now, thank you," Abigail said.

"Sure?"

"Yes." She saw Bodine's face. "Thank you," she said again.

Susanna looked at him. "I got us some coffee for later," she said.

"That's good," he said.

She waited a moment, then looked back at Abigail. "Do you need to go to the bathroom before you go to sleep?"

Abigail was startled, her cheeks flushed a little even in the dim light. "No," she said. "I'm okay."

"Sure?" Susanna asked. "Because you could go outside."

"She isn't going anywhere," Bodine said.

"I just thought—"

"Well, don't think." Bodine paused. "If she needs to go, she can pee in her pants. We're all family here."

Susanna nodded. "I guess we are."

Abigail made a little movement with her shoulders and was still again.

"Why don't you try sleeping for a while?" Susanna asked her. "It'll do you good."

"Okay." Abigail lay down, then sat up again. "I don't suppose you brought a blanket, did you?"

"No, I'm sorry."

"It's not too cold in here," Bodine said.

"It's not too warm either." Susanna answered before Abigail could say the wrong thing.

"I'm all right," Abigail said, and lay down again.

"Sleep tight," Susanna said softly.

Abigail closed her eyes.

The storm strengthened. The wind lashed at the little shack, and Susanna marveled again at how it had survived for so long, and then she heard a cracking from the roof, and the sound of shingles tumbling, and though there were still no windows in the walls, she knew that the dunes were being whipped up and that the air outside was full of sand on the move. She had observed, on their arrival, that one of those dunes seemed flatter but closer to the shack than it had been in her day; and though it was hard to tell, in the dark and with all the noise of the weather, she thought too that the ocean's own voice seemed closer, that the waves' pounding sounded more threatening, more menacing than it had in the past, but it was hard to be sure of anything, and how could she make comparisons? And what use were comparisons, anyway, when what she needed to do was to put aside every single wasteful, useless thought and concentrate on thinking only about what was most likely to get Abigail and her out of the jam they were in?

If we stay alive till morning, she thought at one point, *Pete will call the cops*, and for just a brief moment that thought was comforting to her, until she remembered Bodine's threats and Bodine's knife and Bodine's strength, and she knew, more than ever, that it was up to her, and her alone, and that it had to be over before morning, long before morning.

"This is strange, isn't it?" she murmured sometime later, while Abigail slept in the corner and she and Bodine sat on either side of the little heater.

"Strange how?"

"Like going back, I guess." Susanna smiled. "Except that our baby's grown a little."

For a while Bodine said nothing.

"Do you ever think of her that way?" he asked finally. "As ours?"

"Sometimes."

"I don't believe you."

"But it's the truth, isn't it? No getting away from the truth."

He shifted a little, his joints causing him discomfort.

"You're in pain," Susanna said.

"It's nothing."

"No, it isn't," she insisted. "I can see it in your face."

"Just a touch of arthritis." Bodine shrugged. "Cold and damp aren't exactly what the doctor recommended."

Susanna watched him for a few moments. "That's why you needed the money so badly, isn't it?" She spoke gently. "I wondered."

"What did you wonder?"

"Just that you'd never asked for anything in the past."

"That's not what you said when I asked before," Bodine said.

"No. I know. I was mad at you."

"You certainly were."

She leaned forward a little, her body language confiding, more intimate. "If you'd just told me the truth, you know, that you needed it, that you were sick, I'd have given it to you."

"No, you wouldn't."

"I think I would," Susanna said. "Without all that blackmail nonsense."

Bodine shook his head. "I don't believe you."

"Why not?" she asked, and glanced again in Abigail's direction. "Can't you feel it? What we all have between us?"

"What we have between us," Bodine said quietly, "is the fact that I've brought you both here against your will, that I'm holding you here with a knife in my pocket, and that there's no one around for miles who can help either of you."

Susanna refused to let him throw her off.

"I know that's all true," she said, still very softly, "but it's not what I'm talking about. I'm talking about the one thing that can't ever really be denied, however much I might or Abigail might want to deny it." She paused. "We're family, Bodine. You're my daughter's father. No getting away from that."

"Maybe," he said. "Maybe not."

The words were grudging, but Susanna saw a glimmer of something in his eyes, and it was something she remembered seeing before, just after Abigail was born, when she had realized that she had at last taken him by surprise, that Bodine had never until then anticipated that he might care for his child and for her mother. Yet he had then, and she knew now that in spite of the darkness in him, he still did care, and on this awful night, in this terrible place, it was all the power she had.

Pete was sitting in the Jeep on Small Swamp Trail, shining a small flashlight onto the map he'd begged off a woman in a gas station somewhere just past the Hyannis turnoff on Route 6. It was a map of Cape Cod on one side, with more fleshed-out inset maps of certain key areas on the back, and what Pete was currently engaged in doing was attempting to hazard where Susanna's shack might be located, and probably haphazard might be a better word for him to use since he was beginning to realize that he stood about as much chance of finding it this way as finding a golf ball in Antarctica.

He'd already gotten out of the car, poked around in the Jeep's headlights for clues that they'd been there, but he knew he didn't really know what he was looking for, and even if he had found footprints or whatever, he knew it wouldn't have made a bean of difference because out here in the dark Pete Strauss was way, way out of his depth. And he'd castigated himself, told himself he was the jerk of all time, that he should either have done as Susanna asked or told the police, but then he'd realized that giving himself a hard time wasn't going to get the job done, which was why he was back in the driver's seat, staring stupidly at the map, trying to work out where the hell to go next.

She must have told you something useful, his mind pointed out. In the sessions in which she'd talked about her months in the shack, there must have been some piece of information that stood out, that he could use now. Had she described any kind of building they'd passed along the way? He didn't think she had. Had she mentioned a geographical point, something permanent, like a pond, or had she talked about a pathway or a café or bar, closed for winter but a guidepost for him nonetheless? He was sure she had not.

Wait a minute.

Something was there, something small, but *something*, tucked away at the back of his mind. Pete let the map fall onto his lap and closed his eyes. The rain had eased slightly, but the wind shrieked louder than ever, making it hard to concentrate, but he'd always enjoyed better-than-average recall, especially when it applied to his patients, was accustomed to sifting through what might, to others, seem like trivia, just so much disposable wreckage along the route to something important, but Pete knew that the really important stuff, the key stuff, was more often than not to be found in that wreckage.

A lighthouse. She'd talked about a lighthouse.

He forced himself to relax, made himself go back in time, tuned himself in to Susanna's voice telling him her story, all the tiny twists and turns, all the incongruous but undeniable brief moments of pleasure that had poked their heads up through her childhood calamity like crocus buds in a winter landscape, all the seemingly insignificant details that had enriched the tale for the listener, had brought it to life the way a fine cinematographer enhanced a movie.

Race Point. That was it. There had been a lighthouse at a place called Race Point that had been close enough for Susanna to see its beam and hear its foghorn. Opening his eyes, he scanned the Provincetown segment of the map and found Race Point at the westernmost point of the Cape's hook. Hope died. There were several miles of dunes between himself and that lighthouse, and though he'd found Small Swamp Trail, his map didn't show the type of dune trails he'd been hoping to take the Jeep through, and without any kind of guidance, even Pete knew enough about the nature of sand dunes to know that he'd be lost in no time and probably stuck fast into the bargain.

"So much for the gung ho hero," he said out loud, and slumped back in his seat. The rain came back with a vengeance, and the wind redoubled its efforts.

Now what?

"I can't believe the noise that wind's making." Abigail had been awake for a while now, and the weather was starting to make her edgy. "It's like a grinding; it's getting on my nerves."

"It is a big one," Susanna said, "but that's the way it blows out here sometimes."

"It's just a bit of a gale," Bodine said.

"We have huge storms sometimes at home," Abigail told him. "We had one awhile back that washed away whole houses—real houses, I mean. But I've still never heard anything like this."

"I'm sure there's nothing to be worried about," Susanna said. "I think we're lucky to be where we are, between two dunes. I guess that must be how this little shack's survived for so long when so much else has been wiped away."

"It's a tough little place, all right," Bodine said.

"I've heard people say that in two hundred years there may not be a Cape Cod," Abigail said. "It's all going to be eroded a little at a time, until it's all gone."

"Well, there's a happy thought," Bodine said sourly.

"Two hundred years is awhile away yet," Susanna said.

With a huge crack, the door burst open, and the gale blew in a cloud of sand and dirt and rain. Susanna reached the door first, fought to push it back, but the storm's power was too great for her, and it took all Bodine's strength to shove it back and jam the catch back into place with a piece of broken wood.

"God," Abigail said when it was over.

"You okay?" Bodine looked at Susanna, who was rubbing her left arm.

"Fine."

"Didn't hurt yourself?"

She smiled at him. "It's nothing."

"Want me to take a look?"

"It's just a little scratch."

"Maybe I should put something on it."

She remembered it as if it were yesterday, Bodine making her bandage his thigh, the acuteness of her embarrassment, his persistence—what had come afterward. Involuntarily, forgetting all about faking Stockholm syndrome, forgetting all about making their captor feel secure, Susanna shuddered, a single, whole-body, giveaway shudder.

"I'll do it."

She heard Abigail's voice, very light, very clear, as if through a fog, felt her touch on her arm, soothing, gentle, safe.

"You all right?" Abigail asked her softly.

Susanna looked into her beloved brown eyes and nodded. "I am now," she said.

Bodine was still by the door, ready to move if it blew open again.

"Still think it's just a bit of a gale?" Abigail asked him, smiling as she dabbed Susanna's cut arm with her handkerchief.

"More like a goddamned hurricane," Bodine said, and for the first time he smiled back at her.

Pete, in his trusty Cherokee, was moving slowly, tentatively along what he hoped and prayed would prove to be a trail through the sandy mountains to the shore. He figured that if he got to the beach, he might be able to point the Jeep west and glide along without too much trouble, his own land-facing window wound down so that he could use his eyes and ears to try to penetrate this black, violent witches' brew of a night. And the ocean, even before he reached it, did sound exactly like a cauldron to him, city boy that he was, grown soft and impotent in the face of the great outdoors and all its perils, and each time the gale struck now, like a massive fist whacking into the side of the Jeep, rocking it to and fro, Pete grabbed on to the wheel harder and felt his insides tremble with the crudest kind of fear, deep-rooted and humiliating, because this was the kind of night when soft Manhattan boys were meant to be tucked up in their beds, and this was the kind of storm that snuffed soft boys out, that turned their Jeeps over or sent high-voltage lightning bolts through their bodies or pushed them into the ocean and drowned them.

"Oh, wow," Pete said out loud, braking hard, as a fabulous

spear of brilliance tore the night apart and displayed before him, with shocking suddenness, the Atlantic Ocean, less than two hundred yards away.

"Oh, *wow*," he repeated, just short of twenty years of education and a good decade of oh, so sophisticated head shrinking deserting him, leaving him simply a humble boy again, in awe of a giant, a swollen, thrashing, monumental, city boy–eating monster.

And then he realized that for the past several minutes, partly through the intensity of his concentration, but mostly through his own naked and pathetic terror for himself, he'd forgotten Susanna and Abigail and Matthew Bodine, forgotten all about looking for the little tar paper shack. And once again, staring around, away from the ocean, into the darkness that was ancient America brought back to life, Pete realized the impossibility of his task. Susanna had told him that the shack had been tucked, almost sixteen years ago, between two dunes, and Pete knew, remembered his father telling him on their own trip to the Cape on that long-ago sunny summer's day that dunes moved, slowly, gradually, a little shift at a time, except during big storms like this one, when their form sometimes changed dramatically, when a sand mountain could be transformed into a plateau or be obliterated altogether. And if that was the case, and Pete believed that now, oh, how he believed it, then how in the name of sweet Jesus could that little shack still be standing?

"*He's taken Abigail to the shack,*" Susanna had told him in her message, but that only meant Bodine had told her that. It didn't prove it was true, and for all Pete knew, they could be anywhere, Bodine could have taken them *anywhere*, and his despair made him want to weep like a child, and for just a brief moment or two he did just that, grabbed hold of the steering wheel and put his head down on his arms and cried like a baby.

And then he stopped his bawling and lifted his head again, and there, far away, but there nonetheless, was the light from Race Point. And whether or not there was any purpose to his quest, and whether or not Susanna and Abigail were in the shack and whether or not the shack was still standing, Pete knew he was back on track. He was going to drive up and down this piece of wild, sodden beach, looking and listening, and then he was going to zigzag farther and farther inland, and when he came to a dune, he would drive around it, and if he worked his way around enough of them, and if the shack was still there, surely he stood some chance of finding it?

Otherwise he'd still be here when dawn came.

"I need to go to the bathroom," Susanna said at around four o'clock.

Abigail was dozing again in the corner, and Bodine was eating another apple, and he'd drunk three cups of coffee and seemed as wide-awake as ever, and Susanna wondered why she'd been foolish enough to buy regular coffee when she could have bought decaffeinated and at least stood some chance of getting her daughter out while he slept.

"I need to go to the bathroom," she repeated, her voice low but urgent.

"What do you want me to do about it?" Bodine asked, his tone tinged with humor. "Build you an extension?"

"I'm going to have to go outside."

"No way."

"I have to." She watched him cut another wedge of Red Delicious. "Did you hear me?"

"Sure I heard you, but you're not going outside." He jerked his head toward the door. "It was hard enough getting that damned thing shut."

"You can do it again." She began to get up.

"Sit down, Susanna."

"No." She stood up all the way, looked down at him, the jagged knife in his hand. "Nothing you say or do, Matthew Bodine, is going to make me pee in front of you, okay?" She heard Abigail shift a little in the corner, then become still again. She kept her voice very quiet. "You didn't even make me do that back then, and you're not going to humiliate me now."

"I want you to stay inside, where I can see you."

"What do you think I'm going to do? Run away, in this weather, and leave Abigail alone with you?" She started for the door.

"It's dangerous out there," Bodine said.

"I'll be fine." She looked down at him. "Are you going to help me with the door or not? It'll blow off its hinges if you don't."

Bodine shook his head. "You always were stubborn."

"Was I? I don't remember."

"Stubborn as you dared to be." He grinned. "I guess you dare more these days."

"I guess I do."

Slowly Bodine got to his feet.

"What's happening?" Abigail was awake.

"Nothing," Bodine said. "Go back to sleep."

"I'm going to go to the bathroom," Susanna said.

"You're going outside, in this?" Abigail sat up.

"Your mama's such a lady," Bodine said, still smiling, "she'd rather take her chances with a hurricane than piss in her pants with me in the room."

"Can I go too?" Abigail tried to get up, but her legs were stiff from hours of sitting.

"No, you can't. Stay right where you are." Bodine gave a little jerk of the knife still in his hand.

"Be careful," Abigail said to Susanna.

"I will, don't worry."

Bodine moved ahead of her to the door, got ready to move the piece of wood with which he'd jammed the catch earlier. "You going?"

"Yes."

The power of the wind almost threw Susanna back off her feet, almost ripped the door out of Bodine's grasp. Wet sand and dirt and debris came flying into the shack again.

"Susanna, don't go out there!" Abigail cried out, holding on to the wall beside her.

Susanna fished in her pocket for a handkerchief, used it to cover her eyes and mouth. If her bladder hadn't been so unbearably full, she would have stayed, but she'd meant what she said, and right this minute the risk of being blown to kingdom come by the weather still seemed preferable to mortifying herself before Bodine.

"I'll only be a minute," she yelled against the noise.

"For Christ's sake, go if you're going!" Bodine still hung on to the door with both hands.

"Susanna, *don't!*" Abigail begged again, terrified.

She'd never gone outside on nights like this sixteen years ago, had stayed safe inside huddled beside her little kerosene heater and used the bucket Bodine had provided her with, but then there'd been no one to see her, and she'd grown accustomed to the way things were.

Now she tucked her head down, keeping the handkerchief clamped over her face, and headed for the back of the shack, knowing she must not, could not venture any farther away or she'd be lost. Moving as quickly as the wind permitted, she found a dip at the rear, did what she had to do, then, with nothing else available, used the handkerchief to wipe herself and let it fly away, whipped high into the air in an instant. Sand stung her exposed eyes as she struggled with the zipper of her denims and started back for the door.

And then she saw it. Against the backdrop of a great sheet of lightning, a strange, dark cloud, too low to *be* a cloud, bowling toward her, toward the shack, and she heard a wild, unearthly shrieking in the air, and she realized that the cloud was made up of debris whipped up by the storm, and she tried to scream out a warning, but her voice was lost in the clamor, and she tried to run, but the freak cloud was already upon them, propelled by a massive blast of gale, and her body was slammed against the wall of the shack.

"Abigail!" she screamed. *"Abigail!"*

The roof went first. Thrown onto her back in the wet sand, Susanna saw it go as if in slow motion, the old shingles flying like playing cards, the tar paper ripping and lifting off, whole pieces sucked up into the cloud like dust into a vacuum cleaner, and then one of the beams caved in and the shack just went, caved in on itself.

"Oh, dear God!" Susanna scrambled to her feet. "Oh, my *God!*"

She could move now. The worst of it had passed by, was traveling off into the distance, the dark cloud well fed with fresh debris from the shack but still ravenous for more. Susanna got around to where the door had been, but there was nothing, and she couldn't see and she couldn't hear, and then another sheet of lightning blanketed the sky and she saw Abigail's hair a few yards away.

"Abigail!" she screamed. "Are you okay?"

There was no movement. Susanna began to feel her way across to her, stumbling over the wreckage, through the mess of boards and wet, soggy sand that the gale had dropped as it had slammed through. She tripped on something, fell down onto her hands and knees, and a great prong of fork lightning bisected the sky and lit up the ground, and Susanna shrieked again, because it was Bodine she'd tripped on, and he was just lying there, his head dark with blood, and something had struck him, a wooden beam or maybe the door. And his eyes were open, his brown, cold eyes, and just a few minutes before those eyes had smiled at her, and now he was dead, and a great and curious pang of sorrow passed through Susanna because when all was said and done, he had still given her Abigail.

"Abigail," she whispered.

She crawled on, leaving Bodine behind, found her daughter, and she was alive, but a spear of wood had stabbed her just beneath her left shoulder, and Susanna was terrified it might be near her heart or close to an artery, and she only barely stopped herself from pulling out the spear, just remembered in time that it was better to leave it, that otherwise she might unplug the wound and then anything could happen, Abigail might start spurting arterial blood, and then there would be nothing she could do to stop it.

On her knees in the rubble Susanna sat back on her haunches and began to weep. Abigail's left leg was hardly visible beneath a large segment of timber wall; she couldn't tell if it was broken or bleeding, didn't know if she would be able to drag her free, or if by moving her, she might worsen her injuries.

"What do I do?" she said softly, though there was no one to ask. "What do I do?" She closed her eyes, and tears of purest self-pity rolled down her grime-covered face. "I don't know what to *do*."

Get her out. The voice that had always spoken to her in times of greatest need or self-doubt directed her again now. *You have to get her out of here right now.*

Susanna stopped weeping and reached out for the piece of wood that covered Abigail's leg. She grasped it firmly with both hands, aware that if she dropped it back, it might cause more harm and more pain, and it was heavier than it looked, and her head had begun to spin, and she had to stop for a moment to steady herself.

No time to stop. Get her out.

She tried again, and this time it moved with her, and its base was caught beneath a lump of rubble, but she yanked at it with all her might, and it came away, faster than she had anticipated, almost knocking her flat on her back, but she twisted her body around so that she could drop it clear of Abigail, and the wood fell with a crash, and a fresh cloud of dust and sand flew up into the air, choking her, making her cough.

Abigail moaned.

"Abigail?" Susanna whirled around, stared at her, saw that she was stirring. "Sweetheart, you're all right; try not to move."

Abigail opened her eyes, bewildered, then, almost immediately, terrified. "Susanna?"

"I'm here, sweetheart, I'm right here. It's all over, and I'm going to get you out of here."

Abigail moved her head, tried to sit up.

"No," Susanna said, quickly. "Don't move. We have to get you out carefully, slowly."

Abigail saw the spear of wood in her chest then and whimpered with horror. Her face grew white as chalk, and she closed her eyes again. Susanna reached for her right hand and clasped it, trying to warm her.

"Try to keep calm, Abigail; you have to keep calm."

"Where is he?" Abigail whispered, her eyes still shut.

"You don't have to worry about him anymore," Susanna said softly.

"Where *is* he?"

Susanna held on to her hand. "He's dead. Something hit his head. He's gone."

Abigail said nothing at all.

"Did you hear me, sweetheart?"

There was a faint, weak nod. "I heard you."

"Try not to think about it," Susanna said. "Just think about how it's going to be when we get you out of here. Think of home, Abigail."

For a long moment neither of them spoke, and suddenly Susanna became aware that the storm seemed to have abated a little, and it was as if the freak wind had absorbed the great force from it, and perhaps it had moved away to sea or was simply dying its own natural death.

"You can't move me." Abigail's eyes remained closed, but her voice had become a little stronger, her mind clearer. "I'm too heavy."

"No, you're not."

"We need help, Susanna. You have to get help."

"I'm not leaving you."

"You don't have to." Abigail opened her eyes, turned her face to the side so that she did not have to see the wood impaling her. "He had a phone with him."

"A phone?"

"Bodine had a cellular phone with him. He used it to call you."

Susanna remembered the static on the line when she'd answered the call back at Hawke House, a lifetime ago, remembered that she'd thought then that he might be speaking on a mobile.

"He put it in one of the pockets of his jacket," Abigail said. "Can you reach him? Can you get to him?"

Susanna craned her head, peered through the dark.

"I think so, maybe."

"If you can get to the phone, you can call the police." Abigail's voice was weakening again. "Susanna, let go of my hand and find the phone."

Very gently and carefully Susanna took her hand away from her daughter's and turned herself around, still on her knees. Bodine's cheek was visible, very pale. Susanna felt sick.

"Hurry," Abigail whispered.

Susanna stood up and walked across to where the body lay, picking her way cautiously, afraid of falling. Reaching him, she averted her gaze from his face, looked down at his jacket. She could see four pockets, two zip-fastened at breast level, two lower down. She bent down, took a deep breath, and unzipped the first.

"Got it?" Abigail asked.

"Not yet." Susanna moved more quickly, fighting to ignore the irrational but sickening fear that Bodine might suddenly come back to life, the way bogeymen often did in movies, and grab her wrist or ankle—the way he'd grabbed her ankle years before on that other beach, before he'd raped her. *He's dead, Susanna*—the voice was harsh now—*dead and gone. He can't hurt you ever again.*

The fourth pocket was fastened with Velcro. She ripped it open.

"Got it."

She pulled it out, looked down at it stupidly through the dim light. She had never used a cellular phone, disliked them, the way they intruded in public places, and now one of them was a lifeline, Abigail's lifeline.

"I don't know what number to dial," she said, confused. "What number do you dial to get the police on these things, Abigail?"

There was no reply.

"Abigail?" Susanna stared across at her, saw that she wasn't moving anymore. "Oh, dear God," she said, and hit 911. She put the phone up to her ear, but nothing was happening, brought it down again, peered at it wildly, saw a button marked "Send" and pressed that. Still nothing happened. She tried again, then tried 0 for the operator, pressed "Send," and again there was nothing. No light, no sound. And then she realized that Bodine must have left the phone turned on in his pocket, and the battery had drained away.

She let the phone fall from her hand to the ground.

And saw the heater. About five feet away, on its side.

It was one of those little camping gas devices, with a circular container marked with all the usual warnings that gas cylinders and aerosol canisters came with. "Do not expose to naked flame; do not pierce, even when empty." That kind of warning.

A sliver of sharp stone, something that maybe the wind had deposited, or that the roof had brought down with its collapse, had penetrated the side of the container, just below its label.

Do not pierce.

Susanna thought she could hear gas hissing.

The heater was still alight.

She had never moved so fast before in her entire life.

"Abigail!" Her voice was almost a bellow now, commanding.

Abigail, unconscious again, did not respond. Susanna got over to her, bent down, grasped first her right arm, then her left, mindful of the dagger of wood but forced to choose the lesser of two perils, and began to drag her. She saw that the bloody stain on her chest had grown, but she could not stop now, had to get her out, and Lord, she was heavier than she had dreamed, but didn't they always say that people got stronger when they were in mortal danger? And so she dragged her, and heaved, and at last they were moving, and once she tripped backward over a piece of rubble, and she heard Abigail's unconscious groan, but she picked herself up and took hold of her daughter's arms again and went on dragging; and the rain had almost stopped now, and the wind had died right down, and the night was suddenly so silent that she could hear her own gasping and her own grunts over the sound of the ocean, and they were almost clear of what had been the tar paper shack, almost clear—

Pete, sitting in the Jeep, engine turned off, despairing of ever finding them, resigned now to waiting for dawn, heard the explosion from somewhere over to his left.

His head shot up. He saw, thought he saw, a flash of something bright orange and yellow, a flame—it *was* a flame—and then, almost as quickly, it was gone again. No, it was still there, just fainter, and Pete knew, with absolute, unshakable conviction, that it had come from the shack. It must have come from there because there was no one else around on this godforsaken horror of a night, no one except Susanna and Abigail and Bodine, and oh, dear Christ, if he'd hurt them—

His hands trembling, his whole body vibrating with tension, he turned the key, switched the headlights back on, trained his eyes firmly on the splash of flame and gunned the motor into life.

Less than a half mile away—that was all the distance there'd been between him and them; that was *all*—he saw the weakly flickering flames of a fire deprived of anything dry to feed on. And then he saw the remains of what had been Susanna's old tar paper shack.

And then he saw them.

CHAPTER 23

~

All the way to Hyannis, Pete knew that something was seriously wrong with Susanna, something below the surface, something out of the province of medical doctors or surgeons. Something in his realm.

Aside from cuts, scratches, and an inevitable bunch of bruises that would, within hours, turn most colors of the spectrum, Susanna seemed, superficially at least, to be miraculously uninjured despite having been thrown several feet from the shack by the explosion. But ever since the initial relief and fleeting joy at finding Pete beside her, Susanna had withdrawn alarmingly into herself. For the entire duration of the journey to Hyannis she had hardly spoken a single word, just sat in the back of the Cherokee, cradling Abigail's still head in her lap, murmuring softly to her.

Pete knew that she was desperately afraid for the girl, and he knew too that she was almost certainly in shock, and for all he knew, she might even be hiding a concussion, and he was anxious for the medics to take a good look at her too, once Abigail was being taken care of; but all his instincts about Susanna, professional and intimate, warned him that this retreat, this *absence* was being caused by something more than shock, injury, or fear, something more profound even than the renewed trauma she and her daughter had just endured. He remembered the things Susanna had told him about past encounters with hospitals, remembered that she had suffered an anxiety attack when Hawke had first been hospitalized in Rome, that she'd said to him soon after their first meeting that hospitals made her a "little crazy." But this didn't feel to him like a phobic response. This was more.

"You okay?" he asked her very gently, every now and again, glancing at her face in the rearview mirror.

"I'm fine," she answered each time quietly.

"How's Abigail doing?" He watched her, saw no trace of expression in her eyes, none of her natural mobility in her face.

"She's doing fine too."

"No change?"

"No change."

And then she'd talk to Abigail again.

"You're doing fine," she murmured, "you're doing just fine."

And Pete drove a little faster.

At Cape Cod Hospital Pete left Susanna and Abigail in the Cherokee while he ran inside the emergency care department to get help, but when he came back out with two nurses and an orderly with a gurney, Susanna wouldn't let go of Abigail.

"No," she said. "You can't take her."

"It's okay, Susanna," Pete said. "They're going to help her now."

"No!" Susanna put her arms more tightly around Abigail, and her face became obdurate. "You mustn't take her."

First the orderly, then both nurses tried but failed to persuade her to let go, and finally it was Pete, in some distress, who forcibly had to prize Susanna's hands from her daughter's shoulders, and then suddenly Susanna went limp and let go, and they got Abigail onto the gurney and straight into the emergency room.

Pete looked at Susanna, slumped against the seat, not speaking, not moving, and a chill passed through him.

"Aren't you coming in?" he asked her very gently.

She didn't answer.

"They need some information about Abigail, Susanna," he said, "so they can help her better. I can tell them most things, but I'd like you to come inside with me."

"No."

Pete put out his hand. "Come on, sweetheart."

"*No.*" There was a flicker of terror in her eyes.

"Don't you want to stay with Abigail?"

"I'm not allowed," Susanna said.

"Of course you are."

"No." She shook her head.

Pete hated leaving her there, but he knew he had to get inside, that any more delay might jeopardize Abigail further. "Okay," he said, "I'll tell them what I can, and I'll be right back out to get you. Is that all right?" He got no reply. "Susanna, do you understand me?"

"Yes," she said.

"Is that Abigail's mother?" A doctor, waiting for consent for the surgery the patient needed, nodded toward Susanna. Pete had finally persuaded her into the waiting area, where she sat, like a stone, white-faced and still.

Pete thought about his answer.

"She is," he said. "But she's not her legal guardian."

"Where is her legal guardian?"

"Her foster parents are on their way from Boston. I called them first chance I had after the accident."

"How long till they get here?"

"Could be awhile yet," Pete said.

"But that woman is Abigail's mother."

"She is."

"So I'll settle for her signature."

"I'm not sure she's in any condition to sign anything," Pete said.

"She has to. Her daughter needs surgery now."

"Okay." Pete nodded. "I'll try."

"You have to do better than try," the doctor told him.

Pete sat down beside Susanna. "How're you doing?"

"Fine."

"Good."

He waited another moment, waited as he had ever since they'd taken Abigail away, for Susanna to ask about her, to do anything vaguely normal or comprehensible. If she'd become hysterical, even started screaming or throwing chairs around the room, Pete would have known better how to deal with her than with this total numbness, this apparent insulation of whatever was happening in her mind. Under other circumstances Pete knew he would have wanted her to be given a shot, to be sedated, to enable her to take time out from this immediate period, but with Connie and Bryan still too many miles away to sign the necessary papers, Pete knew he had to get through to her somehow, before he could allow her the consolation of that escape route.

"Susanna, listen to me."

"I'm listening," she said very quietly, hardly audible.

"Abigail needs some surgery to repair the damage done by that piece of wood." He took hold of her left hand, found it icy, squeezed it gently. "She's lost a lot of blood, and they want to get her into the OR right away."

"No," Susanna said.

"Yes, sweetheart, they do. They have to operate now."

"I said no." Susanna took away her hand.

Pete leaned back, more bewildered than ever. "Susanna, I don't think you're taking this in. Abigail has to have this surgery; she *has* to have it. Do you understand me?"

She did not look at him. "It's not allowed," she said.

She'd said something similar outside, when he'd first tried to get her to come into the hospital.

"Of course it's allowed," he said, his confusion growing.

"No," she said.

He took her hand again, kept hold of it when she tried to shake him off, and after a moment she just let it go limp, the way she had gone limp in the back of the Jeep.

"They need you to sign the papers, Susanna." He pushed on, trying to bulldoze his way through whatever was going on in her head. "You have to sign before they can give her the anesthetic."

She shook her head.

"Susanna, you have to sign."

"I can't," she said.

"She won't sign," Pete told the doctor.

"Why the hell not?"

"What's your policy on surgery without consent?"

The other man looked frustrated. "If a patient's life's in immediate danger, we sometimes have to take action, but judgment calls like that are something we do everything to avoid, and when the mother's actually *here*—" He broke off and looked at Susanna. "Is it a religious problem?"

"Not that I know of." Pete too was looking at her. "I think she should see Abigail."

"The shape she's in, I'm not sure that's such a hot idea."

"I'm not sure either," Pete said, "but I think it's the only way of getting through to her. It certainly can't do much more harm."

The doctor shrugged. "Okay."

Pete went back to Susanna, took her hand again, drew her to her feet.

"We're going to see Abigail."

Hope flickered in her eyes. "Are we going home?"

"No, we can't go home, Susanna."

He led her toward the trauma section, and when she saw where they were headed, Susanna tried to stop walking, dug her feet into the floor, but Pete urged her on, gripped her arm, and told her that she had to do this, that she had to help Abigail, that her daughter needed her now, and she stopped fighting again and let him walk her on.

Abigail had come to awhile back, but she'd had a shot of something since then, and she was out of it again now, and there were little oxygen tubes in her nose and a drip in the back of her left hand, and she looked very pale and terrifyingly fragile.

"It looks worse than it is," Pete said.

Beside him, Susanna made a small strange mewing sound.

"She'll be okay after the surgery."

"Oh, God." Susanna swayed.

Quickly Pete put his arm tightly around her waist, held her upright, keeping silent now, waiting, praying that she was coming out of it.

"Oh, dear *God*." Susanna stared down at Abigail, and Pete saw the shock of this fresh horror dawning in her eyes, and it was like watching someone coming out of a trance.

He seized the moment. "Susanna, they have to operate." He spoke as if he were saying the words for the first time, as if she'd never refused. "They need you to sign some consent papers."

Still, she gazed down at her unconscious daughter.

"Susanna," Pete said, sharply. "Will you sign?"

Slowly, half bewildered, she turned her face up to his.

"Of course I'll sign," she said.

While Abigail was still in the OR, the other Van Dusens arrived at the hospital, each of them anxious, relieved, appalled, rejoicing that they were—would be, God willing—safe. Sitting with them all in a waiting room, observing those good people wrapping Susanna in their love and warmth, Pete maintained his own silent, secret vigil over Susanna's battered psyche. Her intellect seemed, mercifully, restored, and her equilibrium too, superficially at least; she was able now to speak to doctors, nurses, and police officers with perfect clarity. With Connie on one side, Tabitha on the other, and Bryan—poor, wretched man, still sick but unable to sit still—pacing before her, Susanna related the events of the past twenty or so hours as best she could, all the way through to the finding of Matthew Bodine's body in the rubble of the tar paper shack.

The police were gentle and courteous, willing, for now, to hold back the many more questions they would inevitably have for her about the relationship to this night's events of old, unreported crimes. And Susanna remained so calm with them, all her fears for Abigail seeming rational now, and she was back to being Susanna again. Yet every now and then her eyes met Pete's when no one else was looking, and he realized that there was a message in those eyes for him alone, that she had things to say to him. He had grown accustomed through the years to reading her, to knowing when another segment of her past was ripe for telling, and it was hard to believe that there could still *be* more. Yet he knew there was, had known that for a long while, and it was only a matter of time, of waiting for the right moment.

Seven days passed before it came. Abigail, recovering well, was discharged from the hospital after three days and went home. Susanna, needing to stay close for the time being, asked Pete if he could spare another day or two out of his schedule to make sure that Joe Zacharias had everything under control at Hawke House, and Bryan, back on his feet now, was giving the police the help they needed. And life was going on as best it could, and they all knew there was unfinished business, that Abigail had still received none of the answers to her questions, that a true balance in their lives could never be struck until those answers had been given, but no one talked about it, no one spoke to Susanna about it, no one wished to torment her further.

On the eighth day she called Pete, now back in Manhattan. He was with a patient when she called, with another waiting to see him, and it was more than two hours before he was able to get back to her.

"You know there's more, don't you?" she said without preamble.

"I know."

"I'm ready now. To share the rest. All of it." She paused. "I knew I was ready before Bodine—" She stopped.

"You want to come down," Pete said, gentle as always.

"I do."

"When?"

"Soon as you'll have me."

Sitting at his desk in his office on Eighth Street, Pete felt something stir deep inside him, part excitement, part fear, part wonder.

"Come now," he said.

CHAPTER 24

～

"We lived in Sandwich, on the bay side of the Cape, a couple of miles from the Sagamore Bridge. The oldest town on the Cape. Incorporated 1639. We learned that almost from birth, I think. It seemed very important, somehow, to our teachers, being the oldest. My mother referred to it often."

Pete waited awhile. "Go on."

"You might have driven through Sandwich on your way to the shack."

He shook his head. "I took Route Six, and it was dark. But I did see it once, on the way to the dunes, as a boy, the time my dad took me."

"What did you think?"

"Of the town? I don't think I thought anything much about it. I was a boy on my way to the beach." He thought. "I do remember seeing a sign to a beach there, come to think of it. I thought we'd arrived—*Daddy, are we there yet?*—you know how kids are."

"East Sandwich Beach, that would have been."

"I gather it's an attractive town."

"In a very respectable way, yes, it is."

"Did you like living there, Susanna?"

"No."

"Why not?"

"I guess because I was so unhappy there."

"Were you unhappy all the time?"

"Not all the time, no."

Pete waited for her again, this time without urging. There was no need to push now; he knew it would come, knew that this time, this session, at long last, it had to come. Otherwise, in spite of all they had been through together, she might still lose Abigail. The magic words, finally. *Abracadabra.* He, as her therapist and friend, had failed to extricate this from her, this missing piece of puzzle, for all these years, but today there would be no turning away at the last minute. It was coming. It was thick in the air, the way a distant thunderstorm might feel to a dog.

She began again.

"Most of the time, until it happened, I don't think I knew that I was unhappy. I was just vaguely aware of not being really *happy*, you know? Uncomplicatedly happy, the way small children are supposed to be." She paused. "Our house was a strange home. It was solid and handsome, like a lot of the houses in Sandwich. White clapboard with gray shutters and a gray front door—not unlike our house in Cohasset." She paused again. "I remember thinking how similar it looked when Bodine first brought us there. I had this tiny flash of memory that made me very uncomfortable for just an instant, but then I saw the roses around the door and the swing seat on the porch and the bicycles leaning up against a wall, and it went away again. Nothing could have been more different."

"What made your house so strange?" Pete asked gently.

"My mother."

"Tell me about her."

"I'm going to," Susanna said.

One last time she paused. Looking at her face, seeing the strain and the effort and the fear, Pete thought she resembled a diabetic child on the brink of her first self-injection; only this needle, he knew, would plunge infinitely deeper than flesh or vein. He wanted suddenly to halt her, to take her in his arms and comfort her, tell her she didn't have to do it after all, didn't have to force herself back into the dark, into the pain. But he had no right to do that, and all he was to her at this moment was a receiver, a receptacle, and so all he could do was to sit quietly, in the prescribed manner of psychotherapists, and wait for the pain to emerge into the light, to be exposed and faced.

"I had a sister," Susanna said.

The house was on Main Street, out of the center of Sandwich, near Shawme-Crowell State Forest. Seen from the outside, the house was as attractive as most in that street, with a cool, clean, tranquil, suburban feel that seemed to signal a normal, regular American family living within. Mom, Pop, two, three, or maybe four kids, and a dog. Breakfasts around the kitchen table, pancake stacks, crispy bacon; games out in the backyard, with Mom checking through the kitchen window; Dad taking time out in the early-summer evenings to toss a softball around or train the boys with bat and catcher's mitt; TV set in the den, the whole family watching Red Sox games and eating popcorn; Thanksgiving dinners in the seldom used dining room, all lovingly polished timber and gleaming family silver; Christmases spent around the tree, strung with lights and surrounded by brightly wrapped packages.

It was nothing like that inside the house on Main Street where Martha King, widow of Joshua King, lived with her two daughters, Susanna Mary and Abigail Sarah. While her late husband had been Catholic, Martha had been raised by Christian Scientist parents—both long dead—in Chatham, believing, as first taught by Mary Baker Eddy, that man reflected God and was spiritual, that the physical body and mortal mind were counterfeit, and that the whole material world, therefore, with all its suffering was a misconception. Like many of her fellow believers, Martha was steadfastly opposed to seeking medical aid, but since she had always enjoyed unblemished health, this had never presented a problem. When she had first become pregnant, however, Joshua had become anxious for her and their unborn child, and frequent arguments had arisen between them. But Martha's mother had borne her without the help of drugs or doctoring, and so it was when first Susanna and then, eighteen months later, Abigail, were born.

Six months after Abigail's birth, Joshua King was killed when a lightning bolt struck him on the eighth hole of Holly Ridge Golf Course. Within three months of his funeral it had become pretty much generally known that the Widow King had gone somewhat awry. Martha became as reclusive as it was possible for a mother of a two-year-old child and a nine-month-old baby to be. She removed herself from every aspect of the local social life that Joshua had encouraged her to enjoy; her acquaintances observed that she appeared, for a while, to be shriveling up into herself, but then, as time passed, she seemed to begin to grow again, her personal convictions, religious and otherwise, multiplying out of all proportion and becoming so rigidly held and formidable that Lettie Forbush, her next-door neighbor, described her on the telephone to her daughter as having turned from a frail birch tree into an oak and then on into a steel girder.

Martha believed she had risen above and beyond the normal confines of Christian Science. Declaring the house on Main Street her own personal house of God, she had begun to create her very own branch of the religion, creating new credos and rules. The bans on alcohol, smoking, or doctoring were no longer enough for Martha King; there was now to be no television, no radio, no music, newspapers or magazines (except for the *Christian Science Monitor*), no books except the Bible and *Science and Health with Key to the Scriptures*, and no photographs except one. Gone from her finest silver frame was her picture of Joshua, and in its place was her most prized possession, her photograph of Mary Baker Eddy, with whom Martha had become obsessed. Morning, afternoon, evening, and often late into the night, Martha prayed to the framed picture; on her knees she prayed for guidance, for discipline, for strength and purity, and for new rules with which to organize her new private church.

"Pray with me now, Susanna Mary," she ordered her older daughter each day, making her kneel before Mrs. Eddy's shrine.

"Yes, Mama," Susanna said obediently.

"Abigail Sarah is still too young to understand," Martha went on, "but the more knowledge of the Lord and Mrs. Eddy you are blessed with, the better able you will be to guide your sister through life." Her face was grim. "We have already seen how the Lord punishes, have we not, Susanna Mary?"

"Yes, Mama."

Susanna knew that the "Lord's punishment" was how her mother had come to account for her father's accidental death. Mama had told Susanna that Mrs. Eddy had come to her in a dream to declare that Joshua had been punished for his wrongdoings: for his frivolity and gaiety, Mama said, for his liking of an occasional glass of whiskey, for his addiction to his pipe, and, above all sins, for his appetite for sex. Mama told Susanna that she was sorry that Joshua was now burning in hell, but on the other hand, when the Lord had seen fit to send a lightning bolt to smite her husband, Martha knew that He had also blessed her with a new clarity of vision.

"Life is so much easier to comprehend now than it was before," she told her daughter happily.

Susanna found nothing easy to comprehend. She was just a little girl, and the way her mother spoke to her scared her; the things she said about the father she scarcely remembered were a mystery to her that made her unhappy. She didn't like the way their house felt, how dark it was, how silent. She felt uncomfortable and ill at ease when Mama made her get down on her knees and pray with her to a photograph. She'd hated it when Mama had gotten rid of the television and then the radio and all her coloring books, but most of all, she'd hated it when Mama had torn up all their old family pictures. Mama didn't know it, and Susanna had been terrified of getting caught when she'd done it, but she'd salvaged one photograph from the trash can, a torn snap of Mama and Daddy on their wedding day, and now that picture, repaired with tape and resting under a pile of underpants in the bottom drawer of the chest in her bedroom, formed Susanna's own private monument to unremembered but happier times.

Susanna knew that people outside the house felt sorry for her, was aware of the pitying glances when she walked down the street. Between the ages of two and four, she had seldom been seen in public, closeted indoors with her quirky mother and baby sister, and when she had emerged, oddly clothed in too-long skirts, sleeves down to her wrists even in high summer, her white-gold hair almost completely covered by a strange Amish-style bonnet, that awareness of the curious stares of passersby often gave her the nervy, blinking, anxious look of a young animal rarely exposed to traffic or humans.

At the age of five Susanna had duties to perform. Solemn and silent, forbidden to speak to anyone outside the house, she wheeled her sister's stroller along Main Street, bought the groceries, and oversaw the delivery of supplies to the house, for Martha no longer went out to do her shopping. Martha no longer did a lot of things; cooking and washing and ironing and gardening and cleaning took up too much valuable praying time, especially when the Lord had given her Susanna to do them instead.

The chores were hard and often dangerous for a little girl. It was difficult to stand on a chair to reach the stove or ironing board or sink, but Susanna grew accustomed to the bumps and burns and tiring work. She liked doing the work for her mother because it kept her busy, out of Martha's way and off her knees before Mrs. Eddy. She especially liked running errands outside, in spite of the way people stared at her, and she understood them better now, knew they stared only because she looked so different from the other children in the neighborhood. So far as Susanna was concerned, anything that took her out of their dark, gloomy house and into the fresh air was a blessed relief, and she knew that she was a sinner for feeling that way, but she couldn't help it.

Susanna lived for her baby sister. Little Abigail, the light of her life, the hope of her future, the most beautiful and the sweetest child in the world, to be protected against all bad things at all costs. Susanna thought she probably did still love her mother, because all children loved their mothers, but in truthful moments she had to admit she was no longer wholly certain of that, for Martha was not an easy woman to love.

"I must be a very bad girl, Abby," she whispered to the three-year-old when they were alone, though she knew Abigail didn't really understand what she was saying. "I must be really bad not to be sure I love my mother."

"Abby loves Mama," Abigail said, her wide lilac eyes a mirror image of her big sister's.

"Of course you do," Susanna said.

"Abby loves Zanna too," Abigail said, though when Martha was present, she had already learned that she must use her big sister's full name.

"And I love you," Susanna said passionately, "more than anyone in the whole wide world."

She watched her sister's sweet, too-vacant face and felt a pang of fear, for she was coming to realize that Abigail, starved as she was of normality, was not developing as even Susanna, young as she was, thought she ought to be. Deprived of the same things as Abigail, Susanna, blessed with greater inner resources, had managed to compensate, had learned to use her duties to her advantage, always pausing for a moment or two in the park on the way back from the stores to watch other children playing or to listen to birds singing, always eagerly tuning her ears to the chatter in the streets, always making a great effort to read the newspaper headlines in the drugstore—for Martha had taught Susanna to read, except that her early diet had been Mrs. Eddy's writings rather than Dick and Jane.

As well as she could, Susanna struggled to bring a little of the outside world into the dim, silent house for her little sister, but in a while now, when Susanna started school, Abigail would be entirely at her mother's mercy, and without her sister to keep her mind active and open, Susanna, who knew little enough of life out in the real world, feared instinctively what might become of her.

She went through first grade and found that she came home each afternoon to a house hardly altered. Abigail remained sweet and untarnished by the unyielding somberness surrounding her; with her beloved Zanna absent, she had found, in the recesses of her own lonely mind, an imaginary friend she named Kooka with whom she chattered quietly as she gazed out the window of her bedroom at the apple tree in the backyard.

In Joshua's springs and summers, the backyard had been a flower garden, awash with color as the seasons had unfolded, but now the soil lay barren and unturned, the lawn cut by the gardener who still came once each month, forbidden by the Widow King to do anything more than mow or weed, and the only splashes of color came from the daisies and buttercups and marigolds that sprang up between his visits, and from the green leaves, white blossoms, and the apples themselves that grew plump and rosy in early fall.

With so little beauty to occupy her eyes, the tree became the focal point of the backyard for Abigail, and during the hours that Susanna was out at school or running errands for their mother, she and Kooka would whisper about its magic properties, inventing tales about the creatures that lived within its trunk and came out only in spring and summer, when it was safe to hide behind its leaves and bouncing apples.

"Kooka says they're fairies," Abigail told Susanna after school.

"Kooka says they sleep inside the tree and sometimes they climb inside the apples."

"Do they, Abby?"

"Kooka says we mustn't eat the apples or we might hurt them."

"I don't think we'd hurt them," Susanna told her.

"I told Mama about the fairies, but she got mad and made me pray."

"I think maybe you shouldn't talk to Mama much about the tree fairies, Abby, or about Kooka either."

"Why does Mama get so mad at me, Zanna?" The eyes were wide and hurt and curious.

"Mama's not well," Susanna said. "That's why we need to mind what we say to her, okay?"

"Okay, Zanna."

Ever since starting first grade, Susanna had done all she could to try to conceal the bizarreness of her homelife from the other children. Martha insisted she go off each day in one of her hideous, long-skirted, long-sleeved dresses, with her hair covered, but even on her first morning Susanna had been well prepared, for she had seen enough in her preschool years to know how other children dressed. Trained by Martha in basic sewing, Susanna had stayed up late every night for two weeks before the start of school, cutting down one of her dresses, as well as her young, still clumsy fingers could manage, to a more acceptable shape; and each morning on the way to school, Susanna hid behind a big old bush by the cemetery near Main Street and Pine to change her clothes hastily, remove her bonnet, and brush her hair loose, stopping each afternoon on the way back to reverse the process.

It was, of course, a small town, so shorter dress or not, her fellow pupils knew all about the crazy Widow King, and the weirdo outfits, and the house into which no normal person was ever invited, but Susanna was so grateful to be in school that she thrived, drinking thirstily from the cups of information and companionship offered her. And at recess, when the children were sent outside to play, she learned so swiftly to take the name-calling and mockery without rancor that she soon began to make friends, astounding her teachers with her self-possession and control. "Six going on sixteen," they said about her, marveling at what adversity could do to a child.

Abigail's fascination with the apple tree grew stronger with each passing month.

"I saw the fairies last night," she told Susanna one afternoon in the spring. "Kooka says that I can visit with them if I'm good."

"I don't think fairies are allowed visitors, Abby."

"Kooka says that only special children are allowed to visit them."

"You are pretty special." Susanna smiled.

"So can I go, Zanna? Can I?"

"Sure you can go." Susanna looked out of their window at the tree and frowned. "When Kooka says you can visit, what does she mean?"

"That I can go see the fairies in their tree."

"Stand on the grass, you mean, and wave at them?"

"And talk to them too," Abigail said.

"You know you mustn't ever try to climb any tree, don't you, Abby?"

"I know that, Zanna."

"You know why, don't you?"

" 'Cause it's dangerous."

"That's right. Climbing trees is very dangerous."

"And Mama would get mad."

"Even Zanna would get mad if you did that."

Abigail giggled at that. Zanna never got angry with her, had often said to her that it was impossible to get mad with the little girl she loved more than anyone in the world.

"Kooka says she may take me to see the fairies tomorrow."

Susanna kissed her. "Tell Kooka I hope you both have a lovely time."

Abigail did not get to see the fairies next day. The first time she and Kooka had ventured out into the backyard, she told Susanna later, Martha had called her into the house, scolded her for idling, and made her kneel before the photograph for a whole hour, praying for guidance. The second time, Abigail said, as she had stood at the foot of the apple tree with Kooka on her shoulder, it had started to rain, and Kooka had told her that the fairies always sheltered inside the trunk when it rained because their wings melted when they got wet and took a whole month to grow back again.

"Tomorrow," Susanna told Abigail. "You'll see them tomorrow." She remembered there was no school the next day. "Maybe we can see them together." She paused. "If Kooka doesn't mind."

"She won't mind," Abigail said eagerly. "Oh, Zanna, do you promise we'll see them?"

Susanna thought about it, and since she knew there weren't really any fairies in the apple tree, she figured she'd better not promise. She knew she sometimes told fibs at school about their home, but she hated being untruthful with Abigail. "I can't promise, Abby."

"Why not?"

"It might rain again."

"It won't." Abigail was confident.

"The fairies might be gone," Susanna said.

"Kooka says they'll be there." Abigail had great faith in Kooka.

Susanna smiled. "Then maybe they will."

It did not rain. The sun came out first thing and stayed out, but Martha came to fetch Susanna shortly before nine o'clock and told her that they were going to take a sanctification bath together.

"You remember what that means, don't you, Susanna Mary?"

"I remember, Mama," Susanna said, shuddering inwardly, for she remembered all too well, because Mama had made her take one of those baths with her after her last birthday. She'd put her into a cold bath and washed her with a rough flannel from head to toe, and then, telling her only to take a deep breath and pray to Mrs. Eddy, Mama had dunked her right under the water and held her under until Susanna had choked and struggled so violently that Mama had realized she was about to drown and let her back up again.

"You must be absolutely silent while we're bathing, is that clear?"

"Yes, Mama." Susanna yearned for escape. "I promised to play with Abigail this morning."

"Abigail Sarah spends too much time playing." Martha, who wore unrelieved black now, each and every day of the year, folded her hands piously. "There are chores for her to do, are there not, child?"

"Yes, Mama."

"Then tell your sister to do them quietly so that our bath is not disturbed."

Susanna's heart sank. "Yes, Mama."

Later, Abigail came to their bedroom and found Susanna sitting huddled on her bed.

"Can we go see the fairies now, Zanna?"

"Not yet, Abby." Susanna was still shaken from the bath. The water had been colder than last time, and she had swallowed a whole mouthful of it when Mama had held her head under, and now she felt sick.

"Why can't we?"

"Because Mama wants me to go to the grocery store for her." Susanna saw the disappointment on her sister's face. "You can come with me if you like."

"No." Abigail was unusually petulant. "I want to see the fairies. You promised, Zanna."

"I didn't promise." Susanna got up off the bed and went to fetch her bonnet from the closet. "And we can still go see them when I get back."

Abigail's chubby hands were on her hips. "I want to see them *now*."

Impatience rose in Susanna. "Then you'll just have to see them on your own," she said.

Susanna went off to the stores with the discomfiting knowledge that she had spoken unnecessarily harshly to her little sister. When she returned, brown bags in both arms, and saw that Mama was at the door waiting for her, a nameless, inexplicable terror struck into her stomach like an icepick.

"The Lord has seen fit to punish us again," Martha said, her voice as calm and bland as if she were delivering news of a passing rain shower.

"What do you mean, Mama?" Susanna asked breathlessly.

"We must pray, Susanna Mary," Martha said. "We must pray to Mrs. Eddy for Abigail Sarah—"

Susanna dropped the brown bags on the doormat, not caring if the eggs broke or the detergent spilled over the floor.

"Abigail—" She stared at her mother. "What's happened to Abigail?"

"She was disobedient, child," Martha said, "and now she must suffer, as all men and women suffer who have not seen the error of their ways."

"What *happened* to her, Mama?" Susanna was near hysteria.

Martha, calm in her own sanctified state, gazed with only mild reproof at her older daughter, who had never before, in all her life, raised her voice to her mother.

"Come and pray, Susanna Mary."

"I want to see Abigail. Where is she?" Susanna ran toward the back staircase.

"Susanna Mary, come back here this minute!"

"I want to see *Abigail*!"

Abigail lay in her bed, her face almost as white as her pillow, her white-gold hair still damp from where Martha had washed away the blood to purify her. For a moment Susanna feared she was dead, but then, moving closer, she observed that her eyelids were flickering, and laying her cheek near to her sister's mouth, she felt her warm breath, and a vast wave of relief flooded through her.

"Abby," she said softly, "it's Zanna."

There was no response at all.

"It's Zanna come home from school, Abby. Wake up."

But Abigail did not wake up, not then, or the rest of that day or that evening, or the whole of that night. Martha told Susanna what had happened so far as she knew, how she had emerged from a period of prayer a little after noon, and had searched the house for Abigail. Until, at last, she had found her, lying on the ground at the foot of the old apple tree, blood on her face and in her hair.

"Did you call a doctor?" Susanna knew, as she spoke, that it was a foolish question, that doctoring was, to her mother, as great an evil as the devil himself. "Mama, did you call anyone?"

"Of course I called someone," Martha said very quietly. "I called on the Lord, and I called on Mrs. Eddy."

"Mama, Abigail needs to see a doctor. I think she's very sick."

"Then she will be healed," Martha said.

"Mama—" Susanna took a gulp of air, for courage. "Mama, a doctor came to school last week. One of the other children took a bad fall, and he helped her—I saw it—he took care of her, and nothing bad happened, and she got better after he came."

"That place is evil," Martha said. "I knew no good would come of allowing you to go there."

"No, Mama, it's not evil. It's a good school."

"Come pray with me, Susanna Mary."

Susanna tried again.

"Please, Mama, just this one time, can't we call a doctor to come look at Abigail's head? I could call him for you if you don't want to; then Mrs. Eddy won't be mad at you—"

"Mrs. Eddy doesn't get mad." Martha interrupted her, hardly angry herself, still quite calm, quite serene. "Mrs. Eddy intercedes between us and the Lord, and she will do so again now, for better or worse."

"But, Mama," Susanna said, and her voice was small and tight and strange in her own ears, "if Abigail doesn't see a doctor, I think she might die."

The Widow King gazed down at her seven-year-old daughter, and there was just a hint of compassion in her cold blue eyes. "Have you learned nothing all these years, Susanna Mary? Do you still not realize that healing is in the mind, that Abigail Sarah's greatest chance of recovering from this act of disobedience lies in her and our thoughts and prayers?"

"But how can she think when she's sleeping, Mama?" Susanna asked, still in the same odd, half-strangled voice. "How can she pray?"

"That's between her and the Lord, child," Martha said.

Had the doctor been called to examine Abigail Sarah, upon seeing the open wound at the back of her golden head and observing her unconscious state, he would have had her swiftly removed to the hospital in Hyannis, where a neurosurgeon would probably have performed a craniotomy to drain the blood from the space between Abigail's skull and the outer layer of the protective covering of her brain, after which he would have prescribed antibiotics to safeguard against the possibility of either meningitis or encephalitis.

As it was, however, during the critical twenty-four hours following Abigail's fall from the apple tree, all the healing that took place came from her seven-year-old sister's hands, stroking her wounded head, and from her sister's voice, increasingly despairing, speaking to her soothingly, beseeching her to wake and be well again, and from a crazed, black-garbed woman down on her knees, praying to a photograph.

At eight o'clock the next morning Susanna was sitting beside Abigail's bed when she observed a flush on her sister's cheeks that had not previously been there.

"Abigail," she called softly, but still there was no response. Gently she touched the little girl's forehead and found it too warm. Abigail's eyelids fluttered, her pretty, unkissed lips parted, and Susanna heard her breathing quicken, heard a faint rasp in her throat.

Quickly Susanna left the room and went in search of her mother. Martha, having slept for five hours, was dressed and already on her knees, her eyes closed, her lips moving.

"Mama, I think Abigail has a fever."

Martha ignored her, went on praying.

"Mama, don't you hear me? I said I think Abby has a fever."

Martha's eyes remained closed. "Come pray with me, child."

"No, Mama, you have to *listen* to me."

Her mother's eyes opened at last, and there was a glint of real anger in them. "Have you lost all respect, Susanna Mary?"

"No, Mama, but I'm afraid for Abigail." Susanna reached out and tried to draw the kneeling woman to her feet. "Come and see, Mama, please. I'm sure she has a fever."

Martha pushed her daughter's hand away. "That's probably the sickness starting to come out of her, child," she said, calm again. "Nothing to worry about."

Susanna shook her head. "I don't think so, Mama. Please come and see her. I'm frightened for Abby."

"Your sister's name is Abigail Sarah," Martha said.

"Mama, *please!*"

Martha stayed on her knees.

At three o'clock that afternoon, while Susanna was dozing in the chair beside Abigail's bed, she was awakened by a strange sound and opened her eyes to see her sister's face and whole body jerking and twitching convulsively.

"Abby, what is it?"

Terrified, Susanna tried to hold on to Abigail's left hand, but it plucked itself straight out of her grasp and continued to thrash on the white sheet. The sick child's eyes were no longer quite closed, but Susanna could tell they were glazed over and unseeing, the rasp in her throat seemed louder than it had previously been, and when Susanna managed to lay her right hand on her forehead, it was burning hot beneath her touch.

"Oh, Abby." Susanna ran to wet the flannel with which she had been mopping her sister's forehead and cooling her palms over the past several hours. "Try to keep still, Abby, so Zanna can help you."

The twitching ceased. For an instant, staring at the suddenly inert figure in the bed, Susanna felt her own heart stop, believed that Abigail had died. And then she saw that the little girl's chest was still moving, still rising and falling, and she saw a pulse in her neck throbbing and heard the labored breathing, and for the next few minutes gratitude overwhelmed her because at least Abby was still with her, at least she was still alive. And maybe Mama was right, maybe this was all part of the healing taking place inside her body, drawing out the sickness, and maybe it was some kind of battle between good and evil, and if that was true, then surely Abigail would recover because there was nothing, not even the smallest, most minuscule grain of evil in her.

And then, from one instant to the next, Susanna realized the real truth.

Abby's going to die. It was a voice in her head, speaking to her, loudly and clearly and precisely. *If a doctor doesn't come soon, she's going to die.*

Susanna stood up from her chair and went over to the window.

The apple tree, all Kooka's fairies vanished, returned deep into the bark of its trunk, deep inside Abigail's unconscious mind, stood there near the house, branches and leaves and buds blowing gently in the spring breeze, just a tree again now, blameless and innocent.

Next door, in her own backyard, Lettie Forbush stretched out her arms up to her clothesline, hanging her washing out to dry. First a wide pale blue sheet, then her husband's white shirt, then a pair of her daughter's scarlet shorts. The shorts and all the freedom they symbolized hung from the line like a waving vivid red banner. Mama was always scandalized when Lettie Forbush hung out her washing, had said, when she was still in the habit of saying anything much that was not directly addressed either to Mrs. Eddy or to the Lord Himself, that the Forbushes were on a highway to hell and that their washing said it all.

Susanna turned from the window and looked back at her sister lying in her bed. *She's dying for sure, whatever Mama says,* the voice in her mind told her. *You have to get help, Zanna. Abby needs you to help her.*

Abigail's cheeks were flame-colored, the shadows beneath her fluttering eyes were deep and dark and sinister.

Susanna thought about trying one more time with her mother.

Mama's crazy, the voice said. *The wacko widow, they call her, and they're right; you know they're right.*

"Yes," Susanna said very quietly. "I know."

She opened the window, slid it right up all the way, and stuck her head through so that her hair blew a little around her face.

Their next-door neighbor was just hanging her last pair of black, silky-looking, decadent panty hose.

Susanna took a deep breath. "Mrs. Forbush," she called.

She never forgot the doctor's face. It was long and narrow, with a sharp nose and chin, but his eyes, behind his gold-rimmed spectacles, were immensely kind, and his mouth, when he smiled down at her, was surprisingly gentle and sweet.

It was she who had summoned him. She who allowed him to enter the house. Mama's house. Mama's church.

Lettie Forbush stood behind the doctor on the pathway, craning her head to try to see into the hallway.

"Are you all right, dear?" she called out to Susanna.

"I'm fine, thank you," Susanna called back in her tight, new voice.

"Would you like me to come in with the doctor?" Mrs. Forbush asked.

"No, thank you," Susanna said.

The doctor came through the front door, and Susanna closed it.

In the room that had long since become the sanctuary that

336 / Hilary Norman

housed Mrs. Eddy's shrine, Martha, hearing strange voices, rose, at last, from her knees and came out into the hall. Her face was pinched and pale from the dimness and from her supplications.

"And what," she asked, "is the meaning of this?"

"I'm Dr. Fried, ma'am," the doctor said, putting down his bag and extending his hand.

Martha did not accept it.

"Out," she said.

"I beg your pardon, ma'am?" the doctor said.

"Out of my house."

Susanna, tucked between the physician and the staircase, said, "He's come to see Abigail, Mama."

"Why has he done that?" Martha asked.

"Because she's sick."

"How does he know that she's sick?"

The doctor intervened. "A neighbor called me, Mrs. King. I understand that your little girl, Abigail, has had a bad fall."

"Abigail is recovering." Martha's lips were drawn so tight that the outlines of her teeth were visible through the flesh. "We have no need of your services, sir."

"All the same, ma'am"—Dr. Fried stood his ground—"I would like to see her, so long as I'm here."

"Which you will not be, in one minute from now," Martha said.

Susanna stared; the part of her that was not terrified was fascinated, for it had been years since she had heard her mother speak to a stranger.

Dr. Fried knew all about the Widow King.

"With respect, ma'am," he said to her, keeping his voice level and calm, "I must insist on being allowed to see your daughter."

"This is my house," Martha replied, "and you are in no position to insist upon anything."

"But, Mama," Susanna ventured, "surely it wouldn't hurt for the doctor just to look at Abigail, maybe just from the door, just to make sure she's all right."

Martha seemed to grow in stature. "Go to your room, Susanna Mary."

"But, Mama—"

"Go to your room this *minute*."

Susanna ran up the staircase, hot tears flooding from her eyes, stopping at the top to listen, her right hand covering her mouth to stifle her sobs.

"And you"—Martha went on, her voice strengthening, like a long-disused instrument finding its purpose again—"will kindly leave my house."

Dr. Fried made another attempt. "Mrs. King, I must advise you to reconsider. If your daughter has been injured and is being refused medical attention, that may constitute—"

"I'm not interested in your advice, sir," Martha snapped at him.

The physician's kindly eyes grew more disapproving. With a small sigh he turned to leave, picking up his bag. Martha moved past him, careful not to let her black dress brush against any part of his clothing or body. She opened the door, saw and feigned not to see Lettie Forbush, hovering on the sidewalk.

"Good-bye, sir," she said.

Dr. Fried went through the doorway.

"Please, Mrs. King, call me." He fished in his coat pocket, found a card, and tried to give it to her, but she kept her hands down by her sides, and so he leaned forward, in spite of her, and tossed it into the house, where it landed on the mat just inside the door. His expression was half curious now, and a little pitying. "If your daughter gets any worse, please call."

Martha closed the door.

That night was the longest Susanna had ever spent. She waited for Martha to come or to call her, but Mama never came near her, not even to order her to prayer, and Abigail, abandoned by her mother and by the outside world, continued to lie, motionless again now, in her bed. Every now and then, as the night wore on and Susanna sat, sleepless, helpless, at her post beside her sister, she reached out to touch the sick child, and she realized numbly that what her fingers sought now was no longer just to bring comfort to Abigail, but to ensure whether or not she was still living.

First light spread up over the horizon, the birds in the backyard and beyond sang their gentle dawn cacophony of tunes, and Susanna had never heard a more pitiless sound, and a little later her stomach rumbled, and she realized that she was hungry, that she had not eaten for most of the previous day, and she looked at Abigail and knew that she might never feel hunger again, might never hear another dawn chorus, might never smile at her sister again with her beautiful, innocent, sweet smile.

Weeping again, she rose and walked over to the window, and saw that she and Abigail had not, after all, been entirely forgotten. Lettie Forbush was already there, in her backyard, watching for her, and Susanna wondered idly how long she had waited there, and she wondered too why she was waiting, with what purpose, since they both had failed, they and the kindly doctor, and she found that she hardly had the strength left in her even to wave back as Mrs. Forbush signaled to her with her right hand up-stretched, fingers spread wide.

The neighbor was asking her something, Susanna realized, mouthing words at her, but Susanna did not understand, and now the tears, of frustration and of grief and of fear, flowed ever more freely, streaming down her cheeks, and she knew that Lettie Forbush saw them, and for just an instant she thought that she too was weeping, but then the woman was gone, back into her house, and the moment's contact, such as it had been, was over.

The police came first, Dr. Fried following on behind, and again it was Susanna who opened the front door, defying her mother, only seven years old but making her choices, fearfully but decisively. Martha attempted to expel them from her house but swiftly understood that this time she had no hope of success and withdrew again, back to her sanctuary, back to her knees. Susanna stood outside the room where Abigail lay, watched the police officers go in and come out again, saw the doctor bend over her sister, could not hear what Dr. Fried said, but recognized a note of shock, perhaps even anguish, in his tone.

He came out to her a few moments later. "Where is your mother?"

"She doesn't want to be disturbed," Susanna said.

"I must see her," the doctor said.

Susanna nodded and led the way. At the door of the sanctuary she knocked softly.

"No," came the reply, rocklike and immovable.

"I must go in," Dr. Fried said, and stooped for just an instant to stroke Susanna's hair before he opened the door.

The Widow King, in her customary black, knelt before the photograph of a long-dead woman who would in all likelihood have been appalled by the use of her image in such a blasphemous manner. The room was dark, the curtains drawn against the bright sunlight, and two stout white candles burned on either side of the shrine, flames flickering wildly as the man entered.

"Mrs. King"—the doctor addressed her quite calmly—"I have called for an ambulance to take Abigail to Cape Cod Hospital in Hyannis. It would be best if you came along with her."

"No," Martha said, not moving from her knees. "It would not be best."

"They'll need you to sign some papers for her admission," Dr. Fried said.

"I'll sign nothing."

"Your daughter is very sick, Mrs. King," the doctor said. "She may be dying." Behind him, in the hallway, he heard the older child suck in her breath and cursed himself for his lack of tact. "The sooner she receives treatment," he added, "the greater her chances of recovery."

Martha did not even turn her head. "I do not give my permission for my daughter to be taken to any hospital, sir, neither will I sign any papers permitting her to be treated." She paused. "I am a believer in mental healing," she said. "Have you heard of Mrs. Eddy?"

"Mary Baker Eddy? Yes, of course, ma'am."

"Then you understand my position."

"As I hope you understand mine," Dr. Fried responded. "There are police officers here, ma'am, and there will be questions to be asked regarding your daughter's injury." He stared at the back of Martha's unyielding head. "Abigail will be taken to the hospital, Mrs. King, and with the greatest of respect, I would ask you to sign the consent forms so that she can be treated."

"No, sir," Martha said.

Dr. Fried sighed. "Very well, ma'am."

He came outside and closed the door. He looked down at Susanna, saw the terror in her lovely lilac blue eyes. "Would you like to go with Abigail when the ambulance comes, Susanna?" he asked her.

Susanna hesitated. More than anything in the whole wide world, she wanted to go with Abigail and never come back until their mama was well again, had ceased being crazy, was a real mother like the others she'd seen at school. But she knew that she had to stay. She had done enough by letting them come in. She had done enough by weeping at the window where Mrs. Forbush could see her.

"I have to stay here," she answered very softly, trying not to cry.

"Are you sure?"

"Yes, sir."

He nodded and put out his hand again, and this time he touched her cheek with two fingers, very lightly, with great kindness.

"Someone will call back later, to see you and your mother."

"Okay," she said.

"Would you like your neighbor Mrs. Forbush to come in and wait with you?" he asked.

Susanna shook her head. "No, thank you, sir." She looked up into his face, right into his bespectacled eyes. "You said Abigail might die."

The doctor hesitated. "It's possible. I hope not."

She kept her eyes on his. "Please don't let her die," she said.

"We'll do everything we can," he told her. "Try not to worry too much."

He might as well have told a bird not to fly.

The ambulance drew up outside the house. Two paramedics brought in a folded-up stretcher, hurried up the stairs, and Susanna, in the background now, forgotten, watched and waited and did not dare think of what would happen once these people had gone.

They laid Abigail on the stretcher, covered her little body with a blanket, put a mask over her nose and mouth, and prepared to take her out.

"Where's the mother?" one of the paramedics asked.

"Not coming," Dr. Fried said.

"Why not?"

"We'll be needing a court order," the doctor said quietly.

"Oh." The paramedic paused. "Hell."

"Yes," the doctor said.

They took her out. Susanna walked alongside the stretcher, as far as the limit of their pathway, then stopped.

"I can't," she whispered.

"I know," Dr. Fried, beside her, said.

Susanna looked down at her sister. Abigail was the color of chalk, all the flush gone from her cheeks, the only signal that she was still living a fine mist that formed and evaporated with her breath on the inside of the mask.

"Can I kiss her?" she asked.

"Of course you can," the doctor answered.

Abigail's cheek was very cool now against Susanna's lips. She bestowed the kiss very swiftly, wanting, with all her might, to snatch her baby sister from the stretcher, to hold her in her arms and to tell them, after all, that they should leave, that they could not take her away.

But it was done now. She had let them in.

Abigail's stretcher disappeared inside the ambulance. The last glimpse Susanna had of her was when a small shaft of sunlight caught the white gold hair, making it glint like a new-minted coin.

Susanna felt a great, boundless, still-silent sob rising up inside her, filling every space in her body, stifling, suffocating, explosive. Yet she held it in, even as the door of the ambulance closed. Even as it drove away.

Martha came out of her sanctuary once more, minutes after they had all gone. She came out into the front hall, where Susanna still stood, just inside the front door. She was pale, with two spots of high color on each cheek. She looked, to Susanna's eyes, different. Some of the composure, the icy detachment she had shown to Dr. Fried had dispersed, and there was something else in her expression that Susanna had never seen before, something new and more frightening than ever.

"I have just one thing to say to you, Susanna Mary."

"Yes, Mama." Susanna's voice was a whisper again.

"Are you listening to me carefully?"

"Yes, Mama."

Martha King came closer, so that she loomed over her daughter, so that her daughter could smell the mustiness of her, of her dress, of her body, and Susanna thought, for the first time, that her mother seemed to be somehow less alive than other people.

She took a step back. Martha took another forward.

"If Abigail Sarah dies," she said, and her voice was like dry paper, "it will be your doing, Susanna Mary. Your fault. You know that, don't you?"

Susanna was unable to speak.

"You *know* that, don't you, Susanna Mary?"

"No." Susanna could hardly breathe. "No, Mama."

"You led your sister astray, Susanna Mary," Martha said. "You let a doctor into this house. You allowed them to take Abigail Sarah to a *hospital*." The last word cracked with outrage.

Susanna stared up at her mother.

"If your sister dies," Martha repeated, "it will be on your conscience for the rest of your days, Susanna Mary."

And then she turned around and went back into her sanctuary.

They were the last words Susanna ever heard her mother speak.

And Susanna never saw Abigail alive again.

The sob that had risen inside her when the stretcher had disappeared into the ambulance rose inside her again, held back again, more than twenty years later, in Pete Strauss's office. Susanna stood at the window, gazing out unseeing onto Eighth Street, where life continued as usual, where people, most normal, a few crazy, many someplace in between, went about their business.

"They came back for me the next day," she said, not turning around. "My father had an aunt still living, a very old lady, but a devout Catholic—much more devout, I guess, than my father was. She arranged with the doctor and the local authorities for me to go to St. Catherine's."

Pete was beyond words. He had ceased smoking cigarettes an hour or so before. He thought that maybe for once in his life he was beyond even nicotine.

"They declared Mama incompetent soon after Abigail died." Susanna went on, so quietly that he could hardly hear her. "I was told she was in an institution, but that she was quite happy. I think they let her do as she wished, so she probably spent most of the rest of her life on her knees, praying to Mrs. Eddy." She paused. "She died of cancer during the time I was living in the shack. Bodine was telling the truth after Abigail was born, when he told me he'd heard that Mama was dead."

At last she turned from the window. She was ghostly pale.

"My fault, Pete. I believed her."

Pete tried to speak, but no words came.

"All my fault," she said again.

Pete rose from his chair.

"No, Susanna," he said very softly. "No."

"Oh, yes," she said. "I let her climb the tree. I let the doctor come into the house." The tears, still to be shed, stood out in her lilac eyes. "I let them take her to the hospital."

Pete held out his arms. She came into them, moving slowly. He wrapped them around her, felt her body against his, rigid and ice cold. He knew it was a chill he could not warm, not yet at least. Perhaps never.

She let the sob go.

That night Pete would not allow Susanna to leave, for she was too bone-weary, brain-weary, to go safely anywhere, even to her own apartment on Beekman Place. All talked out, hardly able to protest, not really wanting to protest, she let him feed her scrambled eggs and lightly buttered toast, all cut up in small squares, as if he were caring for the child who had today emerged at last to tell her tale of woe. And when she had eaten, Pete ran her a bath, making sure the heat was on full, laying over the warm towel rail the never-worn, plump, soft white terry bathrobe from Bergdorf's that had been Leigh's last gift to him before their split, and Susanna lay in Pete's bath for almost an hour, and he left her in peace but for the odd word through the door now and again, to reassure himself that she had not fallen asleep in the water.

"Bed now?" he asked when she emerged, wondrous to look at in the robe, hair wrapped in a hand towel turban. He was reminded of his first sight of her in the waiting room at Hawke's hospital, of how her vulnerability and frailty had surprised him, of how startled he had been at the depth and truth of the beauty that he had wrongly assumed would be superficial and camera-enhanced.

"I'll sleep on the sofa," Susanna said softly.

"No," Pete said. "You'll take the bed. I'll take the couch." He saw her hesitation. "Don't even think of arguing, because you'll lose."

She smiled, a faint wisp of a smile, then nodded. "Thank you," she said.

"*Nada*," he said. Then he too hesitated. "Same room, of course. Do you mind?"

"I'd mind if it wasn't," she said.

"What about Alice and Steinbeck? We all get to sleep together, usually," Pete said apologetically. "Alice never talks at night—she likes her rest—but the mutt sometimes gets a little restless."

"So do I," Susanna said. "He and I can pass the time of night if I can't sleep."

"You'll sleep." He watched her take off the robe, deeply moved by the sight of her in the oversize white shirt he'd given her, helped her into his bed, tucked her in, bent over her, and kissed her still damp hair. "You cozy?"

"Mmm."

"Mind if I keep the small lamp on for a while?"

She shook her head, already half asleep. "Keep it on all night if you like."

"Want me to?" Pete knew more than anyone else on earth about this woman, but there were still so many small yet significant things he did not know. She might be scared of the dark, and if that were all she was afraid of, what a miracle that would be.

"I don't mind the dark." Tired as she was, Susanna read his mind.

"Sleep then," Pete said. He straightened up. "Anything you need, sing out. Anytime."

She looked up at him, eyes half closed. "Why are you always so wonderful to me?"

"You know why."

"Yes." Susanna smiled the faint smile again. "I guess I do."

He slept little. For a while he read or tried to read, but the words were a blur of print, meaningless, his mind filled with images of a young child, ill used by her insane mother, living out her bizarre everyday life as best and as courageously as she could, while her beloved sister escaped into her own mind and then on into death. He gazed, through the dim light, at the woman now sleeping in his bed and imagined that child, in her curious body-covering garments, wheeling her baby sister through the small-town streets, imagined the grotesque mother kneeling at the makeshift shrine in her darkened sanctuary. How, in the name of God, Pete wondered, had that child survived so much—not only that hideous early experience but the monstrous later nightmares—to become the sane, intelligent, caring, brave person she now was? Surely it was too much for anyone, however strong, however deep her inner resources, to bear?

"I let them in," she had said over and over again, telling her story. *"I called the doctor. I let them into Mama's house, Mama's church. I let them take my sister away."*

She knew better now. Of course as an intelligent adult she was perfectly aware that she had only done good, had acted with wisdom and strength far beyond her years. Yet still, in the hospital at Hyannis just a week before, she had suffered that crisis, that brief breakdown, the fleeting cracking of her twenty-three-year-old armor, which only her great strength had repaired in time.

Her mother, the wacko widow, had done her job well, right at the end of that particular horror.

"If Abigail died, Mama said, it would be on my conscience."

Some mothers had a lot to answer for.

Pete sat through the night, remembering aspects other than Susanna's beauty from their first meeting, observations that had come then and much later. He understood so much more now: her fear of doctors and hospitals; her inability to communicate with her husband or with others close to her; her lack of religious faith; her continuing determination, after Hawke's death, to work on the AIDS project. Pete had believed that Susanna had wanted to give something back for Hawke's sake, to make amends for what she had regarded as her own failings during his illness, but he knew now that her desire, her *need* to help, went back much farther, that she had been trying, was still trying, to give something back for the first Abigail.

He thought about the terrible deprivations Susanna had suffered. Oh, sure, she'd fallen on her feet in many ways, first with the Van Dusens, then with Hawke, whom she had undoubtedly loved, and her remarkable career. But the catalog of those deprivations caught grievously, painfully, at Pete's heart as he logged them, out of professional habit, in his brain.

He had attended three Passover Seders during his life, in the homes of Jewish friends or patients. He remembered the section of the Haggadah that had been read mostly in English, listing the many beneficences of the Almighty to the children of Israel, remembered the word that had been spoken, echoed again and again, after each act of grace. *Dayenu.* It would have sufficed. It would have been enough.

Now, this night, as he contemplated the wrongs that had been done to Susanna through the years, those words came back to him. Had she been deprived only of her mother's love, it would have been enough. Had she lost only her sister, it would have sufficed. But she had lost so much more. Her childhood, her innocence, her youth. Her rights: to make normal decisions about her future, to allow her own natural abilities to flourish and take root, to choose her own faith, to be ordinary. She had lost her husband to a monstrous disease, had sacrificed her first career to the uniquely discriminating qualities of that disease. She had lost the right to take care of her daughter.

And now she still feared losing that daughter's love altogether.

Dayenu, he thought, violently. Enough.

Long before dawn Susanna cried out in her sleep and woke to find Pete already crouched at her side.

"I didn't know where I was," she said, her voice on the edge of tremulous, her eyes still fuzzy from some abstract dream. "I was scared of something, but I don't know what it was."

"That's not too surprising," Pete said.

"I guess not." She lay back again.

"Want to get right back to sleep?"

"No."

"Feel like talking?"

"Not really," she said.

"Okay." He began to rise.

"Stay," she said. "Please."

He settled back on the floor. "Of course."

"You don't mind?"

"What do you think?"

"I think you're the best friend any woman ever had."

"Thank you," he said, a whisper of grief cutting his heart like the sharpest of fishermen's blades.

Susanna lay quite still, watching his face, her eyes accustomed now to the pale light that filtered through the curtains from the ever-wakeful city.

"You know what I'd really like right now?" she asked.

"No."

"I'd like you to hold me."

Foolish hope leaped in him, a grown, professional man become an adolescent again, a schoolboy dreaming of his first kiss. Quickly, brusquely he pushed the hope away. *Friend*, she said. *A hug from a best friend.* For an instant he shut his eyes.

"Help me, Pete," she said.

He opened them again, saw tears brightening her eyes, even in the deeply shadowed room. He reached for her, wrapped his arms about her.

"You're freezing," she said, startled by his cold face.

"I'm fine." His voice was muffled, his mouth cloaked by her hair.

"Why don't you get in?"

Again that leap, that unseemly jig of the heart.

"I'm okay," he said.

"Please," Susanna said very softly.

He had undressed for the night only to shorts and T-shirt, but he had seldom felt so naked and exposed as when he climbed between those familiar sheets and felt her body, her silkenness, her warmth. Instantly aroused, he turned himself onto his side to prevent her from noticing, knowing it would destroy everything in the blink of an eye if she were embarrassed by him in this moment of need. He knew within seconds that she had, of course, noticed; that even if he had been abruptly dragged back into some time warp, she was still a thirty-year-old sophisticated woman who knew an aroused, erect man when he climbed into bed beside her.

"God," he said, half under his breath. "I'm sorry."

"What for?"

"Being in love with you." Every trace of chill had vanished from his body.

"Now why in the world would you be sorry for that?"

Pete turned to face her, saw that the tears, like his chill, had disappeared as if they had never existed, and that instead her lovely eyes were brushed with the gentlest humor. "Are you laughing at me?" he asked. "I don't mind if you are—that is, I understand if you are."

"I'm not laughing at you."

"Yes, you are."

"For a psychologist," Susanna said, "you're very insecure."

"Don't you know that all shrinks are basket cases?"

"With patients like me, I'm not surprised."

"We don't get many patients like you."

He had intended it as a throw-away line, yet it hung in the air, rendering them both silent for a while, minds ticking away, separating them despite the closeness of their bodies.

"When will you tell Abigail?" he asked at last.

"Later today. I'll go straight back to Cohasset, and I'll tell it all again before I lose my nerve."

"She's a strong girl," Pete said softly. "She won't find it an easy story to hear, but she'll get through. You'll both get through now, together."

"Do you really believe that?"

"Yes, I do."

They lay very still again.

"More than anything," Pete said after a while, his voice taut, "I would love to be able to return some of what you've lost through the years. But I know I can't ever do that, and knowing that is hard for me."

"No one can undo the past," Susanna said, "or even fix it. Except maybe me. I guess."

Having begun, Pete needed to go on. "What I can maybe try to do is find a way to fill some of those empty spaces inside you." He paused, looking into her face. "I am right, aren't I, about the emptiness?"

Susanna nodded slowly. "I think maybe I'd gotten used to holding it all inside me. It's as if while I had my secrets, all locked away in their boxes, they were keeping me together, like some emotional corset. You are right, I do feel empty." She paused. "Or maybe I'm just confused. Because though I know I haven't really changed, everyone else—you, especially now, since you're the only one who's heard it all—must be seeing me so differently. You can't help it. From your point of view, I am different."

"No," Pete said. "I don't feel that way at all, and I doubt the others will either." He was feeling his way, working it out as he went. "You're filling in the gaps, Susanna, and now we can start to understand you better. But all the things you were to us before, you still are."

They lay for a long time, talked out again, his arms loose about her shoulders. Still, they were so physically close; still, there was that same chasm between them as their minds wandered through past and present, ventured toward future, froze, and returned to old territory. Pete thought about Leigh, his wife, the last woman with whom he had lain in a bed, for he had never been much for casual sex, and in any case, for the past five years there had been only one woman he had really wanted. And when he was done with thinking about Leigh, he gave over all his mind, once again, to Susanna, wondering yet not presuming to ask what thoughts were now passing through her weary yet still wakeful mind. For there was a part of him now that he found almost distasteful: the yearning to know everything about Susanna, the desire to have her soul laid bare. And the analyst in him would claim to want to help her turn over every stone to pick at each last fleck of pain, each worm of anger, each maggot of despair. But the man in Pete Strauss found it invasive and shameful, for suddenly the analyst seemed to him no better than a looter, a scavenger, and wasn't Susanna entitled to her privacy—to those remaining spaces in her not yet quite hollowed out—and even if he did care deeply for her, love her, did that give him a right to visit those spaces without invitation?

While Pete, in motionless silence, lashed himself and longed for a cigarette, characters from Susanna's life flickered in and out of her thoughts; Martha and the first Abigail, her true sister; the nuns in the convent; Matthew Bodine, all his power to wound Susanna gone now, forever; Hawke, with all his talent and style and dynamism and gentleness, illuminating her world for a few years like a wondrous, dazzling meteor; Connie and Bryan, always joined in her thoughts, one seeming unfinished, incomplete, without the other; sweet, strong Tabitha, so candid and loyal, who would never let down anyone she cared for. Only when her mind turned to Abigail, her daughter, did it veer away again, for she, more than anyone, represented the future, which was unknown and, for that reason, however reassuring Pete's prophecies, more frightening even than her past.

And here, meantime, in the present, there was Pete.

"Are you awake?" she asked him as first light began to lift the veil over the city beyond the room.

"Yes." He felt a tightening in her body, a quiver of something, felt the response, immediate and reprehensible, in himself.

"I've been thinking," she said.

"Me too."

"About what we talked about awhile back." She paused. "About whether maybe you should stop being my counselor."

He kept silent, felt his heart beat faster, thought she must feel it too. On the other side of the room, at the base of Alice's still silent cage, Steinbeck stretched and groaned and went back to sleep.

"I think you should," she said.

Still, Pete said nothing.

"What do you think?" Susanna asked softly.

"You know what I think."

At last she stirred, sat up a little, moving out of his arms. "Why are you making me do all the work?" The question was half teasing, half irritated.

"What do you mean?" he asked, deliberately obtuse.

"You know what I mean."

"Yes," he said.

"Then why say you don't?"

"Fear," Pete answered.

"Of what?"

"Making a mistake." He paused, still lying down. "Of misinterpreting." He did not want to look into her face yet, was afraid of what he might see. "Of abusing our relationship. Of spoiling things between us."

"I don't think you could ever do that." Susanna sat all the way up, her shoulders propped against Pete's headboard.

"Sure I could," he said lightly.

"No," she said firmly. "You could not."

Silence lay over the room again, heavy as fog.

Susanna knew it was up to her, knew, with a clarity and simplicity that startled her—for nothing of late, nothing of consequence at least, had been simple or straightforward—that she wanted this. Wholly, without doubt. And if she waited for Pete to make the first move, she might wait forever, and it was not because he was a coward, for she knew he was anything but that, but because of his goodness, his kindness, his values.

For several more moments she sat still. It had been such a long, long time. No one since Hawke. She supposed she'd known Pete Strauss was right for her for a couple of years now, but her need for him as her counselor had been far more imperative, had vastly overwhelmed other considerations. Her emotional burdens had been so heavy; they still were, of course, were likely, during the next days or weeks, to grow even heavier if Abigail reacted badly to the family history that Susanna was now ready to share with her.

A pang of shame struck her. *Ready*. Who the hell did she think she was that the people who loved her had to wait for her to be ready to share herself with them?

"Jesus," she said out loud.

"What?" Pete was startled.

"I was just realizing how selfish I am."

"In what way?"

Abruptly she threw back the covers and got out of bed, walked over to the window, folded back a curtain, stared out, unseeing, and let it fall back. Steinbeck, woken again, thumped his tail, but she ignored him, and again the wise old dog returned to his snooze.

"Expecting everyone to wait around for me." She shook her head violently, turned to face him. "Expecting *you* to wait for me to be ready."

Pete started to get out of bed.

"No, Pete, don't." Susanna stopped him. "I mean, a week ago you took all kinds of risks to save my life and my daughter's, and all I did was send you to Hawke House and then expect you to drop everything and see me today. And now, just because suddenly I decide I am ready—ready for us, I mean—I expect you to read my mind and take the lead and make it all easy for me, and why *should* you? Why in hell should you want to switch from being my shrink to being my lover from one minute to the next?"

Pete sat frozen on the edge of the bed.

"There you are, you see? I'm right. You don't want to." Susanna left the window, paced over to the bookshelves, turned abruptly, walked over to the easel on which Pete's latest work rested. "Pete, please say something."

"I was waiting," Pete said softly.

"What for?"

"For you to be ready."

"And now that I am, you're not, right?"

"No."

Dismay seemed to seal up her throat, to stop her breathing. Finding herself close to the couch where Pete had spent much of the night, she sat down, her legs weak.

"No, you're not right," Pete said, finding a tiny, unexpected glint of sadism deep inside himself, enjoying this moment, the teasing of this wonderful woman.

"What are you saying?" Susanna asked.

"Am I permitted to get out of bed now?"

"Of course you are," she said, irritable again.

Pete stood up, went over to the windows, drew back the curtains. The sun, such as it was, was up now, its light obscured by clouds and buildings. Downstairs, in a shop doorway across the street, an old tramp slept like a dead man, covered with newspaper. Over to the right a young couple strolled, hand in hand, their faces tranquil and sleepy, fresh out of bed, Pete guessed, and turned from the window.

"Would you like some tea?" he asked.

On the couch Susanna sagged a little. "Yes, please."

"Darjeeling okay? Or I have some Earl Grey bags."

"I don't mind."

"I usually make tea around this time," Pete said.

"Do you?"

He went into the kitchen, and Susanna heard the sounds of water, of the teapot and kettle, spoons, the refrigerator door opening, closing. She stayed on the couch, perfectly still, letting the disappointment wash over her, drowning out the last flicker of hope for something good and strong and sane in her life.

Better this way, she told herself.

Who're you trying to kid? her old inner voice said.

Nothing more to be done.

Pete came back in, carrying a tray. Susanna did not look at him, could hardly bring herself to face him. From the floor beside the couch, she picked up a back issue of *Newsweek* and began to flick through its pages.

"I decided against tea," he said.

"That's fine," she said.

"I thought this might be more fitting," he said.

"Whatever."

"Reading something interesting?"

"Mmm."

She looked up then, surreptitiously, from the magazine, saw the bottle in his hands, saw him taking off the wire, twisting the cork, heard the unmistakable soft popping sound, saw the tiny breath of mist in the air.

"Do you mind?" he asked, pouring into two glasses.

The hope came back. Susanna dropped *Newsweek* back onto the floor.

"I've never had champagne at dawn before," she said.

"I've never had anything this special happen to me at dawn before," Pete said, bringing the glasses to her, sitting down beside her.

They sipped. It tasted fresh and cold and invigorating.

"It's better at dawn," she said.

Pete put down his glass.

"Could we go back to bed now?" he asked her very gently.

"Can we take the champagne?"

"We can take anything you want."

It was better than either of them had dared dream it would be. He was in good enough shape for a man who worked out too seldom, who ran only when he remembered to, but he noted with unsurpassed joy that Susanna seemed to delight in his body, to look at it carefully as she touched it or kissed it or as it came into contact with her own exquisite self. He remembered again the first time he'd seen her. *Face of dreams*, he'd thought then. *Body to match.* He hadn't known then that she'd had a child, and Lord knew, as he saw her now, there was little evidence to show the fact, no stretch marks, not a hint of sag anywhere. He knew that since the end of her career with Hawke she had relaxed her regimen, had allowed herself to enjoy food and cut back on the workouts—she seldom even saw her old trainer, Lulu Fiedlander, and when she did, it was usually for lunch—but Pete knew that he'd never before seen, nor ever would again, a more beautiful woman than Susanna, and though he knew, with certainty, that he would love her just as much if she were not this perfect, he rejoiced in it, thanked God for his good fortune.

Lying with Pete, through the lovemaking, even in the midst, at the core of it, and afterward, taking the warmth from his body and spirit, Susanna felt like a young child, told that Christmas never had, never would exist again, suddenly coming across an archetypal New England town at the heart of the holiday season: decorated tree in the main square, church lights ablaze, Santa Claus himself holding out his arms to her, restoring her soul and all her hope. When Pete touched her, stroked her, caressed her, kissed her, when she saw the love in his eyes, the relief in them, the pleasure and the joy, Susanna felt her world tilting, its whole emphasis shifting, felt the burdens and heartaches sliding away. And if the acknowledgment, at long, long last, of the love of this man, and if his presence—his touch, the sight and smell and the sound of him—could push away that heartache and grief and fear even for a little while, then there was so much more hope than she had ever dared to contemplate.

Sometime after nine o'clock, when they had slept in each other's arms for a good long while, Alice woke them, chattering to herself in her covered cage, and then Steinbeck thrust his cold wet nose into his master's sleeping face, and they both stirred, softly, afraid to disturb the other. And then, realizing they both were awake, they smiled into each other's eyes.

"How do you feel?" Pete asked.

"Indescribable," Susanna answered.

"Try anyway." He still held her.

"Happy doesn't cover it."

"Not for me either," Pete said.

"I feel . . . peaceful," she tried.

"Okay," he said.

"Joyful."

"Good."

She drew away, just a little, loath to lose his warmth, their closeness. "So what about you? What do you feel?"

Pete smiled into her eyes. "Like the luckiest man on earth." He paused. "Close to ecstatic, euphoric, that kind of thing, only this is better, because euphoric is over the top and couldn't last, and you and I are real live, flesh-and-blood, enduring kind of people, and finally we're together, and I know I'm home. That's how I feel."

For a moment or two Susanna considered his words.

"Okay?" Pete asked softly.

"Mmm. Just thinking about what you said, about being home."

"That's how I feel."

Susanna nodded. "Me too." She paused. "Me too."

And they were quiet again.

CHAPTER 25

~

On May 12 that year, Pete Strauss, sitting, as was his custom, at his old, ink-stained oak desk, made the first entry in his journal for some weeks. He had not felt as much compelled to keep up his diary since the events of February, mostly perhaps because he had always written alone, late at night, and these nights, thankfully, he was seldom alone.

We went back to Provincetown today, Susanna, Abigail, and I. We went, we decided mutually, to pay our respects to old horrors and to lay them to rest. It was a fine spring day, and we might as well have been in another land, so different was it from our collective memories. The dunes were there, of course, and the ocean, but there were hikers too, and sun worshipers and families picnicking, and the beach grass waved in the breeze, and beach plum and wild cherry flowered.

We found no sign of the tar paper shack. Susanna and Abigail walked around that section of the dunes in which we all believed it had been, searching for some small scrap of evidence of what we all knew had occurred there, but the national park rangers had done their work well and had removed every last stick of matchwood, and we supposed that the weather had done the rest.

I had long believed that the key to Susanna lay in those

dunes, yet I know now that all the time it lay fifty or so miles to the west, in a sedate and pretty little town, the oldest on Cape Cod, as mad Martha used to impress on her daughters.

I asked Susanna and Abigail if they wanted to visit Sandwich, to make the circle complete, but they both declined. I felt then, and I still feel it now, some hours later, that they were right to do so. I am a psychologist by profession, and so I have learned, more than most, to understand the power of the past, but there are some nightmares, I believe, that can never be expunged. And besides, for Abigail and Susanna and myself, the future beckons.

And the present is already glorious.

The typeface used in this book is a version of Janson, a seventeenth-century Dutch style revived by Merganthaler Linotype in 1937. Long attributed to one Anton Janson through a mistake by the owners of the originals, the typeface was actually designed by a Hungarian, Nicholas (Miklós) Kis (1650–1702), in his time considered the finest punchcutter in Europe. Kis took religious orders as a young man, gaining a reputation as a classical scholar. As was the custom, he then traveled; because knowledge of typography was sorely lacking in Hungary, Kis decided to go to Holland, where he quickly mastered the trade. He soon had offers from all over Europe—including one from Cosimo de' Medici—but kept to his original plan, returning to Hungary to help promote learning. Unfortunately, his last years were embittered by the frustration of his ambitions caused by the political upheavals of the 1690s.

WITHDRAWN